ROBER

Robert Wilson was bo.... ....
Oxford University, he has worked in shipping,
advertising and trading in Africa. He has travelled in Asia and Africa and has lived in Greece
and West Africa. He now lives with his wife in
a remote part of Portugal.

The Big Killing is Robert Wilson's second
novel. His first, *Instruments of Darkness*, also features Bruce Medway and is set in West Africa.

ROBERT WILSON

THE BIG KILLING

HarperCollins*Publishers*

HarperCollins*Publishers*
77–85 Fulham Palace Road,
Hammersmith, London W6 8JB

This paperback edition 1997
1 3 5 7 9 8 6 4 2

First published in Great Britain by
HarperCollins*Publishers* 1996

Extract from *'Shadow of War' Collected Poems 1928-1985*
by Stephen Spender reproduced by permission of
Faber and Faber Ltd, London

The Author asserts the moral right to
be identified as the author of this work

ISBN 0 00 647986 3

Set in Meridien and Bodoni

Printed and bound in Great Britain by
Caledonian International Book Manufacturing Ltd, Glasgow

For Jane
and in memory of Peggy

AUTHOR'S NOTE

The French West African currency, the CFA, was devalued in January 1994 from 50 CFA to 100 CFA to the French franc. All financial transactions in this novel are based on the old rate.

Who live under the shadow of a war,
What can I do that matters

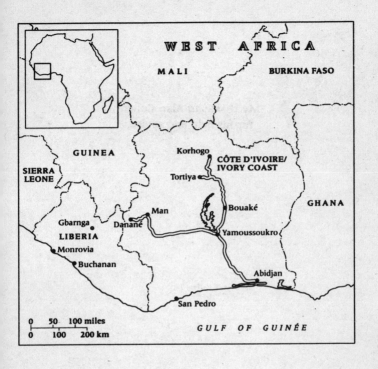

My thanks to Alan Cohen
for his help and advice.

1

Saturday 26th October
We were here again — if you call a hangover company or a slick of methylated sweat a friend — in this bar, this palmleaf-thatched shack set back from the sea in some fractious coco-nut palms, waiting for the barman to arrive. The head I was nursing (the first since last Saturday) had already been given some hot milk — the Ivorians called it coffee, I called it three grains of freeze-dried and a can of condensed milk. Now it wanted a hair of the dog, and not from any of those manky curs digging themselves into the cool sand outside, and not, definitely not, any of that White Horse that was galloping around my system last night, no sirree. An ice-cold beer was what was needed. One with tears beading on the bottle and the label peeling off. I held my hand out to see how steady we were. No horizontal hold at all. Where was that barman? Once he was here, there'd be security, there'd be options. I could decide whether to hold back and make it look pre-lunch rather than post-breakfast.

There he was. I could hear him, the barman, whistling that bloody tune, preparing himself for another day demonstrating the nuances of insouciance which had taken him a life-time to refine. I sat back on the splintery wooden furniture, opened the *Ivoire Soir* and relaxed.

I'd bought the newspaper from a kiosk in Grand Bassam, the broken-down old port town where I was staying, which was a long spit down a palm-frayed shoreline from Abidjan, the Ivory Coast capital city. I normally used it to stave off the first cold beer of the day and the boredom which came from three weeks waiting for the job I was supposed to be

11

doing not to materialize. This time I was actually reading it. There was some ugly detail about a body, recently discovered in Abidjan, which the BBC World Service had told me, at five o'clock that morning, belonged to James Wilson. He had been a close aide to the President of the neighbouring country of Liberia and the President, as everybody in the Ivory Coast knew, had been captured, tortured and killed last month by the breakaway rebel faction leader, Jeremiah Finn.

The World Service had also told me that hundreds of civilian bodies had been uncovered in swampland just north of Springs Payne Airport outside the Liberian capital, Monrovia, and that over the past three days rebel soldiers from Samson Talbot's Liberian Democratic Front had buried more than 500 bodies of mainly Ghanaian and Nigerian civilians in mass graves four miles to the north west of the capital. All this before they rounded off their report on the country's civil war with the positive identification of the strangled and mutilated body of James Wilson who'd been found in the Ebrié lagoon near the Treichville quarter of Abidjan yesterday.

All this on snatches of dream-torn sleep, with a hangover to support, cold water to shave in and a body that was finding new ways to say – 'Enough!' No. It had not been a morning for skipping down to the beach to dance 'highlife' into the long, torpid afternoon. It was a morning for taxing my patience, the beer-foam depth of my resolve, whilst trying to divert myself with the strange facts of James Wilson's death.

He'd been strangled with a piece of wire, which was the conventional bit, but then the killer had strayed into the occult by using a set of metal claws to open out the abdomen. These metal claws were used by members of the Leopard Societies who hadn't been heard of for some time. Their cardholders used to kill people who'd been accused of witchcraft and feed on their innards by the light of the moon. That's what it said. There'd been no moon the last three nights and the police had been informed by the coroner that James Wilson's innards had been eaten by fish. The reporter seemed disappointed. I made a mental note to hold off on the seafood whenever my next remittance came through.

The article finished with some conjecture as to why James Wilson's political career had ended with him as a gutless floater – a state, it occurred to me, that most politicians were making a success out of every day in the 'developed' world. The journo cited unnamed intelligence sources that linked the thirty-two-year-old James Wilson to the handing over of the late Liberian President to the lethal interrogation techniques of Jeremiah Finn and that it was Wilson's own Krahn tribe members who had given him the payback.

A cold beer appeared in front of me. I looked up at the barman who slipped back behind his cane-slatted bar and was giving me his 'eyelids at half-mast' routine.

'*C'est quoi ça?*' I asked, my watch still clipping its way round to 10.30 a.m.

'*Une bière, M. Bru,*' he said, fond of stating the obvious, and added, '*grande modèle,*' meaning it was a full litre bottle of ice-cold Solibra and I should stop looking for philosophy when there was a serious opportunity to deaden myself to existence. I stood up so that I could see more than his flat-calm eye language and used my full six feet four inches to impress upon him that I gave the orders around here and I didn't like barmen making assumptions about my drinking habits. He pointed with his chin across the earthen floor into an obscure corner of the shack.

It was a shock to find that the obese half-caste who'd introduced himself to me yesterday as Fat Paul had managed to rumble in without my noticing. He was sitting there with his buttocks hanging over either side of one of the few metal chairs in the joint, wearing a bright-blue silk shirt with big white parakeets all over it. He gave me a little tinkling wave and a sad housewife's smile. I nodded, sat back down and blocked out the frosted, beading *grande modèle* with the full spread of the *Ivoire Soir*.

Fat Paul was sitting with George and Kwabena who'd been with him yesterday. I'd watched them getting out of a large black 1950s Cadillac with tail fins higher than sharks' dorsals and chrome work you could check your tonsils in. They'd come into the bar and chosen a table next to mine and Fat

Paul had started talking to me as if he was a star and I was an extra in a movie's opening sequence in a bar on Route 66.

'I'm Fat Paul, who are you?'

'Bruce Medway.'

'What they got here that's any good, Bruce?'

'Pineapple fritters.'

'How d'they do that?'

'They dip them in batter, deep fry them and coat them with sugar.'

'Sounds good. I'll have six. What you want?' he said, looking at Kwabena and George.

They'd sat in the same corner they were sitting in now and Fat Paul had ordered a bottle of beer and had it sent over to me. Later he'd asked me to join them for lunch and seeing as I had hell and all to do I went over without bothering with any of the 'no, no, thank you' crap.

Before I'd sat down they'd asked me if I was a tourist and when I'd said no Kwabena had produced a chair from behind his back and had let me sit on it. The conversation hadn't exactly zipped around the table while we were eating but afterwards, while Fat Paul was taking a *digestif* of another four pineapple fritters, he'd asked me what I did for a living.

'I do jobs for people who don't want to do the jobs themselves. I do bits of business, management, organization, negotiations, transactions, and debt collection. Sometimes I find people who've gone missing. Sometimes I just talk to people on behalf of someone else. The only things I don't do are criminal things . . . that . . . and domestic trouble. I won't have anything to do with husbands, wives and lovers.'

'You been asked that before,' said Fat Paul, chuckling.

Soon after that they'd paid the bill and left but, by the way Fat Paul had looked back at me from the doorway, I'd expected to see him again, and here he was, the twenty-five-stone pineapple-fritter bin. He made it look so easy, but that's talent for you.

'You want join us for lunch, Mr Bruce?' said Kwabena, measuring each word as it came out and looming dark in my light so that I couldn't read the paper.

'It's ten-thirty in the morning,' I said, and Kwabena looked back at Fat Paul, lacking the programming to get any further into normal human relations without more guidance.

'You got t'eat!' shouted Fat Paul across the bar. 'Keep you strength up.'

Kwabena picked up the bottle of beer between his thumb and forefinger and took three strides across to Fat Paul's table. The barman turned on the radio, which immediately played the hit of the year he'd been whistling earlier. Its single lyric was so good that they felt the need to repeat it three times an hour. It was the kind of song that could make people go into public places and kill.

'C'est bon pour le moral. C'est bon pour le moral,
C'est bon, bon. C'est bon, bon.
C'est bon pour le moral . . .'

My 'moral' dipped as I looked at Fat Paul's buried eyes, which were like two raisins pressed into some dough so old that it had taken on a light-brown sheen. The mild contour of his nose rose and fell across his face and his nostrils were a currant stud each and widely spaced almost above the corners of his mouth, which had a chipolata lower lip and did a poor job of hiding some dark gums and brown lower teeth. He had a goitrous neck which hung below the hint of his chin and shook like the sac of a cow's udder. A gold chain hid itself in the crease of skin that came from the back of his neck before exiting on to the smooth, hairlessness of his chest. He had a full head of black hair which for some reason he felt looked great crinkle cut and dipped in chip fat.

The one thing that could be said of Fat Paul was that he *was* fat. He was fat enough not to know what was occurring below his waist unless he had mirrors on sticks and a jigsaw imagination. He told me that he had a very slow metabolism. I suggested he had no metabolism at all and he said, no, no, he could feel it moving at night. I put it to him that it might just be the day's consumption shifting and settling. This vision of his digestive system so unnerved him that he lost his appetite for a full minute.

Fat Paul's nationality wasn't clear. There was some African in there and perhaps some Lebanese or even American. To me he spoke English in a mixture of ex-colonial African and American movies, to George and Kwabena he used the Tui language.

George was a tall, handsome Ghanaian who was wearing a white short-sleeve shirt and a tie which he had contrived so that one end covered his crotch and the other stuck out like a tongue from the black-hole density of the knot at his top button. The tie was white with horses pounding across it with jockeys on their backs in wild silks. He hid behind some steel-rimmed aviator sunglasses and did what he was good at – letting his tie do the talking.

Kwabena was a colossus. His cast was probably taking up some valuable warehouse space in the steelworks where he'd been poured. His frame was covered by very black skin which had taken on a kind of bloom, as if it had been recently tempered by fire. He wore a loud blue and yellow shirt which had been made to go over an American football harness but nipped him around the shoulders. He sat with his mouth slightly open and blinked once a minute while his hands hung between his knees preparing to reshape facial landscapes. He looked slow but I wouldn't have liked to be the one to test his reactions. If he caught you and he'd been programmed right he'd have you down to constituent parts in a minute.

'What was it you say you doin'?' asked Fat Paul, the fourth pineapple fritter of the morning slipping into his mouth like a letter into a pillar box.

'When I'm doing it, you mean?'

He laughed with his shoulders and then licked his fingers one by one, holding them up counting off my business talents.

'Management, negotiations, debt collection, organization, findin' missin' people, talkin' to people for udder people . . . no, I'm forgettin' some . . .'

'Transactions,' I said.

'Trans*actions*,' repeated Fat Paul, nodding at me so I knew I'd got it right.

'As long as it's not criminal.'

'And no fucky-fucky business,' finished Fat Paul.

'I've not heard it put like that before.'

'Sorry,' he said, beckoning to Kwabena for a cigarette, ' 'swat 'sall about, you know, jig-a-jig, fucky-fucky. I no blame you. Thass no man's business. But transactions. Now there's somethin'. Somethin' for you. Make you some money.'

'What did you have in mind?'

Fat Paul clicked the fingers he'd been sucking and George opened a zip-topped case and handed him a package which he gave to me. It was a padded envelope with a box in it. The envelope had been sealed with red wax and there was the impression of a scorpion in the wax. It was addressed to M. Kantari in Korhogo, a town in the north of the Ivory Coast, where I was expecting to be sent any day now to sort out a 'small problem'.

'How d'you know I was going to Korhogo?' I asked, and Fat Paul looked freaked.

'You gonna Korhogo . . . when?'

'I don't know. I've got a job to do there. I'm waiting for instructions to come through.'

'No, no – this not for Korhogo.'

'That's what it says here.'

'No. You deliver it to someone who take it to Korhogo.'

'I see,' I said, nodding. 'Is that strange, Fat Paul?'

'Not strange. Not strange at all,' he said quickly. 'He gonna give you some money for the package. You go takin' it up Korhogo side then you up there wid the money and we down here wid . . .'

'Waiting for me to come back down again.'

'That's right. We got no time for waitin'.'

'Why don't you deliver it yourself?'

'I need white man for the job,' said Fat Paul. 'The drop ibbe made by 'nother white man, he only wan' deal with white man. He say African people in this kind work too nervous, too jumpy, they makin' mistake, they no turnin' up on time, they go for bush, they blowin' it. He no deal with African man.'

'There can't be that many white people up in Korhogo.'

'Ten, mebbe fiftee', 's 'nough.'

'The drop? Why did you call it the drop?'

'You callin' it transaction. I callin' it a drop.'

'Where and when is this drop?'

'Outside of Abidjan, west side, down by the lagoon Ebrié, eight-thirty tomorrow night.'

'Why there?'

'The white man no wan' come to Abidjan, he no wanbe seen there, he have his own problems, I donno why.'

'Why don't you just go to Korhogo and cut out the middlemen?'

'We' — he pointed to himself who could easily pass for plural — 'we no wango Korhogo, too much far, too much long.'

'Well, it sounds funny to me, Fat Paul. Nothing criminal. Remember.'

'I rememberin' everythin' and this no funny thin', you know. You jes' givin' a man a package an' he givin' you some money. You takin' you pay from the money an' givin' us the rest. I'm not seein' anythin' crinimal,' he said, getting the word wrong and not bothering to go over it again.

'What's in it?' I asked rattling the package, and Fat Paul didn't say anything. 'A video cassette?'

Fat Paul nodded and said, 'What you puttin' on a video cassette that's criminal?'

'How about child pornography?'

'Hah!' He sprung back from the table. 'This nothin' like that kind thin'.'

I gave him his package.

'You not gonna do it?'

'I'm going to think about it.'

He smiled and raised his eyebrows.

'Mebbe I'm helpin' you think. I'm payin' two hundred and fifty thousand CFA do this job, a thousand dollars, you understandin' me?'

'But none of it upfront?'

'You workin' for African people now, we no have the money 'fore somebody give it. Not like white people, they always havin' money . . .'

'Well, now I know what you want, I'll think about it.'

'You got any questions you wan' aks?'

18

'Tomorrow. I'll have some questions tomorrow.'

'You tekkin' long time think up you questions. How many you got?'

'If I knew that I'd ask them now.'

'You jes' give the man the package. And the man' – he slowed up for my benefit – 'the man he give you an envelope, wax sealed like this one. In the envelope is the money. You don't have to coun' it. Just tek it. Give one hand, tek the other. Is ver' simple thin'. I mean, Kwabena he could do it without troublin' he head 'cept he black. He only jes' come down from the trees. Still scratching hisself under the arms. No be so, Kwabena?'

Kwabena grinned at Fat Paul's insult with a twinkling set of ivories and so little malevolence it would concern me if he was my bodyguard.

'Don' be fool',' said Fat Paul, reading my thoughts, 'he lookin' kind and nice like mama's bo' but, you see, he got no feelin'. He got no feelin' one way 'rother. You go run wid the money. I say, "Kwabena, Mr Bruce go run with the money." He find you, tek you and brek you things off like spider thing. You got me?'

'No ploblem,' said Kwabena slowly.

'Time we goin',' said Fat Paul, looking at a watch on a stretch-metal strap which was halfway up his forearm. 'Leave Mr Bruce time for thinkin'. Time for thinkin' all these questions he gonna aks. I'm goin' rest, lie down, prepare mysel' for the big game.'

Kwabena helped Fat Paul to his feet. The waist of his dark-blue trousers had been made to go around the widest part of his body so that the flies were a couple of feet long, the zipper coming from an upholsterer rather than a tailor. He was bare-ankled and wore slip-on shoes because he couldn't get over his stomach to put on complicated things like socks and lace-ups.

'I like you, Bruce,' said Fat Paul.

'How do you know?'

'You smell nice,' he said, and laughed. He laughed hard enough so that I hoped he wouldn't bust his gut and he was still laughing when he left the shack, hitting the doorjamb a glancing blow and nearly bringing the whole thing down. A dog appeared at the door, attracted by the laughter, thinking it might mean good humour and scraps handed down with abandon. The barman hit him on the nose with a beer-bottle top and he got the picture and took off with his bum close to the floor, leaving us with only a thin thread of music on the radio for entertainment.

2

With Fat Paul gone and the *Ivoire Soir* finished I sucked on the *grande modèle* and fingered my face which still had a few livid marks from a beating I'd taken nearly a month ago. This was just the surface damage and it reminded me why I was even passing the time of day with a lowlife like Fat Paul who deserved the kind of attention you give a dog turd on the pavement.

Heike, the half-English/half-German woman I loved, who'd got mixed up in the ugly piece of business I had been involved in last month, had left Africa and gone back to Berlin from where she'd written saying she was looking for work.

B.B., the overweight Syrian millionaire to whom I still owed money after my last job working for him, was employing me, not on my daily rate, but on a small monthly salary and some expenses, which made the little I owed him feel like a twenty-five-year mortgage.

I was supposed to be handling the sacking of a Dane called Kurt Nielsen who was running B.B.'s sheanut operation in Korhogo. This was what B.B. had called his 'small problem in Korhogo' which didn't seem to be a problem at all, just a way of B.B. amusing himself by keeping me dangling on a string.

Kurt Nielsen had been messing with the local girls, keeping bad books and, worst of all, not calling B.B. I'd asked him what was wrong with playing around.

'Thass what I'm saying, Bruise,' B.B. had said. 'He not playing. He fall in lov'. Dese girls you don't fall in lov', you play. Is nice and light. You fall in lov' an' ever'ting spoil.'

21

B.B. didn't want him sacked until he had a replacement which he was finding hard to get. That's what he said anyway. I knew different. I knew it was because we'd agreed that I would start charging my daily rate when I'd got rid of Nielsen and B.B. hated the sound of my daily rate.

He'd made life sound attractive by offering an all-expenses-paid holiday in Grand Bassam until I was needed. Then I'd found that any expense was too much for B.B. and we'd been fighting over small change ever since. The only expense he considered legitimate were telephone calls which I had to make every day and which would finish with the same line: 'Calm, Bruise. Wait small. Now is not de time.'

Bagado, my Beninois detective friend, who had suffered a cracked collar bone during our last job, had come out of plaster and into continued unemployment in Cotonou. He had no money and the resources of his extended family were already overextended. I sent him money which I was borrowing from my Russian friend, Vassili, who was also helping me run Helen, my cook, who, although she wasn't cooking for me, was looking after a sick uncle of hers who needed medicine.

Moses, my driver, was with me but we couldn't afford much expensive Ivorian petrol so the car stayed put and Moses practised whatever it was he felt he hadn't perfected with the local girls. This was proving expensive for him and therefore for me, and I was threatening to cut out the middleman.

'Who the middleman, Mr Bruce?' he would ask.

'You, Moses.'

He clapped his hands and laughed at this and went through a succession of deep thoughts without finding the hidden meaning.

In an ideal world Heike would come back. Something awkward and sharp amongst all the food that B.B. shovelled into himself would get caught in his throat and he'd pass on into a better world. Bagado would get his job back in the police force. Helen's uncle would get better. I'd get some decent work and Moses would get a short sharp dose of the clap. Only the latter was a serious possibility.

So, I was bored – bored and broke. I needed something to do to take my mind off the things that were causing my brain to plod in tight circles, finding no answers to questions which didn't have any. I needed money. Fat Paul made out he was going to solve both problems.

In the late afternoon I went for a nap in my cheap room in a house on the furthest outskirts of Grand Bassam. It was a narrow cell on the flat roof of an old unpainted concrete block which had no glass in any of the windows and whose shutters had been used for firewood a long time ago.

After I'd jerked awake for the seventh time it was dark. I got up and took two shots of whisky as a mouthwash and then another two to cure the motion sickness. I called B.B. and he gave me the 'wait small' routine again. I didn't bother to check my answering machine at home in Cotonou, Benin, and instead I hit a place with beer and loud music called Le Cafard, the cockroach, a real sleazy joint for men who didn't shave and women who smelled strongly of cheap sex. I had shaved and I didn't buy any cheap sex, but people could tell I had the right temperament for the bar. I had *le cafard*, the blues, and they let me alone to get on with it.

I put away the last quarter of the bottle of whisky when I got back to my room and fainted into sleep, which came in short bursts of violent dreaming, and starts awake in blue-white flashes with instant fears of death, like travelling on a runaway subway train. I woke up face down, twisted in the sheet with sweat cold on my bare back. In the room the darkness was blacker than evil and the mosquitoes had found a note rarely played on the violin which stretched the brain to the thinness of fuse wire. I waited for dawn to paint itself into the room while I marvelled at the size and leatheriness of my tongue.

The bender, which I'd decided was my last, did me some good. I reckoned I'd bottomed out, which worried me because that was what politicians said about economic recessions when there was still some ways to go. I wrote down some pros and cons for doing Fat Paul's work for him and although his offer still looked as attractive as a flophouse mattress, it was beginning to show some merits. You could sleep on it as long as you held your nose and it would only be for one night.

Sunday 27th October

'You got it,' said Fat Paul after we'd been through the drop details for the third time. He leaned over his sloping gut to slap the table top but didn't make it. He settled a jewel-bitten hand on one of his pappy breasts.

He was dressed in the usual five square metres of face-slapping material. The blue and the white parakeets was off today. It was the red with green monkeys for Sunday. He snarled at Kwabena for a cigarette and took a handkerchief out and polished his face with it.

We were sitting at a table in my corner of the bar, which had annoyed Fat Paul because he had his back to the door and I had an angled view out of it down the beach to the sea. It was just coming up to one o'clock but Fat Paul had lost his appetite, maybe because it was hotter than yesterday with no rainfall for the last couple of days, or maybe he didn't like his back unprotected. He only ordered four pine-apple fritters.

'It's not what you'd call a regular piece of business,' I said.

'How so?'

'One, the money. Two, the location for what you call "the drop". Three, the contents of the envelope. Four, the characters involved.'

'Characters?' he asked.

'Fat Paul, Silent George, Colossal Kwabena.'

'Colossal?'

'Very big.'

'Is good word. I like it. Colossal,' he said, trying it out for size. Then he changed, getting aggressive. 'Whass wrong these people?'

'What do George and Kwabena do?'

'They my bodyguards.'

'That's my point,' I said. 'Why do you need your body guarded?'

'I'm not so quick on my feet.'

'Why do you need to be quick?'

'I make money.'

'Doing what?'

'Videos.'

'You got an office?'

He handed me a card which gave the company name as Abracadabra Video, Adabraka and an address on Kojo Thompson Road in Accra, Ghana. The company ran video cinemas. They specialized in showing action movies, mainly kickboxer, to local neighbourhoods. It was a lucrative business, there was a high cash turnover and hardly any overheads. A lot of people were interested in taking over the business but not paying for it. Kwabena provided the muscle to persuade them otherwise and if he couldn't cope George leaned in with the old metal dog leg and people quietened down, talked sensible, played cards and drank beer as if nothing had been further from their mind.

'You look like shit,' said Fat Paul, irritated now and trying another strategy. Trying to get tough with a line I hadn't heard before.

'My mother loves me,' I said without looking up.

'You got no money,' he said. 'No money to chop.'

'How do you know, Fat Paul?'

'You let me buy you chop.'

'You have to pay for what you want. Lunch lets you sit at the same table.'

'You not workin' for you'self.'

'How do you know that too, Fat Paul?'

'No self-respect,' he said.

'I suppose you think you know me pretty well?'

'I know shit when I see it.'

'I've got a good eye for it myself,' I said, looking at his brow which was swollen as if recently punched. Beneath it his eye sockets had no contour and his piggy peepers looked black and aware. Sweat ran down his cheeks as if he was crying. He didn't look as if anything could hurt him unless you tried to take away his plate.

'You just give the man the package . . .' intoned Fat Paul. I held up my hand.

'Thanks, I've got it. Listen . . .'

'No, no,' he said. 'You listen. First I show you where you mek the drop, out Abidjan west side, down by the lagoon Ebrié in pineapple plantation. You go there in the afternoon. The man he comin' from the north, he comin' late, he only get there after dark. You check the place, mekkin' sure you comfortable. Then go down Tiegba side fifteen-minute drive, nice bar, you waitin' there, the other man come. Relax some, drink beer, look at the lagoon. They's a village there on legs, ver' nice, the tourists like't ver' much. Then the time come. You ver' smooth now widde beer and the pretty place an' you gettin' in you car an mek the drop. 'S very easy thing, you know.' He sat back and put a hand up to his face and dipped the little finger in the corner of his mouth.

'Most nights,' I said, 'my motor reflexes put on a good show. I wake up in the mornings alive even if I don't feel it. Then, if I haven't been kissing the bottle too hard I find I have the coordination to stand up and move around. Getting somewhere, putting my hand inside my shirt and pulling out a package and giving it to someone is a cinch for a man with my kind of skills. What's more, I have the in-built ability to take something with my left hand while I'm giving something else with my right. I can also count and eat a biscuit at the same time, but you tell me this job doesn't take such talent.' I stopped while Fat Paul's lip took on another cigarette. 'Now you're beginning to see you're talking to someone who's done a few things in life. Someone who knows the difference between a French-restaurant cheese and a curl of dogshit, someone who knows where the grass is greenest there's twenty years of slurry underneath. So don't pretend to me that this job's a snap. Don't tell me about relaxing with beers and a tourist village on legs and all I've got to do is give a man a package when the postman does it every day and nobody gives *him* two hundred and fifty thousand CFA. Don't tell me there's no snags when there's money . . .'

'Snags?' Fat Paul interrupted. 'What are these snags?'

'Snags are problems, difficulties, obstacles.'

'Snags,' said Fat Paul, weighing the word on his tongue and giving me a good idea of what a cane toad with a bellyful of insects looks like. 'Lemme write these snags down.'

He reached around him for a pen and paper and then pretended to write on the palm of his hand. He knew we were coming to it now. I could see him blinking the shrewdness out of his eyes.

'Are you blackmailing somebody, Fat Paul?' I asked.

'Keep you voice down,' he said, looking up at the barman who didn't understand English. 'Blackmail? I not blackmailin' nobody. This no blackmailin' thing. This a secret thing is all.'

'What sort of secret?'

'I'm tellin' you that, it no a secret no more.'

'I asked you what *sort* of secret, not what it is. Personal secret, political secret, economic secret, arms secret . . . ?'

'Is a business secret.'

'Show me the cassette.'

Fat Paul surprised me by flicking his fingers at Kwabena, who took the package out from under his shirt and gave it to him. With one eye closed to the cigarette smoke he broke the wax seal on the package, took out a wad of paper around the cassette, threw the empty envelope on the table. The heavy-duty envelope was still addressed to M. Kantari, Korhogo. He handed me the cassette. There was nothing unusual about it. The cassette didn't look as if it had been tampered with or opened. I couldn't see anything in it apart from 180 minutes of magnetic tape.

'See?' said Fat Paul.

I folded the wad of paper around the cassette, put it back in the envelope and handed it back to Fat Paul, shaking my head.

'Now you jes' tell me two things,' said Fat Paul, ready for it now and finished with the game. 'One, if you gonna do it. Two, how much you wan' for doin' it.'

'A million,' I said, 'CFA. Four thousand dollars, you understanding me?'

The quality of the silence that followed could have been exported to any library in the world. George glanced across Fat Paul's inflammable hair at Kwabena who looked as if he'd taken a blow from a five-pound lump hammer and was

27

wondering whether to fall backwards. Fat Paul clasped his bratwurst fingers with the implanted rings and checked his watch, not for the time but because it seemed to be hurting him, cutting into his forearm. He pushed it down to his wrist and shook it. He breathed and kissed in the smoke from the glued cigarette on his lip in little puffs. He breathed out and the smoke baffled over his bottom lip.

'Too much. We find cheaper white man.'

'Go ahead. It'd be interesting to see the one you get who's going to make a drop of a "video of a business secret" at night in the middle of nowhere with money involved *and* at seven hours' notice, unless you can delay it some more?'

Fat Paul suddenly started to manage his hair with both hands like a forgetful toupé-wearer. He settled back down again.

'Seven hundred and fifty . . .' he started and I shook my head. He knew it. I had him down on the floor with both feet on his fat neck.

'Show him the place,' he said, smiling, and in that instant I saw that he thought he had won. He clicked it away with his fingers and Kwabena produced a stick of red sealing wax and a lighter and melted off a pool on to the envelope. Fat Paul planted his ring in it as it cooled and then blew on his finger.

'I need some expenses.'

'For a million CFA, you supplyin' you own expenses.'

'So where do we meet tomorrow?' I asked.

'Grand Bassam, one o'clock. There's an old warehouse lagoon side Quartier France, near the Old Trading Houses. You see the car. You find us.'

3

Time was speeding up, now that the theoretical pay scale had jumped a few points, so I went back to my room and lay down to get used to it. There was a lot to do if I didn't want to drift into this exchange unprepared and I reckoned some thinking might help and, although I could do it on my feet, I preferred to be on my back with something liquid in a glass on my chest.

I didn't want to use my own car for the drop. It was a mess, which attracted attention, and it had Benin plates which are beacon red on a white background. I'd have to hire a car. My Visa card was in a hospital burns unit somewhere recovering from a seared hologram and couldn't take a day's car hire without going into intensive care. B.B. was going to have to be tapped. If he didn't come through then I was going to have to rely on the money from the drop materializing. If it did, I could pay the car hire but I was still going to have to be careful. Fat Paul looked like the kind of businessman who, when he got money, thought gross rather than net and let his suppliers talk things over with George and Kwabena.

I found I was thinking more about the money than I was about what was supposed to happen between now and getting it, so I walked to the nearby crappy hotel, which doubled as a whorehouse, where I made my phone calls. There was a woman and a young girl in the lobby, both painted up like Russian dolls. The older and larger woman was asleep with her head on the back of her chair, while the girl sat on her hands and looked across the room as if there was a teacher telling her something useful. She was that young. There was no teacher, but some broken furniture behind the door in the corner which was gradually being used for firewood and above it all an old wooden fan turned with a ticking sound without disturbing any air.

The madame zeroed the meter without looking at it. I dialled B.B.'s number in Accra. She moved off with a sashay shuffle of such indolence that it took her twelve of my dialling attempts to reach the end of the counter which was three yards long. She was interrupted by a large-bellied African in a white shirt with the cuffs halfway up his forearms and a man's purse in his armpit. He nodded at the young girl and the madame's arm struck out for a room key. The man took it and followed the young girl's neat steps out of the lobby.

The satellite took my call and beamed it into Accra. B.B. picked up the phone before it had started ringing.

'My God,' he said, on hearing my voice. 'Bruise?'

'Yes.'

'My God. Is ver' strange ting. I'm tinking 'bout you dan . . . you on de phone.'

'A miracle.'

'Yairs,' he said, and I heard him slapping the wooden arm of his chair. 'What you want?'

'I'm still here.'

'I see . . .' he said, and I heard his fidgeting for a cigarette, the lighter snapping on and the first drag fighting its way down the skeins of phlegm in his lungs.

'I'm short of money,' I said.

'Ever'body short . . . Ka-ka-ka-Mary!' he roared for his housegirl, popping one of my eardrums so that it sang like a gnat. 'Ashtray,' he said, chewing over a forgotten sandwich in his jowls.

'I want you to go to Danish Embassy tomorrow. Ask about Kurt. You got passport detail I give you?'

'Yes.'

'Ask dem. See if dere's problem. You know, mebbe he haff problem back home.'

'You've got a replacement?'

'Mebbe.'

'You want to make it easy for yourself.'

'I'm thinking,' he said. 'I'm thinking I mek *your* job easy.'

'I'm sure you were.'

'What you say?' he asked, catching that change of tone and not liking it.

'About money, you mean?'

'Not about de monny! Bloddy monny! Dis ting. Dis monny ting. Gah!' I sensed him clutching at a twist in his gut. 'Yuh!' He sobbed and then relaxed. 'My God. Stop talking de monny. I know de monny. You yong people got no pay-scharn, you always tinking de monny, always tinking de next ting. You never tinking calm, you always runnin', runnin'. You wok for me, you learn, you learn the 'vantage of pay-scharn. De African he know it but you no' learnin' from him, you tinking he know not'ing, but I tell you, he know tings you never know. Wait small!' he roared and slammed down the phone.

There was going to have to be some money at the drop.

The young girl came back into the lobby, the guy behind her hitching his trousers after what must have been a knee-trembler in the passageway the time it took. He left. She sat down. I called my home number in Cotonou, Benin. The madame walked over and the girl handed her the money and the key. Helen picked up the phone in my house and I told her to make sure Bagado was there between five and seven tomorrow evening. There were some phone messages for me and she put the receiver on the machine and turned it on.

The four messages were all from a guy in England called Martin Fall. Two on Friday, another on Saturday morning and the last when he was roaring drunk on Saturday night. There was nothing from Heike which was crushing. I thought about calling her, but the last time her mother had answered and Heike wouldn't come to the phone. Her mother covered for her, but I could tell she was there. I could even see her waving those long slim arms of hers, the big hands open, the face screwed up.

I started dialling Martin Fall's home number in Hampshire. He was an ex-Army officer who'd quit after ten years in the service and set up his own security company, based in London. He advised despots on how to stay in power, provided weapons training for elite guardsmen and, I didn't know for sure, he probably brokered the odd arms deal as well. He was pretty sharp business-wise; he knew he wouldn't get many repeat orders from these countries when the advice broke down and the despots got what was coming to them so he'd branched out into the commercial world. He now gave corporate executives training on how to be tough, aggressive and competitive. This, as far as I could tell, meant waking them up at four in the morning to drop them in rafts in the middle of the North Sea and letting them cope with the busiest shipping lanes in the world for a couple of days.

He'd got into corporations at a high level and, with a mixture of a fabricated pukka voice and a tough exterior, had persuaded them to let him handle their security arrangements worldwide. So he advised these companies with offices and executives in dodgy parts of the world on how to avoid being blown up or kidnapped.

He'd given me some training late at night once when I'd walked into his study and had found him nodding off in a chair with a glass of whisky in his hand. I'd tapped him on the shoulder and had found myself flat on my back with a forearm across my neck, a jagged whisky glass an inch from my eyeball and Martin's horrible breath in my face.

He'd married an old girlfriend of mine called Anne, and we'd met quite a few times. When I said I was leaving the old country he'd decided that I could be 'his man in Africa'. This had meant nothing until now. I got through and told him to call me back, hearing the word 'cheapo' as I banged down the phone.

'You should listen to your fucking answering machine,' he started off sweetly.

'I did.'

'Once every three days. You must be rushed off your bloody feet. What are you doing out there? This is an Ivory Coast number you've given me.'

'I'm on holiday.'

'You anywhere near Abidjan?'

'Yes.'

'Good. You've got a job.'

'I know that.'

'What do you mean?'

'I'm being paid to sit around by one guy and I'm doing a job for another tonight.'

'Well, you've just got your third job. I've been approached by a guy called – hold on a sec – Samuel Collins of Collins and Driberg. They're diamond traders with offices in Hatton Garden and Antwerp. His son, Ron – is that Ronald? Maybe not – anyway he's twenty-seven years old, young, naive and impressionable; no, I dunno, but young Ron is going on an African trip to buy diamonds. He flies to Abidjan Monday October twenty-eighth on BA whatever, getting in at nineteen hundred hours, I think, but it doesn't matter because you're not meeting him at the airport. There's a couple of fixers who are going to do that.

'He's going to stay at the Novotel, which is good because we have an account with them and you're going to stay there too. He's due to go to a place called Tortiya which is up in the north somewhere, then he either flies out of Abidjan to Sierra Leone where the military are putting up some confiscated goods for tender or he goes to Angola. You don't have to go to Angola because I've got about twenty people out there already but you *do* have to go to Sierra if he goes. OK?'

'What do I have to do?'

'Look after him. His dad's worried about him.'

'He's twenty-seven.'

'A conservative estimate of his father's wealth is two hundred and fifty million.'

'Another poverty-stricken bum.'

'That's the ticket. Straight to the point, Bruce, that's why I picked you. There's one small catch.'

'How small?'

'Three hundred a day plus expenses.'

'How small's the catch, clever bastard?'

'Touchy.'

'Telling me the money before the catch.'

'Play the game, Bruce.'

'The catch, Martin.'

'It really is small. You can't tell him that you're looking

after him. He's an arrogant little fucker and he won't have any of it. That's the catch. Small, isn't it?'

'I'm not going to follow him, for Christ's sake. A white man following another white man in a sea of black faces. You've got to be kidding me?'

'Get close to him, Bruce. Be his friend. You're good at that.'

'How do you know?'

'*I* like you.'

'You like everybody.'

'I didn't like that Somalian bastard.'

'He's dead now.'

'Ye-e-e-s,' he said, as if he might have had something to do with it.

The madame was leaning on the end of the desk with her eyelids falling and her head jerking up when the door banged open and an African in full robes stood in the doorway and roared with laughter so that I looked around the busted furniture in the lobby for a punchline. She pulled off the same key and gave it to him. The girl didn't even bother to look up but stood and set off out of the lobby. The man left a strong smell of cheap spirit behind him, as if he'd been drinking twelve-year-old aftershave. He gave us another roar from the passageway which didn't sound so much like fun as stoking himself up for the big one.

'You still there?' asked Martin.

'Where are you going to send the money to?'

'You're that short, are you?'

'I am, yes, and it's tricky to be somebody's friend if you're cadging drinks all night.'

'There's a Barclays in Abidjan, we'll send it there. A couple of thousand, OK? Give us your passport number.'

I gave him the number.

'I won't be able to go to Sierra.'

'You'll find a way for three hundred a day.'

'Maybe you're right.'

'That just about wraps it up then. Give us a call when it's over.'

'Or, if I have any problems.'

'You won't have any problems. It's a piece of the proverbial. The easiest money you've ever made.'

'Somebody else said that to me today.'

'You're on a roll, Bruce. Enjoy it. I'll book you in the Novotel tomorrow night; you're on expenses from then on in.'

'You couldn't open up that expense account today, could you?'

'That's a little unconventional, Bruce.'

'I need to hire a car. Nothing to do with you. It'd be a help. Deduct it from my fee.'

'You know what *you* need?'

'No, but you're going to tell me and don't say "a proper job".'

'You need a credit card.'

'One with credit on it, you mean?'

Silence from Martin Fall who knew that everybody was in debt but that there was always cash . . . somewhere.

'I'm confused,' he said after some moments. 'I thought you were on holiday *and* had a couple of jobs.'

'I am. I do. But no money.'

Martin said he'd have the expense account open in five minutes. We guffed around a bit more, I asked about Anne, and we hung up.

The door from the passageway opened, the handle hitting the wall hard, and the robed-up African moved through the lobby on the end of a typhoon. The girl came down the passageway doing up her wrap and looking frightened. The madame had come off her elbows on the end of the desk and was standing with her fists balled into where her waist probably was. She said something in her own language which woke the older prostitute, who recognized the tone. The three of them set to it.

I phoned the Novotel from the middle of the cat fight and booked a car for that afternoon. Then I realized what all the broken furniture was about. The madame reached into the pile and brought out a piece of board and gave the girl three hefty whacks on the bottom before I dropped the phone and took the board out of her hand. She turned on me with

35

something in her eyes which I would have preferred to have been murder and I threatened her with the board.

'You pay for girl!' she shouted in French.

'I don't want the girl.'

'He want the girl' – she pointed out of the door – 'but he drink too much, he see the goods, he try but he no pay. You pay.'

'Why hit the girl?'

She blinked a few times at that because she wasn't sure why she was hitting the girl. 'You want to go hit him for me?'

I left money on the counter, which she rushed at, and got out of there leaving the madame pelting the older prostitute with drawbacks of the trade while the girl dropped on her haunches in the corner and cried.

4

It was 2.30 p.m. by the time I joined the Grand Bassam/ Abidjan highway and drove past the handicraft shops, who could sell you a pot for more than you'd pay in Sèvres, and traditional healers, who could put a spell on a troublesome mother-in-law in Tashkent. It was a pleasant drive along the palm-treed coastline, past a seamless *bidonville* of stalls selling tat, bars, and hotels specializing in rooms by the hour. I skirted the end of the airport runway and high up above the departures hall was a team of vultures, their fingers spread at the end of their wings, circling in the thermals, grumbling at the low incidence of pilot error since computers came in.

After the airport the two-lane Grand Bassam road joined a fourteen-lane highway into downtown Abidjan. I drove through the suburbs of Koumassi and Marcory with the Manhattan-style skyline of the financial district called Plateau in front of me. You could forget you were in Africa if you concentrated on the skyscrapers but at Treichville I broke right and the buzz and hot stink of life in the African Abidjan brought me home. I crossed the lagoon, that separated the two continents, over the Pont Général de Gaulle.

Life hadn't been so good in Abidjan recently. Before it was no different to being in any modern city; built around the lagoon the cityscape looked like Sydney and the facilities were much the same. Everything had been accessible on a well-larded expatriate salary and after work the residential districts of Cocody and Deux Plateaux were splashed with gold and silver lamé and rang with crystal laughter. On the other side of those well-clipped hedges the locals were beginning to hit the ground with sticks while they listened to the

President's fading charisma. Then the power workers went on strike. Now there was no guarantee of getting ice in a whisky and cool air to sleep in.

The Ivorians, like all the people along this coast, wanted to run their own country with a bit of democracy. Now that the money had run out, the price of coffee and cocoa had dropped and the value of pineapples foundered, people had taken to thinking they could do no worse than have a crack at it themselves. The army had sensed a mood and had staged a rebellion and the air force had followed. In the confusion a lot of shops were emptied by people with no credit facilities but strong arms and big appetites.

Order was re-established after a few pay rises were promised but not with the same respect for the law as before. Care had to be taken on the streets. There were a lot of fast young men who weren't above a little violence to get a handbag or a gold chain. People ran from their cars to the office and didn't bother to go out for a meal or try to see a film which might not make it to the last reel. Restaurants closed, businesses folded. Everybody stayed in and sweated by candlelight and drank very warm Beaujolais and thought about Geneva and other places of perfect order.

I parked my car in the Novotel basement, picked up the hired Peugeot that blended in with all the other Peugeots that were the only cars in Ivory Coast unless you had a ministerial Mercedes or a bandit's BMW. I worked my way north up to the Banco National Park passing the *fanicos*, a bunch of immigrant workers who stood in thigh-deep water all day washing clothes by pounding them against rocks in the river, and headed west towards the coastal town of Grand Lahou. They were few cars out in the susurrating heat, which meant that I didn't have to eat someone else's dust, picking grit out of my eyes on the graded road.

The drop point was in a pineapple plantation. Tracks had been cut through the fields for harvesting and one of these led down to a landing stage on the Ebrié lagoon, the body of water which stretched west from Abidjan about sixty miles. I decided to take Fat Paul's advice and check it out beforehand

and then drink beer in Tiegba until time came for the drop at 8.30.

I found a left turn with the orange arrow that George had told me about and took the dirt track between the acres of tilled grey earth with a foot-high pineapple every metre whichever way you looked. Three kilometres later the track dropped down steeply through thick vegetation to a large clearing of beaten and sun-baked earth from which a wooden jetty took off out into the lagoon.

It was no cooler down by the water. There was no fresh breeze coming off it, just more humidity and insects. Out on the jetty, down between the warped and loosening slats of the walkway, the water had hardly the energy to slop around the wooden support struts. Through the haze I could just see the opposite bank of the lagoon. The sun, still high even though there was only another hour and a half's light in it, punished the scene and the sweat dripped off my eyebrows. I turned back and something flashed in the corner of my eye from high up in the vegetation on the bank. I ambled back towards the car, casting about like a retired colonel with no troops to inspect, and a fish came up for a fly, leaving concentric ripples. Another flash – high up to my right and I got a fix on it this time.

Looking back from the jetty I could see another track dropped down at the far end of the clearing from where I'd parked. I stepped off the uncertain planking and picked up a stone and sent it on a blasé skim across the water. After a minute's fevered nonchalance I got back in the car and drove fast across the hard earth and up the other track. I broke through the vegetation and out on to the plateau of the pineapple plantation in time to see a whipped-up funnel of dust which hung well and long in the torpid air, making a screen of ash-grey voile through which the car, pulling away, was invisible.

The terrain curved so that I couldn't see the main road to Abidjan and I had to drive a fast and dusty kilometre to find out that whoever had been watching me was in a large dark saloon. The car, off to the right now where the track joined the main road, slowed into a gully, then kicked up on to the graded road and was engulfed in its own dust for a moment before finding a lower gear and heading east, back to the city.

I followed with the windows shut and the dust still finding its way into the car, mixed with the sweat streaming off my face and down my neck. I reached the gully and stopped. The car was too far ahead, and if I'd taken the gully at speed it would have put a kink in the chassis which might have been noticed. I sat back and watched the dust settle in a film over the dashboard and bonnet. A minibus passed from right to left driven by an African with white people in the back holding on to their seats. They were all wearing hats, which meant they were tourists, and they were hunched, grim and tense from a rough ride.

I should have turned right, driven back to the city, gone straight through Abidjan and out to Grand Bassam. I should have found Fat Paul sitting in some broken-down colonial house and given him his package along with some suggestions as to where, on his unchartered anatomy, he could stick it. I let the tourist bus get ahead and then turned left, following it at a distance down to the lagoon village of Tiegba.

Why did I do that, when the first of those snags I'd been on at Fat Paul about had just left a big rent in the threadbare fabric of my inner calm? Why, when Martin Fall was going to start paying me £300 a day plus expenses, did I carry on with a job that stank of disaster? Maybe my sense of honour needed a long stretch in a rehab centre to get itself realigned to cope with a modern world. Or was I just persuading myself that I was all confused with old-fashioned values handed down by well-meaning parents who would never understand the game.

I drove through the purpling afternoon and ran a film clip through my head which was clear as the day it had happened, twenty-two years ago. My father dying in a London hospital. The iron-grey light of a slate-cold, viral January — the month that saw off the parchment-skinned pensioners and people like my father with weak hearts and lungs black, clogged and bleeding from four decades of Woodbines and Capstans. His fingernails were blue, his grey and phlegmy eyes were frightened on either side of the black rubber oxygen mask which covered his dark lips. His hand dragged at the tube of the mask to pull it off and get it over with. The nurse chided him. He beckoned me over. I pulled the mask off a crack and heard the oxygen and then his voice like a radio on the other side of a windy railway track. 'Never do anything for the money,' he said to my sixteen-year-old innocence, 'and if you say you're going to do something, do it.' Those were the last words of a London contract electrician; he survived the night but didn't make it to mid-morning tea.

I'd taken this job for the money, so I'd failed him once. Now that I was following through with something I'd started would the old man be nodding his approval? I doubted it. I had an attitude problem, brought on by being alone too much, brought on by spending too much of my time with a bottle for company. One thing I did know was that I wasn't confused. The truth was, I wanted to see if I could get away with it – tempt fate and still beat it. Maybe Heike was right to stay away from me.

No other cars passed on the other side of the road before I dropped down to the landing stage for the boats across to the stilted village of Tiegba. It was 5.30 p.m. by the time I parked up by the bar where the sound of elderly, annoyed Americans filled the air like frogs sending invitations after dark. Some of them were getting into low flat boats, filming their feet with video cameras while they did it. Most of the rest were climbing up the wooden stairs to the bar.

I asked the driver if he'd seen the last car to pass him on the road. He looked at me as if he'd had a bellyful of something that wasn't food, and I was there to tread on his toes, while he patched up the inner tube of a tyre that wore its tread like a race memory. I left him to it and went up to the bar.

I nodded at a long-limbed guy slouched across a table. He nodded back. I washed in the two-man lavatory packed with seven desperate people jogging on the spot, their trainers squeaking on the tiled floor. The only things that were communicating were pacemakers and brand names.

'The john don't flush,' said a weary voice from one of the cubicles. The room groaned. I got out of there.

I ordered a beer and sat at the old guy's table. He introduced himself as Harold and told me about his trip, told me how many people had died on his trip, without my asking. I cut through it after five minutes and asked him if he'd seen the car. He said he had and that it was a dark saloon which was a big help – probably a Peugeot too, an even bigger help.

It was suddenly dark. Harold still hadn't moved anything apart from his hat across his face. There was an intensity in the atmosphere, a stillness that meant that rain was charging down the coast towards us. Nobody spoke. A woman sighed and a man added a rattly cough – we could have been in the end ward of an old people's home, the ward closest to the Chapel of Rest.

Lamplight flickered across the lagoon in the village. Low African voices coaxed the boats through the water. Toad-talk puckered the darkness and insects worked through the night. The air was stuffed into the room.

'Gonna rain,' said Harold.

The sprung fly-screen door whinged open and snapped shut. Harold's hat stopped for a moment. A younger man in his early sixties came in and told them they were going to leave. They moved as one. Harold straightened and said something about not wanting to die on the premises and an old woman from the group chastised him. He looked through me over my shoulder, out of the slatted windows and mosquito netting into the dark.

'I wouldn't wanna die out here,' he said, and then focused on me as if I was a candidate.

They filed out. Trousers hanging off bottoms with no buttocks, backs curved, forearms withered, breastless concave chests breathing shallow in the deep, thick air. The screen door slapped shut on the last of them.

I moved further into the bar and sat by the window which should have shown the lagoon or given at least the comfort of water lapping but showed only the grey haze of netting on black and the sound of air fizzing. The minibus moved off. A light breeze fanned off the water and guttered the candles on the tables. I had two more hours to kill.

The rain filled in the time. I helped it along with a few beers served by the barman who came from Sierra Leone and who demanded payment as soon as the bottle hit the table. He took the note and flattened it on the table, picking out any folds and creases and then folded it in half lengthways. He talked all the time, concentrating on his work and telling me he had left Sierra Leone because there was no work there and he reckoned the Liberian war was going to drift across the border and stir up trouble in the eastern part of his country where all the diamonds were.

'They look for diamonds, buy guns,' he said.

'Where do they get the guns from?'

'They have logs ... timber ... in Liberia, but no diamonds.'

'But where do they get the guns from?'

'On the east side, they have plenty wood. Fetch plenty money. You work in the logging camps?'

'No. You?'

'The guns,' he said, and stopped. The fly screen slapped behind a policeman wearing a black plastic bin liner which he stripped off. He sat down and the barman served him a drink he didn't pay for.

The rain roared. The water ran down the mosquito netting and the wind blew spray through it on to my face. It was good to breathe cool air with oxygen in it. The barman went behind his counter, the rain too loud for conversation. I felt the policeman's eyes on me as I sipped the beer and replaced the glass on the same ring on the table top.

I was sharing Harold's reluctance to die. His talk, the pointlessness of dying people touring the world when all they wanted to do was sit on the stoop sipping Diet Coke, had weakened my hands. I could barely pour the bottle, hardly grip the glass. The beer had soured my mouth and I began to think I was heading into something which if it didn't finish me off might put some years on me in a single, compact, fear-loaded minute.

Unlike Harold my objection was not to dying out here.

The location wasn't the problem. What did I care? Maybe Harold would rather belly up in the Piggly Wiggly car park in Fort Lauderdale. Me? I didn't give a damn — as long as it wasn't now. That was all I cared about.

My flesh was as chill as a fridged goose and the policeman's eyes were thinning the hair on the back of my head. I started, several times, to think of Heike sitting in a Berlin café stirring coffee, waiting for someone, but I canned each one before I let myself slide into that particular darkness.

The rain eased off, the policeman got up, rolled his bin liner and left. The insects started up again. The barman blew out the candles in the bar. I went down to the car. My teeth itched. I looked for the policeman, but it was too dark to see anything in the weakening light from the closing bar.

With the headlights on I wiped off the number plates and altered two of the numbers with the black tape I'd brought with me. It was probably a pointless exercise now that I'd been seen at the drop point, but pointlessness seemed to be the night's theme. Inside the car I removed the bulb from the interior light and rolled down the window.

I drove towards Abidjan breathing in the cool air full of the smell of wet earth from the pineapple plantation. I found the orange arrow and the track down to the lagoon. I rolled into the thick vegetation which covered the track dropping down to the bare, beaten earth in front of the jetty a few minutes after my 8.30 appointment. Large drops of water fell from the high trees as the tyres unstuck themselves from the mud.

The car skidded, as it came out of the trees, down on to the now puddled expanse of bare earth. My stomach lurched with it at the thought of trying to make it up the steep slope, at the other end of the clearing, if I needed to get away in a hurry.

The cone of light from the headlights was broken by the corner of another car. The radiator grille and mud-tread tyres belonged to a dark-coloured Toyota Land Cruiser. The paranoia kicked in. This was not the car driven by whoever had been watching me that afternoon. The dark saloon was still out there. I cut the headlights and the darkness shut down around us. If he was out there, he had to be close, because the night was black enough to have texture, so black that you knew that any light was inside your head.

I left the engine running and opened the door and, without getting out, shut it. I fixed my eyes on the patch of night where I knew the Land Cruiser's windscreen was and waited, the car in gear, my foot cocked on the accelerator.

A superior lock clicked. A lozenge of yellow light appeared twenty-five yards away. In the barley-sugar glow, head thrown back and mouth open as if napping in a layby, was the driver, a white man. Moving fast out of the passenger seat an African's head joined the night. His dark jacket, white shirt, black tie followed. A thin shaft of light, as solid as a blade, angled out. A white spot wobbled over the vegetation. The beam arced across the night sky, the white spot finding nothing out there, before it slashed through the blackness spearing my windscreen.

I dumped the clutch and picked up speed moving at an angle to the Land Cruiser, no headlights, using the cabin glow from the open Land Cruiser door to aim for where the African stood, a gun in one hand, the torch in the other. A shot – a crack of flame opened and closed. Then the torch was falling, my tyres slapping the puddles. The African's empty left hand gripped the Land Cruiser's roof rack. His right hand, still with the gun, pushed up off the door frame. His legs kicked up behind him. Another shot, another white line across the retina, and brown water burst in a puddle to my left. Then impact – the right corner of my car slammed the jeep's door shut. The cabin blacked out. The Land Cruiser rocked. The man's knees, elbows, toes and heels scrabbled across the roof rack. A body splashed in water. An engine howled.

I turned the headlight on. The track was a hundred metres away. The ground was troughed and shadowed with plateaux of light from the rain water. The car's suspension panicked and jarred, the frame of the windscreen swerved and dipped. Different patches of trees held their leaves up against the light.

I hit the path and cut the headlights to sides only and

eased my foot off the accelerator, still in first gear, the engine not screaming any more. Another shot cracked off. The car crawled up the slope. The front end slid right – the wheel, violent in my hands, snapped at my fingers. The tyres ripped over the slippery ruts of the track and caught on the drier central ridge but slid back and zipped in the mud. The car crabbed sideways and forward, the angle crazed, the tyres chewing at the road not catching, the body slewing and then rearing at the track's edge. The rubber caught, the chassis lunged with the sound of gravel pockmarking the underseal. Another shot – the sound of ice cracking over a river and something with a sharp bite, like a horse fly, stung my neck. The car scrabbled like a desperate climber on a chute of scree. Another shot – the trees closer, my shoulders hunched forward, face up against the glass, the trees even closer but not in them yet, one more shot and then into the noise of the trees, the drops of water slapping and gonging on the metal. A warm trickle dropped below my collar, pooled in the clavicle hollow and ran down my chest.

I stabbed the headlights on, which lit the tunnel of vegetation leading out on to the flats of the pineapple plantation. The car baulked at the rain-filled troughs across the track. The shock absorbers did what they were paid to do. The displaced water shot off into the night with the sound of torn paper. My eyes flickered between the rectangles of mirror, waiting for headlights to appear.

The gully between the track and the graded road was flooded and I hit it at speed, the rain water pouring over the bonnet up to the windscreen. The car clawed its way up the bank as I lashed out at the wipers which swiped the screen in double time. Still no lights appeared in the mirrors. Steam poured out of the wheel arches and the engine faltered, leaving blank spaces in my chest. The fan belt screeched like a stuck pig as the car humped on to the road, the windscreen squeaking dry under the crazed wipers. The Peugeot gripped the road and I rallied through the gears back to Abidjan looking for lights, but the mirrors shone black all the way.

It was nearly eleven o'clock by the time I reached my room near Grand Bassam and the power was off. I flexed my fingers, still stiff from gripping the steering wheel, lit a hurricane lamp and drank from the neck of a bottle of Bell's. I flopped under the mosquito net with it, and stared at the fan which hadn't worked even with electricity.

My thoughts steadied in the yellow light which swayed lazily on the walls. I could see the Land Cruiser's driver, the white man who was supposed to make the drop, not sleeping but dead. There was no blood on him but he was stretched back, stiff, a line across his neck, the garrotte tied around the seat's head rest. The African I'd only seen for a second. His hair was close cropped and he had soft, rounded features with the light skin of a Métis which had shown three tribal cicatrices on the cheek dark against it.

I turned the lamp off and took a final suck on the bottle. My jaw began to loosen off and I went to sleep with Fat Paul where I didn't want him – sitting heavily on my mind.

5

I woke up with a headache, a pain in the neck and a whisky bottle where a lover should have been. The sheets reeked. The room was already hot from the sun pouring through the unshuttered window and I had a film of sweat on my forehead and top lip. I felt a weight at the foot of the bed and started, but it was only Moses striking a maternal pose. I propped myself up on an elbow and saw the blood on the pillow. I kicked my way out of the mosquito net, Moses looking at me as if I might refuse to go to school.

'I'm all grown up now, Moses. You don't have to watch over me.'

'You bleeding, Mr Bruce, please sir,' he said. 'That car, thess hole in window, back one driver's side.'

The mirror showed something that looked human but had been kept underground for a long time. Moses appeared on my shoulder and I told him to look at the back of my neck. He drew the collar down, sucked on his teeth and took a pair of tweezers out of the penknife on the table. After a sharp pain that travelled down my spine to my coccyx and back up again he showed me the diamond of glass that had embedded itself in my neck.

'You be lucky,' he said.

'Maybe I am.'

'You be lucky bullet stoppin' in head rest passenger side.'

'And not in me, you mean?'

'No, please sir, not goin' on brekkin' other window, you pay two and ibbe costly.'

'Thanks for your concern.'

'Your good health is mine. You are my mastah,' he said in a tone of voice I knew well.

'How much do you want?'

Moses grinned. When he used the words 'sir' and 'mastah' it always meant money. He looked off into his head somewhere, pretending to do a calculation when he'd already cheated the answer.

'Two thousand.'

'Cedis?'

'We in Ivory Coast,' he said. 'They speakin' French here and asseptin' CFA. Cedis gettin' me nothin' 'cept Ghana side.'

'Is it cheaper Ghana side?'

'Oh, no, please sir. Ghana girls are very demandin'.'

'These girls sucking you dry, Moses. This rate you never afford yourself a wife, you owing me too much money.'

Moses took the money with his right hand, his left holding the wrist, his head bowed. 'Thanks for your concern,' he said.

He slipped past me out of the door and I called him back.

'I go-come,' he said.

The girl was leaning against the hired Peugeot with a pair of strong arms folded. She saw Moses and stood. Her breasts were high, almost on her shoulders, and the white nylon blouse, with its frilly trim at the shoulders and neck, looked incongruous against the developed shoulders and biceps. She rolled Moses's money in the top of her wrap. Moses was talking fast. She ignored him and pushed off the Peugeot with her rock-hard bottom, and moved off into the trees.

'Strong girl,' I said to Moses, who had returned with the body language of someone now completely at my service.

'Not jes' inne arms, Mr Bruce,' he said, and snapped a finger as if he'd just picked up something hot.

Moses cleaned and dressed my wound after I'd showered. We stripped the black tape off the number plates and packed our things into the car. I had an argument with the landlady who'd heard I was moving to the Novotel which made her push for a full week's rent. She had a baby girl on her back, who looked around her mother's hips at the action, occasionally stretching out a small hand at the money in mine as if she understood the game and couldn't wait to get started. We left at 9.30 a.m., the woman lobbing insults at us while the baby, who'd taken a fat elbow in the cheek, cried.

We found a garage in Zone 4C which could repair the hire car's window. Two young and violent-looking boys wearing sawn-off corduroys and sandals made out of old tyres were slapped away from the car by a more cultured-looking fellow in a white coat who removed the panel from the door. Moses, who'd seen a crowd gathering across the street, pulled me over the road.

We went into a walled compound of a two-storey concrete office block. The sun, already high, was hot and the surface of the red earth in the compound was drying into crushed chillies. Steam hugged the surfaces of large crimson puddles. In a clearing amongst the crowd stood a group of dejected Africans and a large Lebanese in a white robe which was stained red at the bottom. A grey-haired African in a white shirt and lime-green trousers stood next to him. The local witch doctor, they said.

The witch doctor had come to find out who was thieving money from the Lebanese. He told the first man to kneel and, detaching a bag from his belt, poured a mound of sand in front of the kneeling man who leaned forward over it. He looped a cotton noose over the man's head and poked the loose hanging strand into the mound of sand. He asked him in his own language if he had stolen the money and the man with quivering thighs said that he hadn't. There was a pause. Nothing happened. The noose was removed and the man joined the crowd.

The witch doctor repeated the ritual with the others who all passed. The Lebanese was perplexed until somebody suggested the accountant and he perked up. The cry went up and a moment later the small, fine-featured accountant came down the steps of the office building weighed down by his own dignity and an array of pens and a wafer of a calculator in the breast pocket of his shirt. The crowd instantly disliked him.

He refused to submit to the black magic and was rewarded with a low grunt from the crowd. The Lebanese told him there would be no job for him unless he did. The accountant knelt before the mound of sand. The crowd thickened. The witch doctor looped the thread over the man's head and asked him the question. The denial was on the way out of the man's throat when it was strangled by the cotton noose which seemed to have been pulled taut by an unseen hand. It bit into his neck, jerked his head down, popped his eyes and forced his tongue out till the stalk showed at his teeth. The crowd surged and the accountant erupted above their heads flailing, the pens and the calculator already gone from his breast pocket, his shirt torn open and his trousers already down his thighs. Moses pushed me out of the compound.

'They go beat him now,' he said.

It was midday by the time I'd returned the car and checked into the Novotel whose main entrance backed on to the busy Avenue Général de Gaulle, where you could buy hi-fi, hardware and haberdashery during the day but only whores at night. I sent Moses out to buy a blank VHS tape which, after the car expenses, took me down to the last few thousand CFA I had.

Martin Fall had booked me into room 205 on the second floor which the management changed to 307 on the third because an agronomist convention had taken the whole of the second. I asked at reception if they had any private video viewing and recording facilities and the girl said she would set something up for me. I took my bags up to the room and called B.B.; he wasn't there. I left a message with his maid that I was in the Novotel.

I came back down with Fat Paul's package. Moses appeared with the blank tape. I told him to get lost for half an hour. I was taken to a small conference room where a TV and two VCRs had been set up next to a whiteboard and an overhead projector. I broke the seal on the envelope and slotted the original and blank tape into the two machines and played and recorded at the same time.

There was some snow and then the film's title appeared and, in case you couldn't read, a lazy, Afro-American dude's voice told you what it was: 'Once you tasted chocolate . . .' and I realized that this wasn't the film that the Métis was

51

expecting to have to kill for. I watched it all the same, in case Fat Paul's 'business secret' was thrown in there somewhere. It was a tawdry tale, shot on a low-budget set, of a white, heavily wigged and made-up housewife who, having waved her husband goodbye, is immediately visited by two large black plumbers with tool boxes and wrenches for verisimilitude. The three of them went into the kitchen which shook when the door closed. The woman knelt down to show the plumbers what was going on under the sink and the sorry state of her underwear. At this point there should have been something flashing on the screen for the benefit of all plumbers and would-be plumbers like, 'This only happens in porn'. In an indecently short time the woman's skirt was up around her waist and there were two implausibly hung plumbers in front of and behind her. It went on like that. There were a few close-ups of nearly surgical detail and plenty of the rear plumber's view, who ground into the girl's bottom with sickening thrusts, which shuddered a butterfly tattoo she had at the top of the cleft. After a few changes of position and what seemed like half a day but was only fifteen minutes it was all over and they left, that's right, without doing the plumbing job. She didn't seem to mind which is where the suspension of disbelief really broke down badly. You'd have thought after that they'd have done the work for free. Then the girl was on a sofa and hubby came home and he was straight from the office and dead keen but she wasn't having any of it and the punchline came up delivered for the non-readers in the same voice: '. . . you can't never go back to vanilla.' The double negative giving some cohesion to the film. Then there was more snow which I stopped after a few minutes.

The tapes rewound, I boxed them and I went back up to reception to find Moses sitting in the lobby looking hang-dog at his flip-flopped feet.

'What's the matter?'

'I pissing glass, please, Mr Bruce,' he said a little too loudly for a hotel lobby. We watched the pink newspaper that had been sitting next to Moses close and fold and a businessman took his full head of side-parted hair elsewhere. I sat in his place. Moses shrugged and played with his fingers.

'What about the condoms I gave you?'

'They finish.'

'*They* finish?'

'Yes please.'

'No, *you* finish when *they* finish. When *they* finish *you* stop.'

'I don' understand.'

'When you no have condom, you stop, you no stop you go get AIDS.'

'I try,' he said, showing me a pair of clean palms. 'They no let me.'

'I can tell you really protested,' I said, and told him to get the car.

I went up to my room and split open Fat Paul's cassette. There was nothing inside it except tape. I stuffed it back inside the envelope with its broken seal. I dropped the copy into reception and kept the original with me. Moses was waiting outside.

We drove around the Baie de Cocody past St Paul's Cathedral and into the residential suburb of Cocody itself. I left Moses at the Polyclinique and gave him the last of my money.

'This no catch for nothin', Mr Bruce, please sir.'

'It'll have to catch because that's all I've got.'

'You go-come?'

'I go-come.'

''Cause if the money no catch ibbe big plobrem. They callin' police and things.'

'Nobody'll touch you, Moses, when they know what you got.'

I arrived in Grand Bassam *centre ville* just after 1.00 p.m. and turned right past a somnolent *gare routière* and headed out across the lagoon to the Quartier France. This used to be the main trading centre and port of the Ivory Coast until yellow fever hit the town at the end of the last century. The French moved out and opened up the Vridi canal in 1950 which made Abidjan the country's port. The old trading houses still existed, most of them broken down and crumbling like any African economy you'd care to look at. It was in one of these that I was due to meet Fat Paul. I saw the Cadillac parked outside a building which fronted on to the lagoon. It had a large hole in the wall and a drift of rubble down to street level. I turned left 100 metres in front of the Cadillac and parked up on the other side of the building from it.

I walked up some steps through a cracked and splintered wooden door into a cool dark room whose plaster lay shattered on the floor. There was a short passage from the room into a large and warmer warehouse, still with most of its roof on. At the far end, by the hole, was Fat Paul wearing a short-sleeve shirt of cobalt blue with red palm trees on it. He was sitting on a packing case with Kwabena next to him, up on an oil drum, his trousers tight across his thighs, bare ankles showing, his feet just off the ground. George was leaning against the wall by the hole, looking out over the lagoon and fingering his tie.

The warehouse had a wooden pillared corridor three metres wide. The pillars supported a mezzanine whose floor had been ravaged by a type of beetle that did for wood what the pox did for a port whore's face. Through the opiate quiet of the early-afternoon heat came the ticking sound of small jaws undermining the structure and powdering the air with dust motes which hung, dazed, in the shafts of light coming through the roof where the tiles had shifted or broken.

Kwabena pushed himself off the oil drum, picked up a strip of packing-case wood with a nail in the end and went over to where George was standing by the hole in the wall. He tried to push the nail out with his fingers and failed, so swung it against the wall where it made a sharp crack like a festive squib. The thin man inside Fat Paul jumped about a foot, and nearly got away, but his elephant-seal body caught him and set off a crescendo tremble which he quelled manually.

George's sunglassed head turned under beta-blocker control. A gun came from under his jacket in the armpit. He swept the room and put the gun back in his armpit again and turned to look out across the lagoon, thinking he was the Ice Man in some sharp, smart, budget thriller. Fat Paul said something rapid and savage in Tui and restuck a slick of hair that had fallen loose.

'Fuckin' man,' he said for my benefit. 'I send you back to the forest ... you fuckin' person!' he yelled over his shoulder.

'Nervous?' I asked.

'No,' he said loudly, then calm again: 'What you got for me?'

'I'm surprised you're here.'

'Why?'

George's right hand was down by his side, the fingertips tapping the outside of his thigh. Kwabena dropped the strip of wood. Fat Paul held his cheek and chewed the end of his little finger.

'Remember what we talked about on the beach?'

'We said lot of things.'

'Snags. Remember that?'

'Fuckin' snags,' said Fat Paul bitterly, so that I nearly laughed. 'Tell me.'

'Maybe you know already.'

'Tell me anyway.'

I was standing in a shaft of light, the sun hot on my head and a shoulder. I moved towards a pillar. Kwabena moved opposite me four or five yards off, his smell strong in the heat.

'I checked the drop point in the afternoon,' I said. 'Someone was watching. I thought it might be the guy who was going to give me the money, thought he might be checking to see if I was white and reliable. I went after him and got close enough to see he was in a dark saloon. When I went back to make the drop at eight-thirty the other car was there, but not a saloon – a Toyota Land Cruiser. The white guy was in the driver's seat but there was an African sitting next to him. The white man was taking a long nap with a piece of wire around his neck, tied to the head rest. The African had things to say, but with a torch and a gun. That's what I mean by snags. Big snags. Big snags you didn't tell me about.'

'You're here,' he said, as if I was making a big fuss.

'And I wouldn't mind knowing what's going on.'

'Sure you would. Were you followed?'

'I didn't look.'

Fat Paul fluttered his fingers and George disappeared out of the hole and Kwabena set off past me down the pillared corridor.

'Why'd you make the drop out there, Fat Paul?'

'That's the way he wanted it.'

'Like hell he did.'

'You just in it for the money, what do you know?'

'My mistake.'

'You too hungry. No chop enough.'

'So why didn't we do it at a petrol station, or a bar outside Abidjan? Why did we go out there in the boondocks?'

'Boondocks, snags, you teachin' me things I don't know. Is good,' he said, patting his molten-tar hair. 'But you aksin' too many questions, my likin'. What you wan' know everything for? You the paid help.'

George pulled himself back through the hole in the wall, slipping on the rubble outside. He held up a hand, the lump in his armpit visible. I took out the package and shook the cassette out into my hand and threw it on the floor towards Fat Paul. Kwabena came from behind me and picked it up.

'Not what I'd call an "important film".'

'You learnin' fast,' said Fat Paul, now standing and giggling. 'You enjoy the show? They big boys, huh? Mekkin' you white boys feel small?'

'So now you know the competition's out there,' I said. 'One man dead, nearly two. The real thing must be important.'

'You still wan' make some money?'

'I made that mistake already.'

'No, you right. This corruption thing with money too bad. You do it for free this time. Is better for you.'

'You know how to annoy people, Fat Paul.'

'People been annoyin' me all my life,' he said, quick and loud. 'White people tellin' me I'm fat. Tellin' me that all the time, like I don't remember. So I call myself Fat Paul jes' so *they* know, *I* know.'

'I'll be leaving now and I won't be seeing you.'

'You staying right where you are and doin' what you told,' he said.

'Is that right?'

'You got no option.'

'Don't order me around, Fat Paul, and don't make threats. That way we might stay friends the last thirty seconds I know you.'

I walked back down the pillared corridor until I heard a noise like a golf ball being hit into a mattress and a piece of wooden beam in between two pillars disappeared in a burst of powder. I stopped and turned to see George with his gun in his right hand and the suppressor he'd attached resting in his left palm.

'You involved now, Bruce Medway,' said Fat Paul, smiling. George slapped the heavy suppressor on his palm. Kwabena put his hand down his trousers and straightened himself out.

'For the moment,' I said.

'To the finish,' said Fat Paul, shaking his head. 'The only stupid thing you doin' is lookin' too much the money. Mebbe I give you no money you do it right.'

'I lose interest when I work for free.'

'I tell you something might help you,' he said, beckoning me with a flap of his hand. I walked over to him. He took a package off the oil drum where Kwabena had been sitting, identical to the one I'd had, and tapped it on his thumbnail. 'You a clever man, Bruce. It make sense not to use your car. Hirin' the Peugeot was good thinkin', and changin' the numbers a good idea, tekkin' out the light a better idea . . .'

'The policeman?'

'And the bartender.' He nodded. 'You drink three beers. Leave eight-fifteen. They find a Land Cruiser with a dead man down by the lagoon this mornin'. Tyre marks clear in the mud after the rain. They doin' autopsy findin' time of death, should be eight/eight-thirty. This lookin' dicey for you, they find you were there. You understandin' you involvement now?'

'It's coming to me.'

He held the package over his shoulder and Kwabena took it and handed it on to me.

'Another film?'

'You no need to know nothin' this time.'

'Who's it for?' I asked, looking at the blank envelope. 'There's no Kantari this time.'

'Mebbe we findin' there's other people in the market.'

'So where's the drop?'

'We call you.'

'I'm in the Novotel. I've got another job starting tonight.'

'That's nice. You gettin' popular. This thing all over before nine tonight.'

'What time are you going to call?'

' 'Tween five and six. 'safternoon.'

'And if you don't call?'

'I'm only half African.'

'And the other half?'

'American,' he said, stroking his neck. 'My fadder like them white girls. You know them aid workers. He fuck one, she havin' me then leavin' me with my fadder when she go back to the States. They don't like white girls comin' back home with little black piccaninny under they arms.'

'You staying out here in Grand Bassam?'

He thought about that for a moment, shook a hanky out and polished his face round and round getting slower.

'We in the Hotel La Croisette on the front.'

'You don't like Abidjan?'

'They nervous in Abidjan. I like keepin' calm.'

'You mean you don't want to get seen, a man your size in that shirt.'

'Time for lunch,' he said, looking at his watch. 'We no chop yet . . . you?'

I shook my head. He turned and walked to the hole in the wall with surprising speed, Kwabena just in front of him. He took the big man's arm to support himself going down the rubble pile.

'Bon appétit,' he said over his shoulder. 'We call you.' No need to bother about me now. No need to buy me lunch.

No need to work on me any more. Someone calls you a clever man, it's always because he's cleverer.

From the hole in the wall I watched George swing open the Cadillac's heavy door and get into the driver's seat. Kwabena opened the back door. Fat Paul sat on the edge of the seat while Kwabena stirruped his hands. Fat Paul put his foot in them and pushed himself across the back seat into some cushions arranged against the other door. George waited with his hand on the ignition until Kwabena was sitting next to him. The engine roared and then bubbled. The car moved off.

The flat blue-grey lagoon lay stagnant in the afternoon heat. There were no boats out. Two men lay under some palmleaf thatch down by the water, sleeping. A car started, off in the buildings behind me somewhere, and I leaned against the broken wall and thought about how neatly I'd been stitched.

I replayed Fat Paul buying me lunch, opening the package, showing me the contents, resealing it, being open, frank, talking me through it, gaining my trust, letting me think he was a bit of an idiot, letting me bargain him up for a payoff he was never going to have to make. He'd got himself into an all-win situation. If I'd been killed he'd have known he had a problem. I didn't get killed, he still knew he had a problem and he could use me to clear it up. Saved himself some money, too.

6

I picked up Moses at the Polyclinique. He'd lost his hang-dog look and was waving his prescription at me as if it was a winning lottery ticket.

'No money,' I said, and his face crashed.

'I still pissing glass, Mr Bruce.'

'I'm sure you are. Don't drink anything,' I said. 'We might get some money this afternoon. Mebbe you shouldn't have given the girl the two thousand she giving you trouble down there.'

'Two thousand CFA don't catch for this thing,' he said, shaking the paper, 'and I don't know she giving me trouble down there. I know, mebbe I beat her doing this thing.'

'She looked as if she could give *you* a beating, you ask me.'

'Mebbe you right, Mr Bruce. She stroooong woman.'

We parked up in the Novotel garage. Moses gave me his prescription and I told him to come and see me first thing in the morning. I asked reception to put Fat Paul's new sealed package in the hotel safe and went up to my room, double-locked the door and flaked out on the bed. I dreamt, no doubt something meaningful which would catch up with me later, and just as an unanswered ringing had begun to annoy me, I woke up with the phone on the other side of the bed, insisting. Somebody had filled my mouth with those things the dentist puts in to soak up the goo, but it didn't matter because it was B.B. on the line and he was speaking through a mouthful of four bananas.

'You tek your time,' he said.

'I was sleeping.'

'It three in de afternoon.'

'All this leisure tires me out.'

'I see . . .' he said, swallowing something that must have been the size and furriness of a tennis ball because it took him several goes and left him out of breath. 'Ra-ra-ra-ra Mary!' he stammered at a roar to the maid and I heard the slip, slap, slop of her arrival at his side. 'Drink,' he said. He put the receiver on his stomach and I heard some subterranean noises that would have made a potholer rush for the surface.

'What you doing in the Novotel?'

'I'm staying here.'

'For your own accoun'?'

'Unless you want to pay?' I said, hearing that line fizz through his brain.

'I not payin' for dat!' he roared. 'Gah! You tinking for one . . .'

'B.B., calm down. I'm paying.'

'Mebbe you pay me de monny you owe me 'fore you go stayin' in de Novotel.'

'You'll get it, and when you do I'm up to my daily rate, remember.'

'Bloddy daily rate! Bloddy ting! You teef man wid your daily rate!'

'What do you want, B.B.?' I asked, measuring out the syllables. B.B. bubbled some more, chewed over his anger and spat it out like gristle.

'First ting,' he belched. 'You go, you go tomorrow. Kurt, he gone. He not dere. I don' know where he gone. De wife, she say he still dere. I aks to spik to him. She say he always out. You go, you find de problem. You still haf de Kurt passport detail?' he asked, knowing I still had it from the last time he'd asked me. He coughed a quantity of phlegm into his mouth and I felt him search for his hanky. 'Second ting,' he said, spitting the oyster, 'you go to Danish Embassy?'

'Not yet.'

'What you doin' all day?'

'I've got a tight schedule.'

'Mebbe you try wokking in de day like rest of us. Sleep at night, you know.'

'I'll make a note of that.'

'You go to Danish Embassy this afternoon; this Kurt man a criminal, I know it. T'ird ting, de Japanese, dey come.'

'Which Japanese?'

'De company dat buy de sheanut. Dey have de croshing plant in Japan.'

'I know, but what are their names?'

'My God, dis difficult ting. Har-ra-ra-ra-ra . . .'

'Was that one or both of them?'

'No, de udder one is, Ka-ka-ka-ka-ka . . .'

'Fax me.'

'You tinking correck.'

'What about money?'

'Wait de monny!' he shouted, irritated. 'De Japanese . . . you show dem round, show dem de operascharn, you give dem good time, tek plenty whisky. Kurt wife, she help make some food tings an' such. OK?'

'Fine. The money for this?'

'You always aksing de monny!'

'I haven't got any and it often slips your mind.'

'De monny in Barclays Bank. I transfer two million CFA.'

'Is there anything left in Korhogo?'

'No. All gone. You find de books and tell me where it gone. OK. You better horry or de bank it shut,' he finished, the phone clattering into its cradle.

I called the Danish Embassy and made an appointment to see a vice-consul called Leif Andersen at 4.00 p.m. The sky had clouded over by the time I left the hotel at 3.15 and looked ready for rain. I took a taxi to the bank in the Alpha 2000 building and told the car to wait while I withdrew both B.B. and Martin Fall's money. I put it in a plastic carrier bag from Le Coq Sportif that I'd brought with me. The taxi was gone when I came out, which was a small worry. I didn't want to dally too long in the street with a bag holding nearly 3 million CFA — $12,000 doesn't look much like a pair of running shoes.

Up the street a rangy kid of about twenty, in a sweatshirt with a big number thirty-two on it, strolled out of a shop doorway with his hands in his baggy jeans pockets. He had his hair razored up over the ears and cut flat top. Across the street another punk looked over the roof of a car, wearing a baseball cap the wrong way round and a black T-shirt with something white on it. These kids had been watching movies, I thought, and turned to walk down the hill. Two boys walked out of a garage in front of me, one lifting his T-shirt to get some air up there and to show me what he had in the waistband of his jeans, the other with an ear missing. These two were shabbier, old jeans cut tight, faded T-shirts. The one with two ears had Mr Smile on the front without the smile, both with no shoes. I turned back and the other kid was standing by the door to the bank, his friend starting to cross the road now. The taxi rounded the block and started cruising down the hill in no hurry. I walked up the hill towards it, the kid outside the bank with his hands out of his pockets now, wiping them on his shirt front, nervous, like me. I ran at him. His eyes widened, looking for his friends. I could hear a pair of trainers and the slap of bare feet on the pavement. I kicked the kid outside the bank hard on the inside of his left knee and he went down so fast on to the concrete slabs of the pavement that his head hit the ground first. I turned, the taxi coming in front of me now, the kid from across the road in between the parked cars and the one with both ears between the taxi and me, a flash of silver in his hand. The driver, still coasting, opened the passenger door and hit the kid on the point of the elbow. The kid went down and the knife span across the pavement. I got in the taxi, the other two boys backing off.

I told the driver that when a man goes into a bank and tells the taxi to wait it wasn't just out of a feeling of importance. He said he knew that but the traffic police didn't give a damn. Then he thought about it and said he reckoned they were on the take. They were always there for a parking fine and nowhere near a bag snatch. I told him it was the same the world over.

We drove around the block. I pointed him down Avenue Chardy and into a car park at the back of some buildings. I went into a travel agent called PanAfricAbidjan and found a Swiss guy in there who spoke seven languages, one of which was mine. I asked him if he could make 75,000 CFA available in a travel agent called Bénin-Bénin in the quartier Zongo in Cotonou. He made a phone call and said he could. I gave him the money from my Coq Sportif bag.

At the Novotel reception I took some more money out of the bag and asked them to put the rest of it in the hotel safe. I went into a chemist and picked up Moses's prescription and bought a large supply of condoms for him which they were decent enough to wrap. It was a short walk from the chemist's to the Danish Embassy and I was shown straight into the vice-consul's office with its windswept off-white carpeting that looked like snow on its way to sludge.

Leif Andersen was a short, powerful, mid-thirties guy with a friendly brown moustache and a face that had enjoyed a few too many drinks, as it was puffy with vein maps leading nowhere on his cheeks. He was wearing a sports jacket, a white shirt, and some kind of club tie with wine glasses and bottles all over a burgundy background. He sat with his fingers dovetailed across a bit of a belly beneath a painting of some bleak North Sea-whipped Danish coastline which made me grit my teeth in the overstrong air conditioning.

'How can I help you?' he asked.

'Got a visitor's jacket?'

'Sorry,' he said, opening his hands. 'The AC's stuck.'

'At minus five?'

'Plus sixteen, zero humidity.'

'Any chance of something to drink?'

'Tea?' he asked, and I shook my head.

'I'm looking for a guy called Kurt Nielsen.'

'The one running a sheanut operation in Korhogo?'

'You know your nationals pretty well.'

'What's your interest?'

'My client's a Syrian businessman in Accra. He owns the sheanut operation.'

'Kurt Nielsen's wife was looking for him, too.'

'Was?'

'She called a couple of weeks ago. We asked for passport details and photographs and she called two days later and said he'd reappeared.'

'You weren't curious?'

'Not really. Men take time off from their wives. They spend a lot of time together in these isolated places.'

'So the men go off without telling their wives where they're going?'

'We don't do marriage guidance here.'

'So you didn't do anything about it then?'

He shook his head. 'One, he reappeared. Two, there are a lot of Nielsens in Denmark, and Petersens and Andersens. We all have the same names. We need more than "Nielsen" to help us find him.'

I held out the photocopy of the passport details which B.B. had given me and he looked at them for a few seconds and left the room. I did some running on the spot to keep the circulation going and looked around Leif's minimalist office for a drinks cabinet with something warming in it. Ten minutes later he came back with a computer print-out and a pair of black-framed glasses on his nose.

'I'd like to find Kurt Nielsen as well,' he said.

'He's on the run?'

'No, he's dead.'

The Kurt Nielsen who'd owned the passport was born in Alborg in 1954. He left school when he was sixteen and started work on the fishing boats, Danish and later British. He served two short stretches for robbery, the first in '70, the second in '74. After the second term he started working on British ships and spending shoretime in England. He seemed to have developed a taste for young girls and served three years for sexual assault on a twelve-year-old in Middlesbrough. He got out in '85. He died a year later in Nottingham. He had been a lodger with the Cochrane family. Mr Cochrane came back early from his job as a scaffolder after a fall and found Kurt Nielsen having sex with his thirteen-year-old daughter over the sink in the kitchen. Cochrane hit him over the head with a full bottle of cider which had been on the kitchen table and stuck the broken end in his neck. Kurt Nielsen died 3rd June, 1986.

'What are you going to do about it?'

Leif Andersen sat on the edge of his desk with the print-out resting on his thigh and said nothing for several minutes.

'I don't want to rush you, Mr Andersen, but it's bloody cold in here and I don't want to be the first man five degrees off the equator to get hypothermia.'

'Do you drink, Mr Medway?'

'Not tea, for Christ's sake.'

'Aquavit?'

'Now I'm with you.'

He locked the door of the office and produced a bottle and two glasses from his bottom drawer.

'Not what you British would call consular behaviour, but we are in Africa.'

'How do you think the Falklands War got started?'

'I don't understand.'

'Consular behaviour,' I said. 'Skol.'

We banged back a slug apiece and he refilled the glasses. He banged that one back too, catching me on the hop so that he had to wait to fill up for thirds. He nodded and we threw the third one down, and I felt a moment's abandon and thought it might be throwing-glasses-in-the-fireplace time. He put away the bottle and glasses and unlocked the door. He sat back down, gritted his teeth, tensed his biceps and hissed out the pent-up air in his lungs.

'Good. Where were we?'

'What are you going to do about the Nielsens?'

'The Nielsens? Right. Yes, of course. You know,' he started and got out from behind his desk and walked over to the window and looked out on to a dull, grey Avenue Noguès, 'sometimes I look out of the window in the rainy season. The sky is grey. I can hear the wind off the sea around the building, the rain on the window. It's cold in here, as you know. I have a couple of glasses of Aquavit and I think I'm back in Skagen, you know it? Right on the northern tip of Denmark. Terrible place, but I like it around there.' He paused, letting the Aquavit shunt around his system, letting it take the edge off his cares. He swallowed something the size of a crab apple, as if he was trying to keep his longing down, and took his glasses off.

'You know what I think?' He turned to me. 'Mrs Nielsen

didn't call herself Mrs Nielsen, she referred to Kurt Nielsen as her husband but she called herself Dotte Wamberg, she' – he ran both hands through his hair – 'she couldn't find her husband, she called me, I asked for her husband's details, she said she'd have to find them and send them on. Then she must have started thinking and realized that she was going to have some problems if she did that, so she had her husband reappear. How's that?'

'You've done some conclusion-leaping, Mr Andersen.'

'Only since you came in asking about him and we've found that he's on a dead man's stolen passport.'

'OK, I'll buy it. What're you going to do about it?'

'I've a lot . . .' He looked at his watch. 'The ambassador's coming back from Lagos, the agronomists, back to . . .'

'Nothing, then?'

'I didn't say that.'

'Will a fourth Aquavit get us through this hazy patch we're in at the moment?'

Leif locked the door, and took the bottle and glasses out of the drawer again. We had a fourth and a fifth before he put the bottle away, but it didn't make him any more expansive on what he had in mind. He slapped and kicked his desk around a bit and rolled himself back and forwards on his castored chair and laughed about things in his head without involving me, but he avoided definitive action on Kurt Nielsen and Dotte Wamberg.

Somebody knocked on the door and the vice-consul sat up and asked whoever it was to come in. The door was still locked and he said 'shit' under his fiery breath and took off out of his chair, which backed off into the far corner of the room so that he was in two minds as to whether to open the door or go after the chair. He unlocked the door. A woman with straight blonde hair, a light-blue dress and folders held to her bosom, came in. She looked from Andersen to me and then at the chair, which in my vision seemed a long way off. She wore a pair of blue steel-rimmed spectacles whose lenses were the size of throat lozenges. She put the files on the desk and left without turning to see Leif bowing with a flourish from his right hand, which would have given the game away if the alembic fumes hadn't already. He shut the door, breathless.

'She's very attractive, isn't she?'

'Is she new?'

Leif didn't have to answer and he didn't have to tell me why he didn't want to go up to Korhogo and find out what had happened to Kurt Nielsen, who was going to be some lowlife, probably an escaped convict. What did he care about all that? He said he'd fax the passport through to the Danish police authorities and get an ID on who Kurt Nielsen really was and ask them if they wanted any action taken. I said I'd appreciate it if he could give me the dirt on Kurt Nielsen and he gave me his card and said to call him in a couple of days.

7

By ten to five I was back in the Novotel sitting on one of the twin beds in room 307 nearest the window. The high-stacked, bruised clouds of the storm building over Ghana were moving towards me. It would be raining by nightfall. I thought about going out in that storm and doing something for nothing for Fat Paul and that drew me to the secrets of the mini-bar, which I opened but only checked. I needed to be steady for what Fat Paul might have in mind.

I stared at the carpet, waiting for the phone, and had one of those existential lurches when I saw myself – a big man, getting drunk to hold himself together on a small bed in a hotel room in Africa, fresh from a meeting with another drunken bum and about to do something criminal for a vindictive slob. For a moment, I seemed to be on the brink of an explanation for the mystery and absurdity of my situation. Then the god controlling those moments of insight decided I'd be better off without the self-knowledge. A fluorescent light started flickering, pitched at an epileptic-fit-inducing frequency. I turned it off and lay down, relieved that I didn't have to run down to the bar and tell all the other people deadening themselves to reality that I'd cracked it and we could all relax.

I woke up with the rain on the window and it dark outside and in the room. It was just before six o'clock. I phoned reception – no calls. I made sure they knew I was in 307, having moved me from 205 – still no calls. I took a bottle of mineral water out of the mini-bar and sat in the white light from the chamber and drank it until my teeth hurt. I kicked the door shut and lay back down on the bed in the dark, light coming in under the door.

I was missing something which wasn't home but felt like it ten times over. Hotel rooms did this to me. I thought of individuals sitting in concrete boxes stacked on top of each other and the human condition got lonelier. I'd fallen for two women before Heike, one of them was now married to Martin Fall. I've been disappointed just as much as anybody closing in on forty has. I'd always bounced back, though. It might take a few months of rolling into the cold side of the bed before I'd get used to sleeping in the middle again, but I could always get used to being on my own. This time I wasn't bouncing back, I was slipping further down the black hole. I was missing Heike more than an amputee missed a leg and people could see it, smell it, and feel it.

Some footage came into my head, black-and-white stuff, a little quick and faltering like an old home movie. Heike was sitting on the floor of my living room in my house in Cotonou, Benin. She wore her big white dress, her legs were crossed and covered by the dress, her long bare arms rested on her knees. She had a cigarette going in one of her large, almost manly, hands and in the other she held a glass with her little finger sticking out. Her hair, as usual, was pinned up any old how so that every loose strand said: 'kiss this nape'. She sat there and occupied herself smoking and drinking and not saying anything and her completeness brought on a terrible ache, and I shut the film down and drifted off into a lumpy sleep.

I woke up and looked around the darkness in the room, thinking there was a bat flying around expertly missing walls and furniture. I turned on the neon and it blasted the room with light and dark until I'd fumbled around for the light switch by the door. It was 6.30 p.m. The rain still gusted against the window outside and thunder rumbled off in a corner somewhere. The phone went and I tore it off its cradle.

'I thought you said you weren't all African . . .'

'. . . This is Leif Andersen, Mr Medway.'

'Sorry, I was expecting somebody else. Have you got anything for me?'

There was a long crash, one that went on for fifteen, twenty seconds, of falling crockery followed by a roar of approval from down the phone.

'Are you eating Greek tonight?' I asked.

'I'm in a place called Maison des Anciens Combatants in Plateau.'

'War Heroes in Plate Crash.'

'I'm sorry?'

'Nothing, Mr Andersen. You called. Did the Danish police come through with an ID?'

'Not yet. The Ivorian police came through with something. They've found our Kurt Nielsen down by the Ebrié lagoon about eighty kilometres outside Abidjan. In the pineapple plantations off the road down to Tiegba.'

'They found him, what, walking around, taking a leak, out of his head . . . ?'

'Dead, Mr Medway. Strangled with a wire garrotte.'

'Was he a floater?'

'I'm not sure . . .'

'Was he in the lagoon?'

'No, he was in a Toyota Land Cruiser.'

'His own?'

'It belonged to M. Kantari in Korhogo. He reported it stolen this morning. The report made its way down through Bouaké and Yamoussoukro to Abidjan by this afternoon.'

'Have you seen the body?'

'No.'

'How do they know it's Nielsen?'

'He had his passport on him. That's why they called us.'

'Did they find anything else?'

'No, but if they did and it was valuable we wouldn't hear about it.'

'Well, Mr Andersen, thanks for your help . . .'

'One thing more, Mr Medway. We need positive identification of the body.'

'I never knew him.'

'No, but Mrs Nielsen, or Dotte Wamberg, did and we have been unable to contact her.'

'You want a phone number?'

'We have one, but first of all there's no answer and second, these things are better done in person.'

'What about someone from the Danish Embassy?'

'There's no one available. We've informed the local police, but they cannot be relied on.'

'I can't guarantee I'll get there tomorrow. You know how things are.'

'He's in the hospital morgue. He's not going anywhere.'

'Well, I won't put it like that to Dotte Wamberg.'

'You're a sensitive man, Mr Medway, I can tell.'

'How?'

'Anybody who drinks Aquavit in the afternoon understands.'

'I thought it was because I was a drunk.'

'What does that make me, Mr Medway?'

'You get diplomatic immunity.'

Andersen laughed. 'Another thing for you that you should keep to yourself. Kurt Nielsen's stomach had been ripped open by a set of metal leopard claws. I think they found someone called James Wilson in the lagoon here in Abidjan the other day. He had the same problem. Cheers,' he said, and put down the phone.

I phoned reception again – still no calls, but there was a fax from Ghana. Then I remembered Bagado and put a call through to Cotonou. The phone rang and rang for minutes until a dull, thick voice answered.

'Bagado?'

'Yes.'

'You all right?'

'I've some fever. A little malaria. I was sleeping.'

'Do you want some work?'

'What sort of work?'

'Picking bananas,' I said, and he thought about it for ten seconds.

'Forget it,' he said.

'Detective work, Bagado. What the hell else would I call you for?'

'Picking bananas – I don't know. I'm nearly that desperate. My little girl is sick and I have nothing. I open the cupboard, and the cupboard is bare . . . not even any shelves . . . my wife has used them for firewood.'

'Go to a travel agent called Bénin-Bénin in the quartier

72

Zongo; you know it. They have some money for you. Seventy-five thousand CFA. Give some to your wife and use the rest to get yourself to Accra. I want you to check out someone who calls himself Fat Paul who works out of an office in Adabraka called Abracadabra Video on Kojo Thompson Road. He has two bodyguards who call themselves George and Kwabena. The first one is a shooter, the second is just very big. He says he runs a video business, you know, a chain of video cinemas. See what you can find out about him. Then come to the Novotel in Abidjan as fast as you can. OK?'

'What's the hurry?'

I told Bagado about the failed drop, Martin Fall's job and the James Wilson/Kurt Nielsen killings and we signed off.

I put a call through to the Hotel La Croisette and the receptionist there answered in a thick, tired voice which came from a head that must have been asleep on the counter. She told me that Fat Paul and Co were in 208 and tried to call them — no answer. Then she started waking up a bit and told me the key to the room was in reception, which meant they must be out. I asked her to check the bar and restaurant. They weren't there. I asked her if there was a large American car parked outside the hotel and she said that was the only car parked outside the hotel. They were the only guests. The hotel didn't fill up except at the weekends. The phone went dead. I asked reception to reconnect me. They tried, but the woman said the phones were down with the storm. I left a message that if a Mr Paul called, to tell him I was going to meet him in the Hotel La Croisette in Grand Bassam. I said he might call himself Mr Fat Paul, I didn't know, and I heard her writing it all down. I told her if anybody else called not to give them that message and took the lift straight down to the basement.

There seemed to be several storms around taking their turn coming in. Thunder boomed off in the north and the sky lit up in the east over Grand Bassam. When I came out of the Novotel it was raining, but not as hard as it had done judging by the slow trickle in the road gutters and the huge bodies of water that had collected at the bottom of the steep streets of Plateau. The storm drains were choked and cars were cruising with water up to their sills.

I crossed the lagoon. The lights were out in Treichville, Marcory, Zone 4A and C, Koumassi, Biétri and Port Bouët. Just after the airport I had to pull over and let the storm through, the rain a solid wall at the end of the car, the wipers out of their depth even at that crazy double speed when you stop looking at the road and marvel at the insanity. The rain blasted full heavy metal on the roof for minutes, then backed off to light instrumental. I set off on full beam, down the black glass road to Grand Bassam.

There were no lights on there either. People were moving around as if an air raid had just finished. A car horn was sounding off constantly in the streets beyond the *gare routière* and a harsh white halogen light came on by the market, powered by a diesel generator which farted up to full speed somewhere in the dark. The light showed rain slanting silver and people hopping across the streets with plastic bags over their heads. I sank slowly into street-wide puddles and crawled across the lagoon to the Quartier France. I parked next to Fat Paul's Cadillac in front of the Hotel La Croisette. The sea fringe was invisible in the dark. The roar said it was rough out there. A stiff breeze blew on to the shore, snapping at my shirt.

There were two hurricane lamps lighting the lobby and the receptionist was asleep on a chair behind the desk, her head resting on the wall, snoring. I lifted the key to room 208 off its hook and palmed it as the woman woke up. She was dazed. I asked to go up to the room, showing her the key was out. She took a lamp from under the desk and lit it with the slow and gentle movements of someone on automatic.

The lamplight made huge shadows that loomed and wavered down the warm, bare corridor to Fat Paul's room. The hotel was silent apart from the loose change and keys in my trousers and my feet on the strip of sisal carpeting over the polished floor. Several rooms had their doors open, sheets piled on the floor in one, the maids slacking with the lack of business during the week. There was a smell of raw sewage that didn't surprise me after the rain.

Fat Paul's room was at the end of the corridor, the room on the corner, windows on two sides. The bad smell was getting stronger and changing with sweeter nuances over the sulphur that made my face twitch and my empty stomach sick. The hairs were up on my neck, the sweat cold. I went back down and told the receptionist to find the manager.

The manager was annoyed. He didn't like problems on a night with no power and with nobody in the rooms. He knew how little money he was making. He changed his tone when he hit the smell in the corridor; in fact, he shut up and got his handkerchief out. He had a master key which I wanted him to use, but his hand was shaking so much I took it and opened up the room.

The stench exploded out of the room, but worse than the smell was the noise. I'd heard that noise on African butchers' stalls in the market when they flick the black meat with a bloody cloth and with an irritated buzz a skin of flies takes off a foot and relands. That was the first noise. Behind it was something worse. Behind it came the sound of a flap. Something tense and feathery batted the air in the dark. Without thinking, I reached in and turned on the light switch, but the power was still off. I held the lamp in the room and heard the tearing of flesh, and the flap – the flap of a large bird's wing.

There in the yellow oily light, in the black shadows working their way up the walls, were two vultures. The one with its head down, the other looking up, its whole head covered in blood, black and red in the strange light, as if it had been recently skinned.

The manager's vomit slapped the polished floor between the carpet and the wall at the same time as the power came back on. Harsh electric light banged on in the corridor and room. The vultures shrieked at the sudden exposure and danced back into the centre of the room, their wings spread. The red-smeared muslin drapes at the windows open to the sea were lifted and twisted almost horizontal to the ceiling by the wind. The floor was covered in blood, the red and black of carnage. The ghastly yellow of Fat Paul's raw fat quivered as he lay there opened out, mostly naked, his clothes torn off. My vomit, consisting of nothing but soured and burning spirit, joined the manager's. I retched myself dry and breathless.

We went back downstairs and the manager called the police while the receptionist found me a broom. Back upstairs in 208 the vultures had been joined by a tornado of insects circling the light and speckling the walls. I closed all the shutters but one and beat the vultures out of the room – the two of them screeching, mad, angry, their heads bloodied, their wings heavy. I shut them out and they stayed outside and screeched, scraping their talons on the metal railing of the balcony.

Two of the three bodies in room 208 had been shot. George's hand was still inside his jacket reaching for his gun. One eye was missing. A large quantity of blood had soaked into his shirt, the jockey tie and the carpet. Kwabena lay with a collapsed wooden table underneath him, one of his large hands over a huge wound in his chest. Fat Paul's head rested on his shoulder. He had what seemed to be a set of giblets hanging out of his mouth and he'd been opened up the length of his abdomen. Some of his fingers had been sheared off. They lay like cocktail sausages next to him. The ones still attached had no rings on. His gold chain and watch had gone. High up on his chest, against the lighter coffee-coloured skin, I saw the marks that I hadn't seen on George and Kwabena. The leopard-claw marks. As I closed the door I saw the black hole where Fat Paul's genitals had been and realized what the giblets were.

I took my shoes off and washed them in another bathroom and walked through the empty reception into the sea air and the smell of wet tarmac. The manager sat in the hotel bar with a glass balloon of brandy in front of him.

I didn't feel like four or five hours in a police station explaining my relationship with the murder victims. I drove back to Abidjan, windows open, and listened to the wind rushing and the coconut palms clapping, with the smell of carrion still in my nostrils.

8

Whoever had hit Fat Paul and company was not a hotel jewellery thief but somebody with a big axe to grind. Each time I played the hotel scene through my head I saw a clip, alongside, of the African, with the three tribal cicatrices on his cheek, getting out of the Land Cruiser and the white man next to him wired to the head rest. The wire garrotte connected the Kurt Nielsen and James Wilson killings and all of them had been opened up with the leopard claws. Only Kurt Nielsen hadn't been when I saw him. Somebody had gone back to do that, maybe the tribal scarred African or someone he was working for. Whoever it was had decided on the leopard claws as their trademark, but the reason I was sitting in my room ripping through my second Johnny Walker was that the only link that I could think of, between the last four killings, was myself. I'd been at the drop. I'd been to see Fat Paul afterwards and I now had the package. A package of a tape that had probably started life with James Wilson, whose insides were now fish food. The logic had me stroking my whisky-sore stomach.

I put on a pair of blue chinos and a dark-blue shirt and went to find Ron Collins. I was hoping he would be in the bar – some company and more tranquillizing liquor was what I needed. In reception I asked for the fax from B.B. while I remembered it. This took some time as it had gone to room 205's pigeonhole, but it meant that I could look at the reservations book and find out that Ron Collins had checked into room 312 and his key was out. I reminded the girl I was in 307, she nodded, the phone went, she picked it up and started flicking through the reservations book with a pen in her mouth. I used the internal phone to call room 312. No answer.

I read the fax on the way to the bar which gave the names of the two Japanese businessmen, Hanamaki and Yuzawa. It didn't surprise me that the second didn't begin with a 'K' because B.B. had a habit, when he stammered, of using one consonant to pull a completely different one out of the hat.

There were some nervous people standing outside the bar and one of them was the night manager. They looked scared, as if something had got loose in there and that if it got out it might pick up a few of them on its horns and toss them through the plate-glass window into the swimming pool twenty feet below. From inside the bar came the noise of a drunken Irishman who'd got into his stride and was well down the back straight and hurdling the furniture as he went. The night manager looked at me as if I might be a solution, which made me veer off to the restaurant and I saw the hope die in his face. The restaurant was roped off and it wasn't a night for wading through prostitutes out on to the streets of Abidjan in search of a quiet drink and people. So I went back to the bar and hoped that if Ron Collins was in there he wasn't too trampled.

I smelt him before I saw him. It was a cured-bacon-and-whisky smell that I hadn't come across before and whatever the bottle was that he'd got it from he hadn't just dabbed it behind his ears.

'Who the fog are you?' he asked as I walked in.

'Bruce Medway. You?'

'Sean Malahide!' he roared, and turned a wide back on me that he'd just managed to fit into the pillar-box-red shirt which held him tight under the armpits so he didn't fall over.

You'd expect someone with a name like that to have bad skin and Sean Malahide didn't let anybody down. Before he'd turned his sprouting-potato face away from me and presented the room with the fat slab of his porky back, I had enough time to register his livid and cratered features with a large wet mouth and glistening upper lip. I made a mental note not to put myself within slobbering distance.

There was a very tall and slim, blue-satin-skirted, red-vested African girl with a great mane of black *frisé* hair blasting out of her head standing next to him. Her bare legs were stilted up on some backless open-toed red high heels whose colour matched her lips and cheeks. She had a square foot of eye make-up on, as if she was off to a masked ball, but it didn't disguise the wide-open horror she had of Malahide's possible needs.

Next to her was a man who wore his hair long and looked as if he was over six foot when he wasn't perched on a bar stool. His thin, bearded face didn't fit with the good set of shoulders and broad chest he'd packed into a green silk shirt which he wore untucked from his cream, cotton, baggy trousers. There was a wafer-thin oblong of gold watch with a black alligator-skin strap on his left wrist and he had a small gold ring in his ear. He looked as if he kept himself well frocked up and that the Novotel bar wasn't one of his usual hang-outs. He was about thirty years old and judging by the way he was handling Malahide he hadn't had reason to lose any of his self-confidence. He ignored most of the stuff the Irishman dished out, mocked the rest when he could be bothered and kept himself aloof with a mild sneer on his lips as if the bar stool he was occupying had a two-foot spike on its seat.

Malahide directed the mud slide of his gut towards me. Under his failing red hair the scalp was scabbed with tropical disease. His forearms and prizefighter hands were massive and tinged with copper hair. One hand held a bottle, the other a glass. Each knuckle stood out so that you'd have no trouble guessing the impression they'd make on the wrong face.

'This,' he said, pointing the bottle neck at the man standing at the end of the bar, 'is Goldstein.'

'Ron Collins,' said the man in a voice that was well into the twelfth round of a long and ugly bout. We shook hands and his face told me that we were in something together and all it needed was some superiority to see it through.

'It's fogging Goldstein and you know it,' said Malahide, throwing a whisky into a glass and holding it out in my direction. 'Drink?'

'It has been known,' I said.

'You look a little clean for a barfly,' he said, 'but you're all we've got.'

'Is this stuff going to make me start shouting?'

'I'm a bit loud for you, am I?' he hollered.

'No more than your shirt.'

'Ah-ha!' He turned to Ron. 'We'll be having a bit of gentle wit and banter here. We haven't heard any of that for a wee while, have we?'

'You're right there, Sean,' said Ron, in a voice hammered flat.

'I'm not boring you, am I?'

'Don't be so sensitive, Sean.'

'There you go again,' he said, wheeling round. 'You'll be after having another drink.'

Ron slumped on his bar stool and started looking for his second, the one with the bucket of water and the towel. He held out his glass and dropped his head.

'Don't stint me this time, Sean,' he said. 'I'd rather be unconscious . . .'

'. . . than what?' said Malahide, the bottle hovering over the rim.

'. . . than not.'

'That's me lad,' he said, pouring out a measure that looked as if it would do the trick, 'there's no excuse for rudeness. I won't tolerate it when I'm buying. Now where was I?' He looked around him as if he was going to find the thread of his conversation hanging off the furniture. His knees gave and he took two tiny steps which was all the momentum his gut needed to send him rushing to the bar.

'Hup!' he said, crushing a bar stool. He picked up his glass and stuck his nose in it and then took some time refitting it on the level.

'The Liberian civil war!' he said suddenly, the nub of his gist bouncing back.

'Give us a break, Sean,' said Ron, leaning forward. 'Can't you get it into that patchy Irish head of yours that we don't give a shit about the Liberian civil war. In the real world, where I come from, we don't bloody care if a bunch of Afs want to bash each other up. It's their problem. A little local difficulty, we call it, so stow it, will you?'

Malahide frowned at himself, nodded and pouted his lips into a massive cartoon kiss, sizing the situation up. He might have got himself annoyed if he hadn't been so roaring drunk.

'Liberia is the state given by the Americans to their freed slaves in the last century. *They* think it's pretty important,' he said quietly. He blinked with concentration. Ron slumped back. 'So – the Liberian civil war. Samson Talbot and Jeremiah Finn – they used to be chums, you see. Then they split. Old Jerry thought he had a better chance with the Americans without Samson. So now you've got' – he held up his thumb – 'the late President's national guard still in the palace – they're Israeli-trained, Goldstein, and the palace was Israeli-built, so you're represented. You've got the ECOWAS* troops, that's the West African alliance, the so-called peace-keeping force. There's the Americans sticking their oars in. The French are sniffing around. Jerry Finn's getting pally with the Yanks and Samson Talbot's kissing Gadaffi's arse. That's what I call a foggering mess.'

He turned back to the bar and his head dropped on to his chest, his eyes closed and he breathed through his nose and a sheen of sweat appeared on his face which made it look like a plastic horror mask. A long low snore started in his small bowel and finished with a grunt that kicked him in the back and jerked him awake. He looked at us, bewildered for a moment, as if we'd invaded his living room, but the girl triggered something off in him which wasn't the Liberian war and he pulled her to him, growling. She, pliant as an ironing board, didn't resist.

'What's your business?' he asked me, mid-grapple.

'Sheanut,' I said.

'What the fog are you doing down here, then?'

'I'm going north.'

'You'll be going to Korhogo, then?' he said, and I looked into his face, which had now taken on the colour of some-

---

* Economic Community of West African States

thing a butcher would throw into his dog bin, to see if he was thinking of coming with me.

'Not me,' he said. 'No. No. Goldstein here. He's a diamond man, needs to get to Tortiya.'

'The name's Ron, Sean.'

'That'll be short for Aaron,' said Malahide, his head floating about a bit, being annoying, paying Ron back.

'Fuck off, Sean,' said Ron quietly.

'I'm getting in there now, aren't I?' said Sean. 'Getting behind that nice silk shirt of yours, getting behind that nice gold earring in your tab.'

'I bought some diamonds from some Swiss guys in Geneva,' said Ron, picking the words out and fitting them in the sentence. He gave Sean a sideways glance, and then dropped his voice to make him strain. 'Really nice stones and cheap . . . a fucking steal, man, I tell you. They told me they came from Tortiya.'

'Nice of them to tell you where they came from,' I said.

'Well, that's it. They told me if I wanted more I'd have to go and get them myself.'

'Why do you think they said that?' asked Sean, suddenly on Ron's shoulder. Ron shrugged him off.

'They gave me the contact and I fixed myself up with them. They met me at the airport. A couple of guys from Guinea, both called Alfa.'

'That means "king" in Fula,' said Malahide. 'They're all called that over there. A very modest bunch of fellows.'

'These guys pick me up in a taxi and bring me here. On the way they tell me they don't have a car and I'm going to have to hire one to get us to Tortiya.'

'How much did they say?'

'Two hundred and fifty grand,' said Ron. 'A thousand bloody dollars.'

'They're scamps,' said Malahide, laughing, 'absolute fogging scamps.'

'So I told them I was here to buy a million dollars', *at least* a million dollars' worth of diamonds through them and they could hire the goddam car.'

'You don't understand, Goldstein, those poor foggers haven't got a bogger between them.'

'Maybe that's why the Swiss told you where the diamonds came from.'

'Ah-haaaa,' said Malahide, with his eyebrows up to his hairline.

'You still want to go?'

'What sort of car have you got?' asked Ron.

'A Peugeot 504 Estate,' I said, trying to remember the last time somebody asked me that.

'Ah,' he said, trying to picture it.

'Fifteen years old,' I said, developing some small dislike for Ron.

'Mmm.'

'Bald tyres. No aircon and the stereo doesn't work. Still want to come?'

'Sure,' he smiled, making something of a bad job.

'We leave at six,' I said. 'No Alfas, and I don't want to carry a million dollars either.'

'You won't be. There's a Belgian guy here in Abidjan who'll cover me up to a million and a half. If I buy, he'll pay.'

'Sounds like a trusting fellow,' said Malahide. 'Must be Rademakers.'

'How do you know Rademakers?'

'There's only one man who does that business here.'

'Yes, well, that's the way the business works. He knows I'm good for it.'

'That's all right then, isn't it?' said Malahide.

'Rademakers pays out,' I said, 'but what happens to the diamonds?'

'One of the hajis selling the stuff brings them down here. We settle up. Rademakers organizes the export. There's no risk, I'm telling you.'

'You should go in a bush taxi,' said Malahide, 'get some local colour, see the country.'

He went back to the bar and poured himself some more whisky. Ron poured some of the huge measure Malahide had given him earlier into my glass. The Irishman had his arm around the girl and was snoring again, but without jerking himself awake. Ron leaned over and flicked him on the forehead with his finger as if he was nothing more than a little bug. Malahide's eyes opened.

'You're drifting away, Sean,' he said.

'I am. What're we drinking?'

'What about tomorrow? You're supposed to be giving a talk.'

'I am?'

'On pineapples.'

'That's right. We've still time for another.'

Malahide supported himself on the bar and snatched the bottle away from the barman, who backed off. He gave the bottle to Ron and made circular motions with his finger. He beckoned the barman and pulled some notes out of his bent wallet. The barman counted them and folded the notes lengthways while he did a nifty calculation.

'*Encore cinq mille,*' he said.

Malahide pulled out another note which the barman snaffled. He turned to the girl, blinked several times, took out another wad and gave her two notes. She looked at them, tilting her head from one side to the other to get a good 3-D understanding of their value.

'*Encore cinq mille,*' she said.

Malahide wiped his face dead, but the girl fixed him with her lurid mask and showed him a pair of empty hands as if the money had already gone on bills and other expenses. She whipped a note out from the sheaf in his hand and slid it down the front of her skirt with long, delicate fingers which looked torn and bloody but were just shabby with flakes of old varnish.

The bar had filled up behind us and all the comfortable people took time out to watch the girl leave, checking out her stick-thin legs jacked up on red stilettoes, her heels swollen over the edges of her shoes and a black pit in her calf from an old sore. The piped music resumed. Ron's sneer took shape.

Malahide was subdued. His head looked as if it was hurting him already and his scalded face needed a cucumber and

84

yoghurt bath. Sweat marks had appeared on his shirt, even in the air-conditioned cool, and he'd started to scratch the side of his gut.

'I'd give up the drink,' he said, patting his cheek, 'but it'd empty my evenings and the evenings are terrible long in Africa.'

'You live here?' asked Ron.

'I get about.'

'On contract?'

'You're asking a terrible lot of questions.'

'Only two,' said Ron.

'Would you mind putting some whisky on top of this ice,' he said, holding out his glass. Just the sight of him killed any conversation so I told Ron about the witch doctor I'd seen that morning.

'A very interesting thing, don't you think?' said Malahide.

'Mumbo jumbo,' said Ron.

'Well, I didn't expect anything less from a member of the Judaic faith.' He paused. 'Or d'you know what you're on about?'

Ron cranked his arm to tell Malahide to get on with it. Malahide licked his white, crusty lips and told us about the Mandingos' tribal god called Muma dyumbo. When they were captured and sent to the States and Caribbean islands as slaves they took their god with them so that any African religious nonsense was known by the slavers as mumbo jumbo.

'That's very interesting,' said Ron, picking at his coaster.

Sean asked him what he knew about voodoo.

'Zombies. Haiti. *Night of the Living Dead*,' said Ron, with his eyelids closed, the weight of all that disdain making him tired.

Malahide scratched away at a nodule beneath his shirt and, suddenly sober, told him that voodoo came from West Africa, that although there were a lot of Muslims and Christians now, there were still a lot of animists and a fair amount who did both. He told Ron about the fetish markets where you could buy dried split birds, old bones, skulls, jujus to put curses on people, potions to appease gods, get fertile, cure impotence and a lot of other things which a modern medical bill put out of reach for the average native.

'Not that the witch doctor's cheap.'

'You used one?' asked Ron.

'My boys use them.'

'You ever found a red-haired wax effigy stuck with pins?'

'I'll tell you something else . . .' he said, ignoring him, 'something that might help you up there in the north while you're out of civilization. I was working out near Man when a local chief died. My boys disappeared for a week. They all came back thin and starving hungry and I asked them where the hell they'd been. Hiding, they said, because of the heads, they said. They bury heads with the big man's body and they didn't want any of them to be theirs.

'When this president dies, and he's the big man of all big men, the world's greatest Catholic, apart from yer man himself – when he dies, they say he'll need a few hundred heads to keep him quiet. My boys tell me at least one of the heads has to be a white man's. So if the old man dies while you're here Ron, you'd better keep your head down.'

'I didn't know you cared, Sean.'

'I don't, but maybe you have someone who does.'

Ron Collins picked his beard and flicked his hair behind his ear, but Malahide wasn't finished.

'This is something else for you, Ron,' he said. 'Something very relevant to you. Some years ago I supplied a Nigerian who ran a chain of supermarkets in Lagos and Ibadan. The man didn't pay and he didn't pay and I kept calling him and he was never there. I thought he was one of them slippery types you find over that way, so I flew to Lagos to sit on his chest. He was in jail. He'd come back from the Cameroon and his suitcase fell open in Lagos airport. He had a caseful of babies' heads on him. Thirty foggering heads in his suitcase.'

'What's that got to do with me?' asked Ron, sounding bored but listening hard.

'They're for burying. They say it brings on the diamonds. There y'are, you didn't think when you were hunched over your magnifying glass in your smart Hatton Garden office you'd be contributing to the rise in infant mortality on the Dark Continent, did you?'

'But is it true?' asked Ron quietly.

'People get sick, have accidents, drive themselves mad over African girls. Maybe something'll happen to you while you're up there. Watch what you're eating, Ronny boy, or you might start giving a better price for your diamonds than you want to.'

'Now I know you're talking crap.'

'You're probably right there, Ronny. You're probably right.'

9

The bar closed. Ron slid off his stool. Malahide began man-oeuvring himself like a horse and dray in a cul-de-sac. We all made it to the lifts where there was a gathering of loose-limbed people telling each other stuff they didn't need to hear – most of it in Danish. Ron and I ordered a five o'clock alarm call and picked up our keys. Malahide announced his first pee of the evening and went off in search of the con-veniences. Both lifts arrived at the same time.

I ended up at the back of one lift, jammed up against a bleach blonde who was either as tall as me or was just riding up the wall in the crush. She sneered and turned her head to show me a pair of scimitar earrings which promised cas-tration should anyone think of trying anything furtive. The doors remained open long enough for people's breathing to become audible. As they began to close, an African moved into frame, turned his back and pressed himself into the lift and a small woman grunted at my back.

Through the heads I could see the African's small ear. He turned his head to the woman next to him and I saw his profile. Something colder than a toad ran up my back and settled across my neck so that the hackles rose. There were three one-inch scars on his cheek. I turned my face back to the blonde and scratched my cheek on some appliqué on her T-shirt which said 'Heaven'.

The doors closed and a sense of panic moved through the lift. The crush tightened. We went straight up to the second floor. The lift slowed. The doors opened and everybody exploded out. The blonde ripped past me, spinning me back into the lift and I lunged forward and hit the 'Close Doors' button, which didn't respond. In the corridor people fought to get past a couple who'd fallen on each other's lips. The lift doors closed uncertainly and in their own sweet time. I went up to the third floor on my own. The doors opened on to a silent corridor.

I poked my head out of the lift to see if he wanted to shoot that off first. The corridor was badly lit and empty. I walked past the second lift and looked down the short passageway which gave access to the stairs. There was no one. I opened the door to my room and started looking for a weapon.

The owners of this hotel knew a few things about people. The only two appliances in the room that approached being heavy, blunt and movable were the TV and the mini-bar. I took a penknife out and dismantled the towel rail and found myself holding a thin and hollow metal rail which might have concussed a trusting hamster with a thin skull. Then I remembered the fax, where reception had put it, and thought that room 205 might be about to get some room service they hadn't banked on.

In the corridor I found a wall-mounted fire extinguisher. I threw the towel rail back into the room, lifted the extinguisher off the wall and walked to the stairs. I opened the door and listened to the thick humid air sliding down the bannisters. I went down the stairs, weighing the fire extinguisher, trying to decide how hard I was going to have to hit him to knock him out. It wasn't so long ago that I'd killed a man with a lavatory and I wasn't keen to repeat that with another household appliance.

I opened the door and stepped back into the dark shadow of a corner. At the junction with the main corridor was a single downlighter which dropped a cone of light on to the apex. I heard a couple giggling down the corridor and the sound of key tags knocking against doors. Then quiet. Room 205 was right down the corridor and to the left with a view out of the front of the hotel. There were no sounds from any of the rooms. A lift came down and passed straight through the floor. I looked at the dust hanging in the cone shed by the downlighter. It moved, suddenly turbulent. Into it, from the left, moving fast, his feet silent on the carpeting, came the triple-scarred African. His right arm was by his side and in its gloved hand was a gun with a suppressor attached. He didn't stop. I hefted the fire extinguisher, took four steps, turned right into the corridor and, missing my aim, caught him a glancing blow on his right shoulder. The gun fell from his dead arm. He turned and I hit him under the ribs with a right hand and then batted him with the flat of my left hand so that his head cracked sharply against the metal frame of the lift and he collapsed.

I called the lift, picked up the gun and stuck it in the waistband of my trousers in the small of my back. The doors opened on an empty chamber and I dragged him in and pressed the basement button. I frisked him as we went down and found a wallet which I put in my back pocket. On his right leg there was a knife in a scabbard strapped above his ankle. I removed it.

The doors opened on to the oil and petrol smell of the garage and I pulled him out and sat him up against the wall. It was hot and still in the yellow light of the garage but there was a tremendous noise in my ears which reminded me of a jet engine going into reverse thrust. I stopped to listen and found that this was the noise that whisky made when pumped around hardened arteries. Sweat was dripping off my nose on to the man's jacket which I was holding by the lapels as I straddled him. I lifted him and drove him up the wall and hoisted him over my shoulder in a fireman's lift, holding on to his legs, and set off across the car park – so far, so professional.

Ten yards from the car I stopped dead. The two litres of sweat lathering my body iced. The gun was out of the waistband of my trousers and pointing into my spine.

'Slowly . . .' he said, speaking with an American accent. 'Let me down, man, but slowly.'

I still had the knife but I wasn't keen to test my ability with it against a .38. I lowered him to the floor. He was small and it was a long way for him to go off my six-foot-four-inch frame. I still held his right wrist as his feet touched the ground and remembered that he had held the gun in his right hand in the corridor. He must have been groggy still from the smack on the head because he moaned. I felt the gun come off my spine and he twisted his wrist out of my grip. I straightened and he started falling backwards trying to change the gun into his right hand as he was going down. The heavy suppressor tilted the gun and his fingers turned into a full set of dislocated thumbs. Then I was on him. I grabbed his right hand which held the gun and it coughed out a shot. A Mercedes's tyre burst, kicking up concrete dust from the floor and the car slumped on to its right buttock.

I had a problem. The knife was in my left pocket. My left hand held his right, my right was groping around at his flailing fist which was punching me in the head. The gun went off again and this time one of my Peugeot's tyres popped. I dropped my forehead hard on to the bridge of his nose. There was a crack and a bit of a grind, which I felt in the back of my head. I reared back, preparing to butt him again and he said, quietly, as if to himself, 'No.'

The gun fell from his fingers and I picked it up and stood back from him. He sat up and held his broken nose with both hands while blood poured on to his shirt.

'It's broke,' he said. 'You broke my goddam nose.'

I'd given up my English instinct for apologizing a long time ago so I didn't say anything. He told me he'd never broken his nose before in a way that made me think that perhaps we hadn't just been trying to kill each other. He asked me what he should do about it and I told him that was the least of his problems and that he should get on and change the tyre he'd just shot out on my car.

'Me?' he asked, as if this was well below his normal line of duty, and I had to explain to him that I wasn't going to do it because I had the gun, and in those circumstances the one without the gun did the dirty work. He shrugged and said he didn't know how to change a tyre.

For a moment I'd begun to like him. He was sitting on the ground like a youngster who'd just executed a brave rugby tackle and found that, in life, not only is bravery not always rewarded, but it can also damage your looks. I was on the brink of giving him a hand when a movie still came into my head of Fat Paul, George and Kwabena in their hotel room and I kicked him hard in the leg.

'You fuck!' he shouted, rolling to one side, so I hoofed him up the backside. He scrabbled to his feet and straightened his jacket. I lined him up for another message from my size-twelve boot and he limped to the car, overdoing it.

I asked him his name while he got the tyre and jack out and he said it was Eugene, '. . . but they call me "Red".'

'Sounds tougher than Eugene, is that it?'

He didn't answer.

'You a Liberian?' I asked.

'Yeah, I am. What's it to you?'

I took his wallet out of my back pocket and read his ID. Eugene Amos Gilbert, born 1958, profession: businessman. I checked through the wallet which had a little currency in it and not much else. I asked him who sent him and he didn't answer so I asked him who he worked for and he still didn't say anything. Then I told him I was talking to him and he said he was concentrating on changing the tyre because he hadn't done one before and he didn't want to screw it up and get us involved in an accident. I was touched.

He changed the tyre like someone who'd changed a couple of thousand tyres in his lifetime and then suffered a stroke in that very specific part of his brain. I told him I was going to check the wheel nuts and that for every loose one I was going to break a finger. He tightened all the nuts.

I gave him his wallet and told him he was driving. He said he didn't know how to drive so I asked him what the hell he was doing in his car at the lagoon yesterday. He shrugged. I told him to give me his hand. He held it out without think-ing. I took his middle finger and just before I snapped it back he had a sudden and total recall of how to drive.

We got in the car and Eugene looked over the dashboard, steering wheel and gearshift as if he was buying it. I told him to get on and drive it across the Pont Général de Gaulle to Treichville. He responded by kangaroo hopping us up to the garage gates, which made me put the gun firmly in his ribs and explain in his little ear that the safety was off and this was no way to drive, whereupon we smoothed out and he began driving like a president's limo chauffeur. It took some time to raise the *gardien*. He opened up the grille for us with his eyes barely open and we went out into the black shiny night.

I asked him who he worked for and again he didn't respond, except to grunt with the barrel in his ribs.

'Why did you kill Fat Paul?' I asked, and he looked a little surprised.

'I found him and the other two covered in flies with a couple of vultures in his stomach. Why did you kill him?'

He shrugged as if there didn't have to be a reason.

'What're you after?' I asked.

He checked the rearview and tried his nose with the fingers of his left hand as if he was modelling clay.

'OK. How did you find Fat Paul?'

'I followed you, man.'

'From where?'

'The Novotel, where d'you think?'

'You didn't follow me last night.'

'I saw the number of your car at the lagoon in the afternoon. I call a friend in that place in Abidjan where they keep the numbers, they told me it's a hire car and there's only four companies in Abidjan do that.'

'What did you want from Fat Paul?'

He didn't answer.

'What do you want from me?'

He thought about that for a moment.

'I gotta kill you.'

'Any reason?'

'You seen my face and you got the package.'

'We're getting somewhere,' I said. 'What's in the package, Eugene?'

'Red,' he said. 'The name's Red.'

Halfway across the bridge I told him to stop.

'Bad idea, man,' he said.

'It's the only one I got.'

'They's a lotta assholes on these bridges.'

'Now there's two more,' I said, 'and what's a hit man worrying about assholes for?'

He shrugged and looked out the window across the black leathery lagoon. I hauled him across the passenger seat and stood him on the pavement. There was no traffic and no pedestrians. All the assholes had mugged each other and gone to bed, bored.

I hoped Eugene was beginning to realize how bad things were looking for him. He felt his nose with both hands and then asked if he could do his shoelaces up, and before I remembered that he was wearing slip-ons he was down on one knee. I took the knife out of my pocket and tapped him on the head with it and he stood up and nodded. I threw it in the lagoon, asking him who he was working for again and what was in the package. He sighed and put his head to one side.

'Maybe I don't work for nobody.'

'You look like a pro with that ankle knife.'

'Maybe I'm doing things for my own account.'

'But are you?'

He shrugged again.

'What about Kurt Nielsen?'

He looked at me, blank. I tapped him on the forehead.

'You got anything in there?'

'I don't understand.'

'You killed Kurt Nielsen last night down by the lagoon. You just said that's where you saw the car.'

'I forgot. I mean I didn't know him.'

'Why did you kill him then?'

'I don't understand the fuck you talking about.'

'If you're working for yourself you should know who you're killing and why. Or were you just keeping your hand in? Doing some night practice? Getting ready for the big day.'

'I still don't understand the fuck you talking about.'

'It's a British thing. It's called "irony".'

'Irony,' he said. 'Is that heavy or what?'

'How did you know to go down to the lagoon?'

'Uh?'

'How did you know the drop point was down by the lagoon?'

'I followed the white man.'

'You were there in the afternoon.'

'He came early, like you.'

'You knew where the drop point was. Who told you?'

He didn't answer.

'Are you working for Kantari?'

'Who the fuck he?' he asked, and I gave up and told him that if he didn't spew it out I was going to kill him and he shook his head.

'You're not going to shoot me,' he said, which was perceptive given the gun in my hand pointing at him.

'How do you know that?'

'You gave me my wallet.'

He knew I didn't have whatever was needed to put a bullet in someone. He'd seen me looking inside myself for some cold brutality and come back up with warm English custard. I told him to step over the rail of the bridge and asked him again about Kantari while I searched his pockets. I found Fat Paul's rings. He told me through trembling lips that he couldn't swim and I said that he'd forgotten a lot of things that night and then remembered them under a little pressure.

'It's true. This time it's true. I don't know how to swim,' he said.

'You're going for a swim unless you talk. Who's paying you?'

'I told you, I can't swim.'

'You're going to learn,' I said, 'and if you don't . . .' I thumped him in the back.

There was a splash, a moment of quiet, and a light uncertain breeze, looking for somewhere to blow, fluttered my shirt. Over the rail it was black with the odd glint from the lights on the shore but there was no sound. The clouds which had been spraying rain most of the evening still hung around up above, applying pressure but not much else. A car zipped past on the other side of the still-wet road. I sorted through the rings and found the one with the scorpion on it and threw the rest in after Eugene. I waited, listening for the sound of splashing, the sound of Eugene taking a huge gulp of air, but there was nothing but the smell of the sea coming in on the nothing breeze.

I walked around the back of the car to the driver's door and, as I reached for the handle, one of those assholes Eugene was worried about appeared in a black string vest, crouching with his arms out. He showed me a nasty but very white grin and a pair of malevolent eye-whites which flickered to his right hand which held a knife. He pointed the blade at my pocket and grunted the word '*Argent.*'

I put my arm straight out in front of me so that the suppressor ended up a couple of inches from his nose. He stopped moving forward and straightened a little so that the gun was pointing at his throat. He was blinking now and the malevolent eye-whites had turned to lightly fried egg-whites and he'd reined in his greedy grin to a nervous smile. He turned and ran without looking back.

I tucked the gun up underneath the driver's seat and drove back to the hotel. I got into bed with a miniature of Courvoisier in the absence of Johnny Walker. I stared at the ceiling and had the thought that for the first time in four weeks I'd got hold of something and hadn't pissed on my hand.

10

Tuesday 29th October

The phone told me it was 5.00 a.m. My body told me it was
a lie. I crawled to the mini-bar and polished off everything
non-alcoholic, including some very gaseous tonic water
which lodged itself behind my sternum like a heart attack.

I let the shower needle my scalp for some time to see if it
would loosen some of the grey phlegmy stuff that had seeped
into my frontal lobes. I had some success because by the time
I got to the mirror I could see that where my eyes weren't
bloodshot there were pink threads, and you don't pick up
that kind of detail unless you're sharp.

I shaved with a razor that seemed to have been used on
seven women's legs before it got to my face and the foam
ran pink in the sink. By the time I got to reception I looked
like the start of a papier-mâché mask.

Ron was propped up against the front desk as if he was
about to be moved into a window display for safari gear.
There was a Great White Hunter's hat on the desk and there
was nobody else around which meant it was his, and he was
going to wear it. His hair was done up in a ponytail so that
everybody would get to see the gold earring. The oblong
wafer watch had gone and he was wearing the kind of thing
you'd expect to see on a lone round-the-world yachtsman
with time on his hands to work out what everything's for.
He had a pair of Timberland boots on his feet which had
done twenty-five yards of walking on carpet. The man looked
attractive — attractive to people with no money and hours to
spare to think up ways of relieving people with too much of

it. He was dozing on his feet, and enjoying it by the look of his lips which were searching for a bare shoulder.

It took some time to compute the mini-bar takings. The girl, who was wearing a very bright and complicated African print which raked across my eyeballs like a currycomb, fetched my carrier bag from the safe and checked to make sure the paper wasn't going to run out on the printer. I took B.B.'s two million out, along with the sealed package which Fat Paul had given me yesterday. I left Martin Fall's cash in the bag and handed it back to the girl. She felt sorry for me and gave me a little bag of cakes which she told me she'd made herself. I signed the bill. Ron jolted himself awake.

'Bloody hell,' he said.

'Don't worry. I'm just the hangover. He sent me down to settle the bill. He'll be along in a minute.'

'You missed a bit,' he said, looking around the corner of my face, 'and you slept like shit.'

The lift doors opened and Ron glanced over as if he was expecting the real me to come out. It was empty.

'I had a busy night,' I said. 'You got rid of those Alfas yet?'

'They didn't show.'

'They will. I'll get the car. Wait outside and don't forget your bullwhip.'

'Funny guy,' said Ron, fitting the hat on his head.

In the basement I stripped some money off the block and stuck the rest in an old plastic bag. I opened the rear passenger door, unscrewed the panel, and taped the block inside the door and replaced the panel. Fat Paul's package I taped to the back of the glove compartment. At street level Moses was walking towards the hotel, swinging his Ghana Airways bag with as many cares in the world as I'd have liked to have. He didn't recognize me at first with all the tissue stuck to my face but then he slapped his leg and shook his head, marvelling at me as if I'd been up all night preparing it as a school project.

I gave Moses his prescription and told him to load up while Ron and I had coffee and croissants in a café down from the hotel. The Alfas were waiting for us when we got back. They saw Ron and fell on him like a couple of labradors who'd seen someone they knew and had to tell him about their day. I stood back from the tail-wagging and watched Ron give them the kiss-off.

The Alfas were both wearing raincoats, reminding me to look at the weather which had made no impression because it was one of those grey nothing days, neither hot nor cold, neither rain nor shine. Ron surprised me with the flashiness of his brutality in getting shot of the Alfas. I could tell he hurt. They skewered him with a couple of looks that would have made a more sensitive man wriggle.

We made good time on the motorway from Abidjan to Yamoussoukro, once the car had got over being insulted by Ron, and we'd listened to how fast an Alfa Romeo Spyder can go.

Ron slept for the first hour to show how impressed he was. I held my hand out the window and thought about things I shouldn't have thought about – Heike. It didn't do me any good covering that old ground again; I'd never got used to the high hurdles, the deep water jumps and the elephant pitfalls but once I'd got started I had to go through with it.

I was interrupted by a dog which had come out of the dense vegetation at the side of the road and loped along at the edge of the tarmac looking over its shoulder at the passing cars. Just as we pulled alongside it, for no reason at all, it veered into our path and clobbered against the car, dying instantly. Moses didn't stop but looked into the rearview mirror at the body basking on the tarmac. I had a sudden vision of Eugene disappearing into the black lagoon and decided that dark thoughts brought on others and it was time to recapture some of the positivism of last night.

We rolled into Yamoussoukro at around 10.00 a.m. The President of the Ivory Coast had built this huge, expensive, grid-planned metropolis, in which not enough people were living, as a tribute to his mother. He had also made his 'deal with God' here and erected a cathedral so massive it made the Pope nervous that he was going to have to pay for the servicing.

We bought a crate of Aiwa mineral water and six bottles of Black Label from a supermarket and found a garage where

I bought a new tyre to replace the one that Eugene had shot out the night before. Ron stood over the guys and supervised the work so that they looked at each other a few times, as if they were wondering what sort of a dent a tyre iron would make in the white man's hat. When they stripped off the old tyre a piece of metal fell to the floor which Ron picked up and inspected.

'This is a bullet,' he said.

'It is,' I confirmed.

'How did a bullet get in there?'

'I might ask you how you know what an impacted bullet looks like.'

'I've been to the movies.'

'The bullet was fired from a gun.'

'That's unusual.'

'I could go into it if you want.'

He held the bullet between his thumb and forefinger and straightened his hat with his free hand and walked off towards the car doing some kind of breathing exercises.

'Oh boy,' he said, putting his hands into the back pockets of his trousers and shaking his head. 'Here comes trouble.'

'This your first time?'

'What?'

'In West Africa.'

'I've been to Banjul in the Gambia.'

'You went to a five-star hotel and sat on the beach behind the chain-link fencing, you mean?'

'They *said* it wasn't a good idea to leave the compound. They *said* there could be trouble.'

'Trouble's what you get in Africa.'

'Yeah, so everybody's keen to tell me, but this isn't bureau-cratic-red-tape-fill-it-all-out-in-triplicate-and-attach-your-original-birth-certificate-type trouble. I've had that shit before in Russia. This is different, this is sort of serious . . .'

'. . . gun-type trouble,' I said. 'You get that in Russia too.'

'Break it to me gently, Bruce. I'm a nervous traveller.'

'Somebody killed three guys in a hotel room in Grand Bassam last night and then tried to kill me. That's it.'

'I thought, for a moment, you were going to tell me something really fucking terrible.'

'We had a scrap and he shot the tyre out.'

'And after that?' asked Ron, flicking his ponytail.

'We ended up on the bridge, had another fight and he fell in.'

'You killed him?'

'He was a contract killer.'

Ron didn't say anything for a while but searched my face for something that would explain what had just darkened his day.

'Did you kill him?'

'He jumped off the bridge.'

'Jumped or pushed?'

I didn't answer.

'This is thrilling stuff,' he said. 'You know that?'

'I do my best,' I said, trying to lighten things up. Ron blew a valve.

'I'm a diamond trader. I'm a fucking di-a-mond trader,' he said, giving me a syllable count but not looking as hard as he sounded in his shop-stiff safari gear. 'D'you get that? Diamonds are highly transportable forms of cash. You can walk around with five million stuck up your arse if you want. You know what that means? People *like* diamonds. When people *like* things they want to *steal* them. Bullets, guns, contract killers, just those words make me fucking edgy. I don't even have to have the reality, just the fucking words make me edgy.'

'And you think I'm cock-a-hoop?' I asked. He wasn't listening.

'You drive me out of town, you don't say a fucking word, then it's, "Oh, what's that?" "It's a fucking bullet. I had to put someone away last night. Pop him off. Sorry, mate." Was this before or after the drink?'

'After,' I said, and he fixed me with a very steady look.

'Are you all right in there?'

'I'm trying to get a grip . . .'

'I'm relieved,' he said.

101

'. . . like you should, unless you're going back to Abidjan, then you can do what the hell you like.'

'No, no, it's OK, we'll carry on,' he said, feeling his pony-tail, making it smooth.

'If you come, then be calm. If you're not calm, you'll upset the locals and then they'll upset you.' He nodded and stuck his hands under his armpits, tense.

'You want a cake?' I asked.

'Where did you get them from?'

'The girl on the desk. She said she made them herself.'

'No, thanks.'

'They're not going to kill you.'

'I don't know what's in them.'

'Sean getting to you, is he . . . with all his black magic?' He faltered.

'Maybe?' I asked.

'Maybe.'

He sat on the bonnet, picking at his beard, and asked me how I'd killed Eugene. I didn't want to go through it again but he insisted and I slipped up by dropping Kurt Nielsen's name into the story, which opened up another tree-lined boulevard of inquiry. It made Ron even more unhappy, but Ron liked being unhappy. It gave him the opportunity to walk around looking big, to use manly language that made him sound tough. But he never got unhappy enough to give up and go home.

We left Yamoussoukro at 10.45 a.m. and fell off the tarmac on to the graded road north. At the Bouaké police post, 100 kilometres further north, the car was searched by four men overseen by a large-arsed senior officer who had the habit of gripping his own love handles. I offered him money and he asked me in a voice of rehearsed and quiet threat whether I was trying to bribe him. I told him it was more of a donation and he looked at me through half-closed lids as if this was the most suspicious thing he'd heard since the news had broken about Santa Claus. I made a rolled-up 5000 CFA note available to him and he tugged on one end of it while I asked him with the tilt of my forehead to call off the sniffer dogs.

His lids opened, suddenly startled, to show a pair of eyes

which were coated with something you'd expect to see in a pneumonic lung. In the corner of one eye was a small orange worm of the type that burrowed through the foot, made its way up through the liver, laid eggs and, after a tour of duty, exited wherever it could. I let go of the note. He reared back and stumbled to his office calling off the search as he went.

We stopped by the railway station in Bouaké and picked up a meal of kedjenou — spicy chicken with vegetables and rice. Ron seemed to be designing a housing project in his food but not eating it. I told him that restaurants in Tortiya were not well known and this might be the last food before Korhogo tomorrow morning. He said he was a vegetarian. I told him he was going to lose some weight.

We left for Katiola in the dreadful afternoon sun. In the steam-bath heat Moses developed a pimpling of sweat on the end of his nose. Ron and I had dinner-plate sweat patches under both arms, wet hair with the pink scalp showing through, puffy faces, sweat hanging off the eyebrows and beggars' eyes. Ron's ponytail came undone, he let his hair hang loose and took to muttering, 'What a fucking shithole,' at everything he saw.

We had a puncture in Katiola and a small breakdown in Niakaramandougou, whose name caught in Ron's throat like a cocktail stick. We arrived in Tortiya at dusk, about as ready for work as two severely whipped Egyptian mules.

11

Ron gave Moses the name of his contact and we watched his white shirt disappear into the mud huts of the village. I stripped off my shirt and put on a fresh one and offered another to Ron who asked where I'd bought it. I discussed the fine lines of Armani and the fussiness of Christian Lacroix and Ron got the picture and backed off, saying he'd wear one of his own. Where did Martin Fall find this guy?

The sun set unusually, in a crimson streak through dove-grey clouds on the horizon. Then it was dark and the cicadas drew in with it, rubbing out any sound that might have come from the village. Woodsmoke cut the thick night air and the smell of cooking, something viscous and bland, came on the back of it.

The weak light of a cheap torch bounced between where we knew the houses were and took its time arriving. Moses introduced us to someone whose hand we fumbled for in the night and who called himself Borema. We left Moses with the car and crossed the dirt street into an alleyway between mud walls. We walked through the layers of woodsmoke that hung outside the doorways where weak hurricane lamplight painted cracks down and around the doors. There were voices over walls and behind doors, all low, hungry and tired from a long day looking for what the white man had come to buy. The white man was asking me, why these people lived in such shit, why didn't they get themselves organized, why . . . ?

After stumbling along the rough alleyway we came into a round clearing where there was thick, audible drainage trick-ling down a black ditch. We crossed the ditch and went into another narrow alley and then across a wider street into another passage which had been dabbed with tincture of billy-goat sweat. There was bright light at the end of this passage and the sound of an old generator which we found was connected to a forty-foot container.

The container stood in a swept earthen square with a queue of fifteen hajis in long robes and cylindrical hats leading to a door that had been cut in the side at one end. Borema went to another door cut in the opposite end of the container, opened it and turned the light on inside. The generator's tone changed as the air conditioning came on and the apprehension that had hunched Ron's shoulders forward lifted and he held his hands out to receive the miracle before him.

Inside the container was a pristine diamond room that could have been lifted straight out of the Antwerp exchange and transported intact to this dark and miserable place. The floor was polished, the walls painted white. In the middle was a long table with two chairs and on the table two large white blotters. There were Anglepoise lamps by the blotters and, in between, a set of scales. At one end there was even a telephone. The only downmarket element was another table in the corner with a primitive sink and a tap. On the table was a plastic tray and in the tray a bottle of clear fluid in a plastic bottle.

'This is a fucking mirage,' said Ron. 'If these were electric' – he pointed at the scales – 'it would be perfect.'

I picked up the plastic bottle in the tray.

'Careful with that, Bruce. Hydrofluoric acid. Cleans diamonds, burns flesh. We probably won't need it, all the goods around here are alluvial which means . . .'

'They come from the river bed.'

'Right, so you know your Latin. They dig up the river bed, wash the gravel, move on. The goods'll be clean enough to price. When we get them back to Antwerp they'll be deep boiled in hydrofluoric and that stuff you really don't need on your hands.'

He sat down and from the holdall took out a pad, pen and calculator, then a pair of tweezers and an eyeglass. He combed his still-wet hair straight back and straightened his black T-shirt so that the white legend 'Moolah' was clear. He sat up, clasped his hands and bent them back, cracking his knuckles. 'Let's go,' he said.

Borema opened the door and the first haji came in. The haji produced a packet from under his robe and Ron tipped out the contents on to the blotter. In a matter of seconds he had divided the stones into three piles. A single stone on its own, then two others and the remainder in a small pile. He looked at the three main stones through the eyeglass.

'What do you know about diamonds, Bruce?'

'They're forever.'

'Corny.'

'They're a girl's best friend.'

'Which decade are you from?'

'They're not cheap.'

'Yeah.'

'Hoods call them "ice".'

'They're wrong.'

'And they're probably trouble.'

'That's for certain.'

'How about you? You look as if you've done this before.'

'This is the best bit,' he said. 'You ever collected coins?'

'I've never been that interested in money,' I lied.

'I did, when I was a kid. I sifted through pennies, that was all I could afford, looking for the ones I didn't have. When I had them all I looked for ones in better condition, but all the time I was dreaming that one day I'd come across the ultimate: the unaccounted-for, priceless nineteen thirty-three penny. Every time I came back from the bank with a bag of pennies . . . the excitement . . . there's nothing like it.'

'Bags of pennies – well, you've got me there, Ron. I never would have seen it.'

'Funny guy,' he said, looking down. 'You're going to learn something today, Bruce. This isn't about money. This is about beauty and perfection. Money's the scale, nothing more. The reason I'm here is because of the stones. Bigger, better and more perfect stones. I'm not an asshole, I know the money is important but . . . take a look at this.' He held the single stone he'd divided off and handed me the eyeglass. 'That is what we call a sawable. You see that double pyramid form. Octahedron, remember your geometry? It's the best kind of stone because it can be cut and shaped with the minimum of loss, but look inside the stone. You can see blue and yellow and pink in there and behind them all a bright white light . . . That's what it's all about.

'Those are the easiest stones to spot. These are more difficult,' he said, taking one of the two stones from the middle lot. 'This is a cleavage. Sometimes they can be as good as a sawable in quality but there's always going to be more loss because of their irregular shape. You value it by seeing how you can cut it.

'This . . .' he said, putting it down and picking up the other stone, '. . . is a problem. It's a maccle. It looks nice; it even looks a bit like the other one, but you look harder and you see problems in the middle. You're more likely to find flaws in these. Sometimes the flaws are tricky to see. Sometimes I make a mistake and I end up with a piece of shit, having paid for something better. Every stone teaches you something. I won't buy it unless he gives it away.'

'What about the other?'

'They're industrials,' he said, without looking round. 'Nothing of interest, like broken glass. They'll go to make those baguette diamonds you see on either side of better stones to enhance them. Either that or industry. They're no big deal. These three are what we're here for.'

He weighed them and asked the haji to give him a price. Shaking his head, he punched the figure into his calculator, converting it into dollars.

'He's asking for more than I can get in Antwerp,' said Ron, brushing the diamonds back into the packet which he handed to the haji who gave him another figure. Ron shook the packet at him and another lower figure dropped out of the haji. Ron tossed the packet at him. The haji didn't want to pick it up, as if by picking it up he would lose the sale. He told us he was seventy-three years old. He looked fifty. Ron nodded. He told us he had twenty-eight children and his fourth wife was pregnant with number twenty-nine. He gave another figure and Ron folded his arms. The figure was a lot lower and the haji said it was for the whole packet.

Ron opened the packet and poured the diamonds out in an expert sweep. He took a towel out of his holdall and wiped his hands. Then he sat back, taking his time, running his hands through his hair and flicking it up over his collar and using the towel again. The haji, half bent over the table, was locked in position with the tension. Ron picked up the flawed maccle he hadn't liked and took another look at it through the eyeglass, weighed it, and shook his head. He weighed all the industrials, writing down their weights on the pad and a money amount next to each one. He totalled the column. He weighed the sawable and the cleavage but didn't write anything down.

He thought for some minutes. The haji's white-slippered feet shifted in the silence. Then for the first time Ron gave a figure. The haji blinked. This was real money and I could hear his brain ticking through it like a note counter, wrapping rubber bands around it and stacking it off. The haji started to say something, started to try and reopen the negotiations and Ron stared him into the ground. They shook hands.

Ron took a fresh sheet of paper out, wrote the haji's name on it, the agreed price and the carat weight of the parcel. They both signed it. Ron told the haji the name of the Belgian who was financing the deal and the haji nodded as if there was nobody else.

'How was that?'

'Good,' said Ron, his brain buzzing, blinking fast. 'He was too desperate.'

'All those children.'

'Yeah, right. Even with Allah on his side he needed that cash. Shit, they always come down hard, the ones with their opening bids out there in cyberspace. You come in fifteen per cent above the real price and make a man fight for each point – that's the way to do it. They're the tough guys.'

'Where's cyberspace?'

'Up there on the Internet, Bruce. Where've you been the last decade?'

I felt like Fat Paul then, hearing new words, not knowing what they mean.

We shook hands with the haji. I asked him why he was still having children, old age was a time for rest. He laughed and said in French, 'My wife is a young woman. If I don't give her children, she doesn't feed me. I'm too old to go hungry.'

Ron was impressive. He worked for nearly five hours without a break, seeing all the hajis in the queue. He sipped mineral water, used the towel a lot and found some good stones, most of which he had to fight hard for. By 11.30 p.m. he had bought more than a million dollars' worth of product at Antwerp prices and he didn't look unhappy about it – looked as if he was going on holiday this year. He asked the last haji who was going to come down to Abidjan with the goods and they said it was going to be the father of twenty-nine. So Ron called him back in again and they arranged to meet in Rademakers's office at 8.30 the following night.

Ron had just started packing up when Borema looked in from outside.

'*Allons y*,' he said. '*A minuit la police va faire une patrouille. S'ils nous attrapent, on doit payer.*'

He turned off the air conditioner and locked the door from the inside and waited for us by the other door. Borema set off at a pace that made me think he was trying to shake us off. It was close to midnight by now and the few people about were running. We reached the clearing with the audible drainage. More people were running and Borema spoke to them. They didn't stop. Their bare feet thumped across the beaten earth and they disappeared down alleyways.

'*Problème*,' said Borema, the word I'd been waiting for.

We turned back on ourselves and followed Borema at a slow jog through the village labyrinth. He stopped in front of a house and hammered on the door as if it was the tenth time of asking. A woman made a noise which sounded like a local version of 'Keep your hair on', and opened the door. Borema shoved us in, talking to the woman over our heads in her own language, while she looked at us, then back at him, and then back at us again, her mouth set tighter than a belligerent bivalve.

Borema shut the door on us and ran.

'Fucking brilliant,' said Ron.

12

The woman's hair was plaited in straight furrows over her head. She nudged the three pieces of smouldering wood under the pot with her foot and dropped on her haunches to fan them with a piece of rafia matting on a stick. She banged a large wooden spoon on the side of the pot and a gob of glutinous manioc flopped back in.

'Fucking brilliant,' said Ron again.

'What d'you expect?'

'After the day we've had I *was* hoping for a fuck-up-free night.'

'You don't buy a million dollars' worth of diamonds in a place like this and not eat shit for free.'

'I was just hoping.'

'It didn't strike me as a hopeful kind of place.'

'How so?'

'Everybody in here thinks about nothing except diamonds whether they've got them or not. The white man comes and in fifteen seconds they all know about it. In fifteen seconds everybody in this town is thinking of an angle. How to separate you from what you've got. You're a "have" in a sea of "have-nots".'

A baby mewled. Lying on a piece of cardboard in the corner of the room was another, younger woman. The baby was lying on her stomach and she pulled it up, lifting her T-shirt, and torpedoed her breast into its mouth. She stroked the back of the baby's head and played with the sputnik points of her hair looking off at the wall, stoned. Ron picked at the beard on his chin with his thumb and forefinger and looked at her as if she was a life form off the evolutionary scale.

The manioc in the pot chupped and popped steam like a mud geyser. The air was thick with smoke collecting under the corrugated iron roof with no way to get out into the still night outside. The woman came over with a bowl of water and I washed my hands; so did Ron. Then she filled two bowls with manioc and splashed some sauce over it which looked red and chilli-hot. I took one and Ron asked me what I thought.

'It's vegetarian.'

'But, you know, hygiene?'

'It'll take your stomach three days to break the manioc down before it gets to the dysentery.'

'What'd you say it was?'

'In-fill and chilli. She's getting upset now, so decide.'

He took the bowl and watched me eat with my fingers.

'What do we do after dinner?'

'We give it twenty minutes, let the police patrol through, and then we get out of here.'

'You've got a torch?'

'No.'

'How are we going to get out of here?'

'Be positive, Ron.'

'I would be if I could see where I was going.'

'You got a torch, they got something to shoot at.'

'Shoot?'

'They're armed, Ron.'

'Why're they going to shoot at us?'

'Because we're running away.'

'Maybe we should stay put.'

'I need to get to Korhogo and I don't want to spend the night in jail. You don't either.'

We ate the food, the piquant sauce branded my tongue and the manioc re-formed and sat in my stomach like a tumor. The night was stiller than before, the village silent, even the cicadas seemed a long way off or were playing it pianissimo. The woman on the cardboard ran a horny foot up and down her shin. The baby had fallen off her breast and was sleeping.

Since the fire had been going, the room had got hotter and the smoky air was thick and rough on the throat. Ron started dozing with his back up against the wall. The flame from the fire dropped so that the only things visible were the sheen on Ron's forehead and the smooth skin of the woman's arm. The younger woman, abandoned on her piece of cardboard, slept. I felt my head going down, a reflex tugging at it.

Something jerked my string hard and I came awake in a burst of noise and adrenaline. There was a hammering on the door, hard and constant, not fists. Ron was stumbling around the room on stiff knees. The woman unlatched the door which crashed back against the wall and two boys, eighteen years old apiece, walked in. The first one with the flashlight gave the woman a back-hander in the face. She scrabbled across the floor to the corner with the younger woman and her baby. The boy pointed the torch after her and we got a glimpse of pure fear before he turned it on us.

They were both armed with automatic rifles. The second boy, who was stripped to the waist, wore army fatigues but had bare feet. He carried a heavy stick. The one with the torch wore a torn Black Sabbath T-shirt, fatigues and a pair of red and white basketball pumps. He picked up the holdall and pointed us out of the door with his rifle. Ron asked him who the bloody hell he thought he was, and the boy bridged the language divide by showing him the butt of his gun. We stood outside while the second boy gave the two women a beating which they took in complete silence, not wanting to antagonize him with any screaming.

They ran us down the village alleyways in a night that had thickened to tar. We fell, they kicked us. We stumbled, they butted us on with their rifles, enjoying themselves, giggling high-pitched laughter, out of their heads. We broke out of the village at a fast trot and moved towards the electric lighting of the police station's compound. We arrived pouring with sweat and shit-stained from falling into the drainage channels.

We waited at the foot of the steps that went up to the covered concrete verandah of a well-lit building that lacked paint, but had filth and flophouse stains to compensate. The boy with the holdall climbed the steps and walked down a long corridor with a single light. He reached the door at the end and knocked. The door opened, silhouetted him, and closed behind him.

The sweat was beading in Ron's beard and his stomach was pumping after the half-mile run in the heat. He alternated between the words 'fuck' and 'shit' and the kid with the rifle whose age I'd revised downwards a couple of years was telling him to '*Tais-toi*' until he'd had enough and aimed a flashy-looking kung-fu kick at Ron's leg. The kick hit Ron on the hip with no effect, except the boy fell over and fought with his gun in the dust until he ended on his back, the rifle pointing at Ron, who hadn't moved.

'These kids watch too many kickboxer movies,' I said.

The gun pointed at me. '*Tais-toi*!' screamed the boy, who stood up and took two lengths of plastic out of his pocket and cuffed our hands behind our backs.

A door opened in the corridor and a guy in shorts was thrown into the wall opposite the door. Two policemen with bowling-ball guts on each of them came out after him and picked him up by the shoulders and dragged him, blubbering, to the neon-lit concrete verandah. Their tunics were open, showing white vests, and they each had three-foot clubs in their hands and talked to each other as if their minds weren't on what they were doing. The prisoner's mouth was open with no sound coming out and his cheeks were running with tears.

The policemen threw him down and shrugged their shirts loose of their shoulders and gripped the clubs with both hands. They were still talking to each other, about football, or what they had for supper that night, when they started in on the guy on the floor. He found something to scream with and tried to protect himself. They clubbed him, breaking his arms, hands and fingers and kept on clubbing him for some time after he'd turned the scream off. The clubs ran with blood and their white vests were flecked with red. They threw him off the platform into the dark compound and, still talking, went back down the corridor into their room. The heap didn't move. The night painted over him.

'What did he do?' I asked the boy in French.

'Stole a radio.'

'What's French for "fucking hell"?' asked Ron.

'Try "*Sacré bleu*". They'll think you're sweet and old-fashioned.'

'*Tais-toi*,' said the boy, more subdued, prodding us in the kidneys with the barrel of his rifle, a little bored now. He walked over and sat on the steps, looked at his feet and picked his nose.

The two police officers came back out, one of them bent over clapping his hands and laughing at what the other was saying. They turned right on to the concrete platform, walked its length and went down some steps to a cage at the side of the building. One opened the cage while the other shone the torch at the frightened faces of the men inside. The cage door opened and a figure was pulled out. He tried to stand straight and the policeman with the torch kicked his legs away. They picked him up under the armpits and hauled him up the steps. In the light of the verandah we could see it was Borema, shaky on his legs, his tongue working around his lips, trying to get some moisture there, get rid of the dryness. They took him into their room down the corridor.

'Moses is still out there,' said Ron.

'Finding us a lawyer, you mean?'

'Doing something.'

'Hiding in the bush, shitting his pants. He's not coming anywhere near here if he's using his head.'

'You know, Bruce, you're a great travelling companion. A real calming influence.'

'You start relying on other people, you stop thinking.'

'Thinking about how much I don't want to be clubbed half to death.'

'Thinking about how we're going to get out of here.'

'Where's the fucking law in this country, that's what I want to know!'

'Right here,' I said. 'You want to go stealing radios?'

'But *we* haven't done anything.'

'They're thinking of something. Something expensive.'

The door on the left of the corridor opened. Moses came out. Not only was he not finding us a lawyer, he was stark naked with a badly swollen face, a stitched slit for a right eye and blood at the corner of his mouth and nostril. He hunched forward covering his genitals. They marched him back to the cage. He had blood trickling down the back of his leg from his backside.

'What the fuck happened there?' asked Ron.

'Anal search,' I said. 'Moses got nasty.'

'This is going off,' said Ron, 'badly off.'

'We should have moved.'

'Why are they doing this?' he asked. 'I don't understand why they're doing this, I bought some fucking diamonds, what's wrong with that? I mean that's what they want, isn't it?'

'It is. Now somebody's taking their cut. A big man somewhere's got himself short of money. You're loaded. They're softening you up. Showing you how ugly it can get, so when the time comes, you stretch out and let them rub your tummy. How much money you got?'

'Five hundred thousand CFA in the false bottom of the holdall.'

'That'll do.'

'All of it?'

'You can ask for some change if you want.'

'We still don't know what it's about.'

'Money. That's all it's ever about.'

A car's engine that wasn't used to full throttle screamed out not far off. The synchromesh growled and the clutch thumped in. Tyres span in the dust and caught. A rattling, shambolic noise came closer, the suspension finding its limits on a rough road, the undercarriage ripping into and over humps of baked earth. My Peugeot stormed into the compound and just before it hit the concrete verandah of the police station there was the trouser-ripping sound of a hand-brake being applied and the car swung 180 degrees and stopped and rolled forward. Through the tall dust came some high-pitched giggling and a hand slapped the steering wheel.

Two young police officers in uniform got out of the car and started unloading, taking the cases, including the whisky and water, inside to the room at the end of the corridor.

They came back with a torch and lifted a carpet out of the boot and threw it off somewhere. Then they opened the bonnet and looked in the air filter and under the battery. One of them took a screwdriver from the tool box and started to undo the driver's-door panel while the other searched under the dashboard. They called to each other for the torch every now and again. They found B.B.'s block of money in the passenger door, pulled it out, and took it inside.

Borema came out of the room down the corridor, naked, hands cuffed in front of him with the bored look of someone who's had these problems before. A single policeman walked him back to the cage. He didn't look as if he'd taken any sort of a beating.

'Maybe that fucker set us up,' said Ron.

'Possibly.'

'Maybe the little bastard owes somebody.'

'Just think about what you're going to say to those guys in the end room rather than who you're going to brain when you get out of here.'

The policeman came back from the cage empty-handed. A few minutes later the door opened at the end of the corridor and we were ordered up. A rifle prodded us forward. Close up, the corridor looked dirtier, with flying cockroaches performing acrobatics in the light.

In the room four neon strips dropped harsh light on to two policemen, with a metal filing cabinet between them, going through the bags. The boy in the Black Sabbath T-shirt was grinning, sitting with his leg up on the windowsill, playing with his rifle. There was a desk with Ron's empty holdall on it with the false bottom rucked up inside. Behind the holdall was a large shorn head sitting on two fat shoulders with striped epaulettes. A meaty forearm brushed the holdall aside and the shorn head looked up with eyes spaced wide apart, a flat, huge-nostrilled nose and a big mouth with a lot of white teeth in there. He stuck a finger and thumb in each nostril and said, '*Ce que ça pue!*'

He said something fast in African and the kid came off the windowsill with the grin off his face. The senior officer stood up behind his desk, leaned forward with one paw in the middle of it, and swung his arm around like a yacht's boom. He hit the boy on the side of his head with his open palm and the blow sprawled the kid halfway across the room where he landed on his shoulder. There was an explosion which made everybody jump and the metal filing cabinet rocked backwards. Cordite smoked from the boy's rifle. One of the officers knelt down and fingered the bullet hole in the filing cabinet's gut. The boy looked at his rifle and clicked on the safety. Ron and I opened up our reserve tanks of perspiration.

'I am the *chef*,' said the guy in French, running his hand over his shorn head, looking at Ron. 'What does that mean – "Moolah"?'

'Don't tell him,' I said. 'It'll only encourage him.'

'I don't know what it means myself.'

'Think of something.'

'It means bullshit,' said Ron, in French. Everybody laughed.

'They liked that.'

'These guys are easy to please.'

'So far.'

'You stink,' said the *chef*, laughing. 'You stink like bullshit.'

'Laugh till your hernia pops,' I said, and we roared.

When we'd quietened down a bit, and repeated the *chef*'s joke to ourselves a few times and had a few more spurts of laughter and an oh-dear-lordy-lordy, he said we could shower and change.

By the time we got back our clothes had been stuffed back in the cases and the *chef* was swinging a key with a tag on it like a hotel room key and reading a telex.

'We have two problems,' he said, which was a bad sign because in Africa you only needed one and the shit would be piled two feet above your head.

The first was that we hadn't registered ourselves as diamond buyers; whether you buy diamonds or not you still had to register. Ron pointed out that I wasn't a buyer and the policeman nodded and said that was fine, which worried me because it shouldn't have been. It should have been discussed, analysed, joked over and presents given, but no, all it did was bring him to the second problem.

'This key,' he said, 'it's the key to room 208 in the Hotel La Croisette in Grand Bassam.'

'What's he talking about?' asked Ron.

'You thought we were in shit before . . .'

'*We*?' asked Ron. 'I'll take the rap for the gear, but you're solo for the trip he's talking about.'

The *chef* raised an eyebrow. Ron shut up and listened to him reading the telex in his hand. It was a police report about the killing of a Liberian and two Ghanaians in room 208 of the Hotel La Croisette in Grand Bassam. It gave a clinical description of the nature of their deaths, down to the locations of the bullet holes, the split abdomen and the missing fingers and genitals. There was a synopsis of a statement by the hotel manager referring to a white man close to two metres tall, around ninety kilogrammes in weight, dark-brown hair and blue eyes, who the police would like to talk to.

'Explain,' said the *chef*.

A gust of wind drove its shoulder into the side of the building and a couple of doors slammed shut. The *chef* said something to the youngest boy. Raindrops hit the roof like grape shot. The boy produced some hurricane lamps which he lit. He left the room and the generator cut and the lights went out. The rain roared on the roof, too loud for talk, and we stood in the half-lit room which flared on and off with blue-white lightning so that we could see the rain falling in a white wall outside.

The rain gave me ten minutes to think. One minute to sort out what I was going to say and the nine minutes mulling over the response permutations should they look under the driver's seat and find Eugene Amos Gilbert's silenced .38.

When the rain had eased off the *chef* nodded at me and I told them how I came to be in Fat Paul's hotel room on Monday night. I even mentioned the vultures and how I'd beaten them out of the room to show that I was a nice guy with respect for the dead. The *chef* said it didn't explain the key. I told him I took the key when I first came into the hotel so that I could go up and check the room. If the key had been on the hook the woman would have said they

119

were out and I'd have had no reason to go upstairs and see.

The shorn head thought about that and then asked me why the key was there in the first place if the people were in their room. I gave him the scenario of the empty hotel with Fat Paul's car outside, the killer finishing his work, locking the door and putting the key back on the hook. He didn't like it. He asked me why I hadn't made a statement to the police. I said that I didn't want to spend four hours in a police station when I had to drive to Korhogo the next day and anyway, the manager had the story. He produced Fat Paul's ring, the one with the scorpion on it.

'What's this?'

'A ring.'

'Yours?'

'Yes.'

He gave it to me to try on. It might have cut into Fat Paul's fingers but on mine there was a pencil width's difference.

'You've slimmed,' he said, smiling, so that I had to tell him about Eugene Amos Gilbert, also known as 'Red'. How we'd met in the hotel, how I'd disarmed him and seen his ID. How we'd fought in the basement and ended up on the bridge where we'd had another fight and he'd fallen in the water.

'Where's the gun?' asked the *chef*, which was a good and well-timed question and had me thinking that if they find that gun with my prints all over it and make the ballistic connection I'm on my way to a very long time in an Ivorian penal establishment.

'In the lagoon,' I said.

'And Eugene Amos Gilbert's ID?'

'In the lagoon. I gave it back to him.'

He asked for my timetable between three and six yesterday afternoon. I went over that and my story six or seven times until he'd got it absolutely straight. When the storm had passed and they restarted the generator, the neon lights came back on and after several hours of brutal light and step-by-step repetition my mind was like four eggs, scrambled. One of the other policemen typed it out, the guy needing a course badly, and not from the Pick 'n' Mix school. They had it off in triplicate and asked me to sign it. The same typist typed out the statement on the telex, the keys kicking and slapping and the tape spewing. I signed that too. As if this wasn't enough ugliness for one night I had another surprise when I asked the *chef* about the block of money in the Coq Sportif bag that was taken from my car. There were a lot of puzzled faces and muttering of 'Coq Sportif' and one of the boys left the room and came back shrugging.

'So we can go now?' asked Ron.

'I've telexed Abidjan,' said the *chef*. 'We have to wait for the reply.'

It was four o'clock in the morning when they locked us in the room next door with our bags. I still had Fat Paul's ring which the *chef* had forgotten about in the excitement over the two million CFA he'd just ripped off. I lay on the floor and wondered how long I was going to have to work for B.B. now that I'd lost his two million. With compound interest of Christ knows how many per cent it could be a life sentence, a better life sentence than an African prison — unless you knew B.B.

Ron turned the light off and lay down some yards away. We stared at the ceiling like a couple who've rowed heavily over dinner and are doing some light soul-searching, knowing they're going to make up but biding their time, eking out a little suffering.

'I fucked you up,' said Ron, which nearly sounded like an apology.

'I didn't exactly help myself.'

'If we hadn't come here you wouldn't be in this shit.'

'I'd have been in some other shit. It's nothing to do with you. It's planetary.'

'You believe in that crap?'

'No, I'm trying to make you feel better.'

'You think you can get out of this?' asked Ron.

'I notice you didn't say "we".'

'Hey, I didn't register as a diamond buyer, which is not what I'd call a big problem. I pay out some shekels in the morning and I'm out of here. I'm not up for triple murder plus mutilations and theft. *That*'s what I call a big problem. *That*'s why I'm asking you if you can get out of this . . . OK?'

'OK. My answer is: If they don't find the gun.'

'What gun?'

'The gun the hit man used to kill Fat Paul. It's under the front seat.'

Ron went completely silent, so that I could hear the leather of his boots creaking, the noise of a distant dog barking and the rain dripping off the roof outside.

'You had a heart attack, Ron?'

'No, I've got something on my mind. That's all.'

'Apart from the gun?'

'That's just taken up a big chunk of it, but yes, apart from the gun, which should have been in the lagoon in Abidjan and not under the front seat of your fucking car, there's something on my mind.'

Silence.

'You think maybe I did kill them and you're worried about sharing a floor with a mass murderer.'

'No, I think you covered that in there six times over. I'm satisfied . . . even though you did lie about the gun.'

Some more silence.

'You don't mind keeping what it is to yourself? I mean, I've got a few things pressing on me at the moment, making my heart run a little quick.'

'It's not something that affects . . . *us*.'

'Our new-found love for each other, you mean?'

'What I mean is, it's not important to *our* situation.'

'That's the only situation I'm prepared to think about right now.'

'It's something you should know.'

'You crack under torture, is that it?'

'I don't know, I've never been tortured.'

'Are you going to lance this boil or let it burst on its own?'

'I'm getting married.'

'Congratulations.'

'A week on Sunday.'

'That's great. Nice to have some good news. Sleep well on it.'

'I need to be back . . .'

'What's her name?'

'. . . by the middle of next week at least.'

'You going to tell me her name?'

'I have to get a flight to Tel Aviv by nineteen hundred hours on Friday week.'

'For Christ's sake tell me her name.'

'Anat.'

Pause.

'That's an interesting name. Her parents must have spent a long time thinking up a name like that. Amat. You mean, like amo, amas, amat. She loves.'

'With an "n" for November. Anat.'

'She's foreign, then?'

'Israeli,' he said. 'Most people who get married in Tel Aviv are Israeli.'

'Do you love this girl . . . Anat?'

'Yes, I do.'

'That's good.'

'What do you mean?'

'I mean it wasn't the matchmaker's choice. You love her. It wasn't arranged.'

'No.'

'I'm very happy for you, Ron,' I said, rolling on to my side.

'Thanks.'

'Just don't tell anybody else about it, OK?'

'Fine.'

'We've got to look as if we've got all the time in the world.'

'Right.'

'Now I understand why you were so edgy.'

'I was edgy because of the bullet in the tyre, because you said you killed somebody, because there's a gun under the front seat of the car, because we're in jail in the middle of fucking nowhere, because . . .'

'Don't get out of your pram again, Ron.'

Ron shut up. I could hear him blinking. I could tell he was lying there on his back with his hands clasped behind his head looking at the ceiling with the nastiness all shut out and a warm feeling growing up him thinking about Anat. Thinking about life after he gets out of here. His future. A future that was going to be sweet.

'Have you got anybody, Bruce?'

I heard him but I didn't answer. The smell of wet earth came in under the door. The wind tapped at something metallic outside. One of the policemen snored in the corridor. It wasn't long before I found myself running down a long, wet and badly lit passageway, on my own, not scared, just running, but with no light at the end of it.

13

I woke up on the back of a loud bang followed by the noise of splitting wood and turned to see a splinter of the jamb topple away and the door's hinges pop. The door fell on Ron's inert body and one of the big-bellied policemen, still with momentum, blundered over it and stopped himself against the far wall.

'*Qu'est-ce qu'il y a?*'

'*Il a perdu la clef,*' said a voice from the corridor.

'Fuck me,' said Ron, shrugging off the door.

'*Ça va?*' asked the policeman, leaning the door against the wall.

'*Ça* fucking *va,*' said Ron, on all fours, his long hair, a little greasier now, hanging in rats' tails off his head.

The *chef* came in, running a wet hand over his shorn head and told us the phone lines were down and we were going to Bouaké. I asked him why we couldn't go to Korhogo, which was nearer, and he said the phone lines were down there too, and even if they weren't we'd still be going to Bouaké because that was the way it was going to be.

Outside it was a grey, misty morning with the sun just beginning to burn it off. Moses was loading the car, cold and miserable with his swollen eye just open. He said Borema had been released.

A big man in full purple robes and a cylindrical hat the size of a snare drum stood on the backs of his size-thirteen white pointed shoes by the open passenger door, whose panel had been replaced. In his hand he had the Coq Sportif carrier bag which had contained B.B.'s two million CFA. He was introduced as a local chief and we all shook hands. I brought up the subject of my money with him and pointed at the bag. He handed it to me. It had something thick and solid in it but not money. It was a book – *Le Père Goriot* by Balzac.

'*C'est bon ça,*' said the police *chef*. I put the book back in the carrier bag and gave it back to the chief.

'*Non, non, non,*' he said, and with inspired misunderstanding took the book out and handed me the carrier bag, as if I was a mud-hut native who'd die with gratitude to be given a bag like that. We got in the car along with an armed guard.

Moses drove with his good eye on the road while the chief sat next to him with his hat in his lap, moaning deliciously every now and then as if he was getting a gentle rub down from the money on his thigh.

'This is why we're going to Bouaké,' I said to Ron.

'Not the telex.'

'We're the big man's stretch limo for the day,' I said, and on cue the chief let out a long low moan as if he was getting it just where he wanted it.

We arrived in Bouaké just after 1.00 p.m. The sun was shining but not so that I felt like kicking off my shoes and dancing around a pool with a daquiri. We dropped the chief outside the big hotel in town. He walked in there with Balzac held behind his back, looking around as if he might buy most things under his nose. Moses drove on to the police station and the *chef* went in.

Half an hour later the *chef* came back out and told us we were going to Abidjan. I said he'd had his money and it was time to say goodbye. Without bothering to turn round he told us that Ron was free to go but I had charges which had to be answered in Abidjan. I asked what the charges were, and he said he didn't know the exact wording but the Abidjan police wanted to talk to me about a triple murder.

We drove to Abidjan in the heat of the day. The *chef*'s shorn head dropped on to his chest and he slept. The armed guard behind us dozed and jerked awake. Ron seemed to have lost some of his edges overnight. He was looking out of the window without sneering, looking at women with half a hundredweight of firewood on their heads, and babies on their backs, moving at a fair lick with their bare feet on the hot tarmac road.

'They're very resilient,' I said to him.

'Not just physically,' he said, which surprised me. 'Those women last night.'

'They knew we were trouble as soon as they saw Borema.'

'They let us in, fed us and took that beating without a squeak.'

'Women have a very hard life in Africa. They get used to trouble early on.'

'Trouble,' said Ron, nodding. 'That's the first time I've ever had trouble.'

'I thought you'd had some in Russia.'

'Passport, visa stuff. The business is all protected by the Moscow mob. You don't see anything. Just the odd guy standing in the corridor, looking as if he's eaten too many dumplings.'

'You must sense it, though,' I said, and his eyes flicked across at me, 'the ugliness. Like when you stay in cheap hotels, you always know the whorehouses.'

'I've never stayed in cheap hotels,' he said. 'I'm rich.'

'I forgot.'

'Sure you did.'

'You weren't talking like a jerk for a second.'

'I know I am one sometimes . . .'

'*Some*times?'

Ron laughed.

'A lot of people want to get on my back,' he said. 'I protect myself.'

'Believe me, you're good. You must have spent your whole life at it.'

'Look, *you* can tell me about sleaze. You *know* about sleaze. *Sleaze* is your . . .'

'It's not all sleaze. Some of it's called "real life".'

'I don't know about that. Sleaze, I mean, any of it. I can tell you about diamonds, no problem.'

'I was impressed, Ron. I mean it. You don't have to tell me. Last night I was impressed. You're not a jerk when it . . .'

'Think of the diamond trade and think of Beauty and the Beast. I told you last night, I get all excited about the beauty of the stones. I meant it. But what it comes down to in the end is the beast. The one with green backs. And everybody wants my beast. I have to make sure the assholes stay over there. That's how I do it. Believe me, it doesn't discourage them. They still come back for more. They'd take anything for a slice.'

'You're trying to tell me – underneath all that you're not a jerk.'

'You're very . . .'

'Candid?' I asked. 'I don't need your business and I don't need your money. I don't even need your company. What can you tell me that's different? Diamonds. Diamonds and pennies. What else? You going to tell me how to get out of the shit?'

'I don't know how you stand it,' said Ron, trying to cuddle up now.

'It's not like this all the time,' I said, 'and this isn't really shit. Shit is when you don't have the money to get yourself out of it, and it *is* only money, Ron, after all. Small money. I mean, what're you going to clear on one and a half million dollars' worth of diamonds? Three, four, five per cent?'

'Two, two and a half.'

'Two and a half of one and a half million, that's . . .'

'Thirty-seven and a half.'

'Thanks. Glad to see they still teach mental arithmetic. Thirty-seven thousand five hundred dollars, less two thousand dollars for police expenses, less one thousand five hundred dollars for legitimate expenses, less something for Rademakers. Whichever way you look at it you're thirty up for the week.'

'And you?'

'Well, that's the nature of the poverty trap. Once you're down in it, it's hell to get out. You see the sky every now and again but you never get your knee over the lip. Nobody's ever told me about the poverty springboard – you?'

'We can talk about it.'

'What?'

'The money.'

'Forget it. It was bad luck. I'll work it out. I've got something in mind. Anyway, I don't think I could bear to have you negotiate me into a hole.'

Ron went back to looking out of the window and picking at his beard. Maybe his future wife was going to stop him doing that.

'You're worrying something to death in there, Ron. I think it's a better idea you drop it.'

'I'm twenty-seven years old. I'm getting married in a week. I've got a ton of money behind me. I *know* I'm going to have a very nice life.'

'Then sit back and enjoy it. There's plenty of people's lives you don't want. Mine, for instance. All that shit and sleaze. I can tell you about that if you've got some tears to spare.'

'I haven't done anything and I've never *had* to do anything.'

'Don't get morose on me, rich boy,' I said, and Ron grunted a laugh.

'I'm well protected from life. I didn't tell you, my father wanted to send a chaperon with me out here, make sure I wiped my arse properly.'

'I'm told it's not a talent men are renowned for,' I said.

'What it does is drive me fucking crazy. It makes me worse. It makes me more of an arrogant little fucker than . . .'

'You missed out "narcissistic",' I said, which disarmed him and he shook his head and laughed into the hot air coming through the window. One thing I didn't need to hear was a rich boy's hard-luck story.

'I'm two million CFA down. You?' I asked, getting back down to the business in hand.

'I haven't looked, but I guess the five hundred thousand's gone.'

'Have you got any other money?'

'Need my company now, Bruce?' he asked, finding that reservoir of cockiness again.

I asked him to do a few things for me when we got back to Abidjan. The first was to call Leif Andersen at the Danish Embassy and get him to call the Sûreté to confirm that I was with him from 4.00 p.m. until 5.00 p.m. on Monday and that he spoke to me at the Novotel at 6.30 p.m. later that same day. On the money side I asked him if he could get some off Rademakers and I'd sort him out from Martin Fall's float in the Novotel safe. I told him to bring four blocks of 250,000 CFA each. I had a feeling things might get difficult. People were going to get greedy and there could be more than one of them to cover. Ron was still on schedule to meet Rademakers and the haji at 8.30 p.m. It was nearly 2.00 p.m. by now. We'd be in Abidjan by 5.00 p.m. I told him to come to the Sûreté at 7.30 p.m. with the money. I hoped I'd be ready for him.

We slept until we got to the Sûreté in Abidjan at a few minutes after 5.00 p.m. I reminded Ron to be there at 7.30 p.m. He left without saying a word and I thought I might have trodden on him too hard, but then, you can never tread on someone like that too hard.

They took me down to the cells, which weren't air-conditioned and lacked mini-bars but had been cleaned at least three days ago. They put me in the only cell where the occupants weren't lying on the floor and in the only one with just one other inmate. He stood in the middle of the nine square feet and gave me a steady recidivistic look with a pair of hooded yellow eyes which should have been set in rubber in the middle of the road. His stare came off the top of a body which had worked hard for most of its life, including the struggle out of the womb. He had the body of a cane-cutter, or a truck-loader – not white collar, in fact, no collar at all. The jailer let me in and shut the door quickly. I edged around this statue to delinquency and slid down the wall to the floor.

'*T'as assassiné quelqu'un?*' I asked.

His head turned slowly on his body, some complicated robotics going on in there, but he didn't answer.

'Did you kill someone?' I tried, and a huge smile opened up in his face which worried me that I might have triggered off a pleasant memory.

'Ingliss?'

'That's right,' I said, and held out a hand. 'Bruce.'

130

He took what I'd offered him into his own tarpaulin-skinned hand as if it was a fluffy chick. He patted it and let me have it back after a minute or two.

'David,' he said, 'from Ghana side. Kumasi.'

'Ashanti?'

'I'm ver' happy,' he said, which was a cheering turn-around.

'What d'you do? Kill someone?'

'Oh no, Mr Bruce. I drinkin' too much palm wine. Gettin' drunk and brekkin' things.'

'Just things or people too?'

'Mebbe people too. The police, when they come . . . I throw them.' And he gave me an energetic action replay which left me thinking of policeman-shaped holes in walls. 'More police, they come . . . they hittin' me with sticks. I brek the sticks!' he roared, showing me how those sticks went down to matchwood. 'More police, they come, mebbe twenty, mebbe more. They come runnin'. They get me down. They beat me,' he said, and showed me the back of his head which looked like a sack of conkers. 'I wek up in here, my head hurt no small.'

'That's quite a beating you took.'

'No, no, Mr Bruce. From the palm wine. The beatin', I no feel the beatin',' he said, shaking his hangover-free head and making me feel glad that I'd somehow pulled the thorn from his paw.

'What you doin' in here, Mr Bruce?' he asked, sitting down opposite me.

'They think I kill three people, mebbe four.'

David came forward, his eyes out on stalks and he let out a little squeak.

'They go see the error of their ways, Mr Bruce. You don' kill nobody with those hands. They too small for killin'.'

'They think I shot them with a gun.'

'Ah-haaa!' said David, clocking something he hadn't con-sidered. 'But you no do it. You no kill the men.'

'No,' I said, and he sat back satisfied and the tension drained from his body.

Half an hour slipped by, with David telling me a lot of

things I didn't need to know about his brother's petrol station in Kumasi. I kept him going with some grunts and an occasional 'Ah-haaa'. The jailer came and found us sitting next to each other with David counting off gallons of petrol and pints of oil on his massive hands. He called his mate to come and look. They took me away, with David shouting after me, 'I beg you, Mr Bruce, I beg you! Release me! Release me!'

They took me up to the first floor of the building along a strip-lit corridor and into a room with the same lighting. The dark-green carpeting on the floor overlapped some pipes which were four inches off the floor around the gloss-painted light-green walls. There were police-academy photographs on three walls and, on the fourth, a picture of the President which was hung behind a uniformed man sitting at an important desk with green leather inlay. A mug on his desk for pens had the Prince of Wales crest and '*Ich dien*' underneath, which worried me.

'*Je suis le Commissaire Gbondogo,*' he said, and waved the other policemen out of the room. 'Or would you rather speak in English?'

He nodded me into a chair and continued in English while flicking through my passport.

'An unfortunate situation, I think, is how you English would describe your predicament.'

'I hope you're not talking about our capacity for understatement.'

'Alas, Mr Medway, I am.'

'Alas? Where did you learn this outstanding English?' I asked, going for the bootlicking option, given Gbondogo's opening gambit.

'At school. From the radio. I've always had a good ear,' he said, flipping the passport on to the desk and leaning back, hands clasped across a flat stomach. 'A very good ear, and not just for languages.' He let that hang in the air like battle smoke and it had hardly cleared before he was coming over the top at me – bayonets fixed.

'We have some statements here about your activities, and not just on the night of Monday, twenty-eighth October. We have a statement from a policeman in Tiegba, and from a barman too. You were seen there on the night of Sunday, twenty-seventh October behaving suspiciously.' He slowed down. 'Changing the number plates on your car. Removing the internal light. You left Tiegba at eight-fifteen p.m. A body was found not far from the Lagune Ebrié. The autopsy says death occurred around eight-thirty p.m. The body was in the same state as the ones found in the Hotel La Croisette. We have a statement from the hotel manager saying that you were there on the night of Monday, twenty-eighth October at about seven-fifteen p.m. A full explanation is required. And Mr Medway, my ear is well tuned to lies in all languages.'

Commissaire Gbondogo was not a man to be fooled with and worse, he didn't look like a man who corrupted easily. He was small, wiry, intelligent and ruthless. I told him everything from the top and the only detail I missed out on was the package. I still maintained that Fat Paul hadn't given it to me. I had to hold on to my nerve when I asked him if Leif Andersen had called and he kept his laser eyes fixed on my eyebrows and shook his head.

It was just as well I spilled it clean out because the gun appeared from a drawer in his desk on cue. I got a bit of confidence together by the end and, to see if he was going to show a chink for me to fit through, I told him that the Tortiya police had ripped us off, but not by how much, just in case he turned out cheaper. He didn't flinch. I stopped talking and we sat in silence, a long one, of maybe five minutes.

'Eugene Amos Gilbert has not been found in the lagoon,' was all he said before a single blast from the phone made him pounce forward and wrench it to his ear. He stood up and took the phone with him over to the window and murmured in French to it, while looking at the night and our reflections in the glass. After five minutes he stuck the receiver to the phone, repositioned it on the desk and sat down.

'I don't think I've come across such a serious situation

with a member of the expatriate community since I was made commissaire five years ago . . .'

'Was that Leif Andersen who just called?'

His eyes blinked once and I knew my chance was coming.

'It is the lies in your earlier statements which particularly disgust me and the fact that you are in possession of an illegal firearm. Both charges carry heavy jail sentences and punitive fines . . .'

'Perhaps we could come to an arrangement . . .' I said, and stopped when I felt Gbondogo's look open up my forehead. 'It's just that I know what Eugene Amos Gilbert looks like and you need to find him.'

'*That* is true,' he conceded, thawing now that he knew I wasn't so insensitive as to mention money at such an early stage of the negotiations. We kicked around various elements of my story, me concentrating on the positive things like Leif Andersen and the timing, and he emphasizing the gun and the statements.

'I think perhaps we are close to some sort of agreement,' he said, with no evidence for saying it. 'You will find Eugene Amos Gilbert and bring him to me. However, because of your earlier . . . mendacity' – he enjoyed that one so much he had to repeat it – 'because of the *disgraceful* mendacity of these statements I do not believe you can be trusted.'

'What about bail?'

'Bail?'

'Bail and a fine, perhaps.'

'Yes . . .' he said, and assumed the gravity of a judge – one which looked very low and immovable. 'A fine of seven hundred and fifty thousand and bail set at five hundred thousand. I think that is fair.'

'I was thinking more of a two hundred and fifty thousand fine and the same bail.'

'Out of the question. The charges are too serious.'

'I'll deliver Eugene Amos Gilbert within the next ten days.'

'A fine of five hundred thousand and bail set at two hundred and fifty thousand. Bail refundable when you deliver Gilbert.'

We haggled over this for some time and Gbondogo

wouldn't budge off the 500,000 fine which, I assumed, was going straight into his pocket. I still needed to save face in the negotiation but couldn't move him off the money. I came up with a solution which startled him. I asked for the release of my ex-cellmate, David. He buzzed someone on his switchboard and a sergeant appeared at the door. They spoke in their own language and the sergeant was dispatched.

'The charge is not serious. He has already been beaten. It is done.'

It was 7.45 p.m. by the time we went downstairs and Ron hadn't curdled on me so badly that we'd separated. He was waiting at the front desk. We went into the compound and he produced the 750,000. We shook hands and the commissaire laid down his cards.

'Leif Andersen confirmed your story, so did the *gardien* of the Novotel garage and the hotel reception. The autopsy put the three deaths at somewhere between three p.m. and five p.m. We have found the hire car you used from which we extracted a .38 bullet from the head rest and noticed the replacement window. We have not had it confirmed by ballistics yet that the bullet came from the gun in your possession but I expect that to be the case. We are not looking for a white man for these murders. They bear all the hallmarks of tribal killings. We think they may be Krahn people. Let me assure you, Mr Medway, that had you been suspected of the killings, no amount of this would be sufficient.'

'I'm glad to hear it,' I said, feeling as if I'd paid a lot more than I'd have had to with the facts.

He gave us a click of his heels and a brief salute and retreated into the darkness, appearing briefly in the yellow-lit doorway of the Sûreté, the bag in his armpit.

Ron and I had just opened the doors to the Peugeot when there was a roar from the steps where the commissaire had just disappeared and David came running across the compound. He clasped me to him.

'My brother,' he said. 'You are my brother.'

Something which I didn't think many people were going to believe.

14

Ron looked at me across the car roof once David had let me go and disappeared into the night.

'You paid that guy three thousand dollars to . . .'

'Don't tell me, I should have had you on the negotiating team.'

'. . . to get out of *jail*?'

'The corruption, you mean? Public servants don't always get paid on time. He's probably an important person in his village or tribe. He's got responsibilities. It's expensive being a big man. He just uses his position to do a little ripping off to bolster funds. It's not as if he's raping the country or anything.'

'He is. He's just doing it slowly.'

'Maybe he learnt how to do it from us. The colonial powers did some ripping off in their time.'

'We put a hell of a lot back in. Schools, hospitals, infrastructure . . .'

'Somebody'll do the balance sheet one day. Who got what for how much. It'll be interesting. Now can I have a shower?'

We got in the car. Ron reached into a back seat for a newspaper.

'I found this. You've got equal billing with Sunday's election.'

I straightened out the *Ivoire Soir* and read the middle-page headline:

LE MASSACRE DU LÉOPARD;
ENCORE QUATRE CADAVRES!

'They love it,' said Ron.

'Elections don't sell newspapers around here. The President's for life. Did you hear that guy from the opposition on the World Service? No, you wouldn't have. He said something like, "People want to see what an opposition leader looks like. They just want to touch me, see if I'm real." Now, "the Leopard" and four more bodies, that's real. Something they can get their teeth into. Are you fixed up with Rademakers?'

'At eight-thirty – it's still on. You going to come?'

'What's going to happen?'

'You get to see one and a half million dollars in CFA, I buy you a meal and we settle our accounts.'

'Are you telling me the haji takes it out in cash?'

'He's not sticking it in the bank. He turns up with a couple of big guys and drives off with it. That's what Rademakers says.'

'You don't go running off into the night with your diamonds, do you?'

'You're kidding. Rademakers gets them out to Antwerp whichever way he wants.'

'What does that mean?'

'If he sends them back officially he has to show money paying for them. If he sends them back black then he'll make on the money.'

'You've lost me.'

'Rademakers raises the money, the CFA, from local businessmen here who want dollars outside Ivory Coast. Because they want the dollars they give a discount on the CFA. I pay Rademakers in dollars in Belgium. He makes on the discount. Otherwise it all goes through the banks and shit and he buys at standard rates of exchange. Got it?'

'What happens to you?'

'I go to Angola. I was going to a tender in Sierra but they cancelled it, so I've got the weekend off here and I fly to Luanda on Monday and back home Wednesday.'

'Tel Aviv Friday.'

'Looks like it.'

'OK. Let's go to the Novotel. I need to get the smell of that jail out of my throat.'

I showered and changed and drank a beer from the mini-bar and took a call from Martin Fall who didn't want to know if I was still alive, he only cared about Ron. I told him we were meeting Rademakers in half an hour and after that, as far as I was concerned, now that the Sierra trip was off, my assignment was over. I was *not* going to play ping pong with Ron at the Novotel all weekend until he flew off to Angola.

'You didn't get along?' asked Martin.

'If you stripped away the money, the fancy clothes, the fast cars and gave him six months' rehabilitation in the real world he'd be OK . . .'

'OK for a spoilt, arrogant, narcissistic little fucker,' said Martin, 'and that's what his dad called him.'

'You got anything else for me? Same money, better casting.'

'Take him to Rademakers and you're home free. We'll sort out the money business later.'

I went down to the lobby. Ron was waiting for me in the bar. We drove to Avenue Chardy, still in Plateau, and parked in the street and gave a *gardien* some money to look after the car. The street was empty of cars and people. We crossed it and went down a narrow alley between two buildings which opened out into a private car park behind some apartment blocks. The exit to the car park, which was further down Avenue Chardy, was chained off. A man lay on a piece of cardboard near the chain with his arm over his eyes and a knee crooked.

It was hotter in the car park than in the open street. The air was locked in, and the heat was still coming up off the tarmac. We went through a green door in one of the apartment buildings and up a concrete stairway through one floor and then another. We came out on the third and walked along an open balcony with a view down over the car park. We turned right down a dark corridor with a single bell light halfway up the wall on the right. Five yards down the corridor lights came on as we broke the unseen beam of a sensor. There was a video camera high above the door. Ron pressed

138

the buzzer, the door clicked open and we went into an airless anteroom of bare concrete walls and a rough untiled floor. There was a large steel door in front of us which looked as if it might have taken some lifting to get it hung right.

The door opened automatically with the sound of some heavy steel bolts shunting out of the wall. It was helped on its way by a small grey-haired man in his early seventies with thick rimless lenses for specs on his nose. His eyes looked huge behind them, like aquarium fish. He had a white beard and a moustache which joined on his very pale face. He wore a lightweight powder-blue suit, a white shirt and a yellow shantung silk tie. We all shook hands. His were small and snappy, good for drawing innards from small birds. He put one of his small hands on Ron's back and guided him into the office, which consisted of two rooms divided by a glass partition. I closed the door.

The office was cool and noiseless. The furniture was dark and wooden, apart from a sofa which was made of something probably called leatherette. On one wall there was a reproduction Magritte, of the stiff in the bowler with a Granny Smith in his face. Two very big men in giant blue polo shirts and jeans stood on one side of the partition and looked through the glass at the haji, the one with a generation's worth of children, who was sitting on a chair I couldn't see. His legs were spread wide under his white robe and his white slippered feet tapped the oatmeal carpet with no rhythm. A white cylindrical hat sat on Rademakers's desk, as did a closed Samsonite suitcase. Behind the desk was an open safe with a metal box in it. We did another round of handshaking. Nobody said a word. The reverence for money and mineral wealth demanded religious respect.

Rademakers introduced Ron to a chair in front of a table with an electric balance, a light and a blotter on it. The haji got to his feet and reached down into a three-foot pocket which ended by his ankle and produced a white packet which he put in front of Ron.

I sat on the sofa and slid around on whatever it was that the horrible thing was covered in. There was a video screen, wall-mounted, high in a corner and visible from Rademakers's chair, which was now dark but showed a red light on the consul so that he knew his technology was working. On the wall in the other office, just visible between the two heavies, was another repro Magritte, the one of a smoking pipe and the legend *'Ceci n'est pas une pipe'*, which looked as if it was asking for trouble.

Ron sorted through the diamonds, weighing some of them and checking them off against a notebook he'd taken out of his breast pocket. Rademakers sat behind his desk and stroked a pad with nothing written on it. He smiled at the haji, whose expression didn't change. I asked him what it was with the Magrittes.

'He's Belgian,' he explained, rather than give me two hours on twentieth-century surrealism, I supposed.

Ron did a final count, swivelled on his chair and nodded to Rademakers, who stood and opened the Samsonite case and turned it towards the haji. The card on top of the money said 476,656,000 CFA. The heavies' necks didn't look so fat suddenly. They were straining to see the money through the partition. We'd been there twenty-five minutes.

I crossed a leg and the sofa blew a raspberry, drawing attention to myself. I resisted blaming the sofa but looked up at the video screen which was still dark. There followed a fraction of a second when we were all transfixed, silent, tense like deer who've just caught the whiff of something that isn't other deer. Then the room seemed to suck itself in tight and with a short, powerful thump, which knocked Ron on to his arse and drove what felt like a sharp spike through my head, the thick steel door to the office popped out of its frame. It stood for a full second and then fell forward, shattering the glass partition, whose aluminium frame was torn away from the ceiling and crashed over the two heavies in the other office. The one nearest the door took the full force of it against the corner of his head and was out before he hit the ground. The other ducked instinctively but a full glass panel still broke over his head and a shard cut him deep across the side of his neck. From the quantity of blood that hit the ceiling it must have severed his carotid.

The noise was still going on in my head when three Africans in black T-shirts and jeans appeared in the room. The muscles and tendons in their arms stood out, their hands clenched around a variety of small firearms. One man stood by the empty door frame and checked out the two heavies under the glass partition, the other two came into the room. The larger man swept the room with a machine pistol which looked as if it could empty enough bullets per second to saw Rademakers's desk in half. The other man kept his pistol, fitted with a suppressor, firmly aimed at Ron.

'Nobody moves,' said the man from the door in an American accent. The one holding Ron in his sights saw the white packet on the table and pressed it. He opened it up with one hand, checked the contents and slipped it into his pocket. Ron crawled towards him, not using his head.

'Freeze,' said the man from the door, not shouting, just saying it.

The man with the diamonds grabbed Ron by the collar so that he had to scrabble forwards. Ron landed on his face in front of the man by the door. The one with the machine pistol closed the Samsonite suitcase. The haji stood up.

'Siddown,' said the man from the door. The haji kept moving.

'*Asseyez-vous!*' shouted Rademakers. There was a single pop on the word *vous* and the haji sat down this time, his eyes wide open, and a red flower with a black hole in the middle of his chest. He reached for it but couldn't get his hands up there. He nodded his head down at his wound, confirming to himself that he'd been hit. He slipped off the side of the chair, his face ending up crushed against the wall.

The machine pistol was now on Rademakers, whose hands had come up to shoulder height. The gunman nodded him down into his chair and pointed me into another. The man at the door covered us. The others put down their weapons and took out strips of plastic and cuffed us to our seats. The man at the door threw some tape in and they wound it around our heads and over our mouths.

'Move it,' said the man at the door.

They checked the office, picked up their arms and the suitcase, turned out the light and left, taking Ron with them.

I watched them leave on the video screen, the corridor lights coming on this time and staying on for a minute and then the screen went to black again and the silence was complete.

My feet were cuffed with a figure of eight of plastic and my hands attached to the chrome stalk at the back of the chair, which was on castors. I drew myself by the heels across to the light switch and turned it on with my forehead. The blood on the floor of the other office had reached the far wall and the glass, like broken sheet ice, seemed to be floating in it.

Rademakers was bright red in the face, even to the roots of his hair. He was as good as blind without his glasses, which were broken on the floor. His breath tore in and out of his nose, the shantung silk tie pumping up and down on his sparrow's chest. He was frantic.

I dragged myself over to the aluminium frame, wedged the castors against the fallen door and worked the plastic around my ankles against a shard of glass. It took fifteen minutes to get through it. I stepped into the frame and sawed through the handcuffs, which was quicker. Rademakers was in spasm by now, his chair almost leaving the ground with each jerk of his body. I stripped the tape off his face, tore his tie open and ran my hands down the shirt buttons which opened on to a vest through which I could see the brutal scarring of a chest operation. I called an ambulance. I sawed through his cuffs with a Swiss army knife from his desk and lifted him on to the sofa, his legs kicking out wildly. I loosened off his trousers, ripped open his shirt cuffs and rubbed the side of his neck and checked his pulse, which was a fast and wriggly thread. In the middle of his forearm, amongst the white hairs, was a tattooed number: 173628.

I called the police, asking for Gbondogo, and then Martin Fall.

'Do nothing,' said Martin.

'I can't do nothing. I haven't done nothing. There's a dead haji, two dead bodyguards and Rademakers in very bad shape. I've called the police and an ambulance.'

'Fucking Christ! How'd they all get killed? Shit. Don't answer. What were the gunmen like?'

'Three Africans. One with an American accent. The others didn't talk. All fit, looked well-trained, they used explosives to get through the door and they all had their favourite weapons, I'd say.'

'Liberians. Rebels.'

'Christ knows, but they knew what they were doing and their timing was perfect.'

'So who knew what Ron was doing?'

'Apart from me?'

'Apart from us, Bruce – let's think positive.'

'He was talking to a guy in the bar a couple of nights ago. A man called Sean Malahide.'

'Who's he?'

'An agronomist, a speaker at the conference in the Novotel.'

'Talk to him.'

'Probably Borema, who's the fixer in Tortiya, Moses my driver, the police in Tortiya, Bouaké and Abidjan. Maybe the Alfas.'

'Who are they?'

'The fixers who met him at the airport. He gave them the brushoff.'

'And Rademakers?'

'Yes, but he looks like one of those quiet, discreet kind of people who've been in the diamond business for half a century and know that you don't go blabbing your client's diary around the place.'

'Find the Alfas and Borema. The police, Christ. Malahide. And see if anybody works for Rademakers.'

'Haven't you got anybody you can send down here?'

'Why'd you think you got the job?'

'But Martin, when things screw up most people wouldn't carry on using their last resort.'

'I have nobody else I can put down there for a week.'

'What about you?'

'Once they've made their demand I'll make a decision. Meantime, find those bastards and get them talking.'

'Get me the name and address of the Alfas' contact. The Swiss who put Ron on to the diamonds out here should know. Fax me at the Novotel.' I hung up. Rademakers was still breathing, but at the same rate his heart was spasming.

The police arrived in ten minutes, along with the ambulance. The two paramedics checked Rademakers's condition while another stepped through the aluminium frame and shook his head over the two bodyguards. The ashen colour of the haji and the size of the bloom on his chest didn't even merit a shake of the head.

15

I took Gbondogo through it step by step three times over, while another officer sat at Rademakers's desk scribbling it all down on a pad. They took me back to the Sûreté and typed out the statement, which I signed, while Gbondogo gave me more eye treatment than I needed. He asked me my programme for the next few days and released me just after 11.00 p.m. I took a taxi back to my car which was alone in the street. I walked across to the *gardien* who was sleeping by the chained entrance to the car park and asked him if he'd seen anybody and he told me he'd already been asked that and his answer was the same as the last time.

The girl in reception gave me a fax from Martin Fall and another from the hospital asking me to visit Rademakers in the morning. I asked about flights to Korhogo and she looked it up in her book and told me the *published* departure time was 10.00 a.m. She pointed across the lobby to Bagado who was sleeping across three seats, still wearing his blue mac. The dab of white on his hair seemed a bit stronger – Bagado ageing by the week. I booked him in and asked her if Malahide was still in the hotel and she went back to that book of hers and said he'd left after lunch that day.

Bagado rarely slept preprogrammed for danger and I had to bully him awake, so that he came out of it fighting.

'You,' he said, accusing me of something terrible.

'You've got a room. Where's your suitcase? Let's get a drink.'

'So you think I need a suitcase with my wardrobe,' he said, and pulled a carrier bag out of his pocket. 'Socks, pants, toothbrush. Have you got any toothpaste you can lend me?'

'I don't lend toothpaste.'

'I'll use my twig then,' he said, producing a flattened stick.

'I'll *give* you some of the gunk I use if you want.'

'No, no, the twig's fine.'

The bar was closed, due to lack of agronomists on expenses, so we went up to my room.

'I think I'll have a gin and tonic,' said Bagado.

'There's Blue Curaçao, crème de menthe, Tia bloody Maria, Bailey's Irish Cream. A real African mini-bar this one – alcoholic toffee. Don't lie down, Bagado,' I said, and he went rigid. 'I'm not carrying you out of here.'

'My God,' he said, 'I thought you'd seen a bider.'

'Bider or spider?'

'Don't even say the word.'

'I didn't know you were an arachnophobe.'

'Oh, yes,' he said. 'I can't even look at pictures.'

'I don't think I've ever seen one in Africa.'

'If you're scared of them they find you.'

He took the gin and tonic. I settled for the usual.

'Have you eaten?'

'No,' he said, tasting the gin and tonic and drawing a couple of fingers down the ridge running from his hairline to his nose.

'Nor have I. The guy who was supposed to buy me dinner got kidnapped.'

'It really needs lemon, doesn't it?' he said, holding out his glass, his fingers rubbing at the scar on his chin. I found three slices of cling-wrapped lemon on a saucer and offered him one. Bagado took it, shrugging his mac up, getting used to a bit of luxury, some service around here. He sipped the drink again.

'Now we're there,' he said. 'Were you supposed to be protecting him?'

'Accompanying him. To make sure he didn't get into trouble.'

'Like biders and me, Bruce. Trouble always finds you.'

'D'you think I'm in the wrong business?'

'No, no, the right business. No trouble, no job.'

'Well, I'm getting plenty of it now. What happened with you and Adabraka Video?'

'Abracadabra Video, Adabraka, Accra.'

'How many "A"s is that?'

'Eleven,' he said, taking a good pull of his gin and tonic. 'Chairman and Managing Director: Matthew Paul Thompson.'

'*Chairman*,' I said, 'and he didn't want to call himself Fat Mat.'

'I'm sorry?'

'His name's Fat Paul. Fat Matthew's a little weak and Fat Mat, well . . .'

'When I was a detective,' he said, looking wistful, 'I was paid respect. Now I'm a private dick, people feel they can express themselves.'

'Sorry, Bagado.'

'No, not just you. The public. It's becoming clear that I have no authority, no position. This American expression "gumshoe" disturbs me. It sounds very low. Beneath the shoe is a gumshoe. I've ceased to evolve as a life form.' He took out his notebook. 'Where were we? Yes. Abracadabra Video. The premises were firebombed on Saturday night, twenty-sixth October. Nobody hurt. Stock destroyed.'

'That's two nights before Fat Paul, George and Kwabena were found dead, their stomachs ripped open by a metal leopard claw. The night after a Liberian called James Wilson was found in the water near Treichville in the same state and the night before a Dane called Kurt Nielsen was found dead in a Toyota Land Cruiser outside Abidjan.'

'In the same state?'

'Not when I saw him. They came back later and opened him up.'

'Explain.'

I did.

'What was on the cassette?'

'Porn. Hard-core. Full penetration. Two black guys, a white girl and a white guy, but the white guy only had a walk-on part. Low-quality entertainment, but I kept a copy for you just in case.'

147

'In case?'

'You might recognize someone.'

'It sounds a little more serious than blackmail.'

'Maybe the girl's a Hollywood star now, Mafia backed, and they don't want some of her earlier, cheaper work coming on to the market.'

'I don't know any Hollywood stars. No television.'

'Just kidding, Bagado.'

'No. It's a good theory. There may be something in it.'

'Forget it.'

'You didn't look inside the tape, did you?'

'As a matter of fact, I did. Nothing. Just tape.'

'That was very good,' he said, holding out his glass. 'But maybe I need some food, I can feel myself getting emotional. You didn't happen to notice my self-pitying outburst earlier?'

'Yes. You didn't happen to notice that I used to be a businessman until I met you.'

'You are right. I have brought you down low.'

'I used to have a girlfriend who lived in the same country, too.'

'Ah. Yes. We are seeking to apportion blame here. Perhaps the way to the truth lies not in "strong dring" as my fellow churchmen might say.' He held up his glass.

I ordered a couple of hamburgers from room service and made more drinks. Bagado gave me his notes on Fat Paul.

'He's Liberian. Moved to Accra from Lagos four years ago. Still has a video business in Lagos. I haven't covered it yet. I need some money to do that and a motive.'

'A motive?'

'Why are we doing this?'

'I said I'd deliver Eugene Amos Gilbert to the police within ten days.'

'OK, and . . . ?'

'We're following through with the Fat Paul business because there might be leads to the Kurt Nielsen killing.'

'You were hired to give him the sack. The job seems to have been completed with the minimum of fuss. Need we meddle further?' he asked, smiling into his glass, nearly biting off the rim.

'Kurt Nielsen has a wife or partner, or whatever they're called these days.'

'Ah, you feel some responsibility to her?'

'I haven't met her yet, but yes, maybe.'

'What about the fellow who was kidnapped?'

'Ron Collins. My guess is it's Liberian rebels. There's a Liberian connection in this.'

'That's what I wanted to know.'

'Yes, the connections . . .'

'No, the motivation. You're getting the detective disease. "I have to know but"' – he held up a finger and sipped his drink – ' "I'm not letting anybody else spoil the fun." You have to tell your partner what's going on.'

'I'm not holding back on you.'

'Maybe not intentionally, maybe not yet, but later you might. I'm getting my retaliation in first.'

I told Bagado everything there was to know about the Fat Paul drop and the envelope addressed to Kantari, but not about the unopened package Fat Paul had given me which was still taped behind the car's glove compartment. I wanted to keep my options open on that, something Bagado wouldn't let me do. There I was, holding back already. I told him what I thought of Ron Collins, Sean Malahide, the Alfas, Borema and Rademakers. I filled him in on Martin Fall, Leif Andersen and the double death of Kurt Nielsen, and about his wife, Dotte Wamberg.

The hamburgers arrived with a plate of chips. They rattled down into Bagado's stomach like rubble down a plastic chute into an empty skip. It all took seconds. He lay back down on the bed.

'Fat Paul,' said Bagado weakly, a little faint from the food daze, 'as far as the people in Accra know, and they should know, because they're the police and they've been digging in people's dirt since Independence . . . They tell me that Fat Paul was clean. He imported pornography from, they're not sure where, they think America and Germany, but nothing nasty. All consenting-adults type of thing. His video cinema business did well, he had the occasional problem with people muscling in but nobody was ever hurt badly. He, listen to this . . . he imported turkey tails from UK and France.'

'Turkey tails?'

'Parsons' noses.'

'What do they do with turkey tails?'

'Deep fry them in palm oil and eat them with hot pepper sauce.'

'You've tried one?'

'Very fatty.'

'What else?'

'He bought fish from the Russians. They have factory ships off the coast. He bought lump sugar off someone else, but I can't read my writing.'

'What sort of diet is that for a business?'

'Quite.'

'Was he making money?'

'Yes, but not what you'd call cream.'

'Did you see where he lived?'

'He had a rented house in Cantonments. Up Liberation Road to the airport, off on the right somewhere. A smart place, not far from the' – he slowed – 'Liberian Embassy.'

'I see.'

'They tell me he normally drives a black 1950s Cadillac. There was an old Jaguar in the garage. The house itself was furnished how you'd expect a pornographer's to be furnished. Imitation tiger-skin seat covers, shag-pile carpet in white, matching blue glass dolphins on the sideboard, a statuette of Elvis, a blow-up of Marilyn Monroe on the wall. That one of her standing over the grating with the hot air going up her dress. A cardboard cut-out of Aretha Franklin and the only bizarre thing – a lot of body-building magazines.'

'Maybe he buys food supplements through them, keep his weight up,' I said. 'Had the place been searched?'

'Yes. A little more subtle than the firebomb. Professional. Didn't touch a thing.'

'How did you know it had been searched?'

'It looked tense and there wasn't a single video in the place. Think.'

'Somebody goes into the Abracadabra offices and finds a couple of thousand videos there. He can't search so he firebombs. Then he goes to the house and takes what he can find. Is there anything political with Fat Paul?'

'Don't know. I didn't know about the James Wilson angle then. I'll call Accra tomorrow.'

I opened up Martin Fall's fax message and read it out to Bagado.

'The Alfas live on the corner of Avenue eighteen and Rue twenty-three in Treichville. No phone. Contact was through an intermediary, a Lebanese called Elias Hadet of Hadet Kalmoni S.A., Imm. Alfa two thousand, Boulevard de la République, Abidjan.'

'We'll talk to M. Hadet tomorrow, and the Alfas too,' said Bagado.

'I'm going to have to go to Korhogo tomorrow, pick up Dotte Wamberg and bring her back here to identify the body. You've got Accra and Lagos to call. We can fit the Alfas in on the way to the airport. Can you track down Malahide? There should be some leftovers from the conference who can help you. He wasn't a blender, Malahide. He was a clasher. You're bound to find someone who hated his guts. Rademakers, damn, there's Rademakers too. Maybe we do Treichville first thing. The hospital afterwards. It could be tight for a ten o'clock flight.'

'You won't take off before midday.'

'Sleep?'

'I'm awake now,' he said, and walked to the door. He fished in his pocket and came up with a letter. 'Don't hold back on me, Bruce. I know you are, I know you've got something. Tell me about it . . . soon.' He threw me the letter and left.

The letter landed on the empty bed, German stamp, Berlin postmark, Heike. I didn't want all that now, to read it and let it burn a hole in the bits of sleep I was still getting. I stripped and cleaned up and lay on the bed with a glass, the bottom painted amber, what the French call *un fond*.

White square on the dark counterpane. I turned the light out. It was still there, maybe answers inside it to questions I didn't even know about, maybe just more questions, no answers, maybe the kiss-off, maybe some well-worn clichés and *then* the kiss-off. I turned the light on. The letter was written a week after she'd flown back and it was short, thank Christ, no streams of heart-pouring consciousness.

Berlin, 15th October
Dear Bruce,
I'm working at my mother's café. A double shift which uses up the days, six in the morning to midnight with a break 3.00 to 6.00 in the afternoon and I walk all over Berlin. West to East, East to West. I still can't believe we can do that now. I keep moving. If I had sharper teeth and a predatory nature I'd say I was a shark, just moving to stay alive and keep the water running through my gills. I don't feel like a shark. I only say it because I feel isolated and lonely here in Berlin, where it can rain for a week without stopping. Damn. I wasn't going to use that word 'feel', nor 'emotion', nor 'relationship' but there you are — feelings everywhere.

I miss Africa. Everything about it. The people — you know how Africans wrap you up in their lives. They keep their distance here. Who needs people when you've got the rain to keep you company all day? I'm dying to sweat, that free-flow sweat, and drink an ice-cold Eku and ask Moses to buy kebabs. I even miss diarrhoea — they're so constipated here. But . . . I'm staying. Wolfgang is over here and I'm seeing him (not in that way). He wants me to work on a project in Tanzania. He's being (and I know this will annoy you) very supportive. It helps to see an old Africa hand.

The only thing I can't resolve and haven't, the only thing that tugs away at my insides every day that I can't get rid of however much I walk or work — is you. Feeling important now? My mother said you'd called. I was there and I know you knew I was there, too. I can't speak to you on the phone. There are things that, even when they digitalize them, don't fit down phone lines. My mother says it's sex, but that's just because she can't keep her hands off my father (and vice versa). They still go at it three times a week after thirty-five years of marriage. When I left we seemed to be on the brink of something

152

and it's that, I think, which cuts me. I'll never know
what we would have made of it.
    Love, H.

There must be a detective in all of us. We all *have* to know
something – lovers, friends, family. Bagado had seen it. I saw
it in myself. 'What we would have made of it' left a permanent hunger. Other women, like Anne, Martin Fall's wife,
had left me full, up to the neck, couldn't cram anything more
down even with the back of a spoon. Heike left me starving.

There was an opening for me in Heike's letter, maybe you
had to be on the receiving end to see it. There was something
about that 'But . . . I'm staying' which was wavering and
if she couldn't speak on the phone about the unanswered
questions then it had to be in person. A letter from me and
she could either melt into the capital of the new unified
Germany or be sitting at a table opposite me in her big white
dress, with a cold beer and a cigarette in its holder giving the
raggedy wolf a last chance.

Abidjan, 30th October
Dear Heike,
I've been drinking with Bagado, he brought me your
letter this evening. The nights have been dark recently, I
know because I don't sleep in them any more and I spend
them thinking about you. The thinking moves in tighter
and tighter circles so that I feel drilled through in the
mornings. You're right, we were on the brink of
something – it just happened that on the brink there was
a very complicated situation that was my fault and you
should never have been involved in it. It won't happen
again. You love Africa. I want to make it even more worth
your while coming here, but if I can't you shouldn't
abandon both loves because the one can't live up to the
other. Let me try. I should be back in Benin in a week's
time. I'll call, if you don't want to speak leave your flight
number with your mother.
    Love, B.

I addressed the envelope but didn't stick it down. I licked up the *fond* of whisky, turned out the light and slept like a dog that's been out on the hills all day.

16

Thursday 31st October

At 7.00 a.m. Bagado joined me for breakfast in a grey dining room, made greyer by the low cloud over the iron lagoon outside. He sat hunched in his mac, and mumbled through his croissant, looking about a quarter of the size he had last night.

'You're shrinking,' I said.

'I'm getting old.'

'How old?' He looked up. 'You never said.'

'I'll be fifty-four on Christmas day if you want to make a note of it.'

'You're looking good.'

'It's not how you look, it's how you feel and I feel ninety-seven until midday.'

Moses appeared at the entrance to the restaurant. I beckoned him over. Bagado stood. They shook hands.

'My brother,' said Moses.

'He flatters me,' said Bagado, slapping him on the shoulder and sinking back into the chair.

'This food mekking you body weak,' said Moses. 'Mebbe you need African food. Fufu* mek you strong.'

'All fufu does is lower your centre of gravity,' I said.

'Better than Obroni† food,' he said, pointing at the croissant. 'These things all air. They good for nothing 'cept mekking you wind strong.'

We left the Novotel, driving out of the high-rise Plateau

---

* Yam and manioc mash
† Whiteman

155

district across the lagoon on a still, close morning and into the low-level, grid-designed Treichville quarter. The African Abidjan was already humming at that time in the morning, the people converging on the huge marketplace. We found the corner of 18 and 23 and Moses stayed with the car while Bagado and I side-stepped street kids with flat palms and *cadeau-cadeau* on their lips.

The Alfas' room was above a shop selling motor parts. We went through a door at the side of the shop and climbed the stairs up to the first floor. We went into a small dark room with two beds with an Alfa on each. Even in the half light of the room we could see that they'd each taken a severe beating. The pillows were smeared with blood, their faces swollen and split. They told us about the money they owed M. Hadet and how unimpressed he had been with the lack of the Ron Collins commission. They'd had a visit yesterday afternoon. The discussion had been short, the aftermath violent. They had nothing for us and we left them to count their teeth.

We arrived at the Polyclinique at 8.30 a.m. Bagado waited in the car while a crisp nurse took me up to Rademakers's private room. She said he was stable but not to stay too long.

He lay in bed, unconnected to tubes and electrodes. A body barely making a lump in the bed. His face was ashen. His eyes were open but without his glasses they had a far-off look, as if he was enjoying a choir of celestial angels. I gave him his glasses and held up a hand so he didn't have to speak.

'If you want me to find Ron I'm already looking,' I said. 'We think he's been taken by Liberian rebels but we haven't heard yet. Are you strong enough to answer a few questions?'

'It wasn't a local job,' he said, answering my first two.

'How do you know?'

'I keep up my payments,' he said.

'They had information to do the job. They knew abut the office, the security system and the steel door. They knew a deal was going to be done. Does anybody work for you?'

'No.'

'I was just wondering about the other desk in your office.'

'Nobody works for me.'

'Have you had any unusual visitors in the last month?'

'Unusual?'

'Not in the normal line of business.'

'I don't do so much now, you know,' he said, trying to jog his memory. 'I do some diamonds, some currency. Only for friends. Ten years ago it was different. Now . . . I'm an old man.'

'So you know everybody who comes into that office?'

'Yes. But I'm thinking. There was somebody different at the end of last week. A consultant. He came to see me for information on the Ivory Coast diamond business. He was writing a report for a US conglomerate who wanted to invest in a West African diamond mine. Trzinski. That was his name. He worked for himself. He had an assistant called Foley. Americans.'

'Do you have a card . . . know where they were staying?'

'They were in the Hilton. Their card is in the office. Washington DC address.'

'Is there anybody in Abidjan who doesn't like you or wants your business?'

'I told you, I'm an old man, I don't do anything. If you want someone with enemies, Ron is your man. Not well-liked. Very arrogant. Too much money. Samuel, his father, spoils him. All his enemies are up there, though – London, Antwerp, Geneva, New York. This is his first time down here. They would have had to be very organized, and anyway . . . they dislike him, but not *so* much.'

'You said Geneva. What about the Swiss who sold Ron the first parcel?'

'They want to do business with Collins and Driberg again, my friend.'

'What about M. Hadet? He was the contact for a couple of fixers . . .'

'Yes, I know Hadet. He's not in the business. He knows nothing about diamonds. He hasn't been to my office. Those two fixers probably owe him money. He gives them something to do to get his money back. M. Hadet is nothing, a small man of no consequence, not someone to waste your time on.'

He offered me money; I told him not to worry about any money just yet, that I was going to Korhogo and if he had any ideas to leave messages in the Novotel or speak to Bagado. He stopped me at the door.

'This is very important for me. Samuel and I go back a long way,' he said, tapping the number tattoo on his forearm. 'Ron has three older sisters but he is the only boy. You understand.'

I got back in the car and told Bagado that he was going to have to find out for himself who worked for Rademakers because the man didn't want to tell me.

'How do you know he has someone?'

'The other desk and the way he stonewalled me in there,' I said. 'Ask the *gardien* at the car park. Try treading on Hadet's feet too, see if he's got any corns. There's a card in Rademakers's office belonging to a Mr Trzinski, a consultant who operates out of Washington DC. Check it out, see if it's straight.'

I took Martin Fall's transfer out of Barclays Bank and split it down the middle with Bagado. We reached the airport by 10.30 a.m. with the flight not due to take off for another hour. I called Leif Andersen and told him my life's problems and he said that he'd already instructed the local Korhogo police to find Dotte Wamberg, who was out in the bush collecting sheanut. I called the Hilton, too, just in case Trzinski was still there. He wasn't, but his assistant, Deyton Foley, played a cagey game on his behalf until I told him my business. Trzinski was up in the north, looking at Tortiya and staying at Le Mont Korhogo Hotel in Korhogo. He said he'd make sure he knew I was coming. I looked over Heike's letter again and thought it read like hell in the light – those things always do. I asked a Dutch lobster buyer who was going back to Amsterdam to post it and bought an *Ivoire Soir* to read on the plane.

By 2.45 p.m. I was at the reception desk of Le Mont Korhogo Hotel. They knew about me and said Trzinski wasn't going to be there until 4.00 p.m. I went across to the PTT* and found Kantari's name and address in the phone book. The taxi driver didn't know where it was. We cruised around until we found a young boy holding the hand of a pained red-haired albino who showed us Kantari's cul-de-sac.

A jumpy *gardien*, spaced on cola nuts, let me in and pointed me across a large earthen courtyard in which there was a Mercedes, a Peugeot and a three-ton Hanomag truck parked under a corrugated-iron awning.

'*Premier étage, la porte à gauche.*'

High walls ran along two sides of the courtyard and met a long French colonial period house, whose windows were all shuttered against the strong sun. I went through the open door in the middle of the house into a hallway with a naked bulb on a flex and doors to the left and right.

Another light bulb hung out on wires from a rough hole in the wall's plasterwork, halfway up the stairs. On the landing, railed off by some bannisters which ran to the front of the house, were gilt-framed pictures, dusty silk screens, some telescopic stands and rolls of wire extensions, with pieces of red, blue and yellow gel scattered about.

I knocked on the door on the left and it opened a crack on some black hair, a brown almond eye, coffee skin. The crack closed. I tried the door – locked. I tapped again.

'*Oui*,' said a voice from behind the door.

'*Je veux voir Kantari,*' I said.

'Whass your name?' he asked, coming back in English with American threaded in.

'My French that bad, eh?'

'Yeah. Name?'

'Bruce Medway.'

'Whass it about?'

'I'll tell that to Kantari.'

'Tell me. I'll give him the message.'

'It's personal.'

'Lonely Hearts?'

'Fat Paul.'

* Postes, Télécommunications et Télédiffusion

159

'What you got?'

I didn't answer, let the curiosity do the work. The door opened and a Polynesian boy stripped to the waist in shiny shorts leaned against the door and looked at me with nothing in his face.

'You got something?'

'Just let me see Kantari.'

'What for?'

'Fat Paul is dead.'

'So?' he asked, getting over the big tragedy.

'You're annoying me,' I said and knocked past him into the room. He locked the door, turned and blinked for the first time.

The room had a bare-board, unpolished floor with a few tea chests upside down pretending to be tables. There was a fiery dragon desk with red leather inlay. A portable TV and VCR were positioned on a corner facing away at a bed with a mosquito net tied in a knot above it. A blue-bladed fan with a chrome grill and lights dancing up and down its stand moved its head from side to side over the empty bed.

The Polynesian kid walked like a ballet dancer, his back straight and each foot placed with precision and flex. He knocked on the next door and opened it without waiting.

'Patrice?' said a voice which liked saying the name.

'It's him,' he replied, chilly.

I nudged past him into the fridge-cold, artificially lit room where two men were sitting. The one lounging behind the replica of the desk in the other room had very black brilliantined hair which had been combed straight back in rails over his pate. The two black shiny lines he had for eyebrows made him look sad and the spare set he had stuck to his top lip were trying to pass themselves off as a pencil moustache. His skin was pale and puffy and his eyes black with long lashes which added to his foppy sadness. He looked at me with a little bit of his tongue poking out, like a cat that's forgotten to pull it back in.

'I'm Bruce Medway.'

'Dear boy,' he said, without getting up. 'Kantari.' He held out his hand as if I should kiss it. I shook it. It was small and soft and very smooth, as if it had done nothing but stroke alabaster all its life. He flicked his wrist to introduce his companion.

'Corporal Clegg,' said the other man, who sat in a high-backed armchair – covered in red velour – with matronly legs.

'Corporal?'

'Foreign Legion,' he said, putting his left ankle on to his right knee and showing off a bare horny foot that had done some marching and kicking in its time. He was wearing the bottom half of a judo suit and a black T-shirt stretched tight over bench-pressed shoulders. The sleeves were rolled back over globe biceps with knots of veins popping out. The tattoo on his forearm told the world 'I hate Mother'. He'd used the same charm to get his cheekbone broken, his jaw dislocated, and his nose bust. He had thick, loafy hair which looked like one of those cheap wigs performers use to disguise themselves in pornographic movies.

The room was decorated bordello style – lots of red velvet, gold tassles, brocade cushions, a chaise longue, table lamps of negro statuettes, a Chinese screen with three old boys in full gear which blocked off a washbasin. There was a chessboard on the table with onyx pieces halfway through a game. The pieces were all figures in graphic sexual embrace.

'I didn't know bishops could do that,' I said.

'Amusing, don't you think?' said Kantari. 'Look at the Queen.'

'Some other time,' I said, picking up a light-green bowl, which made Kantari stiffen. I put it down.

'Not the ashtray?'

'We don't smoke.'

'I gave up, too.'

'Delighted. Please sit.'

I sat on the taut sofa and found myself at inkwell height to the angry desk. A trick that has always annoyed me.

'You have something for me?'

'I do.'

'Thank you,' he said, flicking the wrist of his duchess's hand.

161

'Who's he?' I asked, nodding at Clegg.

'Security,' said Clegg.

'We're secure. He can go.'

'Who says?'

'I says.'

'Gentlemen,' said Kantari.

'This is private business. I don't need security in on the meeting.'

'Very well.' He flicked his wrist from Clegg to the door. Clegg left, giving me that hard faraway look that legionnaires get from looking over sand dunes too long.

It was a negotiating technique I'd learned from a debt collector on Long Island: never accept anybody else's terms for a meeting and, when you've got your own way, do your best to show that you're really quite mature after all. It was risky when there was someone as congenial as Clegg around, always leaving his brain in his gym locker, but Kantari was straight on to it. He was a player. He sat there in his white starched shirt with black-and-gold silk bow tie, hands in prayer, legs in grey slacks tidily crossed, bare white ankles, black velvet slippers with gold crests, his pink tongue peeping out, his dyed black, failed hair licked into position – a fop, but a player.

He reached over to a bottle of water which sat on a silver tray alongside two glasses.

'Drink?'

'I'd prefer something with more bite.'

'Whisky?'

'If you have it?' I saw him hesitate.

'I only have single malt.'

'I'll force it down.'

'I want to know I'm not wasting it.'

'Water it is, then.'

'You're going to disappoint me?'

'For the time being, I probably am.'

He stood, making little difference to his height, and poured an English barman's measure of Laphroaig from the gold trolley at his side.

'Just to show I can be grown up, too.' He handed me the glass.

'I need some help to clarify a few things.'

'Money,' sighed Kantari.

'Not yet.'

'I like a change. Africa can be so predictable.'

'I work for a Syrian from Accra called B.B. He buys and ships sheanut out of Korhogo. He *used* to employ a Dane called Kurt Nielsen.'

'If you're looking for contacts, I know nothing about sheanut.'

'But Kurt Nielsen did and he was found in your Toyota Land Cruiser down by the Ebrié lagoon on Monday, twenty-eighth October. Dead. I'm taking his wife down to Abidjan to identify him.'

'They said there was a reason they couldn't release it.'

'Kurt Nielsen was in that car waiting to pick up a package for the attention of M. Kantari, Korhogo. He'd been secured to the head rest with a piece of wire and his guts torn out. Not nice on the upholstery.'

'What are you suggesting . . . ?'

'You're not stupid, M. Kantari.'

'I haven't been out of Korhogo for two weeks.'

'Not personally.'

'How, pray?'

'Eugene Amos Gilbert?'

'Is that one man or three?'

'He's a Liberian hit man who likes to call himself "Red".'

'A Liberian?' He thought about it. 'How do you know all this, dear boy?'

'I had Fat Paul's package. I saw the dead man. I saw what "Red" did to Fat Paul the following day and I had dealings with "Red" myself.'

'You think that I sent "Red" to kill Mr Nielsen and pick up the package?'

'And kill me.'

'Why did I report my Land Cruiser stolen?'

'Nielsen wasn't back by morning. Covered yourself.'

'Do you have the package?'

'Not on me.'

'Have you seen the film?'

'*A* film.'

'One thing. This "Red" fellow is a Liberian. Black, I presume?'

'Yes.'

'My agreement with Fat Paul was that the exchange should be between two whites. Why would I send "Red" Gilbert when I have Corporal Clegg who could have killed Nielsen, and, being white, not troubled your suspicious mind when you handed over the package?'

'He might start thinking with all those muscles instead of just doing,' I said. 'Why should Fat Paul send you a pornographic video?'

'I can't think,' he said, his face as dead as a poker player's with a huge hand.

I sipped the Laphroaig and its peaty bite gave me a stab of nostalgia and a longing not to be in front of this dyed queen and his ugly hangers-on.

'You're in the film business as well,' I said.

'As well?'

'As well as Abracadabra Video.'

'For my own amusement,' he said. 'I did a lot, professionally, when I lived in Beirut, before the troubles.'

'How do you make a living now?'

'I trade, like everybody else in Africa.'

'What in?'

'It's true, I've had to learn some new things.'

'Not an answer.'

'Because I don't have to. It's my business.'

'Pornography?'

'It amuses me.'

'I had you down as a little-boy merchant . . .'

'You're being distasteful now.'

'Four people have been killed, five if you include James Wilson. Abracadabra's offices have been firebombed and Fat Paul's house searched. If you didn't have Nielsen done then whoever did is serious. More serious than Clegg could ever be. They know about you. They know about me. They know about the film.'

'I thought you said it was pornography.'

'Not that one. There's another one in Abidjan.'

'Ah-ha.'

'That's the film Fat Paul gave me, saying he'd get back to me with the instructions. You should have seen what they did to him. Snipped off his fingers. Scooped out his genitals . . .'

'What do you propose to do with this film?'

'Sell it.'

'You've said something intelligent at last.'

'But to who? That I don't know.'

'You appear to have only one buyer. All you know about your other bidders is what they'll do to you if they catch up. I suggest you sell and get out before the value of your stock drops further.'

My second sip of the Laphroaig finished it. I stood and put the empty glass on the table.

'If you knew something was going on, as Fat Paul did, then why didn't you use Clegg? He looks as if he could have chewed up "Red" and flossed him out.'

Kantari opened his hands, revealing three feet of nothingness.

'Nielsen was expendable?' I asked. Kantari shrugged. 'Why did Nielsen do it for you?'

'The same reason anybody does anything for somebody else.'

'How did they know where he was going to be? How did they know about the drop?' Silence. 'They followed him from here?' I asked. 'They must be watching you.'

'And you.'

'Possibly.'

'Divest yourself of the problem, Mr Medway.'

'What about James Wilson?'

'Who's he?'

'Come on, M. Kantari, play the game.'

'You're holding cards. I'm holding cards.'

'James Wilson was an aide to the late Liberian president.

165

He was found strangled and torn open in the lagoon in Treichville last week. I think he was killed because he had a tape or something that fits inside a tape and Fat Paul knew you'd be in the market for it. When they caught up with James Wilson he'd already sold out, but they got it out of him about Fat Paul. They torched his office, searched his house, but they couldn't find *him*. So what do they do? The trail's gone cold. Somebody, somewhere, tells them about the drop and where one half of it is coming from. How did they know to follow Kurt Nielsen from here? Why did you and Fat Paul set up a dummy run, and why don't they take you out of the game?'

'I've never had what they want, Mr Medway. You have. It strikes me that you should be a very worried man. The dummy run occurred precisely because I've developed the level of concern that you haven't and was proved correct. How they knew about the dummy run, or how they knew to follow Nielsen from here is a mystery which I doubt you will survive long enough to solve.'

'You seem pretty broken up about Nielsen. Did you tell him he was headed for a meat grinder?'

'If you send someone to make an exchange and offer them five hundred thousand CFA to do it they know what they're getting themselves into.'

'Did you pay upfront?'

'Half.'

'Why Nielsen?'

'The right man at the right time.'

'He needed the cash?'

'Amongst other things.'

'What about his wife?'

'I'm not sure that husband and wife would have clearly defined the status of their relationship at the time. Kurt had a liking for African girls.'

'Perhaps we should talk about money.'

'Yes. It's a pity you didn't bring the goods with you. As time goes on, situations change, circumstances materialize . . . prices go down.'

'And up. What's the offer?'

'Let me see. Five hundred thousand was the delivery charge, I believe.'

'That was the messenger's fee, and anyway, it was a million.'

'Yes, well, you'd never have seen a million from Fat Paul. You met Kwabena? He always handled the rendering of accounts and as you probably realized, his gift was not that of an accountant.'

'Kwabena's dead and if you're threatening me with Clegg, don't. And remember, I'm not the messenger any more, I'm the principal.'

'A principal who doesn't know what he's selling.'

'Not yet.'

'When you're ready, come and see me.'

'I will. Thanks for the whisky. It was a delight.'

17

Trzinski stood out in the Le Mont Korhogo Hotel bar as the only possible American in the joint. His body was as deep as it was wide and the arms coming out of his cream short-sleeve shirt had, at the very least, wrestled bullocks to the ground. His head was hard enough to be loaded into a how-itzer and was covered in a brown fuzz of crew-cut hair which he liked stroking. His nose had taken a thump or two, and had been stupid enough to come back for more, and he had light blue-grey eyes made for looking out over large expanses of sheet ice or tundra. He folded the *Ivoire Soir* he'd been reading and gave me a professional smile with some teeth he hadn't been born with.

'Al Trzinski,' he said, shaking my hand. 'Pleased to meet you.'

I was slow with the handshake and paid for it, so that I was flexing my fingers for the rest of the meeting. I sat and fascinated myself with the width of his forehead and the way his eyebrows bossed out on ridges.

'You're English?' he asked. 'Where you from?'

'London. You?'

'Omaha, Nebraska. That's beef country, if you didn't know it, Bruce. Beef and the birthplace of Marlon Brando. I think that covers it.'

At that moment I didn't see Al Trzinski as a business con-sultant. I saw him clearly, wearing a white coat in a cold store full of skinned carcasses hanging off hooks – the man as big as a beef cow himself.

We small-talked about Africa until the waiter came to the

table and Trzinski unnerved me by ordering cold milk. I had a beer.

'Foley says you want to talk to me about diamonds,' he said.

'I'd like to talk about your particular interest in diamonds in the Ivory Coast and how you came to know about Mr Rademakers.'

'Why's that?' he asked in such a sweet-natured way I was tempted to kick him to the floor. Instead I gave him an undramatic account of Ron Collins's kidnap. He was very interested. He leaned forward, occupying most of the table and a great deal of light.

'That's a terrible thing, Bruce. It surely is,' he said. 'Such lawlessness. It'll have to be in my report, you understand.'

'Who's that report going to?' I asked, and he ignored it.

'One thing I'm not clear about,' he said, rubbing his head, trying to buff some clarity in there, 'is where you fit in. What is your role, exactly? You and Mr Collins were in business together?'

'No, I'm not in the diamond business. I'm in sheanut.'

'And what, may I ask, is that?'

'It's a nut that grows wild at this latitude. The locals pick it and dry it, we ship it and factories crush it and put it in chocolate.'

'That's very interesting,' he said, 'but I'm still confused.'

I clarified it for him and he asked who I was working for. I asked him who he was sending his report to. We smiled at each other for some time.

'What about Rademakers?' I asked.

'The Chamber of Commerce in Antwerp gave me his name, Bruce.'

'You went to see him when? Last Thursday the twenty-fourth?'

'That's right, Bruce. I can understand your concern. You're doing the right thing. Check me and Foley out. You gotta do it.' He sat back. 'Lemme see. Mr Collins was kidnapped Wednesday. I was here. Foley was at the Abidjan Hilton. But that doesn't prove a thing, does it?'

He sipped some milk, smiled and left me looking for another question, which I didn't have.

'You read this?' he asked, pointing at the *Ivoire Soir*.

'On the plane.'

He leafed through the paper and stopped at a piece about the ceasefire Samson Talbot had just rejected because no Libyan troops were allowed on the peace-keeping force.

'You think Mr Collins was taken by the rebels. Take a look at that,' he said. 'Do those guys think we're dumb or what? Nobody's gonna let a buncha towelheads in there. The guns're pouring out of Trip-O-lee faster than he can use 'em and he thinks the international community are gonna put them on the peace-keeping force? Give us a break.'

'What's your point?'

'If I was Samson Talbot I wouldn't wanna ceasefire, that's for sure, so I'd come up with cockamamie suggestions like Gaddafis on the peace-keeping force while I built up a stock of arms. But I'd need some money to do that. Right? You see where I'm coming from. You see how Mr Collins is fitting into the scenario. What I don't like is the way it's done, Bruce. No respect. No respect for the US of A. It gets me mad.'

'I thought Samson Talbot had a lot of Americo-Liberian support? They send him money, don't they?'

'The Liberian president's been killed,' he said. 'That was the main thing the A-Ls wanted, the President outa the game. They got it. Their money's dried up. The problem *now* is that Jeremiah Finn took the President out, not Samson Talbot. Finn's in Monrovia, Talbot's not. Finn's getting financial support, Talbot's out there in the marketplace. Geddit?'

'Have you got a personal interest in this war?' I asked, and Trzinski gave me the full force of his long-distance eyes. 'You seem to know what's going on.'

'When I do a report for a client who's going to put maybe fifty million bucks of investment into a country, I check out *all* the angles and that means ugly political situations in neighbouring countries.'

'Where've you been so far?' I asked, and something like amusement passed behind Trzinski's eyes.

'In Ghana we went to the Birin basin and Akwatia, here I'm due to go down to Tortiya, then I go on to Sierra to Panguma and Yengema but I don't hold out much hope – Talbot's gonna be across that western border by the end of the year.'

'Have you got any military experience, Al?' I asked, the look of the man and the way he talked still bothering me.

'As a matter of fact, I have,' he said. 'You ever been in a war yourself, Bruce?'

'Nothing more than street violence.'

'I was in Nam,' he said.

'How did that leave things with you?'

'Things?'

'I imagine you have a different perspective on life after you've been through a war like that.'

'Yea-a-h,' he said slowly and folded his arms. He stared at his milk. I looked over the *Ivoire Soir* and sipped my beer.

'Nam,' said Trzinski, surprising me after a long ruminative silence, the milk going through his nine stomachs. 'Nam left me with the belief that there is no greater evil on this earth than war. That everything should be done to prevent it. And if you can't prevent it, everything should be done to stop it.'

'Laudable thinking, Al; you'll go down in history.'

'All that time I was in Nam, I never got hit. Not even a graze. I saw men lose their legs, arms, have their heads blown off, their guts torn out but *I* never got more'n a scratch from a thorn bush. And, you know, I came back to the States and I sat there right in the middle of the US. That's where Omaha, Nebraska is, if you didn't know it, Bruce. And I had nothing inside of me. It was like everything had been blown out . . . and then,' he said, and this was the first time I realized what was coming. I should have seen this herd of beef cattle coming from a lot further off, well before it was on top of me. 'And then, I found Him.'

'Who?' I asked, thinking Trzinski might have wrong-footed me after all.

'The Lord, Bruce. I found the Lord.'

'And He told you to get into business consultancy.'

'I'm being serious,' he said, the irony stripped out from behind his eyes.

'Al, this is very personal . . .'

'Yeah, Bruce, it is, but I don't mind telling you about it.'

'No, I mean it's personal to me. I don't want to hear about your experiences with the Lord. It doesn't mean I don't believe. It means I don't want to talk about it.' Hard and firm, it's something I've learned.

'OK. I respect that,' he said, and sucked on his milk while I wrestled with the three facets of his personality he'd thrown at me in the last half hour.

'You went to Tortiya with Mr Collins?' he asked.

'That's where he bought the diamonds that were taken with him in the kidnap. We had some trouble. Spent a night in jail there.'

'That kinda place,' said Trzinski, nodding.

'Some advice for you, Al – even if you're just looking, go and see the police first and be nice to them.'

'Thanks for that, Bruce,' he said, his manner changing, getting more urbane. 'You know anybody there who could help me, like I said, just to look around?'

I gave him Borema's name, he slotted it into his memory and glanced at his watch. I stood and he asked where he could contact me if anything valuable should come to mind. I gave him the compound number and told him where it was.

'One thing, Al,' I said, 'you've been here a long time and not gone down to Tortiya . . .'

'There're people who handle diamonds here. They've been filling me in on the scene.'

'And they don't have a contact name for you down in Tortiya?'

'Not the same as yours.'

'Who are they, if you don't mind me asking?'

'A French guy called François Marin, and a Lebanese called Kantari.'

'It's always useful to know names in Africa, Al.'

'It surely is, Bruce. It surely is.'

172

18

The taxi dropped me off at the compound around 5.00 p.m. Kofi, one of B.B.'s Ghanaian boys, was sleeping by the gate but he woke up to show me around. He explained that 'sistah Dotte' was out collecting sheanut but she'd be coming back because the police had been looking for her since yesterday.

The compound was massive, maybe sixty or seventy yards long, with corrugated-iron awnings on three sides and some unpainted grey and brown accommodation with red dirt spattered up the walls on the fourth side. In the middle were two huge black iron vats which looked as if they'd been used for boiling tar but were now filled with water to boil sheanut. They were surrounded by scaffolding and a walkway of planks. In between the vats was a primitive crane for lifting the cages of sheanut into the water.

Next to the vats was a pile of rusted engine parts and three glassless truck cabs which had been torn from their chassis. Goats nosed about in the interiors, stripping off the plastic door panelling. In front of all the awnings were the old truck chassis with boards on their backs and sheanut drying in the sun.

We walked up on to the concrete verandah of the accommodation block. Kofi showed me the bathroom, which was outside, and took me into a hot, oppressive room with a bed in it where I could wait for Dotte. Kofi was uneasy in the house and left as soon as he could. I checked the other rooms which were all locked, except the one next to mine which was strangely cool without air conditioning or fan, just with the windows curtained off.

It had an identical bed, a chest supported by three hardbacks under one corner and a doorless wardrobe with some musty male clothing in it. I flicked through the clothes in the chest and found some stuff that you'd expect to see from emptied pockets. Kurt Nielsen's cholera vaccination was in there, some gutted biros, an old packet of Marlboro with two left. I opened up a book of matches from Le Mont Korhogo Hotel which had no telephone numbers inside but some doodling from a brain floating on a toke of weed, of which there was a little baggy and some super-long Rizlas.

I looked over the room, under the chest, the wardrobe and the bed – plenty of dust, not much else. I lifted the mattress and saw it immediately, up at the head end – a juju. It was made out of reddish-blond hair and some sort of bone and feathers tied round with twine. I dropped the mattress back down on it.

I lay down on the bed in my room. Sleep came as quickly as waking up, an hour or more later, in a cold sweat. It was dark outside with light from the compound coming into the room. A tight band of headache was wrapping itself around my head and someone was watching me. A young white girl, with long blonde hair, was standing by the door in squares of light thrown up against the wall from the window. She wore a white vest which covered her high, budding breasts and stopped just below her ribcage where there was a lean, bare torso down to the top of her white cotton shorts. Her legs were crossed at the ankle. She fiddled with a strand of hair, using both hands, and looked at me as if I might be danger-ous. I shook my head which released a ball bearing into the bagatelle of my brain and it took forever to drop down the hole.

'Hello,' I said. 'What's your name?'

'Katrina,' she said, and put the strand of hair in her mouth, freeing up her hands which she had no place for on her body. 'What's yours?'

'Bruce.'

She disappeared, leaving me blinking and holding on to the cool metal of the bedstead and running a parroty tongue around the birdcage of my mouth. It was 6.30 p.m.

'That's a funny name,' she said, reappearing at the door, a biscuit in both hands, which she nibbled.

'Not as funny as Brian.'

'Brian?' She tasted it. 'That's a bear's name, isn't it?'

'Could be.'

'Do you like biscuits?'

'Sometimes.'

'You can have one of mine.'

'Thanks, but not now,' I said. 'I haven't got the mouth for it.'

'That's a funny thing to say.'

'You're not wearing my mouth.'

'You're funny,' she said, putting a hand up to her mouth and feeling it.

I'd blinked the crap out of my eyes by now and could see that Katrina was on the verge of being pretty. The features she was going to take into womanhood were all there, but not settled in her face. They were too big, making her gawky. She was tall with a straight body which had started to curve, the hips coming out, the thighs getting some shape. She walked over and sat on the edge of the bed, pushed her bottom back and leaned against my crooked knee. She nibbled the biscuit she was holding with fingers whose nails were down to the quick.

'Is Dotte here?' I asked.

'Mummy's talking to the boys in the yard,' she said. 'She can't find Kofi.'

'He was here an –'

'Don't you like me?'

'' Course I like you.'

'How do you know?'

'I can tell.'

'How?'

'You talk quietly when I'm waking up.'

'I'm sorry I woke you up.'

'How do you know you woke me?'

'I looked at you and said to myself, "Wake up, wake up," and you did. Magic. Do you know how old I am?'

'No.'

'Guess.'

'Fourteen.'

'That's not fair. You knew.'

'No, I didn't.'

'Anyway, I'm not fourteen.'

'There you go then.'

'I'm thirteen and three-quarters.'

She sounded young for her age, but what do I know? Maybe it was a miracle she was talking at all and not plugged into a walkman listening to some hair-sprayed youth bounce around in their jockeys, pretending to play music. I wondered if she was Kurt's daughter, but then couldn't imagine B.B. not telling me about it. Then again, if he'd told me that I was throwing a family out into the street, I wouldn't have taken the job.

'What are you thinking about?'

'Nothing. I've just woken up.'

'But don't you think about things all the time?'

'I try not to.'

There was the sound of a footfall on the verandah and Katrina started and shot off the bed and out of the room. I didn't move and listened to voices outside talking too quickly and quietly to be heard. Then footsteps in the corridor and the door opened wide and standing in the squares of light was a woman. As soon as I saw her I knew I was in trouble.

'You're Bruce Medway,' she said. 'B.B. mentioned you.'

'What did he say?'

'He said you'd be coming. We reckoned you were going to sack Kurt.'

'You were right.'

'Somebody's done your job for you. The police've just told me he's dead.'

'I know,' I said, and she looked at me, her hand creeping up the doorjamb.

'Let's have a drink,' she said. 'You look the sort who does that.'

I liked her even better.

Dotte Wamberg didn't have the looks to slay millions at the box office; if she had she wouldn't have been out here in the middle of Africa shovelling sheanut, she'd be working at a supermarket check-out waiting to be discovered. She had the kind of face that drew a man in, not just me, lots of men. She promised something different, something a long way from mortgages, summer sales, car washes and underwear in packets of three.

She put two glasses on the table and stuffed them full of ice, not thinking about what she was doing. She took a bottle of Red Label with a flow-control stopper and turned it upside down in the glasses, her dark-brown eyebrows frowning a little underneath her blonde hair at something that wasn't in the glass. She put the bottle down and gave me a full frontal with blue eyes, tired after a long day which made them look intense and a little chill for diving into. They were creased at the edges, too, from squinting at the sun or the unseeable distance. Her mouth was her feature. It had a soft, pliable big top lip whose underside caught against the smaller lower one, swelling it, making it look kissable.

'Water?' she asked. I nodded.

She went to the fridge, tearing the towelling band off her ponytail and shaking her hair out, which was still crappy with dust and sweat. She was neither tall nor small, neither fat nor thin, she had a compact body used to hard work outdoors. She wore a white T-shirt, a wrap of African print in dark red, orange and yellow. Her black espadrilles were dusted with red from the compound. She poured the water into her glass and left it for me. I splashed it into mine and sat back, looking at her which she seemed used to from men and which irritated her as well. She was frowning again.

'How did you know?'

'About Kurt? I went to the Danish Embassy.'

'B.B.?' she asked, grasping the situation quicker than I'd have thought.

'He thought it might make my job easier.'

'Sneaky bastard.'

'Him or me?'

'Both, probably.'

'Did they tell you he was murdered? They want you to

identify the body. There's a plane leaving for Abidjan at nine o'clock tonight. We should be on it.'

Her eyes were a lot older than the rest of her and they didn't leave my face. They were eyes that had seen things, that had got her used to suffering, that had twenty more years filled into them than the rest of her thirty-year-old body.

Kofi appeared at the door, shiny with sweat. He started to say something but stopped when he saw the set of Dotte's face, her eyes open and still.

'You all right, sistah Dotte?'

'The police, Kofi.'

'What they want you for?'

'To tell me Mr Kurt is dead.'

'Mr Kurt . . . he dead?' said Kofi, shocked, reaching deep to say the last word and a terrified look creeping into his face.

'As soon as the water's ready, start the boiling,' she said.

I heard Kofi's feet thumping out into the compound and a rush of voices as he explained in Tui to the other boys. Then Katrina was standing at the door, her hair wet, African print wrapped around her body, a towel over her arm and her eyes occupying most of her face.

'Is that true?' she asked. 'Is that what they said?' Dotte beckoned to her but Katrina turned and fled down the corridor. Dotte followed. She came back as I was pouring my third.

'Is Katrina Kurt's daughter?'

'No, but she's known him for the last six years. They were close.'

'But you weren't so close?'

'People talk.'

'B.B.,' I said. 'Mr Kantari, too, and I saw his things in the spare room.'

'Kantari,' she said, surprised at hearing the name.

'You knew him?'

'I knew of him.'

'Kurt was doing a job for him when he was killed.'

'What job?'

'A drop. He was picking – '

'I know what a drop is,' she said quickly. 'How do you know about it?'

'I was on the same drop.' That stiffened her back and got the blues eyes working on me.

'You get around.'

'I live a life but not always the one I want to.'

'Do you know who killed him?'

'He was already dead when I got there. It was a set-up. I thought you might be able to tell me something about it.'

'Are you police?'

'B.B. sent me, remember?'

'Police, but not official.'

'The man who killed Kurt is known in the Ivory Coast now as the Leopard. He killed a man before Kurt and then killed another three after him and then he tried to kill me. He's a Liberian working for somebody – I'd like to know who it is. You might not have loved Kurt any more, but you go back six years and it's probably been a long six years. I thought you might like to help me find out what's going on.'

'The Leopard? Five dead men, nearly six? A long six years? That was a very dense sentence; I think you'd better slow down a bit. Drink some whisky. Space it out for me.'

'The Leopard uses a metal claw to open up his victims after he's killed them, the men were killed because they had something the other wanted and, don't forget, I've been to the Danish Embassy.'

'Another dense sentence. You're a specialist, Mr Medway. What did the Danes tell you about Kurt?'

'That he wasn't Kurt Nielsen.'

She finished her drink, poured another measure and watched the amber filter down through the ice.

'I'm going to have some trouble if I identify his body.'

'That depends on the sort of trouble and if you're still in it.'

'I was in trouble from the day I met him.'

Dotte had met Kurt on a beach in the north of Morocco, just down from the Rif mountains in a small fishing village outside a town called Al Hoceima. She was smoking hash with the same guys Kurt was buying from. He persuaded her to come back on a trip with him to Denmark with a cargo, five kilos packed in beeswax blocks to fool the Spanish police dogs in Algeciras. They got through, no problem. They sold it in Copenhagen, made some money and did another trip and another, taking a bit more each time, expanding. That's what people in business do.

'Katrina and I were his good-luck charms,' she said. 'We even started selling gear up in Scotland. We teamed up with a Glaswegian girl and an Australian guy who were doing it and making a lot of money. We stopped after two trips when some Irish guys came to the door one night, put hoods over our heads and took us up a mountainside, put guns to our kneecaps and said they'd shoot us if we sold any more gear on their patch. IRA, very scary. Very quiet musical voices they had, too.

'So we stuck to our contacts in Denmark. Then Katrina was ill one time and I didn't want to take her down so Kurt went on his own for the first time in two years. He came back in on that road from Hemsburg, which we didn't normally do. The Danes caught him with only seven kilos, which was lucky because they gave him a year per kilo.

'He didn't like prison. I used some money we'd saved to get him a passport and I bought a Hanomag truck in Germany. After he'd done two years he came into his rehabilitation period. In Denmark they let you out for the weekends. One Saturday morning the three of us crossed the border on the train to Hamburg. We picked up the truck and drove non-stop to Marseille and caught the first boat out. By Monday morning we were in Tunis. We drove across the desert to Ghana, lived there for two years, ran out of money. Kurt met B.B. and we took this job here. So you can imagine the sort of trouble I'm going to have.'

'Did you meet him out of prison the day you left?'

'No, different people had been taking him out for the three months before. We didn't want to make it too easy, but it wouldn't have taken them long once they'd found I'd gone, too.'

'Why did you call the embassy that time when Kurt went missing?'

'I was scared.'

'You don't seem the type to scare easy.'

'He'd never done that before, just gone without telling me, for two weeks. When they asked for the passport I stopped it and he came back a couple of days later. He didn't tell me where he'd been.'

'That passport was a turkey,' I said, and told her its history. 'What colour hair did Kurt have?'

'Blond with a bit of red in it. Strawberry blond, you'd call it. His beard was the same colour when he had it.'

'I found a juju under his mattress, with a lock of his hair in it.'

Dotte seemed to judder at that, as if her insides had seized.

'Show me.'

We walked down the corridor, past the main entrance which was open to the compound where two fires burned under the water vats. The smell of woodsmoke was strong, but there was no sign of life out there.

'Where've the boys gone?' she asked, stepping outside and shouting for Kofi. Her voice fell flat into the night and nothing came back. We walked out to the vats in the now unlit compound.

'They're sensitive to this kind of thing,' I said. Dotte was standing close to me, her arms crossed, her hands holding on to her shoulders. She looked vulnerable. We walked back into the house in silence, then down the corridor to Kurt's cool room. I turned on the light and lifted the mattress with Dotte at my shoulder. There was no juju. I let the mattress fall.

'Well?'

'It's done its work. They've taken it away,' I said, looking at the time. 'Are you coming to Abidjan, or running away?'

'What makes you think I have a choice?'

'I'm not going to stop you.'

'No money, no truck?'

'Is that yours in Kantari's compound?'

181

'Kurt sold it to him for nothing. I didn't see any of the money.'

'It's going to be expensive for the Danes to send you back, and expensive to get enough evidence to convict you of aiding and abetting a fugitive, and they might not even be able to do it now.'

She thought about that for a few minutes and said she'd talk to Katrina. I socked back the whisky in the kitchen and went into the compound and out through the gates into the street. It was empty. Across from the compound was some shambolic housing with narrow mud roads in between. There was a distant thump of the bass track from some music. I followed it. It came from a bar about fifty yards into the shanty town. Sitting outside, with his head down and a bottle of beer dangling between his knees, was Kofi. I ordered two more beers and gave him one.

'I'm Mr Bruce.'

'Yessah.'

'You know me.'

'Yessah. Mastah send you.'

'That's right. Mastah send me.'

'You wan' something, sah?'

'This very bad thing here.'

'Is very bad, sah. Very bad.'

'Mr Kurt, you see him dying small-small?'

'I see him. Mr Kurt very sick man. In the head. Somet'ing in dere vexing him, sah.'

'Juju,' I said, and Kofi drained the bottle in his hand and started on the second I'd ordered for him.

'The med'cine here very strong, sah.'

'Who put the juju there?'

'The woman, sah, mebbe the woman.'

'Kurt's girlfriend?'

'Woman fro' Mali side, sah. She sendin' him food sometime'. He don' eat with sistah Dotte. Mebbe she putting med'cine the food, sah. Thassway it happenin'.'

'The woman from Mali. What's her name?'

'Soumba, sah. Soumba. Mr Kurt mekking mistake fallin' in love dis woman. He wan' marry her.'

'Why did she put the juju on him?'

'Mek him sick for love, sah.'

'She overdid it,' I said. Kofi didn't understand. 'What happen when Mr Kurt disappear six weeks ago?'

'Is very bad t'ing, sah. He tekkin' Miss Katrina wid him, sah. Sistah Dotte goin' mad.'

'Why did he take Miss Katrina?'

'Mebbe he sick. Mebbe the med'cine working before.'

'Are you and the boys going back to work?'

'Mornin' time, sah. The men don' work now.'

I told him to start work at dawn tomorrow and that I was taking Dotte down to Abidjan and we'd be back in a few days' time.

Dotte and Katrina were waiting on the verandah, out of their African print and wearing European-style skirts. I changed my shirt and went looking for a taxi, which took us to the airport. I bought three tickets and they told us we could board immediately, that the plane might take off early. We went through the formalities, our names, dates of birth and jobs being entered into a four-inch-thick ledger. The policeman wrote slowly, with his tongue out the side of his mouth. He wasn't too disturbed by what he was writing, which wouldn't have seemed unusual to an African. I checked and rechecked my mental arithmetic because, while I made Katrina 14 years old on January 27th next year, whichever way I tried it, I couldn't make Dotte any older than 28 on the 4th April.

19

Friday 1st November

We didn't check into the Novotel before midnight. We'd had
a forty-five-minute wait in Bouaké so that a 'big man' could
make the flight. While we waited the pilot came back and
sat with us in case we unbolted the seats and rolled up the
carpet to use in the privacy of our own homes. We landed
in Abidjan at the same time as an Air Afrique flight from
Paris and ended up brawling for taxis with some crew-cut
Frenchmen. Six of us got into one cab with Dotte and Katrina
across laps. The exhaust skidded against the road, showering
sparks into the night.

I showered and fixed myself a Red Label and opened up
a Perrier for show. I sat on the bed with a towel around my
waist and a T-shirt on against the chill of the air conditioning.
In the mirror on the dresser I saw a big fight going on between guilt and desire against a backdrop of confusion.

I imagined my letter making its way from Amsterdam to
a Berlin sorting office. A letter that said something that the
writer still felt but whose circumstances were, not changed
exactly, but had shifted. Heike was important to me but there
was a hole there where she'd been. Now I'd run into another
woman, Dotte, just run into her, for Christ's sake, and I was
already trying to fit her into that hole. I was attracted to her
. . . for a bad reason. There it was, the dilemma, no easier
to solve for knowing what it was.

She looked like the kind of woman that a lot of men saw
and started finding holes in themselves where there'd been
none before. The dogs sniffing after the unknowable, loving

the chase except, in this case, for us on the trail, the scent was always there, but the prey no nearer.

The strangeness, the dark vitality of the first hours came back to me. She was the same age as Katrina now when she'd had her, thirteen years old when she'd conceived. Katrina herself, a strange girl standing in those squares of light from the window, eating a biscuit, nails chewed off, leaning against my leg — a mixture of girlishness and early sexual confidence with something off beam, not quite right in the head, the teeth of certain cogs spinning free. Dotte, vulnerable and hard, the child-mother, the drug smuggler, the woman out on her own in Africa, her partner killed and telling Kofi to go and boil the sheanut.

There was a soft knock at the door. I picked up the stool, my brain leaping from the Korhogo compound to the abattoir I'd found in the Hotel La Croisette in Grand Bassam.

'Who is it?'

'Dotte,' she said, and I had that cable-snapping sensation. Her hair was wet and she was back in a T-shirt and the African-print wrap, but this time with two inches of bare waist between. 'I couldn't sleep.'

She made me aware of our bodies under little clothing. I handed her a Red Label, a glass and the untouched Perrier.

'I need to talk,' she said, taking the drinks, parts of us touching — wrists, forearms, a hip. 'I haven't done much of that for a long time.'

She left a smell of clean skin, no perfume. She put the drinks down on the bedside table and propped up a pillow on the unused single bed and lay down, crossing her legs at the ankles.

'You saw, didn't you?' she said. 'At the airport.'

'Your age, Katrina's and that your middle name is Sarah.'

'My mother was English. She died when I was eleven. Cancer.'

'Your father?'

'Half Danish, half German. Dead, too. In an accident when I was fifteen. Are you sure you're not a policeman?'

'You've known a lot of policemen?'

'I've been off the rails enough times, even before I met Kurt.'

'Drugs?'

'And the stuff that goes with them. Shoplifting, thieving. I was a pretty good burglar, too. They called me the Kitten because of the small spaces I could get through.'

'You never got caught?'

'Only once. It was good, though. They got me off the smack which meant I kept Katrina.'

'You're very close.'

'Not just in age. She needs me,' she said, and paused, looking off to the bathroom as if she'd heard something. 'I need her.'

'Is she all you've got?'

'One uncle,' she said, wagging her finger and twitching her face. The uncle was a no-no.

'You're all alone, then?'

'Never for long,' she said. 'Somebody always finds me.'

'Like Kurt,' I said, and she grunted. 'He had twenty years on you.'

'Old enough to be my father.'

'Was he?'

'Yes, he was. To start with, he was. A big, strong, gentle guy, but crazed too − not every father uses his daughters to smuggle drugs. That's what he called us, his daughters.'

She sipped her whisky and looked around the room which was no different to hers and said she didn't like too many questions at once. It reminded her of interrogation rooms and conversations with other men.

'Have you got a girlfriend, Bruce?' she asked. 'I know you're not married.'

'I . . . yes . . . how?'

'Not so easy answering questions, is it?' she said, giving me a flat ironic smile. 'I'm used to it . . . and not answering too.'

'I might still have a girlfriend. I don't know. She went back to Berlin. She got involved in some bad business the last job I was on. She needed a break back in civilization.'

'Do you always get involved in bad business?'

'I didn't used to. It's just the way things have been turning out lately.'

'Am I "bad business"?'

'Not yet. Kurt was. The other job I'm doing is.'

'What's that?'

'I was chaperoning a diamond trader who got kidnapped.'

'Diamonds and all?'

'That's right.'

'Very bad business,' she said. 'Do you want her to come back? Your girlfriend.'

'Yes, I do.'

'What was she doing in Africa?'

'She ran an aid project in Benin.'

'A do-gooder,' she said. 'Do you smoke?'

'Not any more.'

'Pity. I like the occasional one.'

'How did you know I wasn't married?'

'Your ego's a little fragile at the moment.'

'Eggshell right now.'

'People think loners are romantic. I think they're just men who aren't comfortable with themselves. They have to keep moving, keep looking, trying to pick up their own trail. Women don't marry men like that. They have sex with them, give them a little comfort and watch them leave.'

'You're very knowledgeable.'

'Men tell me things about themselves. Without my asking. I recognize the types.'

'You get a lot of attention from men?'

'I'm attainable. Not so beautiful that they feel inadequate. Not ugly. Men find me sexy. They want to get me into bed. You can't imagine how dull it is listening to what they have to say when you know their intention. Some men . . . I let them. They all think it's going to make them feel complete. It never does. They end up finding more gaps in themselves, that's all.'

'What about the ones you comfort and watch them leave?'

'They're all right,' she said, and held up her glass. I poured another measure and one for myself. 'Do you love her? Your girlfriend. You didn't say her name.'

'What's in a name?'

'Something personal.'

'Heike.'

'Do you love Heike?'

'I don't know.'

'You miss her now she's gone.'

'Yes,' I said, watching the conversation swerve out of my control. 'I thought you said *you* wanted to talk.'

'I do. We are. About you. I get bored talking about myself, like I said, answering people's questions all the time.'

'What about listening to men telling you things you don't need to know. Things they hope will get them into bed with you.'

'You haven't started on that yet. And those sort of men were more revealing when they were in bed with me already. They wanted the sex to have meaning.'

'Which it didn't for you?'

'It doesn't when you're on the game.'

'I didn't realize that was what we were talking about.'

'I didn't say. Shoplifting, thieving, burglary *and* occasional whoring. It was the easiest way to make money for drugs. I didn't like doing it, but stealing was time-consuming.'

'And after you met Kurt?'

'What's Heike like?' she asked, knuckling me down again. 'Give me some adjectives.'

'Strong. Resilient. Intelligent. Likes to drink . . .'

'You don't see her as very feminine.'

'Women in Africa . . . working in Africa, don't always have the opportunity to be feminine. But I do see her like that too, it's just that she needs to use other qualities more often.'

'Did you ever see her outside Africa?'

'I broke down in the Sahara. She pulled me and my car out.'

'Your saviour,' she said, and we both thought about that for a moment.

'Kurt,' she said, 'was a lost man. Africa found him out, stripped him down to what he was. Big body, small heart, no morals, no integrity, nothing to hold on to, a hollow man. They could beat him like a drum. I can't find many tears for him. The man who took me off that beach near Al Hoceima was long gone. Too many drugs for too long. That stay in prison – he drank too much of the stuff they make out of potatoes. Before that though, the worst thing that happened, what changed him and the way he was with me . . . he killed a man. He was the big daddy until then, and after that I mothered him. I mothered him in prison, out of it and down here. He hated it. He wanted it to be how it was before the killing. The problem was that he couldn't satisfy himself that there was a reason for it.'

I stared hard at the carpet between the two beds, rolling the killing, maybe the two killings, I'd done over and over. I'd satisfied myself of the reason for killing them. They were both killers who would have killed me, but it didn't matter how long I kicked that rationale around, if I thought about it it did me no good at all.

'I'm talking to you,' a voice said, off somewhere.

'What?' I said, irritated now to find Dotte's eyes on me. She was kneeling on the bed, her face at my level, big blue eyes staring in. 'It's late,' I said quietly.

'I'm going,' she replied, just as quietly. 'Whatever you've done you've coped with it better than Kurt. He still wakes up screaming.'

'Not any more, and how do you know I don't?'

'No,' she said, getting her legs out from under her, standing up. 'Your reason must have been better than Kurt's.'

I felt sick now, sick, strained, probed, opened up and inspected like a post-op or how women tell me they feel after the gynie's been there with a cold speculum. I stood and she put her hand on my shoulder and drew me down and kissed me on the cheek. 'You're a good man, Bruce.'

'You wouldn't know.'

'Katrina told me. She likes you. She might not be all there. But in some things she's never wrong.'

'And you?'

'I'm no judge,' she said, and left.

20

'I spoke to Fat Paul's Lagos partner,' said Bagado, sitting over his breakfast in his mac, looking sullen. 'He'd heard about the firebombing and the murder. He didn't think Fat Paul had any political connections but he said Fat Paul's father was a Krahn and had some kind of government position.'

'So Fat Paul might have known people, even if he wasn't directly involved. Did you ask him about James Wilson?'

'He's never heard of him.'

'But Fat Paul's father probably did and Fat Paul and Wilson were about the same age.'

'Is this relevant?'

'Connections,' I said. 'You saw the film?'

'Pornography. Tame. I didn't recognize any faces. What I saw of them.'

'There's another film,' I said, and Bagado steeled up on me.

'You see,' he said quietly, dabbing his mouth with a napkin and looking out over the grey lagoon, at the sun just breaking through the cloud. 'I was right. You *were* holding back.'

'I wanted to see Kantari first.'

'Did it make any difference?'

'It made me think we should take a look at it, and not just hand it over.'

'So let's see it.'

'After breakfast. Did you hear anything more from Accra?'

'Maybe,' he said, looking around the room for someone more interesting.'

'Come on, Bagado.'

'Don't do that again,' he said. 'Trust is all we've got in this game. You're making a lot of assumptions for someone who used to be a businessman.' He poured himself some more coffee, slowly, getting himself calm again. 'Now *you* tell me about *your* day.'

I told him about the meeting with Trzinski, what happened with Kantari, and in the compound afterwards. I mentioned the few odd things about Dotte and Katrina's ages but not about Dotte's criminal past. I didn't want to prejudice him – that's what I told myself.

'Any ideas on what this is about?' I asked.

'Whatever it is, it's serious. The police in Accra told me unofficially that Fat Paul's house was searched by two white men with short hair and dark suits. They paid in dollars to do it and have it kept quiet. They were Americans and very fast.'

'A bit of a quantum leap there, Bagado.'

'To the CIA, you mean?'

'One minute it's hoods getting whacked in a hotel room, now it's intergovernment business.'

'Liberia is very important to the Americans. It's their eyes and ears in Africa. They've got something called an Omega satellite tracking system and VCA transmitter/receivers there, and don't ask me what they are, I've only just stopped calling a radio a wireless. If there's anything that's going to affect their position, they want to know about it. Fat Paul might have had something. We're just about to find out. Who else is there?

' "Red" Gilbert came after me so he knew. He might have told his boss, or he might have survived the lagoon to tell his boss. But then if he did, why hasn't he come after me again?'

'Gilbert attacked you Monday night. If he survived the lagoon he wasn't going to come back the same night all in his wet clothes. Tuesday morning you checked out of the hotel. Who knew where you were going?'

'Sean Malahide.'

'What's he got to do with it?'

'Nothing. You asked a question.'

'Nobody knows you went to Tortiya. You spent a night

with the police. You didn't get back to the Novotel until late Wednesday night after Collins was kidnapped. You were out again Thursday morning and didn't come back until after midnight. What would you assume if you were "Red" Gilbert or his boss?'

'That I'd left the country. What would you do?'

'If I was them I'd wait in the Novotel for a week.'

'That's your style. Very patient,' I said, 'but not very American. Do you think "Red" is employed by the Americans?'

'Careful what you say,' said Bagado. 'It might not be *the* Americans. It might be *some* Americans, or even *an* American.'

'Like the Iran/Contra affair wasn't anything to do with the Reagan administration?'

'A clever thing to say, but don't say it too loud, especially with what you have in your possession. And I can't remember the last government in the world to admit that their covert operations have resulted in deaths, mutilations, a firebombing and an illegal search, can you?'

'You're tearing ahead again, Bagado. Your Accra police said that US agents bought their silence to do a frisk of Fat Paul's house. What's been happening here in the Ivory Coast could still be a tribal thing. The *Ivoire Soir* wrote that James Wilson was implicated in the handover of the Liberian president to Jeremiah Finn and that's why he got done. The *commissaire*, Gbondogo, thinks the same.'

'And Fat Paul and Kurt Nielsen?'

'Were killed by a Liberian, possibly paid for by Krahn tribe members. Assuming that I've got Wilson's tape, which he'd given to Fat Paul to sell to Nielsen who was buying for Kantari. Then the Liberian was just following the trail.'

'The Liberian, and I assume we're talking about "Red" Gilbert, started at Kantari's end. He followed Nielsen to the drop.'

'How did he know about Kantari, you mean?'

'Maybe James Wilson knew Kantari and gave his name.'

'To protect Fat Paul? Possibly. So why hasn't Kantari been raked by the Leopard?'

'"Red" Gilbert knew that Kantari was the buyer. He knew

that he was *going* to receive the package which was why he followed Kurt Nielsen.'

'How does he know to follow Kurt Nielsen?'

'Somebody told him to,' said Bagado. 'Kantari sounds a slippery fellow.'

'He's a player,' I said. 'Maybe Dotte can help there, she knows *of* him, she says.'

'Americans, Krahns, Kantari. I want to see that video.'

Katrina appeared at my elbow, still puffy with sleep and looking as if she might rub herself out if she continued working her eye over with her knuckle. She pointed over to Dotte and asked what we were supposed to be doing. I said I had to make a call. Her shoulders sagged and she shuffled back through the tables.

'She's pretty,' said Bagado, 'and not *so* strange.'

'Her mother says she can be a little off beam. But then everything about this job is a little off beam. You should have been there last night, the boys felt it and bolted, they knew about that juju. Tell me about Hadet.'

'Hadet is nothing, he just gave the Alfas a beating for not paying up. More interesting is who works for Rademakers.'

'There is somebody?'

'Yes, but perhaps it's not the work you had in mind. Her name is Chantale Leubas. A married woman with expensive tastes, big blonde hair, Parisian clothes, painted nails and plenty of gold jewellery. She has a husband who works in the Peugeot sales department.'

'Rademakers's mistress?'

'Maybe not just Rademakers's. The garage boy says Rademakers keeps a room at the Hotel Tiana in Plateau for "siestas". She works three mornings a week for him, they have lunch and take a "nap" afterwards. The doorman confirmed it and told me about the husband. The Leubases have a nice house in Deux Plateaux. Not cheap. She was picked up by a chauffeur-driven Mercedes around seven-thirty in the evening. I followed her around Abidjan; take my word for it, she's a *fille de joie*.'

'Did you speak to her?'

'I was going to leave that to you. I couldn't see that she'd have anything to say to a fifty-four-year-old unemployed Beninois policeman.'

'What about Malahide?'

'He'd left. No address. Paid cash. The only thing I could get out of the girl was that he had a lot of Libyan stamps in his passport. The rest of the conference delegates left after lunch yesterday and I talked to most of them. They all knew him. He gave a talk about pineapples. I met someone called Dr Felix Bost who lives here in the Ivory Coast and he knew a lot more about him than most. He's a conservationist, which means he doesn't like Malahide because Malahide is in the logging business. He operates out of Man near the western border with Liberia. Dr Bost says that the Ivorian forest has already been decimated and there's barely enough left to make an operation worthwhile. Conclusion?'

'Malahide buys Liberian logs. The logging territory is in Grand Gedeh and Nimba County just across the border from Man.'

'Which is held by Samson Talbot's rebels. Dr Bost told me about an Armenian, called Ajamian, who trades out of Man and can give us better information about Malahide's business. I have Dr Bost's card as an introduction.'

'We'd better go to Man.'

'We're booked — eleven-thirty. Don't worry, it'll be late.'

I called Gbondogo at 9.00 a.m. and asked him if he could have an officer available for the body ID. He said he could, but not before 10.00 a.m. because of a meeting about the national elections coming up. The officer would join us at the University Hospital in Cocody where Kurt Nielsen's body was being held. I called Martin Fall and left a message for him to call me back. Then I called B.B., whose maid, Mary, answered the phone, and she slopped to the staircase and yelled, 'Mastah! Mistah Bru-u-u-u!' which went up the stairwell like a chill wind. B.B. roared back through four concrete walls from what was probably his bathroom, and an image of a pink hippo with his chin on the bath's rim flashed before me. I could hear him stoking himself up from the top of the stairs, the house trembling as he thundered down them, his hand slapping the wooden bannisters.

'Lemme spik to him,' he said, as if he'd ever had to ask Mary permission for anything. He whumped into his chair and those terrible feet crashed on to the table. 'Where you bloddy hell!'

'Abidjan.'

'What you bloddy f-f-fool, what you doing darn dere? You supposed to be in Korhogo.'

'Kurt Nielsen was murdered on Monday night.'

'Get me cigarette!' he roared at Mary.

'Sah!' she shouted, from what sounded like her usual position just behind his right shoulder, where it was an effort for him to turn and see her.

'I donno . . . dis ting,' he said, suddenly subdued and petulant. 'It . . . bloddy hell . . . matches? Tank you. He morderèd. Bloddy f-f-fool. Is no surprisin', de man . . . a uzeless man, neffer doin' what I tell him to do. He always goin' off an' doin' what he tinkin' an' now look. Morder-èd. De wife?'

'She's here with me to identify the body. She's all right.'

'De man, uzeless, he don't deserve de job. But morder-èd. Is locky I organize de replacemarn,' he said, dragging hard on his smoke.

'Where is he?'

'He comin' from Englarn.'

'Has he worked in Africa before?'

B.B. paused.

'No, he neffer wok in Africa before.'

'Does he speak French?'

B.B. rapped the arm of his chair with his knuckles.

'No.'

'Is he the right man for the job?'

'He ver' chip.'

'Sometimes cheap is expensive.'

'Sometimes, Bruise, you tinking correck.'

'I have things to do down here. I won't be in Korhogo for a few days. Kofi is processing the sheanut which Dotte brought in last night. Maybe you should rethink your employment policy.'

'Dis life,' said B.B., depressed down to his long yellow toenails, 'dis life is ver' long. It tekkin' too much time and

195

monny. You get my point? Mebbe is time, you know, mebbe is time . . .' he trailed off, and the phone rattled into its cradle. B.B. was going to hate me by the end of this job, hate me so bad that I'd never work for him again.

The girl on the desk told me that Martin Fall had come through. I ran through Martin's checklist, finishing on Malahide and our planned trip to Man.

'There's a political situation your end, Bruce,' he said.

'Surprise me, Martin.'

'The Americans have been putting pressure on the Ivorians to stop Libyan weapons coming through Ivory Coast from Burkina-Faso to Samson Talbot in Liberia. Talbot holds the Liberian port of Buchanan which ECOWAS are trying, not very successfully, to blockade. They haven't, or rather they can't, stop the rebels' business empire operating out of the Ivorian port of San Pedro, near the Liberian border. The Ivorians maintain that they've frozen Talbot's assets in Ivory Coast and that they're working on preventing arms coming through, but there's no government will behind it, which means the rebels pay and they get their arms. I'd say that they're using Ron, not just for money, but to get concessions to move arms freely, which the Americans and ECOWAS don't like. We're talking to the Ivorians now. Still no news from the rebels or whoever's got Ron.'

I threw Trzinski's views into the pot and Martin scribbled while he asked me half a dozen more questions about how Trzinski fitted in. He told me to stay in the biggest hotel in Man called Les Cascades and he'd contact me there if necessary. I told him the water was getting deeper and hotter and it might be an idea to send somebody more qualified down here. He gave me a lifetime achievement's worth of flattery and we hung up.

I asked the girl at the desk to arrange the video facilities again and went out into the street to buy a blank tape, an identical jiffy bag to the one Fat Paul had given me and some sealing wax. I retrieved Fat Paul's package from behind the glove compartment. I saw Moses in the lobby and told him to bring the car around to the front in half an hour. I told Dotte to be ready to leave then.

Bagado and I took the package down to the conference room. I set up the television. Bagado cracked the seal on the envelope and took out the cassette which was wrapped in crepe paper. He shook out the envelope on to a blotter on a desk and then the crepe paper. Nothing. He looked over the cassette and handed it to me. It was a 180-minute tape. I recorded on to the blank tape at the same time.

There was a minute of white noise and then darkness and a confusion of voices. The screen changed between black, brown and dark green and the voices were shouting in an African language I didn't understand.

'They're arguing about who's going to hold the camera,' said Bagado.

There was a single imperative which silenced the screen and the camera whip-panned on to an impressive-looking man in army fatigues who was drinking Budweiser from a can and having his temples dabbed by a young woman.

'Jeremiah Finn,' said Bagado.

The camera pulled back to a wide shot, and, sitting on the floor in his underpants with his hands and arms tied behind his back and a small head wound trickling blood down the side of his face, was the late Liberian president. He was alert, his head making the jerky movements of a terrified man who didn't know where he was going to be hit next. The camera closed in on his shins, which had several bullet holes in them.

'US Embassy, sah. I got the US Embassy,' said another voice, and the camera moved to the radio operator and Finn, who was now standing there with an earphone held to his head. He moved the microphone around to his mouth and said: 'We got him. We got the President.'

There was a bang and the camera rocked and rolled on to the President, who was flat on his face, his head turned towards camera, the sweat pouring off him now, his neck muscles standing out. The air hissed between his teeth as they applied the rifle to the back of his other knee and, bang, his whole body jerked off the ground so that the soldier fell back into the men watching.

'What the hell's all this about?' I asked Bagado, who was screwed up in his mac.

'I've heard about this film,' he said. 'They tortured him for twelve hours before they killed him. What I don't understand is . . . this is nothing new. Journalists have already seen this, or a version of it. Finn played it to them to show that he had American backing for the President's capture. Their reports showed that they weren't impressed by the quality of human rights on display. When they asked a US Embassy official in Sierra Leone about it he denied any US involvement. He said the tape proved nothing – "Finn must have been talking to his grandmother because he wasn't connected to the US Embassy." I think those were the man's words.'

'So how did Finn get the President?'

'I don't know. We'll have to find a journalist.'

'Where did you hide the money?' asked Finn's voice on the video.

'I am your brother,' said the President. 'Loosen me. I will talk.'

'Bring me his ear.'

One of the soldiers took out a bowie knife and straddled the President, who was sitting up now. He took hold of the man's ear and sawed it off and gave it to Finn, who asked for the other. With four or five cuts the other one was severed. Then Finn forced them into the President's mouth and told him to eat them. The President looked up, shit-scared, chewed. The blood from his ears leaked down his chin and the film turned to snow.

We unplaited ourselves. The snow continued for several minutes. I stopped the tapes, and after fast forwarding the original to check for any more film, rewound them. I handed the original to Bagado and slipped the recorded one into the envelope I'd just bought. Bagado took a penknife out of his sock and unscrewed the five cross-headed screws at the back of the cassette, opened it, lifted out the two spools of tape and checked the spools themselves, which were hollow. The cassette was empty. He put it back together again.

'The film has to be the clue,' he said. 'This is what it's all about.'

'That the Americans were involved?'

'That would be worth killing for, wouldn't you think?' said Bagado.

'I can feel the stakes getting higher.'

'But high stakes for what game? This is a handful of nothing. It looks like a bluff.'

'Then who are we bluffing?'

'*We're* not bluffing anybody, we're somebody else's bluff.'

'You think there's somebody out there who knows we've got a handful of nothing and we're running a diversion on their behalf?'

'Let's hope he doesn't fold his hand.'

21

I asked reception to put the copy and the original in the hotel safe. Dotte sat in the lobby with her head resting against a wall and sunglasses down over her eyes. Katrina leaned on her. I introduced Bagado. We drove to the University Hospital. The cloud had dispersed now and the sun had dried out the roads, putting the humidity up there in the high thousands. We sat in silence and watched the sweat patches grow as we eased through the traffic out of Plateau.

A policeman, a medical examiner and a doctor met us at the door to the morgue. Dotte and I went into the cool room in which there were ten slabs but only one occupied. The doctor checked the toe tag and lifted off the sheet. Even from the murky photocopy B.B. had given me I could see it was a very still version of Kurt Nielsen. Dotte nodded and left the room. I eased the sheet back further and saw Nielsen's roughly stitched abdomen. The scratch marks from the metal leopard claws were still visible around the sternum where they'd grazed the skin before cutting through the soft flesh over the diaphragm.

The policeman led us into an office. Sitting behind the desk was Leif Andersen, his hands clasped together as tight as his crossed legs – tense. We shook hands. Dotte was cooler than Nielsen on his slab. She took the sunglasses off for the first time and gave Leif Andersen the benefit of her blue eyes, which sat him up. He gave his best diplomatic condolences and got to work.

'The Danish police have informed me that Kurt Nielsen is in fact a Mr Søren Tinning who had eighteen months to serve of a drug-smuggling sentence. Were you aware of this, Ms Wamberg?'

'He had told me, yes.'

'The Danish police also tell me you have an extensive criminal record yourself.'

'One conviction.'

'That is true,' he said, looking at papers on the desk that weren't his. 'I've spoken to the Danish police and under the circumstances . . .'

'Which are?'

'The fact that the prisoner is dead, that you are in Africa . . .'

'And they have no evidence?'

'This has contributed to their decision, yes, to let the matter of the Nielsen/Tinning escape rest. You will, however, be required to speak to the Abidjan police about the circumstances that led to your partner's murder.'

'Circumstances I know nothing about.'

'I must still ask you to accompany this officer to the Sûreté.'

After that display of taut diplomacy we all stood. The creaking of Andersen's leather shoes was the only noise. We shook hands and left. When you expect trouble by the truckload it has a habit of discharging itself elsewhere.

I told Dotte to stay in the Novotel until we got back from Man. Bagado and I went to the airport where we caught our flight, which had been delayed by a politician who needed to get to Man for Sunday's elections. We took off at 1.30 p.m. and as soon as we'd flattened out and Bagado had released the arm rests from his white-knuckle grip, the questions started coming from over the blue collar of his mac.

'What did Heike have to say?'

'Why're you asking me that question now?'

'It's my question, I'll ask it when I want to.'

'She said that she was keeping herself occupied, that she was staying in Berlin and she was looking at a project in Tanzania.'

'Don't make me try, Bruce.'

'She said she missed Africa and me, too.'

'And you?'

'It's been better since I started working.'

'An *int*eresting answer.'

'And true. I've thought about her every day almost all day, chasing my tail for three weeks. I've caught it a few times, gnawed it, it hasn't helped.'

'And now you've got a rabbit to chase.'

'What does that mean?'

'Dotte?'

'You're always there, Bagado, aren't you? Watching.'

'It's my job. What about Dotte?'

'She's got something.'

'Think of it as leprosy, it'll help.'

'You liked her.'

'It's not a question of like,' he said, looking down the aisle after a small girl who'd built up some momentum. 'Have you ever been afraid of the dark?'

'When I was as small as that,' I said. 'And you've given me a couple of scares standing in rooms during power cuts.'

'Remember that.'

'Bagado, you're talking in crossword clues again.'

'That woman is a dark person. She's learnt about the dark before the light and it's been from ugly experience. She has depth but it's nothing you can learn from. Leave her alone because she will never bring happiness with her. And don't listen to me, I'm just a silly old African "gumshoe",' he said, trying to get himself used to the word. 'I wish I had my father's voice. When he talked about these things he sounded like distant thunder and we believed everything.'

'You don't think I do.'

'I've never known another human being take advice in affairs of the heart. In fact, they always do the opposite, because they believe in their heart. If they feel something in it, it must be right. And there's no known quantity of talk that can shift that.'

'So you tell me these "dark" things and you dig yourself a hole at the same time.'

'I have to satisfy my conscience.'

202

'That you warned me. Don't worry, Bagado, she's warned me herself.'

'And she can do that because she knows it doesn't make any difference.'

'I'm not getting involved.'

'Those, my friend, sound like famous last words.'

We landed somewhere and took off again. We drank beer and dozed until, maybe for the benefit of the politician on board, we circled the mountains of Man and looked down on the rain-forested ridges surrounding the grid and sprawl of the town before heading south and landing in hot sunshine at just after 3.30 p.m.

We took a taxi and checked into the Hotel Les Cascades, which overlooked the town. Bagado called the Armenian, Ajamian, who said he could see us at 5.00 p.m. We walked into town and ate some chicken in the Restaurant La Prudence in the Quartier Commercial and then took another short walk to Ajamian's office, which looked as if it had been recently shelled.

Ajamian was a large, dark and hairy man who didn't bother to explain why he was working in a room where the rubble from a destroyed wall still remained in a pile in one corner. His office furniture was draped in sheets which he threw off for us to sit on. He poured us a whisky without going through any unnecessary formalities and sat down, putting his feet up on his sheet-covered desk. He fitted an oval-shaped Turkish cigarette into a small bamboo cane holder, lit it and through a very heavy, broom-bristle moustache, asked us, in French, if he could be of assistance. Bagado gave him Dr Felix Bost's card and started to explain about Malahide. Ajamian smoked and looked down his cheeks at the card and the hair sprouting through the gaps of his shirt buttons, raising his eyebrows every so often as if he'd spotted an insect or some birdlife nesting in there.

'Felix doesn't like Sean,' he said, getting himself started.

'Do you?' I asked.

'Sean is very boring when he is drunk and when he has that Irish poet on his mind. Up to eleven and between four and six, after his siesta, he can be very charming. The rest . . .' His arm floated away with the smoke from his nostrils and ended up behind his chair.

'Dr Bost said he's in the logging business.'

'Sean's been in Africa a long time. He's run down the Ivorian rainforest almost single-handed and he and the Lebanese did a very good job in Ghana too. He goes where the business is, and the business is in Liberia and has been, for his kind of operation, for a year or more. He buys logs from Samson Talbot who controls this end of Liberia, and he ships them ex San Pedro in the Ivory Coast up to Europe, mainly France and the UK. As far as I know, the money for the logs is deposited in dollars in accounts held in Ouagadou-gou, the Burkina-Faso capital, but he also keeps money in CFA here . . . so I am told.'

'The money comes direct from European buyers?'

'I think from Sean's offshore European accounts.'

'You know a lot about Malahide's business.'

'If I want to sit at the table I have to know my opponents.'

'And the rebels use the money to buy arms?'

'Yes. The arms come from Libya. They ship them across the Ivory Coast. Some come direct from Tripoli into Buchanan and soon he'll be flying them in when M. Talbot finishes lengthening the runway at his headquarters in Gbarnga, two hundred kilometres north east of Monrovia. M. Talbot has promised to become a good Libyan socialist when he wins.'

'Is Malahide involved in any of these arms deals?'

Ajamian looked at me with coal-black eyes buried deep in their nests. Smoke snaggled on the tufts of nasal hair as he sucked and breathed the bamboo cane cigarette holder. He played with one of the oval-shaped cigarettes he'd taken from the box on his desk.

'Perhaps now you should tell me what your inquiries are about,' he said. 'Now that we know we are not engaged in idle gossip.'

I told Ajamian about the kidnap, the Liberian connection, Malahide's knowledge of Rademakers's office and the nature of Ron's business. When the word 'diamonds' came up Ajamian didn't stiffen but he became very still.

'Is there something wrong, M. Ajamian?' asked Bagado.

Ajamian ran his hand over the burnt stubble on his chin and checked his palm.

'One of the things that the Ivorians have done to keep the Americans sweet is to make it more difficult to move large sums of money out of the country. It's not easy at the best of times. There's a limit. Now it's impossible without outside help. A way round this is to use CFA made in the Ivory Coast to buy diamonds. Moving diamonds is easier than suitcases of cash. This is all very inconvenient. The rebels would like to have more flexibility. It would seem logical that your client has been kidnapped to secure such flexibility and to turn a profit from their work. It will be interesting to see what they ask for in exchange.'

'And Malahide?'

'Well . . . he knows everybody concerned.'

'Does he deal in arms?' I asked.

'I'm told he has a lot of Libyan stamps in his passport,' said Bagado.

'How much logging is there in Libya?' I asked.

'You're answering your own questions,' said Ajamian, removing the spent cigarette and plugging in the fresh one in his hand. 'As you probably realize, we are now talking in areas where certain things cannot be known. I don't know whether it would be of interest to you, but he has a timber yard on the outskirts of town on the Danané road, two hundred metres after the Mobil garage on the right. You can't miss it. It's a very well-protected compound.'

Ajamian let us know it was all over. We finished our drinks and left.

I called Malahide from the Restaurant La Prudence and asked him if he remembered me and he unnerved me by saying I was the sheanut man he'd met in the Novotel in Abidjan. Drunk, but not unconscious. We agreed to meet at 7.00 that evening. He said he lived up in the hills over Man but he'd send a driver to pick me up at the hotel.

Bagado and I took a taxi to the Danané road and sat in a food stall opposite Malahide's oversecure timber yard. Apart from the chain link topped with razor wire there were four savage dogs chained to metal poles in the yard. If a workman came too close they ran at him until the chain clicked tight and flung the dog up in the air and down on to the baked earth of the compound. Bagado retreated into his mac. An industrial saw started to rip through a length of mahogany and clouds of red-brown dust rolled out of the central warehouse into the yard covering passing workmen with a thin red film.

'Do you think you could get in there?' I asked Bagado.

'Not with those dogs.'

'I'm impressed you think you'd get as far as the dogs.'

'Old,' he said, 'but still nimble.'

'I don't want you to lose your manhood on that razor wire.'

'Is that what it is?'

'Maybe you should talk to some people without the white man on your shoulder. I'll see Malahide on my own.'

'You're not going to accuse him of anything?'

'I'm going to ask him to contact the rebels, see what they want. He's our only way in, even if he did set Ron Collins up.'

I slept in my room until they called me to say that Malahide's driver was in reception. I sat in the back of the dark saloon and watched the lights of Man spreading out as we climbed above the valley floor.

Malahide's house was a fifteen-minute drive from Man, but once the car had been videoed going through the gate and I was standing in the courtyard of his wooden, Alpine chalet-style house, the grid-lit town seemed a matter of a few hundred yards away. It was cooler up here, with firm breezes shaking the vegetation. A maid took me up some stone steps directly into a large living room with a complicated structure of beams in its roof which looked as if Braque had been involved. It was glassed on one side with sliding doors and beyond them was a half-covered, railed wooden verandah where Malahide was sitting at a table, staring into space with the back of his red head to me. The maid directed me towards a chair and let me know through some ancient tribal communication that I should sit and contemplate the inverted night that was the metropolis of Man.

'There y'are,' said Malahide, as if he'd been looking for me all day. 'Will you have a drink of something Irish?'

He poured three fingers of Bushmills into a tumbler on my side of the table and topped up his own.

'There's ice if you're feeling weak,' he said. 'Do you smoke?'

'No.'

'That's just as well. I can't tolerate smoking in my house. Can't abide the smell of it. Now then . . .' He roared something incoherent into the night and the maid materialized out of the darkness. Malahide spoke to her in her own language. She backed off. 'When I'm here,' he said, facing me, 'I look out there after dark and I have this tremendous feeling of control, you know, as if I'm operating a foggering great console. Are you with me? Then just as I get to feel like that, I kid myself that the stars have fallen to earth and I reach for the Bushmills and put everything in order.'

'That's very poetic of you, Sean,' I said, keeping it flat and straight.

'Yes, poetry,' he said. 'It's a very important thing to the Irish.'

'Do you have much use for it in your business?'

'In *my* business?' he said, cocking an eye in my direction. 'In my business and in life. I have use for it all the time. Some of us, of course, don't. Like that Goldstein chappy we were with in Abidjan. The man had nothing. The boy had nothing.'

'Ron Collins?'

'No poetry, that boy,' he said. 'No fogging soul. He'll go nowhere.'

'He's gone somewhere, Sean.'

'And what do you mean by that, Bruce?'

'He was kidnapped Wednesday night.'

'Maybe that'll teach him some humility.'

'It seems likely that he was kidnapped by Samson Talbot's men.'

The glass on the way up to Malahide's mouth stopped and he looked across at me.

'And?' he said.

'Apart from being an agronomist talking about pineapples, you buy logs from Samson Talbot.'

'Who've you been talking to?'

I didn't answer. He sniffed.

'I thought as much,' he said. 'You've been talking to that Armenian bastard. I thought I could smell him on you. Those Turkish joss sticks he smokes.'

'He says Grand Gedeh's your second home.'

'He'd know. He's still living in that bomb site?'

'Bomb site?'

'He had a gas explosion in there. Killed a man walking in the street. He's lucky the building's still on its feet.'

'Ajamian says you do business with Talbot.'

'And you want me to find Ronny boy. Ronny Wonder. What're you running after him for?'

'My job.'

'Yes,' he said, drawing it out. 'I didn't have you pegged as a sheanut man. What're you up to?'

'I was asked to look out for Ron Collins. Make sure he didn't get into trouble.'

'Well, you fogged that up a treat.'

'My footwork's not fancy enough to take on three armed soldiers and be sure of winning.'

'How fancy is it?'

'I can get across the road without falling over . . . most of the time.'

Malahide chuckled.

'You'll do,' he said. 'You'll do.'

Which was the same noise as the mosquitoes were making as they gave me a savage going-over. Malahide was exuding something powerful enough to keep them on my side of the table — *Animosité pour homme*. The maid came back with kebabs and salad and two cold beers. Malahide ate and ran beer and Bushmills neck and neck. The pace was fierce, but I kept up. We finished and sat back.

'It's a lawless world we live in,' he said. 'A lawless fogging world.'

' "*Things fall apart, the centre cannot hold*",' I quoted.

'You've read a spot of the great Irishman?'

'A little.'

' "*Mere anarchy is loosed upon the world*" – that's what's happening over there,' he said, pointing towards Liberia. 'I'll talk to them for you, Bruce. See if they've got yer man. That's all. If there's any exchange to be done, you're on your own. And I'm telling you – you'd better be careful, it's gone to fogging hell over there. You'll see.'

'Will you talk to them tonight?'

'I'll try them. They'll want to see you if they're going to do business with you. That means over there. I've some business to do myself. Perhaps we could make a trip of it. I'll call you later at Les Cascades. But get some sleep, because if we go it'll be at three or four in the morning and you'd better be sharp for those bastards.'

He stood up and walked back into the low light of the living room and this time through I saw it behind one of the wooden support pillars. Hanging off a rough piece of hewn wood that was on its way to being a carving of sorts was a full leopard skin with leather straps for human wear.

'The leopard,' said Malahide. 'A very important animal for the Dan people around here. They believe it makes the wearer invisible so that he can wander about the place and see the evil' – Malahide finished his tumbler of Bushmills in a gulp – 'and the good, if there's any fogging left in the world.'

'And what does he do when he finds the evil?'

'He rips it out.'

Malahide put an arm around my shoulder and steered me towards the steps, and, rather than human warmth, I felt something cold creep up my spine and tug at the strange nerve endings attached to the hairs at the back of my neck and the cap of my scalp.

22

'Is that it?' asked Bagado.

'Not quite; as I got into the car he stood on the steps, stared up at the sky and said:

> "A starlit or a moonlit dome disdains
> All that man is;
> All mere complexities,
> The fury and the mire of human veins."'

'Is he insane?'

'Not because he quotes Yeats.'

'*Because* by night he drinks whisky and spouts poetry at the heavens and by day he decimates the African rain-forest, pays money to people so that they fight their wars and . . . is there a Gordon's in there?'

I tossed him a miniature from the mini-bar and handed him a glass with a can of tonic in it.

'What else?' I asked.

'He's shipping arms to Ireland. Nothing serious, more of a gesture. He takes a truckload off the consignments coming across from Burkina. They offload it in the bush into jeeps and pick-ups, he takes it into the compound and packs them in the lining of containers of furniture and ships them out of San Pedro to Cork.'

'Who told you that?'

'I talked to the owner of that food stall across the road from the compound. Four workers were given the sack last month. I tracked them down. The one with six children under the age of eight told me everything I needed to know. I gave him fifty thousand, if that's all right?'

The phone went and Malahide's voice started without introduction.

'You know La Prudence?'

'Yes.'

'Go there and wait.' He clicked off.

'He's enjoying this.'

'I don't like it.'

'What's the worst-case scenario?'

'You get killed.'

'Why kill me?'

'You know things. You've got your nose in their business.'

'It's only a discussion of terms and conditions.'

'You trust Malahide and his puppet leopard?'

'He needs me.'

'I've heard women who've been battered to pulp say the same thing of their lovers.'

It was a hot walk, but not lonely. Business was brisk outside the hospital, with girls selling mangoes and bananas through the windows. There was already a stream of people going into the stadium, where a leaflet told me there was a political rally before the Sunday elections.

There were only two empty tables at La Prudence, which was full of foreigners that night. There was one long table of aid workers who'd been there some time judging from the empties on the table. I took a table next to four Germans who leaned over their huge guts and ate with concentration and precision, only pausing to apply mustard and sink a few inches of beer. They didn't speak. The waiter brought me a beer and five minutes later told me to come to the phone.

'I can't talk to you in that hotel of yours,' said Malahide. 'There's all sorts of bastards in there. It's on for tonight. I'll pick you up at two a.m. outside the PTT. Don't be late. I'll wait for two minutes only.' The line clicked dead.

Bagado didn't keep me up. He gave me a plastic bag and told me to take some clothes for Ron. I put a pack of playing cards in my pocket. I set the alarm for 1.30 a.m. and fell into some ragged sleep at around 11.00 p.m. I woke up sweating, the air conditioning not working in the room. It was just before 1.00 a.m.

I walked through the empty leaflet-strewn streets. There was only me and a ribby, snake-hipped dog out at this hour. I waited ten minutes at the PTT. Malahide was on time. It was a good hour's drive to Danané. The police post there waved us through without asking for papers and we headed south to Toulépleu on a rough road with thick vegetation on either side.

'They say Ronny's dad is a wealthy man,' said Malahide.

'He's been in diamonds a long time.'

'Since the war. Once he got out of Auschwitz.'

'You've done your homework, Sean.'

He shrugged and took a hip flask out of the seat pocket in front.

'Drop of Bushmills, Bruce, keep you steady.' I took a swig. 'You think the arrogant fogging bastard's worth it?'

'I didn't like him much either,' I said, Malahide grunted. 'You got a grudge in there you're honing?'

'I'm not anti-semitic, if that's what you mean.'

'Why all the Goldstein crap?'

'Just teasing,' he said. 'I always behave badly when I'm away from home.' He capped the hip flask. 'We'll keep the rest for coffee.'

We drove through two towns. Just before Toulépleu we came off the road and headed west to the Liberian border, which at that point was the river Nipoué.

It was 4.30 a.m. by the time Sean eased himself out of the car with a coffee Thermos dangling from a finger and we walked down to a landing stage made of wooden planking over lashed oil drums. Malahide checked his watch and sat down, resting his heels on the oil drums. He poured the coffee and laced it.

'We're ten minutes early,' he said. 'So we'll sit ourselves down by this little river here and, *"like the long-legged fly on the stream, let our minds move upon silence"*. How's that, Bruce?'

'Very pretty, Sean,' I said. 'Who am I going to be talking to over there?'

'Well, you might meet the living cliché himself.'

'Cliché?'

'Samson Talbot. They had him in jail in the States, waiting to extradite him back here to face embezzlement charges. Somebody brought him a cake with a file in it and he sawed his way through the bars and let himself down on bedsheets. And that, I can assure you, doesn't happen very often. About as often as you'll see a cat amongst pigeons.'

'What do you think of him?'

'He's a bastard. He has to be. He's started a war with four hundred men against a proper army, and now he's got four thousand men and he's winning.'

'With a bit of help from his friends.'

'I've always been a great supporter of the underdog.'

'Not anti-semitic, but pro-Arab.'

'Now you're using it,' he said. 'Not anti-American, just pro-African.'

'Not anti-British, just pro-republican.'

'Not anti-British at all.'

'And the Libyans?' I asked, hearing him listening.

'A very proud people, the Libyans. A very understanding people. A people with a very good understanding of the underdog, I'd say.' He checked his watch. 'By God, it's black out here. A man might think he was dead if it wasn't for the sound of the water.'

He had a sense of timing, did Malahide; timing and a rare talent for terminating an inquiry with maximum threat.

'History,' he said. 'The human race is always reinviting history on itself. We never learn. We keep going over it, again and again, and we'll keep at it until the end of time and there's nothing you or I can do about it.'

'We don't have to get involved.'

'I've always preferred playing to spectating,' he said, and clicked on the torch three times. A single light flashed on the opposite bank and Malahide clicked his torch back on and held it between his knees. 'Give them something to aim at,' he said, putting the Thermos back together. 'Time to cross the river Styx, Bruce, and give you a sight of hell!'

A few minutes later the *pirogue* bumped into the oil drums.

We got in and they paddled us across to an open-topped jeep waiting on the other side. The driver, in army fatigues, drove with brutal efficiency, flicking through the gear changes, his face impassive, cheeks juddering over the rough road. We came into a village and joined a graded road which went north and then west. We ripped through a couple more villages, heading north again, and at first light we joined the main road.

'This'll take us into Gbarnga,' said Malahide.

The cloud was low after heavy rainfall and a mist hung over the wrecked terrain of dead and broken trees. There were acres of torn mud mashed with splintered wood and uprooted vegetation. Ragged gashes in the earth were filled with stagnant water and pigs scraped around upended tree stumps. After half an hour we slowed down for a checkpoint and the stench of rotting flesh was so strong it lodged itself in the back of the throat like an instant cancer.

Instead of sandbags, the checkpoint had been constructed out of bones and skulls, some with flesh and hair still attached, some being gnawed by rats and dogs which the soldiers ignored or didn't see. The men sat on stools, their eyes dead and unfocused, the smoking reefers dangling from limp fingers at their sides.

A boy soldier who couldn't have been more than twelve, wearing a T-shirt with a Rolling Stones tongue on it and rolled-up fatigues, was searching the car in front, prodding at things and people with his rifle which was only a couple of inches smaller than him. He laughed as he did it, showing a mouth of sharp white teeth which looked like splintered bone. He came to us and saw the white men and pointed the gun and blew us away with cinematic ease.

'I like to kill,' he whined, then more shrill laughter which, now that it was closer, broke in my head like a glass hangover. I was glad to be in an official jeep until I looked at the driver, who was more scared than we were. Malahide gave the boy a five-dollar note and he waved us through. We passed through the walls of human remains and watched a dog skittering off into the bush with a severed hand in its mouth.

There wasn't much traffic and we made good time until we got caught behind a truck with the slogan 'Here comes dead body trouble' painted on the back. It was filled with armed men dressed in pink towelling dressing gowns and day-glo tracksuits, some of them wearing blonde curly wigs, others with crash helmets on, some of them dancing, others hanging from the bare metal tarpaulin supports, passing joints to one another. We overtook them hitting a pothole which lifted Malahide clean out of his seat.

'As fine a bunch of fighting men as ever I've seen,' he shouted over his shoulder.

We made it to Gbarnga by 7.45 a.m. and drove through the streets filled with people starting the twelve-hour scavenge for food. There wasn't a piece of fruit in the town. There were leaves for sale, leaves and weeds. Dazed children with bloated bellies stood beside huge puddles in the road. Old people propped themselves up against destroyed buildings, their shattered faces staring out of rags, an empty plate in front of them as if they were guys and the kids were out collecting for them.

'They're selling water on the streets in Monrovia at ten dollars a litre,' said Malahide, as if it was a business we might get into.

We went to the police station and were shown into a room with a desk and a chair and a lakeside view of the empty compound. Malahide poured more coffee and heavier stiffeners and gave me another small flask for Ron. At 9.00 a.m. Malahide left for his meeting. An hour later I was taken to another office with three men in uniform with pips on their shoulders sitting behind a single desk. The middle one spoke, a pencil held in two hands, his eyes glancing down at a single sheet of paper on the desk.

'I am Colonel Joseph Aguma. I've been appointed by President Samson Talbot to negotiate on behalf of the Liberian Democratic Front. The terms for the release of the prisoner are as follows: The Ivory Coast government to unfreeze all LDF funds in Ivory Coast and allow free passage of arms from Burkina-Faso to Liberia. The equivalent of two million dollars in uncut diamonds with a value not less than forty thousand dollars per carat to be delivered to a prearranged location in Liberia where the prisoner will be exchanged. That is all.'

'You said "negotiate".'

'These are the terms.'

' "Negotiate" means we can discuss it.'

'No discussion.'

'In that case I want to see the prisoner.'

'Impossible,' said the officer on the left, which the other two weren't prepared for and they started to talk about it in Tui, so I joined in, silencing them.

'What're you people from Ghana side doing here?' I said. 'I thought this was Liberian war, not Ghana war.'

'We getting paid,' said the colonel, 'in dollars.'

'Better than Ghana job,' said one of the others.

'What about the killing? This big killing no be so?'

'The killing is very bad, but that between the people. The Gio and Mano people want revenge on the Krahn people. We not doing nothing for that.'

'But you see it.'

'Sometime, but most time we're not looking for the killing.'

'What about the checkpoints on the road to Gbarnga?'

'They are sick people, their heads in a muddle from cola, and weed.'

'You can't talk to them. They are lost people. They gone for hell,' said the colonel, and in those few short sentences I knew they wanted me to think better of them.

'Are you going to let me see this prisoner?'

'No problem,' the three of them said, and all looked at each other, amazed at the consensus.

An orderly took me out across the compound to another low building where the stink of incarcerated humanity hit me from thirty yards off. The jailer checked the bag of clothes I had for Ron and took me down a filthy shit-stinking corridor with cells on either side and hands coming at me through all the barred windows in the doors. The jailer cracked the arms and wrists with a thick, heavy cane. He opened up the penultimate door and showed me into a room which looked like it had been under dirty protest for a month. The light coming through the high window in the cell lit about a foot of ceiling and nothing more.

'What the fuck do you want?' said a voice from low down.

'Sounds like you, Ron.'

There was a sudden movement and Ron's head and bare shoulders appeared in the light that had crept a little further into the room.

'Fuck me. It's you.'

'You smell like an old badger. What happened to your clothes and your earring?'

'They left me with my Calvin Kleins. Nicked the rest.'

'Africans don't believe in fifty-dollar underpants. If they did you'd be naked. Do you fancy a nip?' I said, and handed him the hip flask. 'How did you pitch up in this hole?'

It was a long story with more horrors thrown in than I'd seen coming into Gbarnga. They'd crossed the Cavally river into the south east of Grand Gedeh and went into a village where two Krahn men had recently been captured. This being logging country, there was no shortage of chain saws and Ron had witnessed the execution of the two Krahns. The first by having his arms and legs sawn off, the second, who was naked hanging upside down, his wrists and ankles tied to a wooden frame, was sawn in half from the crotch to the cranium.

'The noise,' said Ron. 'You wouldn't believe the noise a chain saw makes going through flesh and bone.'

They'd got drunk on palm wine and smoked some grass, which took the edge off things. He'd been stripped at the same checkpoint we'd stopped at. There was a truck with a flat tyre with the legend 'Death no problem' and soldiers in women's clothes – dresses and housecoats, with bras on the outside – dancing to heavy metal. He'd been glad to get into the police cell.

I gave him the clothes, the belt I was wearing and the playing cards. He asked me why I was here.

'To get you out.'

'Now?'

'Soon. A few more days.'

'I've been thinking of Anat . . . a lot.'

'Play cards instead.'

'I have to marry that girl.'

'You will, Ron.'

'I don't and my life will go to shit.'

'Don't even think about it. Patience is a time-consuming game.'

'I want to tell you something. In case it all fucks up.'

'Don't tell me; it's not going to.'

'I want to tell you anyway.'

'Then tell me.'

'I love her . . .' he said, which was all that came out because something the size of a football got lodged in his chest and after those three words all he could do was swallow. I put my arm around him and he took a standing count of about thirty seconds, breathing it down, and then he asked about the terms.

'Two million dollars in uncut diamonds,' I said, which cheered him up, so I told him he'd be unbeatable at patience by the time he was released and he nearly fell for it.

I went back across the compound and into the colonel's office again. He was on his own, pretending to read some papers.

'We take good care of the prisoner?'

'He's OK for a man who's been in his underpants for a week,' I said.

'Those terms of yours. You're talking to the Ivorians about the first two?' He nodded. 'Where and when for the exchange?'

'On the border. We'll give you the time and location when we've finished talking to the Ivorians. *You* will make the exchange, nobody else. No guns, only the diamonds.'

After a courtesy knock Malahide came in, looking as if he'd just lapped the cream.

'Are you done, Bruce?'

'You're winning, Sean?'

'I'm not losing.'

We drove back to the regular border crossing in the same jeep, a light drizzle falling. We had little trouble from the checkpoints. Some of them were strangely silent, with just the sound of the light rain on leaves, the smell of woodsmoke, the sight of a pair of boots still on some feet, lifeless in a doorway, the dogs and rats going about their business and the shattered forest standing back, looking on.

23

Malahide's driver met us at the border and drove us back to
Man with a fresh bottle of Bushmills on the back seat
between us, our heads and shoulders soaked through and
the rain still coming down, but heavier. They dropped me at
the PTT. I called Martin Fall, who hit me with a couple of
hundred questions until I was blethering anything that came
into my head.

'We're talking to the Ivorians too,' he said. 'So are the
Americans, and now the French have got involved, which
has pissed the Yanks off mightily. The French put up a trans-
mitter/receiver for Samson Talbot some months back and
the Yanks didn't much like that. The Ivorians are going to
say one thing to keep the Americans happy and let everything flow for Samson Talbot. They think they're backing a
winner. All the Americans can think of is Libya — Libya and
Lockerbie. If Talbot's Libyan-backed they don't want him.
As for the diamonds, well, I don't think that's going to be a
problem for Collins and Driberg.'

I told him I was going back to Korhogo via Abidjan until
the exchange; he could leave messages at the Novotel and I
gave him the Korhogo number.

Bagado had been sleeping, his face was puffy. He lay under
a cold towel and said he'd been boozing all afternoon.

'It's the only thing to do on a wet afternoon.'

'It was work.'

'My kind of work.'

'Where were you when I needed you?'

'Who were you drinking with?'

'Two businessmen from England.'

'Not many of them around here.'

'They don't speak French, either. They were cagey about what they were doing until we started drinking. I told them I was in sheanut and we were doing development work up north and around Guinée. They said they sold educational and scientific equipment. Like what? I asked them. Rain gauges, they said. They were both wearing hand-made shoes, thousand-pound lightweight suits, one's got a Rolex, the other a Patek Philippe. I thought, "We should be in the rain-gauge business". Then after an hour or two they told me they work for IMIT. International Machine and Instrument Technology based in Nuneaton. I remember the name but not what they do, but I know it's more than rain gauges. I call Brian, my detective friend in London, and he tells me they make weapons. They're arms salesmen.'

'Another supplier. They could be working with Malahide to take away some of the business from the Libyans. He was looking pleased with himself this afternoon.'

'It's another piece on the board,' said Bagado. 'This game's filling up.'

He gave me the bad news after that, which was that we'd missed the flight out of Man and there wasn't another until Monday. We were on the overnight bus to Abidjan. I went to my room and showered and slept. A knock on the door tugged me out of it.

It was a man I didn't know. A white man with straggly long grey hair and matching beard who smoked a cheroot which he must have rolled himself, using dried dung. He took it out of his mouth and spat on to the floor.

'Howard Corben,' he said, in an American accent, holding out a claw. He was wearing brown and very damp clothes. The shirt looked as if it was the first he'd ever made and he'd done it from memory rather than go through the fag of using a pattern. He had a leather satchel, stained dark from the rain, and a camera with a macramé strap. His trousers had a six-inch tuck in the waist and were held up with string, the bottoms were stuffed into woollen socks whose furred ends were iced with chocolate mud.

'Bruce Medway,' I said. 'I'd ask you in . . .'

'It might be better,' he said, and side-stepped past me into the room.

I dressed and shaved and asked Corben if he wanted a drink, but he was already in the mini-bar.

'I saw you coming out of Liberia this morning,' he said.

'Who are you?'

'Howard Corben. I told you.'

'Where'd you learn that sense of humour?'

'I'm a freelance journalist.'

'How'd you find me?'

'I saw you at the border. So I took a bush taxi to Man, came here, paid some money and they told me where the two-metre white guy's room was.'

'And now?'

'I thought we could talk about what you were doing in Liberia with Sean Malahide.'

'You know him?'

'Sure.'

'Ask him, then.'

'He lives out of town and I don't have his home phone number.'

'You mean you've got a better chance with me.'

'Could be.'

'You tell me something, Howard. I'll tell you something back.'

'How 'bout vice versa.'

'Bye-bye.'

'Shoot.'

'James Wilson. Found dead in Abidjan last week.'

'Guts ripped out by the Leopard.'

'The paper I read said he was involved in the handover of the Liberian president to Jeremiah Finn and the President's Krahn tribe paid him back. What can you tell me about it?'

'You got something to blow that story open again?'

'We had a deal, Howard, don't go falling at the first fence.'

He poured himself a whole miniature and remembered to offer me one.

'Beer to chase?' he asked. I nodded. 'You got any real

cigarettes?' I shook my head. He sat down. Comfortable.

'James Wilson. Now that is a can of worms, a goddam drum of worms with a nest of vipers on top. Shit. The first thing is I gotta go back to June this year. In June James Wilson went to the States with a delegation of Krahn supporters of the Liberian president. They wanted to tell the US what a great guy he was and the US told them, you gotta be kidding.'

'Who in the US?'

'A unit of West African specialists.'

'Appointed by the US president?'

'The President of the USA is well clear of this shit, not even in the same room as the fan. So, the US, I mean this policy unit, says the Liberian president has to go. That's the only way the fighting's gonna stop. On to the stage walks Godwin Patterson, an Americo-Liberian who's a friend of the Liberian president, same masonic lodge and all that shit, organized funds for him from the other A-Ls in the States. My Washington pals tell me Patterson and Wilson had meetings with each other, with none of the other delegates present. When the delegation goes back to Liberia, Patterson is with them. He introduces Wilson to the President, so Wilson goes from peripheral Krahn supporter to ace buddy.

'Now, that is something I found out after the President was captured in the port in Monrovia on September the ninth by Jeremiah Finn at what was supposed to be a three-way peace settlement between Finn, the ECOWAS peacekeepers and the Liberian president. I also found out that James Wilson visited the port twice in the morning before the President turned up on September the ninth to talk to the ECOWAS guys and Jeremiah Finn visited the US Embassy in Monrovia three times on the same morning . . . September the ninth.'

'What was the peace settlement?'

'The President and his guard were going to get free passage out of Monrovia with US visas and money. Finn was going to get the bits of Monrovia he hadn't already secured. And ECOWAS were going to implement a peace plan, including an interim Liberian government. That, as you know, did not happen.

'From midday on September the ninth Finn's men were going around the port evacuating people, telling them something's gonna happen at two p.m. The presidential convoy turned up at the port at one-forty-five that afternoon. The ECOWAS troops disarmed the guard. At two o'clock Finn turned up with his troops and they let them in fully armed. They killed something like seventy people in the presidential guard, shot the President in the legs and took him. How does that sound to you, Bruce?'

'Everybody knew what was going on except for the President and his guard.'

'Right. A set-up. But there's no proof.'

'There's that film of Finn torturing the President and speaking to the embassy on the radio.'

'I've seen that piece of shit. Makes out he's got the embassy on line and says, "We got him, we got the President." It doesn't stand up. It's a crock.'

'So why'd James Wilson get it?'

'This is it. The can of worms I was talking about. This is the bit that nobody knows except for a few journalists who were still hanging out in Monrovia after the President bought it. I'm not sure *I* even know it. I mean, I don't know how I know it, if I do. You get me?'

'Drink some more whisky, Howard.'

'This is fact: An embassy cleaner called Joe Biécké was found dead in the Sinkor quarter of Monrovia, September the twelfth. He'd been shot in the head and his abdomen ripped open. His heart and liver were missing.'

'What about the wire garrotte?'

'One of the few differences.'

'What's the bit you don't know how you know?'

'Joe Biécké found a wire in the cistern in the men's bathroom in the US Embassy. No tape, just the device.'

'Not the kind of thing that comes out in a press briefing.'

'No. That's why I don't know how I got to know about it. It kinda flew into the circle of journalists I was with like

224

airborne bacteria; we all caught it, but nobody knows where from.'

'What happened to Godwin Patterson?'

'Back in the States. Left a couple of days before the President was taken.'

'Anybody else turn up dead?'

'Plenty, but not with their guts ripped open.'

'Why didn't you stick at the story?'

'First off, we were all looking for Wilson. Can't find him. The guy's gone to ground. We figured he was trying to get out of Liberia and to do that he had to get out of Monrovia first, which was controlled by Finn, so maybe it took some time. Nobody saw him at the port that afternoon, so he might have already started running. Whatever, the first we heard was when he turned up dead in Abidjan nearly seven weeks later and the story was kinda cold by then.'

'How do I know you're who you say you are and what you do?'

Howard took out some press accreditation, a US passport and some cuttings from the *Philly Bulletin*.

'How do I know you're a straight journo and not doing anything extra-curricular for the US government?'

'You're difficult to please, Bruce. How about thinking about what I just told you?'

'Do you know anybody on the World Service?'

'Try Mike Carter, you hearda him?'

I called the number Howard gave me from his book and got through to Mike Carter, who said he couldn't think of anybody less likely to be working for the US government than Howard Corben. He added that he was a complete bastard and to tell him, which I did.

'We don't always see eye to eye, Mike and me,' said Corben. 'I can be a bit too underground for his BBC ass. You know what I mean?'

Bagado knocked and I ran him through what Corben had said, and it set him off like something clockwork, pacing up and down the room clicking his thumbnail against his teeth, while Corben and I sat between the beds and drank. I filled him in on Fat Paul, Kurt Nielsen, Kantari, 'Red' Gilbert and the package. Corben was writing it all down in a notebook, in shorthand that looked like bird prints in the snow, and he was cackling to himself as he did it.

'One thing,' he said, flipping his notebook shut, 'you know where James Wilson was staying when he got killed? The Hilton. The guy was on the payola.'

'But what's so funny?' asked Bagado.

'There's nothing in the package.'

'We *think* there's nothing in the package. We didn't know about the wire, we weren't looking for an audio tape,' I said.

'Wilson might have taped a meaningful conversation, he might not have. He might have had a tape, he might not have had one, too. The important thing is that somebody thought he did,' said Corben.

'What about Patterson?' asked Bagado.

'He's in the States.'

'I mean if Patterson put Wilson close to the President so that he could set him up and paid him for it. Who instructed Patterson?'

'Patterson established contact with Wilson during a delegation visit to Washington. That sounds like he's taking orders from, or he's in the pay of, a US agency,' I said.

'And a US agency, if it didn't firebomb Fat Paul's office, definitely searched his house,' said Bagado.

'What about checking the names of the US West African policy unit and advisers against people who were in the Monrovian US Embassy around September the ninth?' asked Corben. 'That way we might find out if there was a connection between the Wilson/Patterson link made in Washington and what happened on the ground in Monrovia port.'

'Can you do that, Mr Corben?' asked Bagado.

'I surely can, Mr Bagado,' said Corben. 'It might not prove anything, the CIA can be dumb but not all the time.' He paused then, just long enough so that we were both looking. 'There is one consideration that might make the forward progress of this little investigation . . . problematic.'

We didn't say anything.

'I'm broke, guys, no more of the green-backed monster, fresh out of spit to lick.'

'What about the *Philly Bulletin*?'

'They terminated my contract. I am really extremely free-lance right now. I came here to do some pieces on the election tomorrow, the refugee camps and arms traffic to the rebels, but I have no certain buyers for the work. I'm staying in a fat cow's back room with no bathroom for one thousand five hundred CFA a night. This has been my first whisky in three weeks. I don't eat. This is not my shirt.'

'It's OK, Howard, we're weeping already.'

Bagado and I each gave him seventy-five thousand CFA and the telephone numbers in Abidjan and Korhogo. Corben stashed the money all over himself.

'It's been very interesting talking to you about James Wilson and that,' he said, 'but as you know, that was not my original line of inquiry. It's scratch-my-back time, Brucey-babe. What were you doing with Malahide?'

Bagado was standing behind Corben now and shook his head. Corben had the full range of journalistic sensitivities – the rhino skin, a cat's gut and a nose for rats.

'Don't go holding back on me, you two, now that we're friends.'

'Malahide's contacted the rebels for us.'

'Well, Bruce, I kinda guessed that, but I also know that two and two never equals four. Why d'you need to speak to the rebels, and if it's not too much of a cliché – who *are* you guys?'

'That,' said Bagado, 'is a very good question.'

'I'm in the question business,' said Corben, 'and when I don't get answers . . .'

'You make them up,' I said.

'Only if the truth's a bit constipated or what I come up with is more interesting. The truth, you know, can be awful dull.'

'We're freelancers,' I said.

'Freelance what?'

I looked at Bagado, who was checking out the ceiling.

'Investigators,' I said.

'You know, Bruce, you don't sound very sure to me. Maybe I should ask who's payin' you to investigate what.'

'The official line is that we're a charitable organization.'

Corben fell back on the bed and roared. I didn't think it was that funny, but then I hadn't been dipped in cynicism and hard-boiled in china glaze like he had.

'You done some kinda media training to come up with that kinda bullshit?'

'I'll tell you what we're doing,' I said. 'But not now.'

'When?'

'Next week.'

'Monday?'

'I doubt it.'

'OK. I tell you what. I give you the stuff from Washington when you give me the Malahide connection.'

'I can give you *some* dirt on Malahide now,' I said, and Corben's notebook flipped open. 'He's doing some small arms shipments . . .'

'. . . to Ireland,' said Corben. 'I been to the timber yard.'

'You spoke to Ajamian?' He nodded. 'The only other thing we know is that he has a lot of Libyan stamps in his passport and he's a great supporter of the underdog.'

'I'm smelling something,' said Corben. 'I'm smelling something bad from that guy.'

'Here's a theory,' I said, 'nothing to do with the Krahns paying Wilson back, nothing to do with the Americans setting the President up. Malahide. Malahide has access to Liberia. He *could* have killed Biécké. He was in Abidjan at the time of the Wilson, Nielsen and Fat Paul killings. He could have an interest in the tape, if it exists. That tape buys him influence. He has a leopard skin draped over a carving in his house which he tells me makes the wearer invisible so that he can observe good and evil in the community. When he sees the evil . . . he rips it out.'

Corben nodded, sizing us up.

'You still want me to talk to Washington?'

'It's all circumstantial.'

'So what colour is the Leopard?'

'Black,' I said.

'White,' said Bagado.

'I'll go for spotted,' said Corben, finishing his drinks.

He packed up his satchel and asked to use the bathroom. Bagado's hands hung limply at his sides, his shoulders sagging. Corben came out of the bathroom.

'Don't smoke in there for a few minutes,' he said, and left.

'Is Malahide the Leopard?' asked Bagado. 'Do you think there's a connection between the James Wilson package and the Ron Collins kidnap?'

'Don't waste your brain cells on that one, Bagado. It was just something to throw in the pot.'

'If he is then he must know who you are, he must know that you have the tape to send "Red" after you, but . . . he's letting you off the hook. Why would he do that?'

'The diamond deal is more important than the tape. The tape would be useful. It would improve his business position but it doesn't implicate him in any way. It's not *his* arse on the line if the world knows that the Americans were involved in getting rid of the Liberian president. Diamonds and arms are money.'

'If you were the Leopard would you hang your uniform in the living room?'

'You haven't met Malahide.'

'I asked you if he was insane.'

'No, he's just a teaser. He likes to stir things up.'

'You know what I would do if I was the Leopard after that tape? I'd watch Kantari. He led them to Nielsen. They must know he's the buyer.'

'I've already been to see Kantari.'

'Which means they're not watching him, or they're watching him and biding their time, or Kantari has already met the Leopard and we don't know about it.'

'Why don't we stop talking about this until we've taken the package to pieces and found that audio tape . . . if it's there.'

'All right,' said Bagado, lying down on the bed. 'Let's talk about something else.'

'What did you have in mind, Bagado?' I asked, recognizing the tone of voice.

'Let's talk about Heike.'

'One of my other unsolved problems,' I said. 'Do we have to? She must be paying you to do this.'

'She doesn't need to. I know a good woman when I see one.'

'And a bad one.'

'Just the wrong one.'

'When did you appoint yourself my guardian angel?'

'The day I met you.'

'Was it that obvious I needed one?'

'We all need one at some time or other.'

'Some more than most.'

'Only when they've decided to diverge from their destiny.'

'Christ, I didn't know it was that serious. I thought I was just taking an interest in the condition of another fellow human. I really had no idea I was diverging from my destiny. Had I known —'

'What happens in the next few days will decide whether you're going to be a lonely man . . . or not.'

'How do I know Heike is going to come back?'

'If she does and she finds you with Dotte, you will be a very lonely man.'

'But if she doesn't.'

'I didn't realize you were that afraid,' he said, sitting up.

'Maybe it *would* be better if we talked about Malahide.'

'Yes. I've always found solace in solving crimes. It's as nothing compared to the detection work you have to do on yourself.'

24

Sunday 3rd November
The bus arrived in Abidjan at 6.30 a.m. We took a taxi from
the *gare routière* to the Novotel in Plateau, where it was sunny
with a stiff breeze blowing off the sea. It was election day
and people were out in the street getting excited, but not
so excited that they'd attract the attention of the *loubars*,
military-dressed thugs, paid to beat some sense into opposition FPI members.

At the Novotel the girl who'd given me the cakes was off
and had been replaced by a tougher, middle-aged woman who
worked with her elbows out. She gave us a room and said we'd
have to be out by 4.00 p.m. I asked her for the packages from
the safe and she stonewalled us until Bagado hit the desk hard
enough for her complicated hairpiece to take off into the back
office. We got the packages and went up to the room.

Bagado unscrewed the cassette and lifted out the two
spools. He checked the casing, which was clean, and the
inside of the spools, clean too. Then he unwound the tape.
Close to the end he saw a lighter brown audio tape stuck to
the inside of the darker VHS magnetic tape. Bagado peeled
off the slice of Sellotape securing it and unwound the rest.

'Now we need a dictaphone, a cassette and some Sellotape,' he said, looking at me, letting me know I was the
younger man and it was time to get on with it. He said he
was going to shower and for me to take the room key.

I went down to the lobby and out into Avenue Général
de Gaulle and found my way blocked off by the widespread
arms of David, the cocoa-cutter I'd got out of prison last
Wednesday.

'My brother,' he greeted me, giving me the fluffy chicken handshake followed by the finger click, Ghanaian-style.

'I'm busy, you know that,' I said, walking down Rue du Commerce with him at my shoulder, following a tall, slim African woman holding her wraparound western dress in a sheaf halfway up her thigh, the wind wanting to tear it off her back.

'Is jes' I'm thinkin', I like you, Mr Bruce. I like to work for you.'

'I haven't got a job for you.'

'You must have job.'

'What can you do?'

'You have car, I clean it.'

'I have a driver, too.'

'Ah-haaa,' he said, letting that sink in. 'I'm ver' strong. I proteck you.'

'I don't need protection. What makes you think I need protection?'

'Ever'body need protection. Why you in jail? You doin' somethin' dangerous. You doin' dangerous thin's, you need protection.'

'I haven't got the money for it, even if I needed it.'

'Money no problem.'

'You work for free?'

'Noooooooooo,' he said, 'free trial mebbe.'

'Mebbe,' I said and clapped him on the back. I told him to come to the Novotel at 2.00 p.m. I went into the only open electronic goods shop and bought a dictaphone. They sold me some used Sellotape they had in there too. On the way out somebody bumped into me from the side and I stiffened as I felt a hard nozzle jab me under the ribs.

'Let's go for a walk,' said an American voice with a heavy cold. 'Look straight ahead, keep calm, and move it.'

The nozzle moved to my kidney and nudged me forward and I walked back down the street to the Novotel. I crossed the street again when the voice told me to, and turned left just before the hotel and walked down a steep side street towards the lagoon. We turned left into a dead-end alley and stopped.

'Turn around,' he said.

'Eugene,' I said, almost pleased to see him. 'What took you so long? It's been nearly a week.'

'The name's "Red",' he said. 'I been busy with other things.'

'You couldn't find me?'

'It took some time. You a lucky man, Bruce Medway. Been moving around, making things hard for me.'

'I've spent a couple of nights in the Novotel. It shouldn't have been too difficult.'

'I been sick.'

'The lagoon?' I asked, and he nodded. 'You lied to me, Eugene.'

'I did? How come?'

'You said you couldn't swim.'

'Oh, right. What I meant was, I don't like to get wet. Misunderstanding, you get me? Where's the package?' he asked, tightening up.

'In my room.'

'What's in the bag?'

'A dictaphone. I have some letters to tape.'

'Sounds like you found something you shouldn't have.'

'What would that be?'

'Is there somebody else in the room?' I didn't answer. 'Right, so there's somebody else in the room,' he said. 'We get there, you tell him to lie on the bed, face down, hands behind his head. You open the door and stand in the doorway. He not on the bed, I'm gonna put a bullet in the back of your leg. He on the bed, we go in. You pick up the tape. We leave.'

'You going to shoot the guy on the bed or make it worth his while?'

'We'll have to see.'

'No deal.'

'Whaddyamean, no deal?'

'I'm not going to do it.'

This was not in Eugene's script, so he decided to give himself some more time by aiming the gun at my right leg, just above the knee. The wind was thumping around the alley and making him nervous with odd, unexpected noises. An empty plastic bag ripped past his back and took off into the sky and his head twitched. He wasn't wearing gloves this time.

'Keep calm, Eugene . . .'

'Red.'

'I don't say it to annoy you. I just forget. You don't look like a Red to me, that's all. Too sensitive for a Red.'

'Shut the fuck up. We going to the room.'

'I'm not. I told you it's no deal and I don't know how you're going to make me do it. You shoot me in the leg and I'm definitely not going to do it. I'm going to sit down and cry. So let's have a talk.'

'The man said, "If he get difficult, kill him." You gettin' difficult's my opinion.' He raised the gun, aiming at my head this time, with a different look coming down the barrel.

'He said that, did he?'

'Hm-mmmmm.'

'Who's the man? Maybe we could talk about this with him.'

'He don't want to see you,' he said, his voice weak and a little distant for my liking. 'He just want the tape.'

'What happens after I give you the tape?'

'You free to go.'

'Is that what Mr Malahide said?'

'You think I got pigshit for brains, don't you?' he said, and fired a bullet across my face about four inches past my right ear, which took a chunk of concrete out of the building five yards behind me. 'Heee, this wind strong. I don' normally miss this kinda range. Lemme try again. Get it right, Red. Get it right.'

He moved to his left and leaned against the wall, the gun still head high, his arm out straight. I was looking hard at that gun, the sweat coming off me in pint drops into my eyes so that I wasn't sure if my vision was on the button or not. It looked as if David had appeared at the corner of the alley, a couple of yards behind Eugene.

'OK, Red,' I said, 'we'll go and get the tape.'

'Now you talking sense at last,' he said, and pushed himself off the wall lowering his gun arm. David closed in on it. Eugene, suddenly aware of shadow in the alley, pulled his arm up and swung round, his wrist slapping into David's massive palm. I leapt forward, there was a thud from the gun and a chip of concrete flew, then there was a cracking and grinding noise which was Eugene's wrist, both radius and ulna, snapping in David's cocoa-cutter's hand. The gun fell to the ground and I side-kicked it towards the opening of the alley. David was holding Eugene, who was sagging to the ground, by his broken wrist. I told him about the knife and David cuffed Eugene across the face with a short six-inch jab from his other fist and Eugene's head clicked back as if it was broken at the neck.

'Mebbe this a good time to aks you the job again?'

'You've got the job, David. Now wait here. Don't touch the gun. I'm going to call Gbondogo.'

It wasn't so easy to get through to Gbondogo on election day. Maybe he had his hands full terrorizing voters. I told him I had Eugene Amos Gilbert and he said he'd have two officers and a car around there in ten minutes. By the time I got back to the alley Eugene still hadn't come round.

'I hope you didn't kill him, David,' I said, trying to get Eugene's eyes to work on their own inside his slack face.

'I only smack him small like pikin.'

David was wearing some oily shorts and a T-shirt that was running about him trying to keep the whole thing covered. I gave him some money and told him to buy some trousers and T-shirts that fitted.

'And no palm wine or beer,' I said. 'You work for me, I can't afford the furniture.'

Eugene started coming round out of the black and into some bright, white pain. His eyes were pinched closed and his mouth racked open tight at the corners.

'What the fuck happened?'

'You got hit by a train. Now listen, Red. Who's the tape for? I need a name.'

'Go fuck yoursel',' he said, looking down at his wrist which lay at an impossible angle on his stomach.

'When the police arrive I can either say you've been cooperative or you've been a pain in the arse. You talk to me and they might even fix up your wrist so that you can use it. You don't and you'll never make a hit with your right hand again. You'll never get out into the fresh air to make a hit with your right hand again. What's it to be?'

'Like I said, go fuck yoursel'.'

'OK. If you can't give me a name, just nod. Is it Sean Malahide?'

The air hissed between his teeth. His wrist was swollen, fat as a puff adder and a lump had appeared on the side of his face.

'Suck my cock, kwi man.'

'I'd tell you to go and see some decent movies, improve your vocabulary, but you're going to a dark hole, Eugene, and you're never going to come out.'

The police arrived and bagged the knife and gun. I didn't need to tell them Eugene was a pain in the arse, they knew. They threw him in the back of the van and cuffed him and he passed out. I told the officers that if he talked to Gbondogo I wanted to know what he said and gave them 2,000 CFA each to make sure.

Bagado was clean, in bed and asleep when I nudged him. He looked at his watch from under a hand held to his frown as if it was a long way off.

'They gave you a choice of seven and you had to read all the manuals?'

'I met Eugene and I've employed a monster.'

'You youngsters,' said Bagado, taking the bag.

Bagado spliced the tape into the cassette. We sat on the bed and listened to it. It opened on a toilet flushing, a tap running, hands being washed, people talking about a pre-season game between the Cowboys and the 49ers and none of it that clear because whoever was wearing the mike had it located under clothing. Footsteps in the corridor, the man sat down. Other footsteps approached, quicker, staccato with heels. A woman's voice said, 'Hi, Jimmy.'

'You're looking very nice, Miss Callahan.'

'Thanks, Jimmy.'

Some throat-clearing. Then back to the toilet. Locking the booth. The wire was clicked off, then back on again. Toilet flushing again. Back down the corridor, taking a seat. A door opened.

'You can go in now, Jimmy,' said Miss Callahan's voice. Footsteps. Another door opening. Then a voice, distant, boomy and indistinct.

'Hi, Jimmy, take a seat. You OK?'

'Bad stomach . . .' He spoke as he sat down and if he said the man's name we lost it.

'OK, I'll be quick,' the other man's voice said, pacing up and down now and speaking, the voice coming and going. 'ECOWAS can vouch for port security for one hour between fourteen hundred hours and fifteen hundred hours in the afternoon tomorrow, ninth September. The President and his entourage should get there fifteen minutes before fourteen hundred hours. It's gonna take that kinda time for them to disarm. So latest thirteen-forty-five, you understand? How many in the entourage, Jimmy?'

'A hundred and twelve.'

'That's a lot of people to talk peace, Jimmy. Does he need that many?'

'There's nothing I can do 'bout it. They just decided that today. The guard go where he goes. They don't want him running away without them.'

'I see. So. Fourteen hundred hours, Jeremiah Finn arrives.'

'How are ECOWAS gonna play it in the port?'

'Whaddyamean?'

'I mean, they're gonna have enough soldiers on the ground to move a hundred and twelve palace-guard troops away from the gates, so that when Finn arrives . . .'

'They won't see a thing. We'll put up a wall of twenty-foot containers. Finn's men'll arrive and the ECOWAS people'll be out there. Finn's men have the layout of the port. They know exactly where everybody's gonna be. They'll walk in there and take the big man out.'

'I don't want them to take out the whole of the palace guard.'

'I hope they won't, too. But that is not under our control. Now, you've got the President primed. He's coming to the port to discuss standing down. That means: when he's gonna do it, when he's gonna leave the country, the number of visas he wants for his people, his future, their future. No talks unless that is understood. Right? You gotta keep that side of the story straight. You start making other things look possible, he's gonna smell something. The guy's paranoid enough as it is.'

'Everything's OK.'

'Once this is over the ECOWAS troops will assume control of Monrovia. An interim government will be appointed and free elections will take place within one year.'

'What about Jeremiah Finn?'

'Jeremiah Finn is in control of some key locations in and around Monrovia. He has to allow the transition of power. Don't worry . . .' We lost the end of that sentence under door-knocking and opening.

'Miss Truelove, what can I do for you?'

'General Akosombo is here, we're taking him down to the conference room.'

'I'll be right along.'

Door closed.

'You got the money, Jimmy?'

'I got it.'

'Get the President there for thirteen-forty-five tomorrow afternoon and prepare yourself to become a part of the history of your country.'

Barely audible under the rustling of clothes, the footsteps and the door opening came the line, 'Blessed are the peacemakers . . .' The rest was lost. James Wilson returned to the toilet and the tape finished.

'James Wilson sets himself up for life,' I said.

'He did that very well. It's not so easy to get somebody to say something when you're wearing a wire, and he got him to say what he wanted, except the most important thing. He didn't get him to say his name.'

'He did, we lost it. It doesn't matter, somebody's going to recognize the voice. We'll try it on Corben.'

I put the video cassette back in its envelope and sealed it, using Fat Paul's scorpion ring and the wax I'd bought; the copy I threw in the bin. The audio cassette I put in my pocket.

I called Martin Fall at his Hampshire farmhouse and got Anne, his wife, my ex, who sounded affectionate and cosy, which wrenched at the thought of what might have been if

. . . If I'd been a different person. She told me that he'd gone, not out of the country, just to the London office. He was due to call before takeoff. He was flying private, she said, in a Lear jet hired by Collins & Driberg. That was all I wanted to know.

I called Rademakers at the hospital but they said he wasn't available to talk. I arranged to see Chantale Leubas, Rademakers's 'secretary', and as I drove out to Deux Plateaux to see her I felt the trail cooling on me.

Once Chantale Leubas had let me in, puffed her hair, played with her diamond rings and tamed her loose and disobedient gown, she set about disarming my questions with amused honesty. She told me what she did for Rademakers, how she served him coffee and allowed him certain privileges. How at other times she had to be a little stricter.

'He has very fast hands,' she said. 'I think from playing with small things for too long.'

I didn't stay long. She told me what I already knew. That I was sniffing in the wrong place. She stopped me with her arm as I was leaving and whispered in my ear, her lips making contact.

'Ce n'est jamais la putain.'

She opened the sliding doors for me and tapped the aluminium frame with her rings.

'Have you ever done anything for a man called Sean Malahide?' I asked.

'No,' she said, the rings getting impatient on the metal, so that I was reminded of someone else with an interest in diamonds.

'Al Trzinski?'

She grunted and shuddered.

'That man is an animal,' she said, and slid the door shut.

25

We rolled into Korhogo at 10.00 at night and the post-election parties were swinging. We drove through streets full of people who'd just exercised their democratic right in what passed for a free and fair election. We'd had another hard day on African roads and the six of us looked as if we knew who'd won and had come to poop the party. The compound was dark and empty but we could hear the thump of the music coming from the bar in the middle of the shanty town across the street.

Everybody went to bed. I sat in the kitchen and listened to the bass track which came into my head via my feet, and a heaviness came over me – not physical tiredness, but a malaise, a soul sickness that settled on me whenever I was in this house. I poured whisky over a handful of ice and sipped it and waited to ease into the cure, looking at the striplight reflected in the window. Dotte came in with wet hair, a wrap around her waist and a very loose-knit vest on top, through which her nipples were protruding. She found a pack of cigarettes on a shelf, lit one and leaned against the sideboard.

'Do you like this place?' I asked.

'It suits my mood sometimes.'

'You don't look the suicidal type.'

'Let's go and sit outside with the bottle,' she said. 'Wait for the rain. It's coming. That's what does it.'

We sat facing each other, leaning against a post each on the verandah.

'Aren't you going to start?' she asked.

'No questions. I'm all quizzed out.'

'Been asking too many?'

'And answering.'

'It would be good to just be, wouldn't it?'

'If they'd had prelapsarian pizza Adam would never've gone for the apple and we wouldn't have any of this crap.'

'You believe in original sin?'

'People's sins are getting more original every day.'

I drank, poured another measure and looked into the night to see if the storm was coming to loosen up the atmosphere.

'Talking in the dark is easy,' said Dotte.

'Listening is easier.'

'You're not helping me.'

'All right. Tell me what happened to Kurt. You said he killed a man.'

She took a couple of long drags on the cigarette, gathering herself.

'We were in Hamburg. Kurt was doing a deal with a guy who ran girls at a live-performance sex club just off the Reeperbahn. They bought the stuff by the kilo, I mean, a girl has to get out of her head to go on stage with a pig. Kurt had just bought a gun. A guy had pulled a knife on him and taken him for half a kilo and twenty-five thousand marks, so he bought a gun. I was watching from the car. Kurt went up to the guy at the back of the sex club, where they kept the bins. They talked. The guy didn't pull a knife or anything. He was leaning against the gate with his hands in his back pockets, looking cocky — stubborn. Then they stopped talking. Kurt took his gun out and pointed it at the guy. The guy took his hands out of his pockets and shook his head. He had the money for the dope in his hand. Kurt shot him and took the money. He got in the car, and we drove out of Hamburg. He didn't say a word. He never said anything about it. I watched it play on his mind, break him down, but he never let me talk about it with him.'

She got up, went into the kitchen and came back with the cigarettes.

'We don't *have* to talk about this,' I said.

'It's on my mind. He's dead and it's on my mind.'

241

'Was that what was on your mind when we came out here?'

'No.'

The light from the kitchen picked out the strands of her wet hair, but kept her face in shadow. Then she turned and the half light opened up her cheek and painted round an eye socket, the corner of her mouth, the cigarette going up to it. She seemed as far away as the night she first stood in the squares of light from the window . . . and yet . . .

'Do you remember the first thing that changed you?' she asked.

'There are degrees of change . . .'

'I mean the first time you realized that innocence was not a permanent state.'

'My father died when I was sixteen. That was the end of childhood, but it is for most people anyway.'

Dotte smoked. I took an inch off my watery whisky and replaced it with an inch of neat stuff. Bagado was right. There wasn't much light coming from this woman. Especially now, talking about this stuff – Kurt killing a man because the guy wanted to talk money. Dotte's head clicked back against the post.

'You saw when we left Korhogo the first time . . .'

'You don't have to tell me this, Dotte. I don't *need* to know. I'm curious but you don't *have* to tell me.'

'They all want to know,' she cut in. 'They all want to know why I'm like this. The "mystery woman", some of them call me. I'd ask them if they really wanted to know what it's like being me. I'd give them a look and they'd get scared. They didn't really want to know, you see. They'd prefer it served up as a fiction. If it's too brutal they think that some of it might rub off on them. Taint their lives. But to me there's no mystery. It's a very simple tale. But they never saw that because they were thinking how much it would enrich their lives to know it.'

'That's why I'm saying, Dotte: you don't *have* to tell me.'

'But I want to tell you,' she said. 'That first night in Abidjan I saw the same in you . . . and Kurt's the only person I've told and he's dead now.'

242

'Is it going to help?'

'It's not a question of help or understanding, if that's what you mean. I don't know what it's like to have killed a man, but doesn't it help you that somebody ... sympathetic knows?'

'You mean empathetic ...' I said, and thought about that. I thought about if Bagado hadn't been there when I killed the man in that warehouse over a month ago, if there hadn't been someone who understood why it had to be done, the circumstances. I thought about the relief at seeing Eugene, a death that could have played on my conscience because I hadn't needed to do it.

'You'd better tell me,' I said, and she lit another cigarette for strength.

'When I was ten I found myself looking through a crack in my bedroom door at my father coming out of the bathroom. He knew I was watching. He turned, his towel fell away and I felt my whole body blush. I threw myself back into bed and lay there with the sheets over my head, the cold sheets on my hot body with the first sight of my father's penis in my head.

'It was like coming alive. I was fascinated by it. A silly girl's fascination with no brother to help out. I didn't think about it any more after that. But my father did.

'He'd come into my room while I was dressing. He'd pull me on to his lap and I'd feel him hardening underneath me. He'd take a pee while I was in the bath. Then the next summer my mother was diagnosed with cancer. She had a hysterectomy and that was the end of their sex life. My father had cooled off a lot since my mother was at home all the time. Then she died and he was broken up by it. I slept in his bed to comfort him. I was lonely myself. And that was how it happened. I didn't know how to say no. I couldn't say no to my own father.

'After a year or so I got pregnant and that was the end of it. He tried to make me terminate it. I wouldn't. I felt so bad by then I didn't want to feel worse. I was just under fourteen when I had Katrina. A year and a half later my father was killed in a car accident. I went to live with his elder brother

243

and it would have happened all over again, but I was older by then. I knew how to say no.

'So you see, it's a simple tale, with a long repercussion. People from the social services told me it explained a lot. Why I took drugs, why I stole things and prostituted myself. It never explained anything to me.'

'How much does Katrina know?'

'She doesn't know that my father is hers. She hasn't asked for some time. She attached herself to Kurt as if he was her father. He was very good with her. I told you, she's not quite right, but Kurt – OK, she couriered drugs for him – but he gave her a lot of love.'

The last cigarette was finished. She threw the butt into the compound where it sparked and smouldered in the dust, the smoke hanging over it in the still night air. The music was still thumping off in the darkness. The first flickers of lightning appeared in some stacked clouds which were some way off, but coming. The thunder rumbled around us. Dotte poured herself some more whisky. David came through the gates and walked across the compound past the water vats. He went into the drying sheds, where he lay under one of the chassis which the boys had already pushed in, expecting the rain.

More lightning, a lot closer than we'd expected, made Dotte turn suddenly. The edges of things in the compound looking jagged in the blue-white light.

'Where did that come from?'

'A different storm. It's coming from the east.'

The music stopped. Dotte eased herself off the verandah and came over to me. We were eye to eye, with me sitting.

'I don't want you to think badly of me,' she said, and kissed me on the lips. There was nothing warm or seductive or lingering about the kiss. I was expecting a more chemical reaction but the kiss sat on my lips, going no further than if it had been stuck there like joke lips. Then a wind bolted through the compound, plastering Dotte's hair across her face and whipping the strange moment away with it.

She swung herself up on to the verandah just as the first rain kicked up the dust.

'What are you doing tomorrow?'

'We should look at the books early; I might have to go to Man.'

'You have to go back?'

'Sometime.'

'Why?'

'The kidnap. The guy is going to be released as soon as the Ivorians agree to the terms and I turn up with the diamonds.'

'Is it rude to ask how much they want?'

'Two millions' worth.'

'He's not cheap.'

'He can afford it.'

'I'm going to bed,' she said. 'I can't add unless I have eight hours' sleep. Not that there's much to add in those books, you'll see. Good night.'

She went back to the kitchen, whose light failed as she reached the door, along with all the other lights in Korhogo. I leaned against the post and watched the rain and let the sound of it, on the rusted corrugated-iron roofs, drum my brains out.

26

Monday 4th November

It was still dark at 5.40 in the morning, and cool. Cool enough to wake up wrapped in a sheet with no sweat in the scalp and the unusual feeling of having rested. I dressed and went into the corridor with my shoes in my hand. Dotte's bedroom door was ajar. I listened and then pushed it open – nobody home. The bed was made, there were crossed ironing creases on the pillows, and a dent in the edge where someone had sat.

I put my shoes on, swigged a cup of coffee and at first light walked across the puddled compound to where the boys slept and found Kofi blowing on some kindling. I told him I wanted to go and see Soumba, Kurt's old girlfriend, and asked if she lived far. He said he would take me.

We drove through a hungover Monday morning in central Korhogo to an old colonial house on the other side of town. It looked derelict behind its high walls. There had been a fire in one half of the house. The rooms inside were blackened by smoke and only a single charred shutter remained on one window. A group of women and children sat outside in the compound between the house and what had been the servants' quarters.

I asked after Soumba and nobody answered, a little hostility rankling on the back of the woodsmoke coming in my direction. Two young women who'd been pounding yam stopped and looked at the white man. A kid with his finger in his belly button leaned against the thigh of a seated mama who was holding a small baby in swaddling.

'*Où est Soumba?*' I tried again.

A tall, slim young woman in a smart African print suit, of red and green cloth with a European-style cut, appeared at the door of the main house. She had gold sandals on and turned a heavy bronze wristlet on her left forearm. I introduced myself and followed her into the house, which had nothing in it except a red spray-painted slogan of the FPI opposition party on a blackened wall.

'Trouble?' I asked in French.

'The Ivory Coast is not yet a democracy.'

'Your men have been taken?' She nodded. I decided to make it quick. 'You know Kurt?' She nodded again. 'He's dead. Murdered last week.' No reaction. 'You were lovers, weren't you?' She shrugged. Tougher lines needed. 'I found a juju under his mattress.'

'It wasn't mine,' she said as a matter of fact, barely opening her mouth.

'Whose was it, then?'

'Ask the whore.'

'Which whore?'

She batted me away with her hand and walked off towards the wall with the slogan.

'I finished with Kurt some time ago,' she said.

'When did you last see him?'

'I saw him every day. He stood outside the gates there, looking in. He was a lost man. I told him he would be. Too weak.'

'Too weak or too poor?' I said, and she shot me a look that took most of the back of my head off.

'I don't have to speak to you, M. Medway.'

'You're wearing nice clothes. Good cloth. Good tailor.'

'I'm not bought, like you think African girls are bought.'

'How are you bought? *Cadeau-cadeau*?' I asked, needling to get an answer. It incensed her and she came at me with her arms flailing. She caught me on the side of the head with the bronze wristlet, but I got hold of her arms and held her close so that our noses nearly touched.

'The juju, Soumba?'

'It wasn't mine. He had his own juju. He didn't need any from me.'

'What does that mean?'

'He was already spoilt, broken.'

I let her go, pushing her away and shook my head to try and get the things to stop popping in there. She held on to her arms, looking over her shoulder at me, not so cocky, but not burnt out either.

'Ask the whore,' she said.

'Which whore?'

'The white whore,' she said.

I drove back to the compound; Katrina was at the gates, down on her haunches with a group of local kids. She was talking to them in their own language and they were looking at the words coming out of her mouth as if she was spewing pure silk.

Bagado was still sleeping; Dotte was having breakfast.

'Where've you been?' she asked.

'I went to see Soumba.'

'How did you know about her?'

'Kofi told me, said she might know something about the juju.'

'Did she?'

'She said ask the whore.'

'That's it?'

'The white whore.'

'She never liked me.'

'You knew each other?'

'Of each other.'

'That's quite some hate she's stoking.'

'I controlled the money. Kurt wouldn't have been nice about me.'

'So what about the juju?'

'I haven't got anything to say about the juju.'

'Why did she call you a whore?'

'It's her way of trashing me,' she said, and sat at the table, close to me, staring in. 'What's going on in there, Bruce?'

'I don't know. I'm confused. Maybe I'm worried about the Leopard, about this kidnap business, getting strange thoughts about them,' I lied.

'Don't think about it. Just like you don't have to think about the juju. It could have been anyone. And anyway, I thought you'd found Eugene.'

'Yes, but not who he was working for.'

'Are we going to do these books?'

'I have to call B.B., make things look good.'

She threw me a bunch of keys. I unlocked the office and the phone lock and dialled B.B. a dozen times before I got through. As usual he had his hand resting on the phone, waiting for it to ring.

'Yairs?'

'Bruce.'

'Where you been?'

'Around and about. I've had some police trouble.'

'I see,' he said, slurping his drink. 'Now den, Bruise, de replacemarn, he comin'.'

'That's good.'

'You no like de wok?'

'I was just thinking of you having to pay my daily rate . . .'

'Shut up de bloody daily rate! Bloody ting. I no pay't. You no done bloody not'ing earn you bloody daily rate. You drife me mad . . . f-f-furious . . . you sayin' dis ting!' he roared. I held the phone off my ear and he grumbled around until he got a cigarette going and smoothed out.

'Now den. De replacemarn. His name John Smith – from Newcastle.'

'He's a Geordie, you mean?'

'I don' know what bloddy Geordie ting is.'

'That's what they're called, people who come from Newcastle. You said he didn't speak French, they don't even speak English up there.'

'I see,' he said, his brain ticking.

'What?'

'I was jus' tinking. You say correck. I no understand a bloddy word he say.'

'You won't, unless you're a Geordie,' I said. 'You said he was cheap?'

'T'ousand parn a month plus expenses.'

'He probably used to be a shipbuilder.'

249

'Yairs. How you know dese tings?'

'All the shipyards are closing up there.'

'I see.'

'They're good people, though. Hard workers and you never know, maybe the locals here will take to speaking Geordie. When's he coming?'

'Arrive Abidjan T'ursday British Airways. You meet him?'

'I'll meet him. What about the Japanese?'

'I don't know where dey gone.'

'I'm going through the books now.'

'You put de monny in de accoun'?'

'Yes,' I lied, and he put the phone down.

Dotte and I started on the books. They were a disaster. It was a relief to get a call from Sean Malahide telling me to be in Man by 10.00 p.m. that evening at the latest. The Air Ivoire rep in the Hotel Kedjana organized a ticket for me on the midday flight to Bouaké and on to Man. There was going to be a three-hour wait at Bouaké, but it had to be better than the bus.

By the time I left for the airport there was over one million CFA unaccounted for. This was the period before Dotte took over and there was still another month of that to go. No wonder Soumba didn't take to Dotte, and no wonder she slammed the door shut on Kurt. The only thing – if I'd been Soumba, I'd have taken Dotte out with the juju, not Kurt.

Bagado took me to the airport. I told him about Soumba. He stared over the top of the steering wheel without blinking.

'Why is this juju troubling you?' asked Bagado. 'It's black magic. What's it got to do with anything?'

'It worked.'

'You think that whoever planted the juju told the Leopard to follow Kurt from Kantari's.'

'It's possible.'

'Dotte?'

'You really don't like her, do you?'

'It's not a question of like. You're either in her orbit or not. You're either attracted to her or not. You are, I'm not. She only operates with those who are.'

'You think she's manipulating me?'

'She's working on you. You have your little talks. Maybe she's seen something she wants to exploit. A weakness or two.'

'Don't drag me into that fight again,' I said. 'Just tell me what Dotte's motive is for serving up Kurt? She said he was a broken man. Soumba said the same. Why bother to have him killed?'

'She was desperate enough to contact the Danish Embassy when he disappeared. Does she strike you as a desperate woman?'

'Kofi told me he took Katrina with him.'

'Kurt was punishing Dotte.'

'There's plenty of history there for that kind of thing.'

'Why don't you tell me some of it.'

'You wouldn't want to hear it, and anyway, there's not enough to want to kill the man. Just personal stuff.'

'Intimate?'

'Is that a word or a question?'

'You know.'

'Yeah, and I'm not answering.'

We pulled up outside the airport. Bagado got out and sat on the bonnet with his arms folded.

'You be careful now, with those Liberians,' he said.

'Dotte didn't sleep in her bed last night,' I said, thinking I was throwing Bagado a bone. It didn't deflect his attention for a moment.

'Did you ask her where she was?'

'No.'

'Ask yourself why you didn't, and you don't need to tell me the answer.'

'We still haven't spoken to Borema to see if there's a connection to Ron.'

'My day is already planned,' said Bagado.

251

27

The mountains of Man had been rained on most of the night and the clouds still hung around their shoulders. I took a taxi from the airport just as night was falling and checked in at Les Cascades. Martin Fall was already installed. I cleaned up and went to his room. He'd been lying on the bed in a polo shirt and blue jeans with a weak whisky on the go, reading a stack of old *Ivoire Soir*s.

'What's this, then?' I asked.

'Always do my homework, Bruce. It's automatic. Read the papers wherever you go, find out what's crackling.'

'What is?'

'Multi-party election fever. But it looks like a put-up job to me. I can't see the old man standing down. You?'

'It's a step in the right direction. He won't see out his next term anyway. Too old.'

'There's some international observers staying here. They say the old man'll get in by a hair. They all know.'

'What else?'

'The Leopard seems to be all the rage. They said on the news the police'd caught him. Eugene Gilbert.'

'The police are making a pre-election splash. They've caught the Leopard's shooter but not the man himself.'

'You're on top of it, Bruce.'

'You could say that. I gave them Eugene Gilbert, but he wouldn't tell me who he worked for.'

'Got any ideas?'

'Some.'

'There's a diamond dealer who's been kidnapped too. How did that get out?'

'People talk when there's money around.'

'The rest is cocoa and coffee. They like their football here. Very disappointed in the Nigerian referee, they were – very disappointed.'

'I don't watch it myself.'

'I went to Brentford last week.'

'You don't still watch them, for Christ's sake.'

'The Bs? Course I do. They're on a roll.'

'They won?'

'Yeah. I heard a new chant too.' Martin started singing to the tune of 'Guantanamera':

> *"One referee, there's only one referee,*
> *Two-o-o-o linesmen*
> *But only one referee-e-e-e."*

'And you know the great thing about it was that when the ref heard them, he got a spring in his step. He thought, "They like me". You ever heard of a crowd liking a ref?'

'You're very ... what's the word ... chirpy, Martin. You're very chirpy.'

'You, I notice, aren't. The rainy season getting you down. A drink, perhaps?'

'Never known you so slow on the uptake, Martin. How's Anne?'

'She's great.'

Martin poured me a drink. I needed something to get me through his energy blast. He was looking good. Still in fighting condition, probably did more press-ups in a day then I'd done in the last decade. Still had all his hair, very black it was, too. Maybe he dyed it. It gave him a narrow forehead, though, made him look a bit thick, not much room to fit the brains in. He once told me he'd never read a book. I think he was just showing off, letting me know he was different. He had a whole library full of them, all hand-tooled by Moroccan craftsmen and gloriously bound in scivotex. What did I care if he read or not? He handed me a whisky, the water held like a question mark. The muscles ridged in his forearm under the dark hair and he still had triceps up by the sleeve of his shirt instead of blancmange. I shook my head at the water.

'You're looking fit, Martin.'

'I work out. Everybody does. Even Anne. You?'

'It's not the climate for it. You can lose three pounds reading a book.'

'I wouldn't know,' he said, dropping it on me again.

'Have you got the diamonds?'

'I was wondering when you'd get to it.' He handed me a metal tube, the sort you'd expect to find a top-grade Havana in. I unscrewed it and pulled out a length of soft pimpled plastic, the diamonds set in the pimples.

'How'd you get them into the country?'

'Tochas express, as they say in the business.'

'Who's Tochas?' I asked, stuffing the plastic back into the tube.

'Tochas means "anal".'

'I see,' I said, giving him back his tube, concerned by its warmth.

'What do you know about this Malahide chappy?'

I told Martin about the logging, the money in Burkina, the Libyan arms from Ouagadougou, the way Malahide creamed off a truckload to send to the IRA. I gave him my 'Malahide as the Leopard' theory, from the package I was supposed to hand over to Kurt Nielsen, down to the skin hanging in the Irishman's living room.

'So, as well as dealing with the man who probably set Ron up, we could find ourselves exchanging glances with someone who's arranged to have maybe five men killed and their guts torn out. He might have even gone for the hands-on approach with some of them.'

'I'm looking forward to snuggling up to him,' said Martin.

'He's not so lovely.'

'What's in the package?'

'A tape of a conversation between two men which shows some American involvement in the handing over of the Liberian president to the people who tortured him for twelve hours and then killed him.'

'Where's the tape?'

'In a bank vault in Abidjan,' I lied, for no other reason

254

than to keep the numbers who knew about it down to a minimum.

'Well, let's call Malahide,' he said. 'Get this thing over with.'

'I assume the Ivorians have agreed to unfreeze the assets and let the arms through,' I said. 'How do the Americans feel about that?'

'It's not been written down anywhere, Bruce.'

By 8.00 p.m. we were standing in Malahide's sitting room, with Martin fingering the leopard skin and Sean telling him that it was real. I went on to the balcony and tried to iron out my goose flesh, smooth my hackles.

'What's in the chest?' I heard Martin asking.

'That's just the box it came in,' said Sean, who joined me out on the verandah and helped himself to a tumbler of Bushmills. 'What can you see out there tonight, Bruce?'

'The stars are still stuck in the night, Sean. If that's what you're asking.'

'What about some more Yeats, Bruce? You got any more up your proddy sleeve?'

> ' "The unpurged images of day recede;
> The Emperor's drunken soldiers are abed." '

'Wishful thinking. Is your friend Martin a man of letters?'

'He tells me he's not, but he might be lying for effect.'

Martin came out from the living room and sat down in front of an empty glass. Malahide poured him a length of Bushmills.

'D'you like poetry, Martin?' asked Malahide, direct, a man who'd lived on his own in Africa a long time, not feeling the need for social timing; let's get down to it – who are you, are you all right? Martin knew the answer. He didn't give a damn about poetry. I saw him struggle with propriety for a moment and then toss it away, strangled.

'I try to avoid it,' he said. 'It messes up the head.'

'I've always thought it clarified things,' said Sean.

'I'm not an abstract man, Mr Malahide,' said Martin. 'I like tangible things.'

'Yes. I can see that. You're a professional. A soldier, maybe. A man to be careful of.'

Martin liked that, even though he knew it was pure Irish flannel coming his way. I wasn't so keen. Malahide was the man to be careful of around here – Irish trickster. And out came the Yeats on cue to annoy the ex-soldier.

> ' "*The darkness drops again but now I know*
> *That twenty centuries of stony sleep*
> *Were vexed to nightmare by a rocking cradle,*
> *And what –* " '

'That's as maybe,' Martin cut in. 'Perhaps we should concentrate on the situation in hand. We have a man kidnapped and it's time to get him out.'

'Yes, yes, yes,' said Malahide. 'All in good time. I said to get here by ten but there's nothing to be done till three. Company's rare out here. I thought we could have a drink, some chat, some crack. Get to know each other.'

Malahide buried his top lip into his Bushmills and sucked hard. Some tense moments passed when it could have gone either way and then Martin decided it.

'Is there any reason why we should?' he asked.

Malahide looked at him for a full minute in a silence broken only by the twinkling of the stars in the black velvet night.

'You're not in your office now, Mr Fall. You're sitting round my table drinking my whisky. You don't want to be civil, you can leave. This matter only concerns Mr Medway here. *He* is the man who will make the exchange. If you think you are going to have any part to play in this, think again. Anybody who goes down to that river tonight apart from Mr Medway will get himself and Mr Collins killed. We are not dealing with very understanding fellows. Am I clear?'

'We're getting there,' said Martin.

'My driver, Kwame, will take Mr Medway to Danané. Outside the town on the road from Man is a hotel called the Tia Etienne. He'll wait there at one-thirty for further instructions. I don't know where the exchange will take place.

They'll string a liana bridge across the Nipoué somewhere. It'll only take them a few hours. Your contact will take you to the bridge. It'll be off that road between Danané and Toulépleu. That's all I can say about the location. When you get to the bridge your contact will take you across. There'll be a tent on the other side and someone to check the value of the diamonds. When they're satisfied they'll release Mr Collins and you walk back with him across the bridge. Kwame will take you back to Les Cascades. D'you have any questions?' Malahide tipped his drink back and refilled it, not offering any more, annoyed.

'I don't like it,' said Martin. 'Why can't they bring Ron across and check the diamonds on the Ivory Coast side of the Nipoué?'

'Because,' said Malahide slowly, 'that's the way it's foggering well going to be and there's no changing it now.'

'Are they straight, Sean?' I asked.

'They'll play straight as long as you play straight. As long as Mr Fall here doesn't start playing British professional soldiery out there. He does and you're all dead men. I can assure you.'

'We're not going to do it,' said Martin. 'Tell them the deal's off.'

'In that case, Mr Fall, your Mr Collins will be floating down the Nipoué tomorrow morning with a bullet in his skull,' said Malahide, his voice soft and gentle. 'That was the deal. The diamonds delivered as specified or Mr Collins dies. If you don't turn up, it's all over for him.'

'Bruce?' asked Martin.

If I hadn't known how useful Martin was with his hands I might have tried to punch him out over the balcony.

'Is there any way you can contact the rebels now, Sean?'

'No, there isn't,' he said, flat as a pan in the face.

'Then we're in a very fine negotiating position,' I said to Martin, letting him know.

'It stinks,' said Martin. Malahide held his hands open. I finished my drink. Martin stood up. 'Let's go.'

'I'll send Kwame at twelve-fifteen, should you decide to use him. Good night.'

We drove back down to Man. I kept some hard silence going in my corner while Martin dented the night air with squaddy language. At the hotel the insect life were working through the night, sawing and planing and rasping off each second towards morning, the noise filling every corner so that if you started listening the brain could get feverish and the nerve shaky. I still hadn't spoken and Martin had run out of words to hate the Irish with. I opened the door to my room and stood in it with some 'no entry' body language.

'You're a professional, Martin. This is your job. I'm employed by you. And I just want to say I thought you handled that like a man right at the top of his game. Brilliant strategy, tactics, vision, anticipation, originality. . . .'

'Fuck off, Bruce,' he said conversationally. 'How many tours of Northern Ireland have you done? Right. You don't know them. Tricky little bastards, they are. It's all poetry and Guinness and then they'll blow your legs off in the name of a united Ireland. You don't trust them, you play hard ball with them because it's the same game they play.'

'You don't think Malahide could have talked to the rebels tonight. You don't think he's got a radio in his back room so that he can discuss business with them on a daily basis. You think he's sending runners round with slips of paper in cleft sticks, or what! We had an outside chance of negotiation before you spat in his drink.'

'I can tell you now, you'd have sat there all night kissing each other's arses with poetry and you'd have got no further with him.'

'Maybe I'd have had a decent drink,' I said. 'Now will you get me the diamonds, I'm going to bed.'

He gave me the tube, more subdued now, and wished me luck.

'I've lost a lot of friends to the kind of talk he was giving us tonight,' he said.

I went to bed and listened to the alarm clock clipping off the seconds for half an hour. Then there was a knock – Martin thinking of another reason he was justified in knee-capping Malahide tonight. It was Corben.

'You've got a sense of timing, Howard.'

'I saw you'd checked in. Thought I'd buy you a drink on your expenses, go through a few things with you, but I see . . . you're in bed. Kinda early, isn't it?'

'It keeps me young and my complexion smooth. I'll see you tomorrow, say ten. There's a flight leaves at eleven-thirty. I want to be on it.'

'It's happening tonight, isn't it?' he asked, his little black peepers suddenly alive in his shaggy grey head. 'Where?'

'Don't even think about it, Corben. They'll kill the lot of us. I'll see you tomorrow.'

I went back to bed and slept for an hour and a half and woke with a jolt at midnight, the air conditioning off again, the sweat beading and the insect workshop closer than before, rubbing down the dark.

28

Tuesday 5th November

It was 1.30 a.m., Kwame sat rigid, his head back as if he'd been speared to the head rest of the front seat. I sat in the back counting traffic — three taxis, two trucks — the lights illuminating the car with rushes of geometry as we sat on the verge outside the Tia Etienne hotel. The back door opened and a young African wearing a white shirt got in and sat as far away from me as possible in his corner.

'You're not going to catch anything, make you white,' I said.

'Danané,' he said to Kwame, ignoring me. We pulled away.

At the two police posts we went through they checked the boot. Kwame dashed them something small. We came out on the Toulépleu road. The young man's second word of the night being 'Left', his third 'Right'.

We came off the road between two towns, Zouan-Hounien and Bin-Houyé, and headed west down a dirt track, passing through some thatched huts and only stopping when the rain-forest blocked our way. The young Liberian got out and set off into the trees down a narrow path which dropped steeply at first, then flattened out. I heard the river, swollen with the heavy rains, rushing past on my left. My guide had no torch but he knew the path and I could follow his shirt in the clear night, the air smelling strongly of the rain-forest's rot and renewal.

The path climbed high above the river, and we were moving at a pace that was making me sweat and breathe heavily, which was no pace at all. Maybe I should 'work out' as Martin said. I was at the age when the extra pounds got belligerent, the heart started to want some time off and might take it without asking. I was nervous, the brain setting off on tangents. What did I care about a few extra pounds? Martin thought I was a dead man doing this. I tried to think of getting back to Les Cascades with Ron, keep my head focused. I couldn't see it and it worried me. I could see Dotte and Katrina, Bagado and Heike. I could always see Heike. The footage I had of her, I'd need a foundation to archive it. Was she in Berlin? Could I see sweat patches on her?

I couldn't see anything for a moment; we were running away from the river back into the trees, still following the path but it was darker now and I had a job to keep my eyes on the white shirt flitting in the forest. Through a break in the vegetation I saw it for the first time, out there in some strange light with no apparent source, the liana bridge, about thirty yards of it, across the river. It was 3.00 a.m.

The Liberian stopped at the four wrist-thick liana cords which had been tied to trees within the forest, securing the bridge to the bank. He shook one of the liana railings and a flash of light came from the other bank. He shook the railing again. Two flashes. He stepped on to the bridge's planking, holding on to both rails, and we both started walking down to the centre of the bridge. It wasn't as easy as it looked, the bridge keen on tipping you in the water unless you kept time with the man in front. It wasn't too bad with the light out there in the open, but I made it more difficult for myself looking for the moon which wasn't there.

The tent was up on the other side, the brown canvas lit from inside and shadows standing and sitting, motionless. The Liberian put a hand on my chest. He went into the tent and two soldiers came over and frisked me in places I didn't think it was possible to hide a weapon. They took an arm each and manoeuvred me into the tent.

A wooden trestle table was laid out with a blotter and some scales. A neatly dressed, smiling fellow sitting behind it. Ron, with cropped and spiky hair, stood in the clothes I'd given him on the other side of the tent with a guard. There was an officer, but not one I knew.

'You OK, Ron?' I asked. 'Apart from that haircut.'

'Fine. It's my new rebel look . . .'

'The diamonds,' said the officer. I handed the tube to the smiler at the table. He pulled out the plastic and popped the diamonds out of the pimples.

'I hope they're good,' said Ron. 'There's not too many of them.'

'I want him next to me,' I said to the officer, who nodded Ron over.

'Very nice,' said Ron, looking over the smiler's shoulder. 'Where'd they come from?'

'Somewhere where the sun shines,' I said. 'They're supposed to be forty thousand dollars per carat.'

'They look it.'

'I didn't think your old man would stint you.'

'Have you spoken to him?'

'No.'

'How did you . . . ?'

'Forget it, Ron.'

'Sure. I'm nervous, that's all.'

'You'll be in Tel Aviv Friday night.'

'Do you want to come?'

'I'm broke.'

'I'll pay.'

'Maybe I will, then.'

'Bring someone with you, too.'

'I don't know whether I've got anyone to bring.'

'I geef you my seester.'

'I don't know how she's going to feel about that.'

'Her husband won't like it either,' he said.

There was something different coming off Ron. It wasn't something born again, with that frightening light behind the eyes and the labrador smile, but it was something new and clean, uncreased. He wasn't bored or aloof any more. He seemed vulnerable and didn't use his arrogance to hide it. He had humility about him but it didn't taint his self-respect. He hadn't found God in his shitty cell in the middle of the civil war, there wasn't much of Him about. He'd stripped off the layers like onion skins and found he was one of the lucky ones with something there.

'What're you looking at?' he asked.

'You,' I said. 'D'you want to step outside, make something of it?'

'Yeah, I think I do.'

'We're going now,' I said to the officer. He looked at the smiler, who nodded.

'Best I've seen in a long time,' said Ron and we stepped out of the tent, the officer shouting something to the soldiers outside who backed off.

I went down the bridge first, Ron following my steps five yards behind. The light still there, as if there was a floodlit stadium off behind the rain-forest somewhere, illuminating the sky, silhouetting the branches of the trees. We reached the lowest point of the bridge and started to climb and I looked down through the liana rails at the water flowing fast beneath, roaring, boiling in parts, the white foam highlighted against the greater surge of oily blackness. Then the bridge shook violently.

I turned and lost my footing. Ron was on his front, his face over one side of the planking, his feet over the other, a hand still holding on to a liana strand, a black mark on the light shirt on his back. His hips slid over the edge, the bridge twisting now, helping him along, and I had to throw myself at him and grab hold of anything to stop him sliding over and down into the water. I had a hold of his waist but his weight was dragging him through my hands. I secured one of his flailing arms and locked on to his wrist, my leg hooked around one of the liana cords connecting the rail to the planking.

The bridge turned through ninety degrees and Ron was hanging free fifteen feet above the water. I was upside down now, my leg feeling the strain of our combined weights and slipping, burning against the liana cord. Ron looked up at me, his eyes wide open, amazed. He had a black carnation on his front as well. Terrible noises came from his throat, his lungs filling up with blood. His eyes said it to me. His eyes said what came up through his throat on the back of a black gout of blood that spilled over his chin and down on to his chest. And then we fell. In the fall, rather than the fear of losing my brains to some rocks in the Nipoué, I thought of

263

how I hadn't heard anything. I hadn't heard the shot. He was there and then he was gone.

We hit the water and the impact separated us. Now noise was everywhere. The water crashing and rolling, filling every orifice, wrapping and twisting itself around my body, dragging at me, pitching and spinning me until I didn't know what was up or down, along or across. For a second my head came clear into the open and I caught two shots of a tree, one upright, the other horizontal and then I was down again. I got my feet pointing down river and felt myself being channelled through a rocky gully, getting a crack on the shoulder and an elbow on the way down, the water crashing overhead, my lungs raw and slashed.

At the end of the gully my feet connected with solid rock, the impact juddering through my knees and hips straight up to the back of my head. I popped out into the night air, the water pushing me in the back so that I was falling forwards.

Out of the water, life was moving much slower. I saw the bank close by, and a tree. They were still, but coming towards me, each motor-driven frame clear in my vision. Then I hit the tree and knew, suddenly, how fast I was going, branches, twigs and foliage crashing and flapping past me to blackness.

I came to in a rush of fear, startled by why I was lying up to my waist in a pool of stagnant water with a smell of soap in my nostrils and the noise of nearby water crashing over rocks. Odd yards of what had happened came back to me, flickering through my head with too much light behind them. I pulled myself out of the water and crawled around the edge of it. I'd been in a pool hacked out of the bank by the locals so that they could wash their clothes and themselves without ending up twenty miles down river. The smell of the harsh carbolic and the beaten earth meant that there had to be a path up to the village. I found it and zigzagged up the steep incline, thinking I was going to have trouble with my left knee later on. I came out of the trees and saw where the car should have been. No car and no Kwame.

I limped up the rough track to the Danané/Toulépleu road. It was close to 5.30 a.m. by the time I got there and twenty minutes later I was sitting in the back of a pick-up with two women and a dozen chickens hog-tied for market. The women looked sullen, depressed and the chickens knew what was coming, too. They dropped me in the centre of Danané at 6.30 a.m. I walked out towards the Tia Etienne, found the *gare routière* and bought a ticket with some sodden money on the first bush taxi to Man.

The day had come up with some fierce sunshine and clear air so that my clothes were almost dry when I got back to Les Cascades just before 9.00 a.m. Martin was pacing up and down outside his room.

'Where's Ron?'

I didn't answer and went straight into my room and knocked back a Red Label. Then I ran a bath, ordered a room-service breakfast and opened another Red Label. Martin sat on the bed asking: what happened, what happened, for God's sake?

'Somebody shot Ron,' I said. 'I don't know where the shot came from. I didn't even hear it. The bullet went straight through him, through the chest. We came off the bridge. I lost him in the water. I got lucky, made my way back to the village. No car, no Kwame. Think about it.'

Martin didn't say anything. I stripped and got into the bath. The breakfast came. Martin brought coffee and cognac into the bathroom.

'And you?' asked Martin.

'Bruised, battered, and concussed from the piss drilling into my head from a great height.'

I sank the laced coffee and went underwater. Martin was there with more when I came up.

'What we're going to do, Martin, is go into town and see if we can buy a couple of steel baseball bats and then drive up to Malahide's crow's nest and snap him off at the knees.'

'Who needs steel baseball bats?'

'Whatever, we're going to alter him for good.'

At 9.20 a.m. we were in a taxi going up into the mountains. As we started climbing, just on the outskirts of town there was a group of people at the side of the road looking down a steep bank. Some men were scrambling down the bank while women stood with their fingers in their mouths and anything from pineapples to a water butt on their heads. The driver wanted to stop. We said he could, but on the way back.

Malahide's gates were open. The taxi driver stopped across the threshold when he saw the police car and reversed out saying he'd rather wait outside. In the courtyard two young policemen were standing over a body in the flowerbed – the *gardien*. Malahide's car was parked up with the boot open. Kwame's body was in there, his head at a grotesque angle to his body. We walked up the steps into the living room where a group of four officers stood in a huddle, all talking at the same time. They parted when we came in. I told them we had a meeting with Sean Malahide and they all looked down at what they were standing over.

Malahide was in a pair of red and white striped pyjamas, the jacket wide open and his stomach torn apart, the guts straggling in his crotch. They'd thrown the leopard skin over his face which they now pulled off. Malahide's eyes bulged out of their sockets, his tongue purple and swollen between his teeth and around his neck a wire garrotte. There was an open book on the floor not far from the body, something that Malahide had been reading when he died. A book bound in red leather and much used, judging by the way most of the gold-leaf design on the cover had rubbed off. The collected poems of William Butler Yeats.

They asked us when we'd last seen Malahide and we told them about the fifteen-minute drink last night. They asked us where we were staying and we said Les Cascades and they lost interest in us. I told them that this looked like the Leopard's work. They thanked me for my help. I said that the Abidjan police, Commissaire Gbondogo, was already talking to a close associate of the Leopard and they told me that they watched the news as well.

On the way back down to Man we stopped at the crowd of people. A taxi had come off the road. The driver was dead, broken neck, the car was a write-off, too. It was turning into a magnificent morning.

Howard Corben was waiting for us, leaning against the wall between our rooms looking hungover and irritable.

'The fuck you been?' he asked.

'Making sure I was ten minutes late for you, Howard,' I said, and introduced Martin.

'Make it worth my while.'

'Malahide's dead. How's that?' I said. 'The Leopard.'

'Shit. The police say they got him in Abidjan. It says so in the fucking newspapers. Can't believe the fuck you read these days. Journalists,' he tutted.

'I've got a tape I want you to listen to.'

'You're looking kinda morose, you guys. D'it all fuck up for you last night?'

I gave him a long, steady look.

'Guess so,' he said and the three of us went into the room.

I took out the dictaphone and checked the tape.

'Did you get the names?'

'Yeah, I did. You want 'em?'

'Listen to this first.' I clicked on the machine. 'The guy wearing the wire is James Wilson. Who's he talking to?'

Corben listened, irritated by the sound quality, telling James Wilson, the stupid fuck, to sit still and say the guy's name.

'Rewind,' he said. 'I wanna hear when the dumb bastard sits down again.'

Then a few minutes later: 'Truelove, I know her. Legs right up to her can.'

Corben was leaning so far forward now his head was nearly between his knees. He was nodding though, not pained. We were nearly at the end of Wilson's meeting. Truelove had gone. We'd had the bit about 'a part of history' and then the last line and Corben sat up.

'Got him,' he said. ' "Blessed are the peacemakers: for they shall be called the children of God." That's Al Trzinski.'

29

Howard Corben took a folded sheet of paper out of his breast pocket and handed it to me. There were two lists of names.

'The guys on the left: the first eight are the West African policy unit responding directly to the Oval Office, OK? Underneath them are four more names. They're military advisors seconded to the policy unit – tell 'em which way the guns are pointing. The first three are straight military guys. My friends in Washington tell me that the last one, Big Al, or Colonel Al as he's called, even though he's never made full colonel, has been with the Agency.'

'Why call him colonel if he isn't?'

'It gets him real pissed. The list on the right are non-government and non-military and have nothing to do with the Agency, as far as my friends know, but they help out. They do business. They offer specialized advice on shit the policy unit think they need to know about, so they can fuck up their decisions.'

'You've got a guy called François Marin on this list. You got anything on him?'

Corben flicked through his notebook.

'Shit. He's a trader from the north. That's it.'

'What's this line connecting Trzinski on one list to Godwin Patterson on the other?'

'Patterson is the Americo-Liberian I was tellin' you about, the friend of the late president. Right? The one who put Wilson close to his old buddy. Patterson and Trzinski are close personal friends, if you know what I mean?'

'They kiss and hug and hate each other's guts.'

'I'd pay ringside to see it, believe me, 'cause Patterson's

blacker than a coalminer's asshole and Big Al has a red strip across the back of his neck a mile wide.'

'How'd you know it was Trzinski on the tape?'

'I interviewed him yesterday in a refugee camp outside Danané and his last words to me were: "Blessed are those fucking peacemakers: 'cos those assholes shall be called the children of God."'

'He was in Danané yesterday?'

'That's what I said, Bruce. I wanted to interview him today after we'd had our pow-wow but he said he had to get back. Affairs of state and all that shit.'

'Did he say where he was going?'

'No, he didn't. We didn't get on, Al and I, did not see eye to eye, asshole to asshole. He thinks I'm a pinko which, given that he can't stand journ-O-listas, puts me stratospheric on his shit list.'

'Did you ask him what he was doing here?'

'I sure did, Bruce, and he told me to quit bein' an asshole and ask some proper questions. Been to media school. The big fuck.'

'It's time I was getting out of here,' I said.

'You gotta spill your guts first, Brucey. The deal. We had one. Remember you're English – fair play and all that shit. Come on, let's have the tiffin or whatever you fuckers call it.'

'You've got the tape, Howard. Trzinski is the Leopard. You're going to tell the world.'

'Is somebody going to tell *me* what's going on?' asked Martin.

'Al Trzinski,' I said, 'has some very strong views about war. He thinks war should be stopped in any way possible. I don't believe he is the kind of man to discuss his ideas with people in authority, he just gets out there and does what he thinks is best.

'He arranged for Jeremiah Finn's troops to go into the port in Monrovia fully armed and take out the Liberian president who was supposed to be there for peace talks. He found out that his mole in the President's entourage, James Wilson, had covered his arse by making the tape of their conversation. He then went on a killing spree to try and get that tape, which he still hasn't succeeded in doing.

'I met Al in Korhogo; he said he was a consultant looking at diamond mining. My guess is that he was monitoring arms movements from Burkina-Faso across Ivory Coast to the rebels. The consultant cover was so that he could find the money source for the arms and who was delivering. He was also trying to find the James Wilson tape.

'He must have wet his pants when I came into the Le Mont Korhogo Hotel bar. The man with his tape comes to sit in his lap. Then I tell him about the Ron Collins kidnap. He decides I'm worth keeping alive, worth keeping an eye on. Remember, the guy wants to stop war at all costs. Any exchange of money for Ron Collins means money in rebel coffers to buy arms. According to the Trzinski anti-war policy this must not be allowed to happen. He has Ron Collins killed and screws up the deal.'

'I'm confused,' said Corben. I explained to him what happened last night.

'I'm still confused,' he said. 'Why kill Collins? Why not kill the guy bringing the diamonds? That's you, Bruce, in case you're as confused as I am. That way he stops the cash flow into rebel coffers, and the diamond guy gets maxed for non-payment of ransom. A nice clean piece of CIA business.'

'The man has a point,' said Martin.

'Unless,' said Corben, scratching at his beard, 'and this is not an unlikely scenario amongst American military folk, Trzinski or the men on the ground fucked it up.'

'He'd have to be clinically insane to fuck it up,' said Martin.

'We know he's that,' said Corben. 'What I'm saying is, maybe he missed Bruce going in with the diamonds and did the next best thing, which is shoot the guy coming out. That would blow one element of the arms deal, which is the free passage of weapons from Burkina trans Ivory Coast, and it would guarantee the freezing of rebel accounts held in the IC. Fuckload of good that is when they've already got their money out.'

'I'll clear it up with Al tonight,' I said, 'if you will just let me go to the airport and get my flight.'

Martin said he'd have to start work on retrieving Ron Collins's body and getting the paperwork together to airlift the body back to London. I said I'd call him from Korhogo. Corben and I went to the airport together. I asked him to do two things for me. The first was to find out when Malahide died and the second was Trzinski's movements in and around Danané after he interviewed him.

'How do you know you're going to see Trzinski tonight?'

'I know where he'll be looking for me.'

I didn't sleep on the way back to Korhogo, a ganglion of pain in my left knee made sure I didn't stop thinking about Trzinski. Flying north out of Bouaké we hit some turbulence and even after a 200-foot free fall during which a woman let out a scream loud enough to remind God he had a job on his hands, I didn't for one moment stop thinking about Colonel Al Trzinski.

In Korhogo I bought some heavy-duty painkillers and took four straight off so that by late afternoon I could walk across Kantari's compound without a limp. I had a single light-brown, red-wax-sealed package in my hand for all the world to see. It contained a video showing the torture of the late Liberian president but no audio tape. I went into the house. The door to the left was open. Inside was a large high room about thirty yards long. There was a basic lighting grid in the roof with ladders going up to it. Below that were a number of free-standing lights around a set of a kitchen. The same crappy kitchen set from Fat Paul's porno film about plumbers. Someone slammed the door shut.

Before I knocked on the door upstairs I arranged one of the old heavy-duty telescopic light stands so that it was within easy reach. I went through the usual performance with Patrice, who, I could see when he opened the door a crack, was wearing a long blond wig. He let me in and showed me he knew how to walk in a short black leather skirt and high heels.

'Am I interrupting something?'

Patrice sat down on his bed and looked at himself in a hand mirror. I walked through to Kantari's office, shut the door and then opened it again when I saw Clegg coming out from behind the Chinese screen, drying his hands.

'Run along, Cleggy.'

'You and I are going to meet one night,' he said.

'Not unless I go to the same sleazy pick-up joints you do. Now go and be muscly somewhere else.'

I shut the door after him, sat on the sofa and showed Kantari the sealed package.

'I don't suppose you have any of that Laphroaig left?'

'Teacher's only.'

'Blended for the big deal. You're kidding. Break open the single malt and let's have a dram. We're celebrating.'

'What, exactly?'

'You're getting your package. I'm getting four million for delivering it safe and sound.'

Kantari stuck the tip of his tongue out at me and poured me a glass of Teacher's.

'Think cheaper,' he said.

'Like?'

'The million Fat Paul was going to give you.'

'This isn't a question of greed, M. Kantari. Just need. It took me some time but now I know what I'm selling. The thing is, I can't put a value on political influence so let's talk about need rather than value. My need. I need four million and I think that's cheap.'

'Two,' said Kantari through the steepled point of his fingers at his mouth.

'Now *you're* being cheap.'

'You talk about need. I talk about risk. I'm taking a risk getting involved. We all read the newspapers, watch the television. I'm buying a big risk.'

'If you listen to the news they'll tell you they've caught the Leopard.'

'They're fools.'

'And anyway, risk improves value.'

'Three,' he said. 'That's my last offer. Three, or you can keep the damn thing.'

'Three it is. Now. Cash.'

Kantari opened a drawer in his desk and took out a carrier

272

bag. He slid back a section of bookcase behind him and opened a safe. He took out three blocks of money and put them in the carrier bag. He held out his hand. I gave him the package. He checked the seal, put it in the safe, closed it and span the dial. I took the carrier bag.

'How did you and Fat Paul get to meet?' I asked.

'We have the same interests.'

'Porn, you mean?'

'Erotica is the technical term.'

'How did they know Kurt Nielsen wasn't just doing another porn deal with Fat Paul?'

'*That* is something I do not know.'

'Why did Fat Paul send the dummy with me?'

'Because they found James Wilson in the lagoon. He was playing safe.'

'Who're you going to sell the tape to?'

'The Libyans like this kind of thing.'

I picked up the light-green Chinese bowl on my way to the door.

'That wasn't in the deal,' said Kantari, holding on to himself.

'You're right,' I said, and lobbed the bowl back at him so that it would drop short of the desk. I opened the door, hearing Kantari squawk, and saw Clegg lying on the bed where Patrice was sitting. I opened the next door, ripping the key out, and got myself round the other side of it and locked it just as Clegg's shoulder thumped into it. I put the money on the floor and picked up the light stand. Clegg was through the door in a matter of seconds and I jabbed the six-foot length of the light stand into the washboard rack of his stomach. He folded. As he went down I clipped him across the back of the head with the foot of the stand and watched it bounce up off the floorboards. Patrice appeared in his whore's gear in the broken frame of the door. He took the scene in, clicked open his compact, and tugged at the fringe of his wig, concerned.

I told the cab driver to take me to the back of the Banque Société Générale where I hammered on the door until the manager opened it in a pair of slippers and a dressing gown.

I asked him if he would accept a deposit of two million CFA into B.B.'s company account. He wasn't thrilled but he did it.

Back at the compound I took a shower and sank a half tumbler of whisky with four more painkillers, just to see if the body could take it. I got into bed naked and slept like a fallen statue.

I woke up flailing at something that had run me to ground. I had no strength in my arms and my left knee had a G-clamp, but no pain, across it. Two hands held my wrists and pressed them to my chest. A face, Dotte's face, leaned over me.

'You were dreaming,' she said. 'Badly.'

'What now?' I asked, confused, my head all over the place, feeling drugged.

'I was watching you. You've been still as stone for quarter of an hour and then the last two minutes you started.'

I shook my head, which didn't shift the thick dullness, the strange distance.

'What time is it?'

'Nine o'clock.'

'At night? Where is everybody?'

'They haven't come back.'

'From where?'

She shrugged. 'Do you want a drink?'

'I don't know. Probably.'

'How was Man?'

'A disaster. I don't want to talk about it.'

She ran her hand through my hair, stroked my face — maternal. Then she pushed herself away from the bed and left the room, passing through the squares of light that were slapped up on the wall again from the light in the compound. I tried to squeeze some reality into my forehead, blink away the strange distance. Dotte came back with two glasses and put one on my chest. I sipped the whisky and felt instantly languid, the spirit slipping into my veins like a lethal injection.

Dotte was wearing a loose sleeveless cotton blouse with just a single button done up. I could tell from the way the material shifted that her breasts were hanging free under-

274

neath. She'd split her wrap open and brought her heel up on to the metal frame of the bed. Her chin rested on her knee and she rolled her whisky glass over her foot.

'I've been packing,' she said. 'Time to move on.'

'Do you know where you're going?'

'Not far on the money I've got.'

'I can stand you some.'

'You see, I told you you were a good man. Katrina's never wrong.'

'I've got a place you could stay, too. Until you get yourself organized.'

'In Cotonou?'

'There are worse places.'

'Lagos, Luanda, Kinshasa, Bangui . . . Monrovia.'

'Abidjan, too. They're all going to hell.'

'And Cotonou isn't?'

'Best of the lot right now.'

She sipped the whisky and licked it off her lips. There was something different about her. She'd found some hope. The idea of moving on, getting out from under the shadow of things that had happened here. She turned to find me watching her. She smiled though, not annoyed to have my attention on her.

'A fresh start,' she said. 'I need a fresh start.'

Something warm and prickly was moving in the lower part of my back. She put her whisky on the chair and leaned over me.

'What do you think?' she asked.

'You could use one.'

'I've had some in my time.'

'You're free,' I reminded her.

'That's a word to roll around with,' she said, and kissed me on the mouth; this time her lips were warm, pliant and wet. Her tongue played over mine.

'This hasn't happened to me before,' she said, stroking my chest.

'What?'

Silence. I felt the weight of her breasts on my chest. She collapsed on top of me and lay her head on my shoulder. I felt her thin warm tears trickle off my skin on to the sheet. I rubbed the back of her neck. The cicadas filled in the rest.

'I never let go – never had anybody to let go with,' she said, standing up. 'I'll finish my packing.' She left the room.

I sat on the edge of the bed, looked at the door and thought that it might not have happened. I socked back the whisky left in the glass. A door clicked shut off in the house somewhere. I went to the window and looked out into the compound where flames flattened against the bottom of the boiling vats and steam joined the darkness. It wasn't the clichés that nagged. We, the movie generation, have rafts of them that we talk in all the time. No, it was me. Was I being 'a good man'? Nobody's that good. I put my forehead against the cool glass and steeled myself up again.

'Mummy doesn't love you, you know,' said a voice from the doorway, bristling the back of my neck with its shrillness. I whipped the sheet off the bed and covered myself. Katrina was leaning up against the doorjamb, giggling. Her legs were crossed at the ankles, she was wearing a pair of small white knickers and nothing else that I could see. Her head and a shoulder were in the squares of light on the wall. Her hands were up to her mouth, her arms covering her upper body.

'Why're you peeking at me?'

'I wasn't *peeking*,' she said. 'I was *looking*.'

'Do you like peeking at people?'

'I *wasn't* peeking.'

'You should knock.'

She tapped the door cheekily, showing me her left breast, high and taut by her shoulder. She grinned.

'Go and put some clothes on, Katrina.'

'No,' she said, and dropped her other hand to her hip and gave me a 'dare you' look.

'Go on, get out of here.'

'She doesn't love you, you know. Just because you did it, doesn't mean she loves you.'

'We didn't do it,' I said, and she laughed. It fluttered her stomach and broke over my head like sheet glass. Silence and something ugly was in the room.

'Did she love Kurt?' I asked.

'No . . .' she said quickly, shaken by the question. 'Yes.'

'And you?'

'Sometimes.' She laughed again, high, shrill and penetrating, putting her hand back up to her mouth now. 'When he was being nice,' she said, misunderstanding my question and opening up a cold black hole in my stomach.

'When was that?'

'When we were together. The two of us on our own. Do you want to be my daddy?'

'I can't be your daddy.'

'Kurt was. You could be my daddy too. We could do things together, like Kurt and me did . . .' She faltered and coughed. 'I like you. You're funny.'

She made a noise like a kid pretending to fire a tommy gun and began clawing at her face and speaking in the local Senoufo language.

'We can do things together,' she said, desperate, 'like me and Kurt did. I can make you happy.'

'No, Katrina,' I said gently, moving towards her. 'Go back to your room now. Go to bed. Try and get some sleep.'

A startled, terrified look came into her eyes. She tried a grin, but it came over as a snarl, as a cat's hiss. Then she threw something which missed me but clicked against the window. She turned and ran. I heard the lock snick in her door. I turned the light on. Kurt's juju was lying on the floor below the window.

277

30

I scooped up Kurt's juju in a dustpan, took it out to the vats and threw it on the fire. David was out there stacking wood. There was one cage, still hooked up to the crane but on the ground, empty.

'Is this the last load?' I asked.

'Yes, Mr Bruce, I go puttin' this wood on, then sleepin' small. Tek um out morning time.'

'When you sleeping tonight, you listen for me. I'm expecting trouble. Big trouble. Trouble with gun.'

'Something wrong this place, Mr Bruce,' he said. 'Everything wrong here. Is bad place.'

'I know. We're leaving. Soon.'

I went into the kitchen and poured a drink. There was a note on the table from this morning saying: 'Bagado called from Tortiya. Will call back.' I sipped the drink and left it on the table. I took the mattress and mosquito net out of my room and set them up on the half-lit verandah. I took the bottle and glass from the kitchen and sat on the concrete platform and leaned against the post. I drank without enjoying it, while some mosquitoes tuned in on my frequency and I got under the net and watched them nudging into it, whining, frustrated.

I've woken up in the dark before with something evil in the room, some red-eyed beast looking over me reminding me of the loneliness of the human condition, something you don't need at two in the morning with your hangover flinging weights around your head. I'd run film clips of the good things in life, a family holiday in Norfolk, the coolness of summer grass on my bare back, taking the foam off my father's beer – a treat that got me started on a lifelong affair. I tried the same trick now, running clips of Heike in her big dress, legs crossed underneath her, puffing on the cigarette holder, drinking, looking at me with those aquamarine eyes. Then wrapping her slim arms around my neck telling me she'd been waiting for hours. I always kept her waiting, and it was always for hours. Then stepping out of that dress, sitting astride me, feeling her soft breasts rising and falling against my chest and losing ourselves together in the hot African night. Like some kind of subliminal advertising, illicit frames cut into that world – Ron's face staring up at me, the blood on his chin and the flower growing on his chest, the skinned heads of the vultures in Fat Paul's hotel room, Malahide's torn gut and bulging eyes, Dotte's lost tears, and the frail, abused body of a little, mad girl.

The phone rang the bell on the outside of the house. Nobody answered it except me. It was Bagado.

'Where are you?'

'In the police station in Tortiya.'

'I've been there.'

'They're being very difficult.'

'Haven't you got enough money?'

'Not for the problem in hand,' he said, calmly. 'Borema's dead.'

'You found the body?'

'They're being very awkward.'

'I'll come down. It'll have to be tomorrow. I've got something on.'

'Listen to this. Between Wednesday, thirtieth October and Friday, first November three and a half million dollars' worth of diamonds left Tortiya.'

'Sounds a lot.'

'They've never had it so good. There's hardly a diamond left in the place. Borema left with some clients and went down to Bouaké with them on the Friday. He didn't come back until Sunday. Then he turned up dead on Monday. A lot of his face had been burned away with hydrofluoric acid before he was strangled with a wire garrotte and . . .'

'. . . his stomach torn open by the Leopard.'

'Exactly. The diamond buyers were all from out of town. A place in the south, a port called San Pedro.'

'Samson Talbot using his Ivorian assets to buy diamonds. I thought they were still frozen then.'

'This is Africa, Bruce. Nothing stays frozen in this heat,' he said. 'How did it go with the Lib –'

The line went dead. I got back under the net. Sleep didn't come easy, lying there expecting a redneck with a leopard claw and a wire garrotte. I fell into it like a decabled lift plummeting ten floors before the emergency brakes left me hovering, in extreme tension, above an empty shaft. It wasn't exactly a relief to be woken up by Trzinski's snub-nosed .38 fitting itself into the hollow behind my right ear, but I didn't lash out wildly and get a crack in my jawline for the trouble. He was down on one knee staring over me, sweat pouring down his forehead, cheeks and neck.

'What're you doing sleeping out in the open like some jig?'

'Making it easy for you, Al, so you don't have to go trying all the rooms and waking everybody up and killing them too.'

'Walkies,' he said, pulling me up by the hair.

We faced each other on the verandah, the .38 in his blood-stained fist was pointed at my gut as he wiped his eyes with his spare hand, thinking about what he had to do. He shook his head and the sweat flicked off into the night.

'A hot night to be out working, Al.'

'Just one more job and I'm done.'

'Got your tape?'

'Yeah, and it didn't come cheap.'

'Didn't you use that negotiating tool you've got in your hand there?'

'Sure I did. Got the price down some.' He looked at the blood on his fist. 'Had to pull rank on Corporal Clegg. Beat up on those good looks of his a little more. Got himself a bit of a headache now. But I figured the colour of blood was the only thing'd help Kantari make up his mind.'

'What did you settle on?'

'I'm a reasonable man.'

'You didn't kill him?'

'No point.'

'Too useful? Like me.'

'Like you used to be, Bruce, but not any more. You're a pain in the ass. You see, I buy my expensive tape and I find it don't include a special offer I was expecting and that's really got me pissed, you see. So now all you gotta do is tell me what you done with the fuckin' audio tape. The one you shoulda given to Red a few days back when he asked you, and kept your nose out of my goddam business.'

'Eugene had an attitude problem.'

'Red's like a lot of jigs. He's good at one thing. He can kill people if they're standing in front of him and he's told where to point. You ask him to do anything else an' he can't do it, can't think on his feet. He's a jig. That's what they're like. You musta been out here long enough to know that.'

'But he's one that won't talk.'

'No, he won't, 'cos I keep his family sweet. Thirty bucks a month buys you a lotta loyalty in Liberia. Now, let's have the tape, fuckbrain.'

'Your language has got a little less biblical, Al. What happened to all that stuff you were trying to interest me in?'

Trzinski enjoyed that. He laughed and rubbed the bristles of his crew cut up the back of his head, finding some folds of skin he liked feeling. He looked across the yard at the flames under the vats.

'What's goin' on out there?'

'It's sheanut boiling, that's all.'

'You weren't giving me any shit with all that sheanut stuff,' he said, staring across at the vats until I began to see a nasty idea creeping into his head.

'Let's go,' he said. 'Let's go have a look at the sheanut boiling.'

The noise of the water roaring and the sheanut pinging against the metal of the vats was loud enough for Trzinski to have to get up close to me and let me know what sweating Omaha beef smelt like.

'I seen something like this in Vietnam,' he said. 'Now you get in that cage there, see, and keep still.'

I stood in the cage which came up to the top of my thighs. Trzinski pulled out a length of plastic and cuffed me to the frame.

'Now then, let's start again, and I don't want you gettin' smart with me, understand. Where's Jimmy Wilson's goddam audio tape?'

'It's out of my hands now, and yours. There's nothing you can do about it . . . Colonel Al.'

Trzinski's fist, the one with the gun in it, thumped into the side of my head and I slumped to the side of the cage on my knees.

'Shut your mouth, you little piece o' shit!' he roared. 'I'll be the fuckin' judge of that. You just tell me where it is. I wanna know where my trouble's comin' from if I'm gonna take the stand like good ol' Olly North did.'

'What's in it for me?'

'I shoot you, don't boil you to death.'

'Don't claw out my guts.'

He reached behind him and took the metal claw out of his back pocket.

'You won't feel it.'

'Why the claw, Al?'

'Kinda things jigs do to each other, ain't it?'

'What were you doing in Man?'

'You're playing for time, Bruce. It won't work.'

He put the gun in his pocket, went over to the crane and pulled on the rope, taking me up into the air. He tied the rope off and swung the crane around so that I was hanging in the steam coming off the sheanut. He climbed up on to the scaffolding and stood on the wooden planking of the walkway between the two vats and lined the cage up over the water and took his gun out again and looked at it.

'What's it to be, Bruce?'

'Just tell me what happened in Man, and I'll tell you who's got the tape.'

'Look, I know you're all upset. I heard your diamond man got himself killed and all that. But I've got a war that needs stopping and that's a helluva lot more important than individuals. Now shut the fuck up about Man and tell me where you put the tape.'

I pulled myself up on to my feet again. I was getting worried about the depth of David's sleeping patterns. I couldn't see a damn thing up here in the steam with the sweat pouring down my face into my eyes.

Trzinski eased the rope off a couple of notches so that the bottom of the cage was below the surface of the water and I could feel the heat pooling around my shoes.

'What's it to be?' he asked, clicking the safety off. 'You won't feel a thing.'

'What did Borema tell you, Al? After you burned his face off?'

'He gave me a few names. Some of Talbot's finance guys. Been down in Danané talking it through with them.'

'So why did you shoot Ron? The guy was on his way out, why the hell did you . . . ?'

He didn't answer because the wooden planking bucked underneath him, lifting him two feet into the air and knocking him sideways. His arms and legs reached out for something, anything, his body twisting, his eyes and mouth wide open but no sound coming out. His feet kicked out in a strange spasm, as you'd expect a hanging man would do trying to regain the floor. Then he was in the steam and he must have realized it was the end and fitted the .38 into his mouth. He hit the water. There was an explosion and a dark black mess spurted from the steam.

David sprang up on to the scaffolding, straightened the plank, swung the cage back over the ground and lowered it.

'You tellin' me you no need protection, Mr Bruce.'

'I know, David, I need plenty.'

'You needin' more than plenty.'

31

It was first light, just before 6.00 on a cloudless morning. I sat in the kitchen with a cup of coffee painted with something stronger than milk. Dotte was standing at the door, looking across the compound at the sheanut cage which David had lifted out of the vat. Trzinski was lying across the top of it, a fist-sized wound in the back of his head and his face and arms red-raw.

I went to the office to call the police and the phone rang. It was Howard Corben.

'They just came through with the autopsy on Malahide. They reckon he died between five and six in the morning, the *gardien* too. They haven't done the driver yet. Trzinski . . .'

'Trzinski's dead. Shot himself.'

'Wow. Couldn't have happened to a nicer guy. Did he suffer?'

'Not a lot.'

'You can't win 'em all.'

'What took you so long?'

'The autopsy. I don't know what the matter is with these people around here, but they didn't get started on it until four this morning. The fuck they start then, I don't know. That's Africa, a very surprising place. It took me most of yesterday to find out what happened to Trzinski. Thought the guy must have disappeared up his own asshole and I should start looking for that. I checked all the police posts and found the guy had gone to Man; I even found out he'd been drinking in the hotel bar at Les Cascades, but I couldn't make out how he left. Then somebody at the police post to

284

the airport told me that there'd been a military plane there on Monday. So I went down there, did some asking around and found Trzinski hitched a ride on it. It left eight-thirty Monday evening.'

'Monday evening?'

'That's what I said, Bruce.'

'Before Ron Collins got shot, before Malahide got ripped open by the Leopard?'

'The fuck you telling me for, I just told you.'

I slammed the phone down. Things were clicking in my head. I slumped in the chair behind the desk and sat for a full ten minutes, counting things off, linking information that I thought Trzinski had to information that only one other person could have had. Very complicated but well-oiled combinations slotted into position and they opened up a single door. I phoned Les Cascades and asked for Martin Fall.

'Did you find the body?'

'That's an awesomely terrible opening line, Bruce.'

'I'm not so cheerful. I've got a dead Trzinski in my back yard. Shot himself.'

'Christ.'

'Did you?'

'Yes. Some village women found it twenty miles downstream. They took it into Toulépleu yesterday morning. The police packed it in ice and sent it up to Danané. It's in the hospital morgue in Man now. They'll get the release papers this afternoon. If the weather holds I should be out of here by evening.'

'We never sorted out the money.'

'Keep it. You deserve it.'

I exchanged some small-talk about more work and Anne. We hung up. I phoned the Hotel Kedjona to ask about flights to Man. The next one was tomorrow. I opened up a map. It was 700 kilometres to Man on the main roads and just over 400 kilometres across country. It was 6.10 a.m. To get to Man on the main roads could take anything from 10 to 14 hours, across country it could be better or a hell of a lot worse. Dotte appeared in the doorway.

'I've got to get to Man,' I said. 'Where can I get a car?'

'Le Mont Korhogo Hotel. They're not cheap. What's happened?'

'People tell you to look further than the end of your nose,' I said, ruminating over the map. 'But not always to check under it first.'

'Is this about your diamond trader?'

'I thought Trzinski had Ron Collins taken out but there was something that didn't fit. We couldn't figure it out. They killed Ron on his way out, after I'd given the rebels the diamonds. If Trzinski was involved, he'd have shot me going in so that the rebels didn't get the diamonds. The rebels would have killed Ron. The arms would stop moving across the Ivory Coast. Trzinski wins. It didn't happen like that, it happened exactly how it should have done. It was something to do with money coming *from* the rebels, not going *to* them.'

'Which means?'

'It means the guy I was working for set me up and now I'm going down to Man to talk to him about it.'

'You're driving?'

'There're no flights.'

'Did you sleep?'

'Not much.'

'You're not going to make it on your own with your leg like that. I'll come with you, share the driving.'

'What about Katrina?'

'She'll come too.'

'It could be dangerous.'

'We'll stay out of it. Go and hire the car. I'll put some food and drink together.'

I went out into the compound, glad that I hadn't called the police and then had to spend three days with them plodding through it all. Standing at the foot of the steps up to the verandah were two men, small but formed with the very latest genetic technology. They both wore white shirts and company ties, suit trousers, the jackets folded over their arms, a briefcase in the free hand and a holdall each at their feet. They had straight black hair, wire-framed spectacles and they were standing out in the hot morning sunshine without a pimple of sweat between them.

'Medway-san?' they asked.

'Hanamaki-san, Yuzawa-san?' I asked, thinking: Christ alive.

They head-butted the air, catching me on the hop. Hanamaki pointed over to the cage with Trzinski lying on top and Yuzawa asked: 'Industliar accident?'

The car I was driving was a brand-new Toyota Land Cruiser which had cost me 240,000 CFA, nearly $1,000, for three days' hire and it was worth every bit of that. It chewed up those dusty back roads between Korhogo and Mankono, spewing it out behind in a towering cloud that ensured a reception committee in each village. Men, women and children lined the road, the kids yelling: '*Toure-e-e. Toure-e-e. Cadeaux-cadeaux.*' Chickens came from miles around, timing their sprints from hundreds of yards off to see if they could sustain some terrible injury and claim compensation. Cattle battled towards us like the phalanx of a distant army looking for conversation.

Then we hit the mud, 150 kilometres from Man just outside Séguéla. The Land Cruiser sucked it in and trowelled it out, so hungry it would have been a shame to deny it. It took us just under eleven hours to get to Man, with one puncture and a fifteen-minute stop for food and painkillers.

I slept for six of those hours, curled in the open boot. Katrina didn't sleep at all. She glued herself to the seat and stared out of the window, the grey charcoal smudges under her eyes growing darker.

Dotte opened up – a scarf tied around her head, sunglasses on, she laughed and looked as if she was on her way to marry Cary Grant. She reached back now and again to squeeze Katrina's leg. Katrina didn't turn a hair.

We drove straight to the airport outside Man, the sun still just there but getting ready for the sharp drop into darkness. I limped through the terminal, trying to get some mobility into my stiff knee, and saw the Lear jet that Martin Fall had hired with Collins & Driberg money. It was 200 yards from the terminal on its own stretch of new tarmac as if it was a VIP and got carpeting in its own lounge.

There were ten people in the terminal, including the ground staff and cleaners. The only customers were a long-haired white guy sitting with his arm on his rucksack, picking and smoothing his ratty moustache, and three Ivorians in western-style suits who talked as if they were outbidding each other at an auction.

Dusk came. Night fell. I went back out to the car and took an adjustable spanner out of the tool box supplied, thinking if Martin was flying he wouldn't be armed. Not that that made any difference when the guy could kill in his sleep with two fingers.

Katrina had finally slumped across the back seat, exhausted. She slept, her hands pulled into her chest, as if she was keeping something from us. I sat with Dotte outside under the trees and told her about the juju, about last night's visit – Katrina half naked and talking about Kurt like that. Dotte listened, impassive, and all the animation that had crept into her body during the day drained out of her.

A taxi turned into the airport entrance, its lights slashing over the car. Dotte was as still as if her core had turned to ice. The taxi pulled up in front of the terminal and Martin Fall got out and stood at the back of the car, sorting through some currency and waiting for the driver to open the boot and take the cases out. He paid the driver, who wanted to take the cases inside, but Martin told him to leave them. I gripped Dotte by the arm, pulled her to the car and pushed her across the front seats.

I walked over to the terminal. The taxi pulled away and Martin folded his wallet and slipped it into the lightweight jacket he was wearing.

'Evening,' I said to the back of his head, keeping clear of him, knowing he could be quick and violent.

'Bruce?' he said, surprised and delighted.

'That's me. Don't tell me – I've grown. Let's go for a walk.'

Martin looked at his cases and selected one to bring with him. We walked with a couple of yards between our shoulders, across the tarmac, beyond the parked cars and into the trees. Martin was relaxed, confident. I wasn't.

'You're not going to do anything with that spanner you've

got in your pocket,' he said, quietly so I'd believe him. 'I'll take it off you and fuck you with it before you get it out of your pocket.'

'That's nice,' I said. 'You're nice. This is nothing like that. Only a precaution.'

'I didn't think that phone call of yours was social. What happened? Did Trzinski come up with something? They told me he was in Man "talking" to one of Samson's financial guys.'

'Corben told me Trzinski left Man eight hours before Malahide had his guts torn out.'

'I see,' he said. 'You should have let me go, Bruce. Forgotten all about it, got on with your life. You know what's got to happen now.'

'Does it, Martin?'

'Oh yes, Bruce.'

'What happened to you, Martin, that you have to do this kind of shit?'

'It's a competitive market out there. You have to have an edge. Samson Talbot told me if I wanted to supply him with arms I had to supply him with money to buy them. Not all of it, but some. He's a businessman. He plays the game. You want to play, you have to put down your ante.'

'You didn't have to kill Ron.'

'I did if I wanted repeat business. Have to stop those arms coming across from Burkina, just like your friend Corben said. We're going to be Talbot's exclusive suppliers by ship through the ECOWAS naval blockade and by air when he's lengthened the runway at Gbarnga. Anyway, what do you care, you said yourself Ron was an arrogant shit.'

'I don't remember saying I'd like to kill him.'

'A side effect. It happens.'

'And Malahide, another side effect?'

'I didn't like him.'

'You hid that well.'

'It added to the confusion, too. Those Leopard killings. I got lucky when you linked that to Trzinski, and Corben said he was in town at the time. We're going to pick up Malahide's logging business, too. Samson was getting pissed off with him as well — he didn't like the poetry shit, either.'

'You said "we".'

'I did?'

'"*We're* going to pick up the logging business," you said.'

'Me and IMIT.'

'And the leopard claw? Where'd you get that?'

'It was in that chest at the foot of the leopard skin. There were two of them. When Malahide said it was the box they came in, I checked it. Two claws joined together with binder twine. I only went for the wire garrotte after I read about it in the *Ivoire Soir*; as you know, I prefer to use my hands.'

'How did you get out of Malahide's place?'

'I had a taxi follow me up. Kwame was in the boot. I told the taxi to wait down the hill. I did the job.'

'That was the taxi we saw — the guy with the broken neck and the car a write-off?' He nodded. 'What's in the case?'

'Eight and a half million in diamonds. Five million dollars from the Ron Collins deal. The rest from the frozen CFA they had in Ivory Coast.'

'They've got the weapons, then?'

'Docked in Buchanan last night.'

Three hundred yards from the terminal building we stopped and faced each other. Some light came off the airport, not much, but enough to see the edges of Martin's face.

'Why me, Martin?'

'You're incompetent. Not as incompetent as I'd have liked. You got a lot further in than I intended, but one of my own people would have screwed it up for me good and proper.'

'That's bullshit. You could get your own people to be as thick as you liked. Why me?'

'Because you were there,' he said, and I could feel him shifting in the dark.

'Is it something private, Martin? Something there in your macho soul you don't want to talk about, maybe?'

'Fuck off, Bruce.'

'The book thing? The poetry shit? No, not even you are that pathetic. Kill a man because he's read a half-dozen books.'

Martin was on the boil now. The heat coming off him. The professional soldier who didn't like someone tinkering with his emotions. I hooked my finger through the spanner's handle.

'Shut your fucking mouth now, Bruce. It needs some rest. Always fucking yapping, that's you.'

'Anne. Maybe it's Anne. Does she talk about me? We were very close. Very close to getting married. We would have done if I'd been up to it. A beautiful woman. Intelligent and very affectionate. She'd have made a brilliant wife. I was a fool. A bloody fool to let her get anywhere near –'

'You little fucker. I've had you up to my fucking hairline. Bruce does this. Bruce does that. Bruce would never do that. Bruce always said. Bruce always knew fucking best. You don't know how many times I've had to listen to your fucking name.'

There was a noise off in the trees from the direction of the terminal. Martin turned his head. I slipped the spanner out and in one movement swung it up to his face and caught him with its heavy head right on the point of his chin. He grabbed at it, tearing it off my finger. He staggered, flung it off into the trees and then crouched, spacing his legs, trying to keep himself upright, shaking his head. I kicked him hard in the crotch. He caught hold of my ankle and twisted. I went with it and lashed out with my bad leg as I rolled over, catching him with my heel on the side of his head. The pain in my knee flashed blue-white in my brain. I prayed that Martin had gone down.

He was close to the ground but not on it. It must have been his training keeping him upright because the two blows I'd hit him with were enough to have made jellied eels of anyone's legs. He came at me again, catching his foot on something in the grass, the case. This time he went down on to his hands and knees. There was the clicking sound of a revolver being cocked and I thought for a wild moment it might be Bagado bringing out his one and only trick. Then Dotte's voice came from the dark.

'Hands on your head – you on the floor – hands on your head – face down, lie down, Martin, isn't it?' she said, coming out into the clearing. 'Tell him to lie down.' Martin didn't move. He was gathering himself. I inched back.

'Do as she says, Martin. She has a gun.'

He was panting, his head hanging over the case like an animal that's had to run hard for a kill, only to find others interested.

'Give me the gun, Dotte,' I said.

'Back away from him, Bruce.'

As I moved back, Martin let out a roar and came at me, locking his hands around my neck. I was ready for it and hit him hard in the diaphragm but his hands held on. His split lip, close to, spat blood on to me. There was a flash to my right, a loud explosion, then another. As the two bullets thudded into Martin's body I felt his hands jerk at my neck, trying to get some strength into them to do their work, but nothing came through and he dropped to his knees.

'Oh, Christ,' said Dotte.

Martin held on to his side under the armpit where the bullets had gone in. He slumped back on to his heels and this time when he coughed a huge black haemorrhage came up and a word like 'not' or 'shot' on the back of it. Then he fell to his left and was silent.

'I shot him.'

I knelt down at his side and felt for a neck pulse. Nothing.

'He's dead.'

'I killed him.'

'If you hadn't he'd have had us both.'

Her chest was pumping up and down, the air hissing through her nose and mouth. The gun was pointing at me now.

'Dotte?'

'Pick up the case,' she said, her voice steady, on automatic. 'We've got to get out of here now.'

32

The gun was Trzinski's. She hid it in the back somewhere and rested Katrina's head on her lap as we went through the police posts to get out of the airport sector — Dotte using some of that cool she'd learnt going through Customs with ten kilos in the door panels. We headed south of Man to Duékoué and then east to Daloa.

There was thick forest on either side of the road and the night was a dense, palpable black, torn open by the Land Cruiser's headlights. Dotte's face flashed in the rearview as the oncoming traffic shot past — frame after frame — her head three-quarter profile, eyes unblinking, drinking in the blackness, not needing to see anything, enough pictures in her head.

It was about 200 kilometres to Daloa, the tension easing with each kilometre until we found ourselves exhausted and unable to go further. We pulled into the Roc Hôtel at 10.30 p.m. and took a couple of cheap clean rooms there. The owner grilled us two steaks and gave us drinkable Beaujolais. Katrina didn't eat. The bar/restaurant was still full after our meal. Dotte took Katrina to bed. I bought a bottle of whisky and put a call through to Bagado.

'You got out,' I said.

'No thanks to you. Where were you?'

'Man. I'm in Daloa now. Martin Fall's dead.'

I gave him a compressed account of what had happened. Bagado clicked his thumbnail against his teeth. He stopped twice; the time when Katrina came into my room, and when Dotte shot Martin Fall.

'The line went dead before I could tell you last night,' he

said. 'I found out where Dotte was going at night. It was a house belonging to a Frenchman called François Marin. Does that name mean anything to you?'

'François Marin was on Corben's list. Trzinski knew him too. He mentioned him the first time I met him. Said he handled diamonds. Does he?'

'He does. But more than that – he handles information.'

The steak started crawling up my stomach wall. I felt sick with acid and onions in my mouth. I opened the whisky bottle and took the first two inches out of the neck.

'There's a motive now . . .'

'Don't say any more, Bagado. The woman just saved my life . . .'

'What did you say to me that time?'

'When?'

'When we first flew into Man, what did you say to me?'

I didn't respond.

'Famous last words,' he said.

'I'm *not involved*.'

'Aren't you? What are you going to do now? Walk away? Hold out your hand? What?'

'She didn't sell me to Trzinski.'

'How do you know? How did Red Gilbert know your name?'

'Fat Paul. Gilbert clipped off his fingers until he told him.'

'Is that what he said?'

'How did he know to come after me in the Novotel? My room number. He must have known my name.'

'When was the first time he used your name?' I didn't say anything. 'Persuade yourself, Bruce. You're the only one who can.'

I hung up, took another pull from the bottle, went to my room and tried for five minutes to get Martin Fall's briefcase open, without success. I stripped and showered and sat in my towel. Ten minutes and one and a half inches later there was a knock on the door. Dotte came in wearing a towelling robe. She was calm, with a strange lightness about her manner as if she'd popped a pill.

'How's Katrina?' I asked.

'Sleeping.'

'Do you think she's going to be all right?'

'She seems to be in shock.'

'What are you going to do with her?'

'Take her out on the first flight to Paris.'

'Paris is an expensive place.'

She shrugged.

'Can I have a glass of that?' she asked. I poured one for her. 'Do you mind if I smoke?' She took out a pack and a lighter.

'Go ahead.'

'I've taken a valium,' she said. 'It's helping.'

'Maybe you shouldn't drink.'

'One's OK.' She lit her cigarette, took two long drags on it and blew rings into my room, keeping her eyes on me all the time.

'Did you know someone in Korhogo called François Marin?' I asked.

'Yes, I did. He was about the only friend I had in Korhogo. He liked to stay up late and play jazz. I used to join him when I couldn't sleep. I didn't know you knew him?'

'I don't. I know *of* him.'

She sat next to me on the bed, the towelling robe falling open a little. She was naked underneath. She reached across me and stubbed the cigarette out that had only half an inch taken off it.

'Tastes bad,' she said, and registered that I'd felt her body on mine. Her eyes opened wide. I looked in at the fear, the excitement. 'I don't want to be on my own,' she said, a crack beginning to appear in her lightness. 'I can't sleep with what's in my head. Will you hold me for a moment?'

I put my arm around her shoulder. She fitted herself into my chest and then pushed up slowly, kissing my neck and jaw, until our lips touched. Hers were electric, mine, with questions all over them, itched. She took my hand and eased it under the lapel of the robe and shivered as my palm stroked across the erect nipple.

'Can we sleep together?' she asked. 'Just once?'

She stood up, letting the robe fall off by its own weight

around her shoulders and on to her finger. I swallowed, keeping that red meat down. She hung the robe on a peg on the wall by the bed. Words, images, ideas crammed themselves into my head and closed off all speech. I didn't know who I was any more. She lay across the bed on her side, rolled forward on to her front and reached out for the towel around my waist. The shock of what I saw, looking down her back, just at the top of the cleft to her bottom, threw me hard against the headboard, my head cracking against the wall. Dotte, startled, scrambled to her feet, her arm across her breasts, panicked by the horror in my face.

'What is it?' she hissed.

I struggled to wipe that grimly lit clip from Fat Paul's porn video. The thick, brutal, black cock slicing through the cleft to that small, shuddering tattoo.

'The butterfly,' I said.

'It was Kurt's idea,' she said, the sex now out of the room, down the corridor and miles away. She put on the robe, knowing it, her hands in the pockets. 'What is it?'

'You said you knew *of* Kantari.'

'What's happened to you?' she asked, the fear bringing a growl into her voice.

'You knew *of* him,' I said, the anger at myself heating up my voice.

She backed away to the wall.

'The butterfly,' I said. 'I saw it in a film. It was called "Once you've tasted chocolate" . . . It was the film that Kurt was sent down to the lagoon to pick up, to see if he got killed. I had the film. When I saw that a man had been killed for it I played it back. I saw the butterfly. When I went to Kantari's I saw the kitchen set.'

Her hand came out of her pocket – in it was Trzinski's shiny black .38.

'I nearly believed you,' I said, strangely relieved to see that gun, glad the beast was out of the long grass.

'You wanted to believe me.'

'My mistake,' I said. 'You were paying Kurt back.' I took a pull on the whisky. She eased a cigarette out of her pocket and lit it, the gun still on me. 'You were the reason Trzinski knew to follow Kurt down to the lagoon drop. Trzinski didn't know Kantari was a buyer. He didn't know Kurt was the bag man. Somebody told him. François Marin. And *you* told François Marin during your late-night "jazz sessions".'

'You're right, they weren't late-night jazz sessions,' she said, with a glassy look in her eye that put her some way off from the rest of humanity.

'How did you know the drop at the lagoon was going to be a set-up?'

'When Kantari asked me if I knew a white man who wanted to make some money I knew he wanted me to ask Kurt. I didn't know what it was about so I spoke to Patrice. Patrice and I are close.'

'That figures.'

'Patrice told me about the tape and he told me that it was a dummy run. I made sure by telling François Marin about the tape. I just missed out the bit about the dummy run.'

'Did you sell him any other information?'

'About you?' she asked. 'The man with the tape down at the lagoon. You were so stupid, Bruce.'

'I was.'

'The thing about a good man who wants to do the right thing is that he's so predictable.'

'Not everybody has found me so predictable.'

'No. But this time you were vulnerable as well. No Heike. Do you think I don't know a lonely man when I see one? They're all over Africa. Every bar you go into there's half a white man looking to get whole. You get Heike back, Bruce. She's saved you once. She'll do it again.'

'And last night – "This hasn't happened to me before", "I never let go – never had anybody to let go with". Clichés *and* tears. You must have been confident to trowel it on so thick.'

'I'll tell you, Bruce, it's been a strange day for me. I had a brush with happiness. Driving. You know how soothing driving can be. That illusion that you're going somewhere, that you have a purpose, that the past is only the road you've just been on and the future is all ahead. I had that. With you. I had the feeling, just for a moment, of a clean slate.

Then we got to Man. The drive was over. The past caught up. The past covered those four hundred kilometres of rough road in no time. Everything I thought I could get away from jumped straight back on. My little girl and the juju.

'I've known all along. My type never get away. I was just kidding myself for a moment. I'll never be able to stop the cracks opening up between who I want to be and what I am because I know I'll never be good. There's just too much badness. One of the things about being abused is that you know somewhere, right in your middle, you know it with a certainty that no therapy can move. You know that it's your fault. That you tempted him. That you're bad.

'Katrina put the juju under Kurt's bed. He'd abused her, then he'd left her, went back to Soumba. He'd done what he wanted to do. He'd got his power back. All that strength he'd lost being mothered by me. He raped my daughter. He paid me back. I didn't know that Katrina had planted the juju, but whatever the spirit was she summoned, it found me. There was justice in that juju and it knew where to look to find someone bad enough to do its work.' She stopped for a moment, transfixed by some fine, sharp blade of rage. 'How could Kurt do that to her when he knew what had happened to me?'

'Humans are always reinviting history on themselves,' I said, remembering Malahide's words down on the Nipoué river before we crossed into Liberia for the first time.

' "Reinviting" – what sort of word is that?'

'Not mine.'

'It's not history "reinviting" itself. There wasn't even a generation between what my father did to me and what Kurt did to Katrina. It's just evil and it's here and all around, all the time.'

'What are you doing about it?'

She didn't answer for some time.

'I'm embracing it.'

'Is that why you've got that gun in your hand?'

'You didn't really think I wanted sex, did you? I've had enough of that for three lifetimes. I'll be reincarnated as a nun. I came for what I *do* need. The money.'

'It's not an impulse stick-up then?'

'Why do you think I'm here with you?'

'You thought there were possibilities after my phone call.'

'Possibilities to solve a little financial problem. Treatment for Katrina.'

'Take it.'

'I can't trust you.'

'I haven't been able to get it open.'

'Not that.'

'I'm too tired to squeal.'

She shook her head and produced some handcuffs from her pocket.

'One of François Marin's little perversions,' she said. 'So useful.'

We went into the bathroom and she locked my hands behind my back and around the base of the toilet. She stuffed a hand towel in my mouth and told me the key to the cuffs was on the bedside table. She took the briefcase and the Land Cruiser's keys.

'You know,' she said, as she was leaving. 'You might not think it but you've done something for me, Bruce. I was going to shoot you out there with Martin Fall. But I couldn't do it.'

33

Sunday 10th November

We left Abidjan at dawn. The four of us, Moses, David, Bagado and I, grim and silent in the cool morning which was still dark with low cloud just off the tree tops. Driving down to Grand Bassam the sea looked cold and hard with no waves, no spray and the sand still pock-marked from the drilling it had taken from a heavy storm the night before. The coconut palms were depressed, their heads hanging limp like mad people after an exhausting night revisiting traumas in their dreams. Some traders had begun to put up their stalls, but most people sat around, morose, preparing for a day's zero take. We skirted Grand Bassam and thick vegetation closed in on the road to Ghana, darkening the morning further.

The maid had found me at 11.00 on Thursday morning. I hadn't been able to get that hand towel out of my mouth and she wasn't prepared to oblige me. The owner came through as if he'd seen most things in hotel bedrooms and a naked man, gagged and handcuffed to the toilet, wasn't even going to break his stride. He honoured me by listening to my story without believing a word.

The Land Cruiser was found in the Treichville district of Abidjan and by some miracle hadn't been broken into. Martin Fall's briefcase had been forced open, his papers were scattered over the interior and the lining of the case had been torn away. There were tape marks underneath the torn lining, indicating that something had been stuck there and ripped away.

I had a drink with Leif Andersen that night. I was angling for an informal chat about Dotte. He gave me some privileged information instead. An Englishman called Martin Fall had been found shot, but not robbed, outside the airport in Man. His body had been autopsied in the presence of a British vice-consul. They'd removed two .38 bullets, one from the left ventricle of the heart and the other from the fourth rib on the other side of the left lung. The victim had emptied his bowels into his trousers and a metal tube had been found. It contained, at a conservative estimate, $6.5 millions' worth of diamonds.

I did John Smith, Kurt's replacement, the service of exorcizing the house and compound, which didn't come cheap. A Senoufo witch doctor said the medicine required was very strong and he needed a day's work to dislodge the evil spirits. I paid, and I paid big because I didn't want B.B. calling me and sending me up there to box John Smith back to Newcastle.

I spent an evening with John Smith in Abidjan. We were just about communicating by the end. He'd taken some French lessons so I let him order in the restaurant. The Ivorian waiter prepared himself to memorize the order. John Smith set to it and the waiter looked at him as if experiencing pain in his root canals.

We flew up to Korhogo the next morning. I spent the day giving him a seven-hour induction course on Africa. I introduced him to Hanamaki and Yuzawa who had already revolutionized the sheanut process. That night they took him off and showed him how they drank whisky in Yokohama. They understood every word he said. He was still warm when I left for Abidjan the following morning, but so pale he was translucent.

The election results came out. The President won with eighty-two per cent of the vote which, if you wanted to take a positive view of things, meant that he'd lost eighteen per cent of his popularity since 1985, when he'd regained the presidency with the first ever hundred per cent victory in African history. The FPI opposition leader made a few comments about stuffed ballot boxes and voter intimidation, delivering a final message which would have appealed to Martin Fall: 'It's like a game of football. We're about to score and they close the goalmouth.' It was touching that he even thought there *was* a goalmouth, that nobody had told him that the one he thought he could see was a hologram of his own.

I called the Collins family and they gave me Anat's telephone number in Tel Aviv. She seemed very young; young enough to start again, but who could ever cope with what might have been? She asked me about the trip and the kidnap. She was shocked at what had happened in the police station in Tortiya, and lapsed into silent terror at the Liberian hell. We both had trouble when I came to my last two meetings with Ron. She cracked when I told her what he'd said to me in the prison cell on that rainy day in Gbarnga. Then silent while I recalled the strange light as we crossed the bridge back into the Ivory Coast, but when I told her what I'd seen in his eyes when we were hanging from the liana bridge, she put the phone to her chest and I heard the wound opening up.

We crossed the border into Ghana. The sun came out west of Takoradi, just after we'd passed an advertisement for beer saying: 'It's a good life'. We felt ourselves coming out from under the shadow.

We arrived in Accra at two in the afternoon and I left them at the Hotel Shangri-La to drink some of that stuff that made life good.

The church next door to B.B.'s house was quiet for once. I parked up in the carless garage, knocked on B.B.'s door and let myself in. He was sitting in front of his Swiss Alp hoarding in his string vest and unbuttoned shorts with a bowl of nuts in his lap.

'Ah, Bruise,' he said, and prepared himself for the big one to call Mary.

'I'm in a hurry,' I said, stopping him with my hand. 'Here's your money.'

'Tankyouvermush,' he said, and counted it. He smoothed his hair down over his forehead and got his fingers caught up in the wire wool of his eyebrows.

'Beer?' he asked, flicking some empty nut shells out of his chest hair.

'No, thanks.'

'Groundnut?' he asked, and cracked off a shell and threw the nuts in his mouth. I shook my head.

'Smock?' he asked.

'I gave up, remember?'

'Like me,' he said, and threw some more nuts into the black hole. 'You know Kurt . . .'

'Let's not talk about Kurt.'

'No,' he said, pinching his nose. 'You know, I'm tinking. I'm tinking you giff me dis monny but I owe you someting small for de wok. No be so?'

'That's right,' I said and stopped. More nuts had hurtled into oblivion but this time they rattled down the wrong hole and B.B.'s eyes came out of their sockets. He stood up, the nuts in his lap spraying across the floor, and clutched at his neck with one hand and clawed at the air with the other. This is it, I thought, the moment. He kicked over the table and staggered to the centre of the room, his shorts slipping down his thighs. He pirouetted, both hands at his throat, and faced the Alps. I took four strides and dealt him a terrible blow on his back and the nuts came out like shrapnel – tock, tock, tock – and he set off across the room as if he'd forgotten to let go of a bowling ball. He thumped into an armchair head first and collapsed.

I righted him. He looked at me as if he'd just come up from the abyss and I suppressed the thought that B.B. would do anything rather than pay my daily rate.

'My God. Now I understand how de acorn kill de oak,' he said. Well, *I* knew what he meant, anyway.

I left B.B. asleep on his sofa and picked up the others from the hotel. Moses drove us across the Ghana/Togo border in the late afternoon. We crossed into Benin at dusk and it was dark by the time we reached Cotonou. The power was off in the town. We dropped Bagado in a dark and silent street and watched him open his door to get mobbed by his three children. My house was darker and even more silent. David installed himself with Moses in the ground-floor apartment. Moses made it clear to him that this was temporary, that he had an extensive love life to catch up on. David gave him some encouraging noises and looked around for a good place to dig his trench.

I walked up to my apartment and found it unlocked and thought Helen must be cooking in there by candlelight. As I walked in the light from a hurricane lamp came up slowly in the room. Heike was sitting on a cushion on the floor, a low table next to her with a bottle and a glass on it and a pack of cigarettes. She had a Bic lighter in her hand with which she tapped the table. She looked across to the bedroom. There were her four cases, a two-hundred pack of cigarettes and an empty Glenmorangie cylinder. She picked up her glass and took a sip.

'Do you know how long I've been waiting?' she asked.

'Hours?'

'Seven minutes.'